THE PRINCELING OF NANJING

THE TRIAD YEARS
AN AVA LEE NOVEL

IAN HAMILTON

SPIDERLINE

Published in Canada in 2016 by House of Anansi Press Inc.
Published in the United States in 2017 by House of Anansi Press Inc.
www.houseofanansi.com

This is a work of fiction. Names, characters, businesses, organizations, places, and
events are either a product of the author's imagination or are used fictitiously. Any
resemblance to actual persons, living or dead, is purely coincidental.

House of Anansi Press is committed to protecting our natural environment.
As part of our efforts, the interior of this book is printed on paper that contains 100%
post-consumer recycled fibres, is acid-free, and is processed chlorine-free.

21 20 19 18 17   1 2 3 4 5

Library of Congress Control Number: 2016962168

Book design: Alysia Shewchuk

 **Canada Council
for the Arts**   **Conseil des Arts
du Canada**    ONTARIO ARTS COUNCIL
CONSEIL DES ARTS DE L'ONTARIO
an Ontario government agency
un organisme du gouvernement de l'Ontario

*We acknowledge for their financial support of our publishing program
the Canada Council for the Arts, the Ontario Arts Council, and the Government of
Canada through the Canada Book Fund.*

Printed and bound in Canada

 MIX
Paper from
responsible sources
FSC FSC® C004071
www.fsc.org

For the wonderful women of Richmond Hill,

Samantha Heiydt, Susan Pons, Kim Short, Lena Foot,
Sherri Himelfarb, Ann Gomez, Anne Goodfellow,
Kirsten Webb, and Lisa Flood,

with me from the beginning and never flagging
in their support.

IT WAS EARLY EVENING WHEN AVA LEE AND MAY LING
Wong exited the elevator on the eleventh floor of the
Peninsula Hotel in Shanghai. Ava had arrived in the city
that afternoon, and now she and May were going to a reception that was a prelude to the launch of a new clothing line
called PÖ. Ava, May, and Ava's sister-in-law Amanda Yee
had financed the creation of PÖ, the brainchild of Clark
and Gillian Po, through their Three Sisters investment firm.

"How many people are we expecting?" Ava asked as they
followed the signs to the Palace Suite.

"More than a hundred."

"Can we get them all into the suite?"

"Maybe not all of them indoors, but there's a wraparound
terrace that can comfortably accommodate two hundred
people. Amanda had a marquee put up outside in case it
rains."

Ava spotted Amanda standing just inside the doorway
to the suite, talking to a group of familiar-looking women.
"Are those the women I saw working at the old sample

factory?" Ava asked.

"Yes, we hired them to work in the new one. Clark invited them tonight. I'm quite sure that they and Clark and Gillian's friends are the early arrivals," May said.

"That was considerate."

"Chi-Tze wasn't so sure it was a good idea, but she was sensitive enough not to say anything to Clark. He adores those women and they love him to death. They're also coming to the show tomorrow."

"How many fashion industry types are you expecting tonight?"

"At last count we had about thirty people from various publications, websites, and social media, and I'd say about twenty who either own major chunks of various retail chains or work for them. There are also some real estate agents who control the malls, in case we decide to go with standalone PÖ boutiques."

"How many of them are your friends?"

"Acquaintances more than friends, but a fair number of them," May said. "I see Gillian. I'm going to go say hi."

Ava followed May into the suite. She had taken only a few steps before Amanda was by her side. She noticed the long, thin scar that ran across and just above Amanda's eyebrow. It was the only physical evidence of the brutal beating she had endured in Borneo. In Ava's opinion it enhanced rather than detracted from Amanda's delicate beauty.

"I just got off the phone with Michael," Amanda said. "He sends his love. He wanted to come, but things are crazy for him and Simon right now."

Michael Lee was Ava's half-brother from her father's first

wife, and Simon To was his business partner. "Crazy good or crazy bad?" Ava asked.

"They don't need you to bail them out of trouble, if that's what you mean," Amanda said with a smile.

"That's kind of what I meant."

Amanda laughed and then stopped and stared. "With the exception of at my wedding, I've never seen you in a dress before. You look so damn sexy."

"It's a gift from Clark. It was in my room when I arrived."

"I figured as much, but I only saw the outside of the garment bag. He told me not to peek."

"This is snug but still very comfortable," Ava said, pointing to the form-fitting bodice of the black silk crepe dress. Then she moved her hips, and the lower half of the dress floated out around her knees. "I'm not used to wearing clothes this loose — it makes my legs feel completely naked. I have to say, though, I think I could get used to it."

"Clark said he also left a special message for you."

It was Ava's turn to smile. "Inside the dress, just below the neckline, there's a thin red ribbon with words stitched in gold."

"What does it say?"

"*Ava Lee has my heart.*"

"He does think the world of you."

"No more than he does of you," Ava said. "Now, how was he today at the rehearsal?"

"Excited but in control, and still being critical about his designs."

"You've obviously seen them all."

"Several times, and please don't ask me for an opinion. I find it impossible to be objective."

"We're all eager."

"None more so than the factory ladies. They're here to scream and shout, and they'll do the same tomorrow."

"Did you meet your friend from *Vogue*?"

"Yes. She's just sent me a text saying she'll be here in about fifteen minutes."

"May has just finished telling me about Lane Crawford."

"My god, how terrific would it be to get our clothes in there," Amanda said. "It almost gives me chills thinking about it. Not only are they the leading retailer in Hong Kong, now they have Lane Crawford stores in China and more than fifty Joyce Boutiques across the region. Chi-Tze says they're the perfect bridge between East and West when it comes to fashion."

"Evidently a woman who works there knows me."

"*A woman*? Carrie Song is vice-president of merchandising, which is like being God. Chi-Tze and Gillian tried and failed for more than a month to get an appointment to see her or one of her staff. Finally May used a board of directors connection to get in, but even that didn't go very well until your name was mentioned. All of a sudden there was interest, and then out of the blue one of Ms. Song's assistants advised us that they're coming to the launch."

Ava shrugged. "I have no idea who she is."

"Maybe you'll recognize her when you see her."

"I hope so."

"Now why don't you and May go inside and get a drink and mingle. Gillian and I are on door duty."

"Let me know when Carrie Song arrives."

"Count on it."

"And my friend Xu, if he makes it," Ava added. "I was told earlier that he might be tied up in a meeting."

"*Momentai.*"

Ava walked over to May and Gillian, who were deep in conversation. "We should go in," she said, touching May's arm.

Ava glanced around the spacious suite and saw about twenty people standing around a grand piano that had a bar set up beside it. Just beyond, a sliding door opened onto a white-tiled terrace, where most of the guests had chosen to congregate around another bar and a table laden with hors d'oeuvres. The sight of it made her stomach rumble, and she realized it had been a while since she'd eaten. She walked out to the terrace and was examining the food when Gillian appeared by her side.

"Carrie Song is here," she said.

"Where is she?"

"At the door, chatting with Amanda."

Ava walked back through the suite and looked towards the door. Carrie Song was several inches taller than Amanda and much broader, solidly built, with thick legs and torso. She was what Ava's mother would call "sturdy." Ava felt embarrassed for using one of Jennie Lee's code words and banished the thought from her mind.

Song's hair was pulled back tightly and secured by what looked like a platinum pin set with a row of small red stones. She wore a red silk dress with a high, straight neckline, sleeves that came to the elbow, and a mid-calf hemline. Like the pin, the dress looked to be worth a small fortune. Her eyes were heavily made up and a swath of bright red lipstick gleamed on her lips. Ava searched her memory but didn't recall ever having met her.

Amanda turned towards Ava and smiled. Carrie Song

also looked in her direction, and then her eyes blinked in confusion. *I don't think she knows me either*, Ava thought as she walked towards the door.

"You can't be Ava Lee," Song said when Ava reached her.

"I am," Ava said, extending a hand.

"But you're far too young."

"I most certainly am Ava Lee, and I'm not quite as young as you might think."

"You did work with Uncle Chow?"

"He was my partner, my mentor, and the most important man in my life for more than ten years," Ava said. Those days of collecting debts now seemed so far away, even though Uncle had been dead for less than a year.

Song shook her head. "It was eight years ago that my family hired you and Uncle. I just assumed then that you were older."

"I was in my mid-twenties when we became partners. I felt old enough at the time. And the job had a way of accelerating experience."

"Knowing what you went through with my family, I can understand that."

"Carrie, you have me at a disadvantage," Ava said. "The name Song means absolutely nothing to me."

"It's my married name. My brother is Austin Ma, and my father was Ma Lai."

"Was?" Ava said, as the faces of the two men appeared in her mind.

"My father died three years ago."

"I'm so sorry."

"At least he died with his business, his money, and his pride intact, thanks to you and Uncle," she said. "And I can't tell you how many times my brother has said he owes his life to you."

Ava felt words of protest form in her mouth but then swallowed them. Uncle had always said that false modesty was a ploy used by egotists to gather more praise. "Yes, we did retrieve the money and rescue your brother from his kidnappers. We did as well by them as was possible."

Carrie became quiet. Amanda, who had been listening to their conversation, edged closer to them. "Perhaps we should move away from the door," she said. "And neither of you has a drink. We have excellent champagne."

"Champagne sounds terrific," Ava said.

"Yes, for me too," Song said.

"There's a seating area in the corner of the suite that will give the two of you some privacy if you want to continue this discussion. Why don't we go there, and I'll have some drinks brought to you," Amanda said.

Ava nodded, pleased with the subtle manner in which Amanda had taken control.

Carrie and Ava settled into chairs separated by a small round table. Amanda waved at a server carrying a tray of champagne flutes. Each of the women took a glass.

"To health," Ava said.

"Health," Carrie and Amanda said as one.

"Now I'll leave you two," Amanda said.

Carrie Song perched on the edge of her chair and turned sideways so she could face Ava. "When I told my brother I thought I would be meeting you in Shanghai, he became quite excited," she said. "He said he saw you at Uncle's funeral but doubts you'd remember him being there."

"It was an emotional day. The names and faces were a blur."

"I understand. I was the same at my father's funeral."

"But I do remember your brother and father from the case. It was a tough one."

"I was in my last year of university in the U.K. I didn't know anything about the problem until it was over. I was really angry when I found out they hadn't told me about something so important. But father explained, very patiently, that there was nothing I could have done from the U.K., and that my knowing about it would only have caused him and my mother extra stress. He was right, I think."

"Your father was very calm and thoughtful in the face of considerable adversity. After all, the thieves had most of his money and his son. He showed a lot of bravery. So did your brother."

"My brother doesn't feel that way. He says he was so scared when they grabbed him off the street that he wet his pants."

"That happens to a lot of people, and after the initial shock he carried himself well. I remember speaking to him on the phone when we were negotiating the ransom, and he was in complete control of his emotions."

"Our family owes you a tremendous debt."

"We were paid well for what we did."

Carrie shook her head. "My father went to several organizations for help before he found Uncle and you. None of them would touch us once they found out who'd made off with most of our money and was holding my brother ransom for the rest of it."

"Most debt collectors want only low-hanging fruit. Uncle built our business by taking on jobs that they wouldn't handle. He liked to think of us as a last resort. It was a bit romantic of him, I always thought, but in some cases it was the truth. And we did have some expertise and contacts that other companies lacked."

"*Expertise*. You make it sound so academic. My brother said you risked your life to save his."

"That's a bit dramatic. The guys guarding him were amateurs."

"There were three of them, no?"

"I think so."

"And they had knives, and one had a gun."

"True, but I had Carlo and Andy — two of Uncle's men — and Carlo had his own gun."

"Austin said you were wounded by a knife."

"It was a small cut on my arm. It looked worse than it was."

Carrie lifted the glass to her lips and sipped. "No matter how much you want to downplay it, both my brother and I think the Ma family owes you more than the money you were paid."

"That's very kind. But I hope you're not here just because of that."

"I am."

"That makes me quite uncomfortable," Ava said softly. "This new business has to stand on its own merits or it won't be sustainable."

"Thank you for saying that," Carrie said. "I can't tell you how many invitations we turn down every month. If we accepted even a quarter of them, I'd never be in my office. So my coming here is a bit unusual. But the bottom line is still that we'll do business only if the clothes meet our standards — and those standards are high."

"That makes me feel a bit better."

Carrie smiled. "Good. Now let's hope the clothes are exceptional."

"They're wonderful."

"Is that dress you're wearing a PÖ?"

"It is."

"Then we're off to a good start."

Ava saw that Carrie's glass was empty and looked for a server. Before she could find one, Amanda reappeared.

"Excuse me, but May Ling wants Ava to know that Mr. Xu is here."

"That's perfect timing," Carrie said. "Please go and see your guest. I'm going to mingle for a while and then leave early. I'll see you tomorrow."

Ava smiled and walked away, feeling satisfied. She had no doubt that Carrie Song would be fair, and that's all they could expect.

She saw Xu standing just inside the doorway, talking to May. He was dressed, as was his habit — which Ava was sure he'd picked up from Uncle — in a black suit and white shirt. But instead of his normal black tie, he was sporting one in light blue silk patterned with red and white dragons. About six feet tall, he was slim and elegant. His fine features were accented by strong eyebrows and a thick head of hair that he wore swept back. He looked every inch the successful professional. And so he was, except that his profession was running the triad organization in Shanghai and functioning as chairman of the triad societies across Asia.

May was standing close to Xu, looking up at him with her hand resting on his arm. It unexpectedly occurred to Ava that May was flirting with him. If she was, Xu didn't seem to be discouraging it.

"Hey, what's going on with you two?" Ava asked as she drew near.

May stepped back, looking a bit flustered. "I was just telling our silent partner how well the money he put into our business is doing," she said quickly.

Ava was slightly taken aback by the comment, and she glanced around to see if anyone else might have heard it. Xu had put $150 million into Three Sisters. He had carefully assembled the money from his many enterprises, including factories that made knock-off electronic devices and designer bags and clothes. Then he had separated the money as far as possible from its triad roots before transferring it to them.

"I'm quite sure that comes as a surprise to him," Ava said, relieved to see that no one was in earshot.

Xu smiled at Ava, but in a way that she thought looked a bit tentative. He had dark circles under his eyes and his face looked gaunt. She wondered if he was having lingering health issues from the knife wounds he'd received in Shenzhen five months before, when his main competitor for chairmanship of the triad societies had tried to take him out of the running.

"*Mei mei*, it's good to see you," he said.

Ava stepped into his arms. "And you."

"May said you were meeting with a very influential woman from Lane Crawford. I hope I didn't drag you away from her."

"Our business was done."

"How did it go?" May asked.

"Well enough, I think."

"How do you know her?" Xu asked.

"Uncle and I did a job for her family."

"It was successful?"

"Yes."

"And she feels indebted?"

"Enough that she came here. For the rest of it, she has to see and like Clark's designs. I told her that's the way it should be."

"Getting her here was a feat in itself," May said. "Ava is always teasing me about my *guanxi*, but now she's demonstrating her own."

"Don't exaggerate," Ava said, and then turned back to Xu. "There's champagne and other drinks and food on the terrace if you want some."

"I'm sorry, but I can't stay."

"Suen told me you have visitors from Nanjing."

"I do, and I have to take them to dinner."

"You're coming to the launch tomorrow?" May asked.

"That is still the plan, and I'll be bringing the manager of our main clothing factory with me. His name is Wu."

Ava couldn't help but notice how intently May was staring at Xu. For his part, Xu seemed detached, and his face, as well as being gaunt, looked weary. "May, I don't mean to be rude, but I have to leave soon, and I would like a word alone with Ava, if you don't mind." Xu spoke so softly that Ava wasn't sure she had heard him correctly.

"No, of course not," May said.

Xu looped his arm through Ava's and gently led her away from the door.

"What's this about?" she asked.

"When the reception is over, could you possibly join me

at the restaurant where I'm taking my guests?" he said.

Her surprise at his question must have showed.

"I'm sorry for dropping this on you so suddenly."

"Is it a business dinner? I wouldn't want to get in the way."

"It isn't supposed to be about business, and even if it is, you are never in the way."

"They won't find it strange that you invited a woman?"

"That's one of the reasons I would like you to come. I was told a few minutes ago that Pang Fai is going to be there."

"The actress?"

"Yes."

"I love her work," Ava said. "I must have seen ten of her films, and I don't think there's anyone better at drama. But she's so famous. What's she doing at your dinner in Shanghai?" She saw his brow crease ever so slightly. "Oh, Xu, I hope that didn't sound rude. You must know what I mean. It is Pang Fai, after all."

He smiled. "She's the girlfriend — or at least a friend — of one of the most prominent men in Nanjing."

"He must be wealthy."

"He is, and powerful."

"Would I know him?"

"His name is Tsai Men. His father is the governor of Jiangsu."

"I've never heard of him."

"There's no reason why you should have."

Ava hesitated. The idea of arriving late at a dinner party held little appeal, but she was intrigued by the prospect of meeting one of China's biggest movie stars. "I have no idea when this reception will be over, and I can't leave early."

"Come whenever you can. I've made a reservation at

Capo. It is next door, on the fifth floor of the Yifeng Galleria. You can walk."

"Capo? That doesn't sound Chinese."

"It's Italian. That's where he always wants to go, even though he never orders anything Italian. He says they have the best fresh oysters and steak in Shanghai."

Ava shook her head. "Xu, I'm not sure —"

He squeezed her arm gently. "I don't care when you arrive. Knowing Tsai, it will be a long night anyway."

"And look at the way I'm dressed."

"You look stunning. I've spent time with Pang Fai before, and believe me, she does not dress down. You'll fit right in."

"Okay, I'll be there," she said, giving in to his persistence.

"Thank you."

"But arriving in the middle of dinner is going to look odd. How will you explain it?"

"I'll tell them you were at a reception."

"And how are you going to introduce me?"

"As my girlfriend."

"Girlfriend?"

"Don't be alarmed. It is the simplest explanation. If I told Tsai Men the truth it would only lead to a whole bunch of questions that I don't want to answer."

2

IT WAS ALMOST EIGHT THIRTY BY THE TIME AVA WALKED out of the Peninsula Hotel. The reception was still going on, but about half the people had left, and Ava felt she'd fulfilled her obligations. Besides, the energy in the suite had turned her initial reluctance to go to Capo into something that bordered on enthusiasm. She was looking forward to meeting Pang Fai. It wasn't every day you got to sit with a genuine movie star, and in China there weren't many bigger than her.

The reception had been wonderful. Elsa Ngan from Hong Kong *Vogue* had arrived early, attached herself to Amanda, and was openly supportive. Ava met with Suki Chan, their partner in the Shanghai warehouse and distribution business, and for twenty minutes she listened to Suki's plan to expand operations. Suki was in her late fifties or early sixties and had a penchant for grey Mao jackets and black slacks. Despite her minimalist attire, she had incredible energy and imagination.

At just past seven, Clark Po's arrival brought all conversation to a halt. He and Chi-Tze arrived together. She entered the suite first, a shy smile across her face and her cheeks flushed, while he waited near the door until he was noticed. The women from the factory immediately rushed to him. Clark hung back as the crowd gathered, and then strode into the room with a smile and his right hand waving in the air.

He was tall, thin, and slightly awkward, and he wore his long hair swept to one side, where it fell past his shoulder and was tied with a red ribbon. His skin was clear and pale, almost a translucent white. His lips were stained with a heavy layer of rouge, and his eyes were lined with kohl. He was dressed entirely in white: a long-sleeved shirt decorated with a train of brightly coloured buttons and loose, wide-leg slacks.

The factory women began to chant his name.

He lowered his head towards them.

Ava saw Carrie Song smiling and clapping at the edge of the crowd. Ava caught her eye.

How wonderful, Carrie mouthed.

Ava spent the next hour mingling and getting caught up in the excitement. By the time she left for the Yifeng Galleria her appetite had grown and she was ready to eat just about anything.

She could see the complex from the hotel entrance and started towards it. She hadn't gone more than five steps before she felt a presence. She stopped and saw the man named Suen closing in on her. He was immense, at least six feet six inches in height and half as broad. He was one of Xu's most trusted deputies and sometimes also functioned as a bodyguard and enforcer. Ava had met him for the first time in Borneo, where he saved her life.

"The boss asked me to walk over with you," he said. "The restaurant is a bit hard to find once you get inside the galleria."

"That isn't necessary," she said.

"He asked me to do it, so let me," he said. "I don't need him getting angry."

"Okay," Ava said.

"And just so you know, I'll be hanging around outside after we get there and I'll be walking you back to the hotel."

The Yifeng Galleria was in a century-old office building on Beijing East Road, opposite the Peninsula Hotel. The building had been gutted and turned into a mall full of high-end designer boutiques, restaurants, and clubs. Ava and Suen entered the marble lobby and went up the elevator to the fifth floor, where she found herself in front of the Muse nightclub. There was no sign of a restaurant.

"Follow me," Suen said, leading her down a corridor that took them almost directly behind the club.

When they came to a halt, Ava found herself looking at a wall with a massive reproduction of *The Last Supper*. On the table in front of Jesus was a runner with the name *Capo* on it. To the left was a host stand.

"I'll see you later," Suen said.

"I'm here to join the Xu dinner party," Ava said to the woman at the stand.

"Are you Ms. Lee?" she asked.

"Yes."

"Then follow me, please. They're in the VIP room."

The restaurant's decor was fashionably austere, with floors that alternated between oak and grey tile, exposed brick walls interlaced with arches that provided a view of the open kitchen, and small windows that looked out onto the Shanghai skyline.

The dining area was laid out with corridors that created the impression of discrete spaces, and Ava had no idea they'd reached the VIP room until she saw Xu. He sat at the head of a long, narrow table lit up by a metal fixture that looked like an industrial mobile. Behind him was another enormous rendering of an old Italian painting. Aside from the painting, the room was stark.

There were six seats at the table. To Xu's right were two grey-haired men dressed in cheap-looking suits. On his left was Pang Fai, and next to her was a man who looked to be about the same age as Xu. He was cutting into one of two enormous steaks that sat in the middle of the table. She assumed that was Tsai Men.

"Ava," Xu said. All eyes turned in her direction.

"I'm sorry to be late," she said.

"You can move now," Xu said to the man sitting next to him.

The man pushed his chair back and moved to the other end of the table. Ava walked around and took his place.

"This is my friend Ava Lee," Xu said, standing and wrapping an arm around her shoulders. "And Ava, this is Pang Fai and Tsai Men. The other two are Feng and Ling. Feng works for me."

She smiled at Pang Fai. The actress looked at her with a blank expression and then turned her attention to Tsai, who was still busily cutting the steak. The other two men stared down at the table, either in disinterest or because they knew their place.

"Some wine?" Xu asked.

"Please," Ava said, sitting down.

"Red or white? We have both."

"Red, please."

Xu filled her glass. "Do you want to eat?"

"I do," she said.

"This is an Australian Mayura full-blood wagyu that's been grain fed for almost two years," Tsai said. "I like this cut. It's called the tomahawk because of the bone and the shape."

"One of those steaks looks large enough to feed a family," Ava said.

"More than three pounds each, but we'll share. I insist you join us."

"Gladly," Ava said.

Tsai smiled, his eyes flitting up and down between Ava's face and her chest. In the cozier environment of the suite she hadn't realized the dress was cut quite so low. Now she began to wish she hadn't worn it to dinner.

"Your friend is lovely," Tsai said to Xu.

"I know," Xu said. "I doubt there's a table anywhere in Shanghai — no, make that anywhere in China — with two more beautiful women."

"To our beautiful women," Tsai said, raising his glass.

The others joined in the toast and Ava saw Pang looking coolly at her.

"I'll serve now," Tsai said.

"I adore your work," Ava said to Pang as Tsai apportioned the meat.

Pang nodded as if nothing else could be expected, but then Ava saw her shoulders relax. Ava knew Pang was in her early thirties and had been a star since she was nineteen.

She'd probably been in close to twenty films, ranging from gangster movies to melodramas to period pieces, from costume dramas to martial art pictures. She had been married, briefly, to the director who discovered her, but as soon as stardom beckoned she moved on to better directors and wealthier patrons. She had never remarried, but the Chinese tabloids and gossip magazines detailed a list of boyfriends who always had money or power or both. Ava couldn't remember ever seeing Tsai's name associated with Pang's.

She was a beauty, with fine features and large, round eyes. There were rumours that she had *laowai* blood, but she always denied it. What couldn't be denied was her talent. She was a magnificent actress, given to subtle, refined performances, and was able — as Jennie Lee said — to draw tears from a stone.

"Are you doing a film now?" Ava asked.

"I've just finished one here in Shanghai," Pang said, her voice soft and husky and incredibly sexy.

"Let's eat," Tsai interrupted. It was an order more than a request.

Pang shot him a look that was far from pleasant.

The steak was tender enough to cut with a fork and as good as Tsai had promised. Ava emptied her plate and might have had more if there had been any left. Tsai had taken a huge portion and was still eating when Ava finished. She examined him. She noted that he used the knife and fork properly and with some dexterity, he chewed with his mouth closed, and he used his napkin to wipe the bloody juice from his mouth. His good manners were matched by a tasteful appearance. He was clean-shaven, and his short hair was parted on the right, with every hair in place. His face was slightly round, and he had a long, thin nose and a strong chin, though Ava noticed that his eyelids drooped slightly. He was wearing a grey suit with a white shirt and Hermès tie. The suit looked as though it had been tailor-made, fitting perfectly across his broad chest and shoulders and his thickening waist.

"I'm going to the washroom. Would you come with me?" Pang Fai said.

Ava blinked, knowing the question had to be directed at her, but she was still caught off guard. "Of course," she finally said.

When Pang Fai stood up, she towered over the table. She was wearing a sleeveless blue silk dress cut with a deep slit that exposed one of her famously long legs.

Ava pushed herself to her feet and trailed the actress across the restaurant. The blue dress moved over Pang's body as if it was fluttering in the wind. Ava heard people murmuring as the movie star floated past them.

There were two women standing at the sinks in the washroom. When they saw Pang, their mouths flew open. Pang stood back until they left. Then she walked to a sink and Ava joined her. They stood side by side as they washed their hands. Ava couldn't help but watch Pang as she examined herself in the mirror and reached into her small handbag for lipstick. Ava did the same.

"Where are you from?" Pang said. "Your Putonghua has a distinct accent."

"I'm Canadian, and there we most often refer to it as Mandarin."

"Yes, I've heard that," Pang said. "Are you from Vancouver?"

"No, Toronto."

"I didn't mean your dialect is poor. It's just different. In fact, I kind of like it."

"Thank you."

"What do you do?" Pang asked.

"I'm in business," Ava said.

"I thought so. How much are you charging him?"

"Charging who?"

"Xu."

"I beg your pardon?"

"I didn't mean to insult you. We're all working girls. No shame in that."

"I'm Xu's friend and I'm here on business, but not that kind of business."

"And I'm an actress who's here to make a movie, and now I'm making more money for last night and tonight than I made for three months on set," Pang said. "I've always found the bigger the pig, the more he's willing to pay. And Tsai is one large pig."

"I wouldn't know — about him or your theory," Ava said, trying to hide her dismay.

Pang laughed. "You're a lot like Xu."

"What do you mean?"

"Tight-lipped."

"Maybe I am."

"That part of Xu makes Tsai crazy. Not as much as the fact that I have a little thing for Xu, but crazy enough."

"How often have you met Xu?"

"I've been seeing Tsai for the past year. Every time we meet in Shanghai, there's a dinner or lunch with Xu. How long have you and Xu been friends?"

"About the same length of time."

"Then why have we never met?"

"He and I are great friends, but we have a different kind of relationship."

"What does that mean? A quick fuck or a blow job at the hotel and then nothing to eat? That's cheap of him."

"No fuck. No blow job."

"Poor you or lucky you, I don't know which one," Pang said, and then hesitated. "What kind of business are you in?"

"We own a warehouse and distribution company here in Shanghai, among other things."

"Do you have a business card?"

"Yes, but it only has my Canadian cellphone number on it."

"Can I have one?"

"Sure," Ava said, not quite sure why it would be of any interest to the great actress.

"Where are you staying while you're here?"

"The Peninsula."

"Are you going to see Xu after dinner tonight?"

"I think so."

"Does he ever discuss business with you?"

"Sometimes."

"Can you be direct with him?"

"Yes."

Pang Fai nodded. "Well, I know he runs the triads in Shanghai and that he's smart and tough. But Tsai is maybe smarter and might be just as tough. He's also a great actor. You need to tell your man that Tsai is no friend of his."

"Why?"

"That's all I'm going to say," Pang said. She smiled at her

reflection and then turned and headed out the door.

When they returned to the table, Feng and Ling were in a deep discussion about the cost of a permit to build a factory near Nanjing. Tsai and Xu were listening, and their focus was intense. Pang looked across the table at Ava with raised eyebrows. Several times during the next hour Xu tried to shift the conversation to Pang's films and other more general topics, but Tsai kept bringing it back to business of one kind or another.

Finally, Ava stood and said, "You know, I'm quite jet-lagged, and I've got to get back to my hotel. I have a big day tomorrow."

"It was nice to meet you," Pang said.

"You too," Ava said.

"Don't leave so early," Tsai said with a wave of his hand. "We're going to Muse in a few minutes."

"I am really exhausted," Ava said.

Xu rose from his chair. "Let me walk with you to the door."

"No, I can manage," she said.

"I insist."

"Xu, stay with your guests. I'll see you tomorrow."

He shook his head, put his arm around her shoulder, and walked her to the entrance. "I'm sorry," he whispered. "I didn't expect this dinner to be so awkward and boring."

"It wasn't so bad."

"Tsai is fixated on some business issues right now. I thought having you and Pang at the table might be enough of a diversion."

"Evidently not."

"And I'm sorry you didn't get much of a chance to talk to

her. She can be very pleasant and entertaining."

"We did chat a bit in the washroom," Ava said. "She asked about our relationship."

"And?"

"I told her we're good friends, but that I have my own business."

"That was the extent of her curiosity?"

"Yes, but Xu, you do need to be careful, because the last thing Pang said to me was that Tsai is no friend of yours."

"She doesn't know a quarter of it," Xu said, and then leaned down and kissed Ava on the forehead.

3

THE ROOM WAS LIT UP WHEN AVA WOKE. SHE LOOKED at the clock, saw it was six thirty, and then groaned and burrowed under the duvet. Fifteen minutes later she gave up and got out of bed. Her mind was telling her it was early evening in Toronto, and her body was coursing with energy.

She went directly to the bathroom to brush her teeth and wash her face. Then she went to the front door to pick up the newspapers. She brewed a coffee and took it to the window. Ava had a corner suite that overlooked Suzhou Creek, a public garden that had once been part of the British consulate, and a sliver of the Bund, a mile-long stretch of historic buildings that faced the embankment along the Huangpu River, the last significant tributary of the Yangtze. Dating back to the nineteenth century, the Bund had been part of the International Settlement, and its architecture was a mix of Beaux-Arts, Renaissance Revival, Romanesque Revival, and Art Deco styles, reflecting that time period and European tastes. Fifty-two buildings were officially listed as original. They had initially housed mainly banks and trading houses from Europe, Japan, and the United States.

Technically they were on Zhongshan Road, but everyone referred to them by their number on the Bund. The Asia Building was 1 Zhongshan Road and also 1 The Bund. The Shanghai Club was 2, and so on. It amazed Ava that their unique designs and architecture had survived in the heart of China's largest city.

The Bund and the gardens shimmered under an early morning light that was streaked by rain. There were worse things, she reminded herself, than waking up early in a five-star hotel in Shanghai. During her years with Uncle she had woken up many times in hotels that hardly rated one star; the view from the room was a brick wall or a dirty street, and the wake-up call came from cocks at sunrise.

She stood up and stretched. She wandered to the desk, turned on her computer, and started to read emails. A couple of minutes later her emotions were roiling.

Her mother, Jennie, had written to say she was going to Casino Rama and might be hard to reach. It was bad enough to read "Casino Rama," but the words "hard to reach" almost sent convulsions through Ava's body. Jennie's love of gambling knew no limits. When Ava and her sister, Marian, were young, Jennie had to live within a monthly allowance that her husband, Marcus, sent to Toronto from Hong Kong. There were times when the allowance was gone before the middle of the month — the result of a long game of mah-jong or baccarat — and the girls were told it would be rice and vegetables for the next two weeks.

Ava started to write a reply and then stopped. There was nothing she could say that would make any difference. All she would do was aggravate her mother and frustrate herself.

Even more unsettling was an email from her girlfriend, Maria Gonzalez.

I was just told by the Consul-General that he's asked Bogotá to extend my appointment here for another two years, Maria wrote. He's expecting a positive response, and he's expecting it quickly. I hope this makes you as happy as it makes me. Love, Maria.

Maria was an assistant trade commissioner at the Colombian consulate in Toronto. Her current appointment would be completed in less than a year, and this looming end date had been causing her to panic. She and Ava had been a couple for more than a year. It was the longest relationship of Ava's life, and while she loved Maria, she was starting to feel pressure to make a stronger commitment. Maria had been hinting that they should consider moving in together. Several times the word "marriage" had crept into the conversation. Ava wasn't ready to take either of those steps. A two-year extension to Maria's appointment would at least give her some breathing room, but she knew it was unfair to keep Maria dangling, and she would have to make a decision soon.

I've just arrived in Shanghai and the trip was uneventful, Ava wrote. I think the news about the appointment is fantastic. Now let's hope it comes to pass. Love, Ava.

She sent the message, got up, made another coffee, and walked to the window. The rain was coming down harder now, and people were scurrying along the Bund with their umbrellas held at an angle to deflect it. She returned to the desk and picked up the newspapers, then settled into the green leather easy chair and worked her way through the international *New York Times* and the

Shanghai Daily. She was reading a story in the *Daily* about the ever-increasing Chinese exports and China's trade surplus when thoughts about Suki Chan intervened.

For someone who looked so ordinary, there was something compelling, almost electric about Suki. Clark might have a more visible and obvious charisma, but Suki made an impact in her own way. Ava began to reconstruct their conversation and then paused. Suki had put all of her proposals in writing — those proposals, along with Amanda's analysis of them, were in Ava's bag. She took the documents out, along with a Moleskine notebook in which to record her impressions and questions.

She pushed the green leather chair closer to the window, pulled a small table alongside, and began to read. She took her time, expanding on the notes and adding questions as went. She remembered additional facts and figures that Suki had thrown at her the night before and added them to the proposals. She had no idea how long she spent poring over the numbers, but she had drunk two more coffees before she felt satisfied that she fully understood where Suki wanted to take the business and why she was so excited about the prospects. She was starting to recalculate how much more money would be needed when her room phone rang.

"Hello," she said.

"I'm downstairs in the restaurant," May said.

Ava glanced at the bedside clock. It was almost eleven thirty. "I lost all track of time," she said.

"Are we still on for lunch?"

"I'll be there shortly," Ava said, and then shook her head as if she was trying to clear it of Suki's numbers. She couldn't remember the last time she'd been so absorbed.

4

THEY ATE LUNCH IN THE LOBBY RESTAURANT. THE RAIN had stopped, and the sun poured through the twenty-foot-high windows that framed the north side of the dining room. May had chosen a table near these windows, set against one of the room's giant pillars. As the sun lit the room, Ava saw subtle changes in colour and form and shape in the floor-to-ceiling wall murals, which had been created by Hong Kong artist Helen Poon. The murals were almost a living thing in the way they responded to the light.

May had a bottle of sparkling water, a cheese plate, and a tray of finger sandwiches in front of her. "Help yourself," she said as Ava sat down.

"You're wearing your PÖ clothes again," Ava said.

"You too, and I have to say that dress looks even more stunning in this sunlight."

Ava poured some water and reached for a smoked salmon sandwich. "I'm happy to see the sun," she said. "When it was raining earlier, I began to worry that it might have a negative impact on the launch."

"It would take more than a bit of rain to dampen spirits around here. I poked my head into the Rose Ballroom. Clark looked like he was floating on air."

"How were the girls?"

"They've been here for hours with the producer and his staff. The last models are arriving now," May said, pointing at two willowy brunettes walking through the lobby.

"How many models did we hire?"

"Twenty. Most of them are Chinese, but the producer brought six women from London with him."

"What a production."

"You've no idea. Chi-Tze took me on a tour yesterday before I went off to meet with Suki. They've taken over the back rooms and hallways that lead into the ballroom and have turned it all into a dressing room. They built a stage at the far end of the ballroom and a runway that's thirty metres long. We've got a hundred and fifty seats, and the producer ordered special lighting and a sound system that he brought in from Europe. When Chi-Tze saw the cost, she asked him if it was really necessary. He told her, 'This is show business. You've got one chance to make an impact. The clothes may be great on their own, but the right lighting and sound can make them otherworldly.'"

"So we obviously spent the money."

"We did, and then we spent more again. The models cost a fortune."

"How long will the show last?"

"About half an hour."

"You're kidding. I thought it would be longer than that."

"Me too, but the producer was insistent that the length of time is appropriate. He was equally firm that the show start promptly at one and that we parade one model every thirty seconds. Everything has to be done with precision. When I heard this, I thought Clark might bristle. It was the opposite. He told Chi-Tze that it's a joy to be working with a professional."

Ava poured more water. "I'm just doing some basic math," she said. "The show runs about half an hour and we're showing an outfit every thirty seconds, so that means sixty outfits in all?"

"Closer to fifty. It's a moving target that depends on Clark's mood. Two days ago it was fifty-six, and yesterday after the rehearsal I heard we were at fifty-four."

"That means each model wears only about three outfits."

"Yes, and don't try to calculate what it's costing us every time one of them walks down that runway. I started to but gave up when Amanda told me we can't look at the numbers that way."

"Because we're in show business?"

"Exactly."

"And you said . . ."

"Absolutely nothing."

"Wise."

"I thought so."

"Are you worried?"

"No, I'm excited."

"Me too," Ava said, and then reached across the table to grip May's hand. "I have to say I'm also very excited about Suki's ambitions. I listened to her last night and was impressed. This morning I reread her plans. May, I think we have to find a way to finance them."

May closed her eyes and slowly shook her head. "I can't

go back to Changxing and ask him to give me more money from our business."

"I know, and I'm not asking you to do that."

"And I don't want you to put in more money. We started out as equal partners. I want it to remain that way."

"I do as well. I was thinking of Xu."

"Did you discuss it with him last night?"

"No, we didn't have a moment alone."

"How was the evening, by the way?"

"Pang Fai wasn't quite what I expected, and the big shot from Nanjing was a bit of an asshole."

"Tell me about Pang Fai."

"Maybe some other time, May," Ava said. "It was kind of sad, and I don't want that clouding our day."

May took two cucumber and watercress sandwiches from the plate. "How much money would you ask Xu for?"

"Suki needs at least another hundred million."

"And you can get that?"

"I can try."

"Aren't you concerned about dilution?"

"No, I think I can maintain the status quo."

"How?"

"He owes me a favour or two."

"Then see what you can do."

"I'll call him. Maybe we can meet before the show," Ava said, reaching for her phone, but before she could access her contacts, it rang. She looked at the incoming number. "Speak of the devil."

"It's Xu," he said.

"I know. May and I were just talking about you."

"Kindly, I hope."

"Of course."

"You may not feel that way when I tell you that I can't make the launch."

He said it casually, but she felt some tension in his voice. "Is there a problem?"

"There are some minor issues in Nanjing that I couldn't resolve last night. I have to go there today. I'm on the road already."

"If they are minor, can't they wait?"

"If I wait, they won't be minor for very long."

"Tsai is still in Shanghai?"

"He left last night."

"That sounds ominous."

"It wasn't that dramatic."

"Did Pang Fai go with him?"

"No, she was a Shanghai rental."

"I have to say I was surprised by her, and by that."

"Acting in Chinese movies doesn't pay that well, and competition for roles is fierce. She probably has to augment her income, and having rich and powerful friends can't hurt when it comes to getting parts."

"She told me that she has a bit of a crush on you," Ava said.

"The women I attract tend to have complicated lives. They're usually more than I can handle, and she sure is."

Ava glanced at May. She was eating a sandwich and appeared uninterested in the conversation. "Enough about that," Ava said. "Where does this leave us as far as today is concerned?"

"The plant manager, Wu, will be there, and I told him to take his assistant with him. Her name is Fan. She's young and talented, and I have plans for her. She's excited but nervous about going to the launch. I'd appreciate it if you could look out for her."

"Okay, I'll find her and be sure to make her feel part of the team."

"Thanks."

"That isn't necessary," Ava said. "Have a safe trip."

"Did Xu just cancel on us?" May asked when Ava put down the phone.

"He did. He still has problems in Nanjing that need to be resolved."

"Oh."

"You sound disappointed," Ava said, remembering May's hand resting on Xu's arm the night before. "You wouldn't be —"

"Oh, look," May said, her eyes leaving Ava. "There's Amanda."

Amanda walked towards them with a tight smile across her face. She wore wide-leg teal trousers and a white linen blouse with billowing sleeves that were fastened with delicate purple glass buttons. Her mood didn't reflect the brightness of her PÖ ensemble.

"You look stressed," Ava said.

"It's bedlam backstage."

"Is there anything we can do to help?"

"That's why I'm here," Amanda said. "Chi-Tze and Gillian were going to greet people at the ballroom door and make sure they were properly seated. But we need them to help with the models and clothes. One of the dressers is ill, and they've sent her home. It'll take both of them to replace her."

"How's Clark holding up?"

"Better than me."

"When do you need us?" Ava asked.

"Now."

"Let me look after the bill, and we'll be there," May said.

A few moments later Amanda led them across the lobby to the foyer. The doors to the Rose Ballroom were closed. She opened them and stepped inside. Ava followed and then froze.

"This is unbelievable," she said. "Where did you get all those silk pennants and banners? Did you raid a movie set about a Chinese warlord?"

"They were custom-made. We ordered sixty of the long banners to cover the walls and surround the stage, and forty of the pennants to put on poles. There will be a soft breeze flowing through here when the show starts. They look even more spectacular when they flutter."

The pennants and banners were a blaze of colours. The backgrounds were solid white, red, or gold, and running down the middle of each one in a contrasting colour was Chinese script that read A SINGLE SPARK CAN SET THE WORLD ON FIRE.

"The front rows on each side of the stage are reserved for our VIPs," Amanda said. "There's a name on every seat. After you greet people at the door, help them find their spot. Here are seating plans. You and May have assigned seats, but you should probably stay by the door. We don't want anyone trying to come in once the show starts."

"Unless it's Carrie Song from Lane Crawford or Elsa Ngan from *Vogue*," May said pointedly.

"Of course," Amanda said.

"I assume people who aren't on the seating plan can sit where they want?" Ava said.

"Yes."

"Any other rules we need to be aware of?"

"Such as?"

"Can people use cellphones?"

"Cameras, cellphones, tape recorders, notepads — they're all permitted. We want people to have something to rely on other than their memories."

"Is that our camera crew that's set up now?" Ava asked, pointing inside.

"Yes, we're filming the show. We'll send a DVD to everyone who's here, and we'll use the footage for all kinds of marketing campaigns over the next few months."

"You sound like you've been doing this for years," Ava said.

Amanda raised an eyebrow. "I'm just obeying orders, and believe me, neither the producer nor Clark is shy about telling us how things have to be done. I feel like I'm back at Sacred Heart Academy in Hong Kong with the nuns."

"We'll try not to disappoint," Ava said and smiled.

"One last thing," Amanda said. "We want noise."

"Really?"

"The factory ladies and a lot of Clark and Gillian's friends are going to be here. We've told them already that we want to hear them clapping and cheering as loudly as possible. It won't hurt to remind them."

"How will we know who they are?"

"If they're not on the seating plan, then assume that's them," Amanda said. "I'll see you both after the show."

"So much for our front-row seats," May said as Amanda left.

"I like feeling useful," Ava said.

"Me too, I guess."

Ten minutes later a group of about twenty factory ladies arrived. It was still early, and they hung back from the ballroom door. Ava saw no reason why they should have to stand in the lobby, so she urged them to come inside. "You can sit anywhere except the front rows, and be sure to make lots of noise," she said.

"Don't worry, you'll hear us," one of them said. "We've been waiting years for this."

Soon after, Clark and Gillian's friends began to arrive. May and Ava took turns issuing instructions.

Around a quarter to one, Xu's plant manager, Wu, and the assistant, Fan, came to the entrance and asked for Ava. Ava introduced herself. The manager was deferential, while Fan looked painfully shy. She looked like a schoolgirl in a plain black skirt and white cotton blouse and with her hair in a ponytail. Ava walked them to the front row, where she showed them to the seats that would have been hers and May's. "You can take pictures if you want, and please don't be afraid to clap," she told them.

When she got back to the entrance, the rush had started. She and May took as many people to their seats as they could, but were soon simply directing them. Ava recognized Elsa Ngan from the night before, but the others who were seated in the front rows were just names on a piece of paper. May did know many of them and introduced some to Ava. One, a real estate tycoon from Hong Kong, made Ava laugh when he asked May if her new ushering job paid well.

Just before one, Carrie Song arrived with a young woman who Ava assumed was her assistant. As Ava guided them to their seats, a light breeze began to circulate through the ballroom, and the pennants and banners fluttered.

"This is very well done," Song said, looking up and around the ballroom.

Ava just made it back to the entrance as the lights dimmed. The strains of a traditional Chinese opera song began to play. The rather laborious melody surprised her. But then the room became completely dark, and a few seconds later the song ended.

The silence was almost eerie. It felt as if they were drenched in blackness for much longer than the ten seconds or so it actually was.

Onstage, a single sparkler came alive. When the sparkler went out, the room fell dark again. Ava counted to five, and then there was a crashing *boom*, and all at once the runway and the stage were dramatically lit. Clark stood in the centre of the stage with the dead sparkler held between the palms of his extended hands. He was shirtless, wearing only tight white linen slacks with a red scarf belt. His hair hung long and loose to his shoulders. He bowed, turned, and walked behind the curtain. Jacky Cheung's voice filled the room with the opening words of the song "Blue Rain," and the first model started down the runway.

"I just felt a chill run right down my spine," May said.

Ava glanced sideways. Her friend's eyes were locked on the stage.

The factory women and Clark and Gillian's friends were now standing, clapping and cheering. Ava felt their emotion; she thought about how many years of study, work, and struggle Clark had endured to get to this precise moment and her eyes began to water.

Ava had seen only one collection of Clark's clothes, and that was months before at the sample factory where they were deciding if they would invest in PÖ. The clothes had been made almost exclusively from linen, in a host of bright, vibrant colours. Now he'd expanded his use of materials to include textured weaves, silk jersey, and silk crepe, and he'd balanced the bright colours with black, grey, and muted browns.

The clothes she'd seen at the factory had also been presented haphazardly. Now they were grouped by look, and it was obvious to Ava that the money the company had invested in hiring the producer and his team had been well worth it.

Of the clothes she now saw on the runway, the jackets and coats were particularly inventive and breathtaking. They were of various lengths, many with asymmetrical hems, and were layered and wrapped and belted in an almost primitive way. Some had collars inspired by cheongsams. Many were softly structured, with voluminous shoulders and sleeves.

Ava was pleased to see that Clark hadn't abandoned the beautiful needlework and intricate stitching that had characterized the early designs she'd seen, and his signature oddly shaped buttons of glass and semi-precious stone continued to make his pieces unique.

As the show progressed, the music of Jacky Cheung morphed into that of Eason Chan and then Zhou Xuan, keeping the factory ladies and the Pos' friends on their feet and making noise.

"It's almost over," May said, looking at her watch. "I've never felt time move so fast."

Almost as soon as she spoke, the runway emptied and the song "Stand Up" blared from the speakers. It had been a hit for Leslie Cheung, one of the kings of Cantopop, who had committed suicide. Ava wondered if the final song was a tribute to Cheung, who was gay. The guests in the front rows were now standing. Ava wondered if Clark was waiting in the wings before coming out to take his bow. Then a model walked onto the stage and stood with her head lowered. She wore a white, almost sheer linen coat that flared like a trumpet from her shoulders to her feet. The linen was lightweight, almost gossamer, and verged on translucent. An intricately embroidered high collar partially masked her face. The coat was cinched at the waist with a toggle that looked as though it was made from green jade.

The music stopped.

The model walked down the runway and stopped halfway. She was close enough now that Ava could see the words A SINGLE SPARK CAN SET THE WORLD ON FIRE stitched down both sides of the coat's front.

The model paused, threw her head back, and reached for the toggle. The coat slipped from her shoulders and onto the floor. Underneath she wore an evening dress that looked as if thin strands of liquid silver had been wrapped around her, strand by strand.

The crowd began to chant Clark's name.

A group of models carrying red silk bags walked onto the stage. They moved down the runway and then parted to each side, revealing Clark standing alone in the centre. He raised his arms high and slowly turned to acknowledge the entire room. He was wearing a simple white cotton T-shirt with "PÖ" printed on it in red. The models reached into their bags and began to toss T-shirts into the crowd.

"Don't worry, we have enough shirts for everyone," Amanda said from behind them.

Ava jumped in surprise and turned to see Amanda, Chi-Tze, and Gillian. Each of them had bags stuffed with shirts.

"We're going to hand them out to everyone who didn't get one," she said.

"Where did you come from?" Ava said.

"Through the back corridors. Tell us, was the crowd this enthusiastic throughout?"

"The audience was like this right from the start. You didn't hear them?"

"We were working, and it was so busy that we couldn't concentrate on anything else."

"The show was unbelievable," May said, her voice rising. "Gillian, you should be so proud of your brother. And the three of you, you should be proud of everything you've done to make this happen. I don't care if we sell a single coat. The experience of this last half-hour was worth every dollar we've spent on PÖ since day one."

"We will sell coats," Chi-Tze said. "I promise you that."

"And this won't hurt," Amanda said, looking at her phone. "I just got a text from Elsa. She wants to do a feature on Clark. She says she's going to stay a few extra days, and she's already asked the Hong Kong office to make arrangements for a photographer."

Before the group had a chance to react, the audience began to file out of the ballroom. The women offered T-shirts that were rolled up and tied with a strip of silk. Ava took one and opened it. The words THE SPARK WAS

LIT and the date were printed under the PÖ logo. Ava stared at it. It was only a T-shirt, but she'd never owned one that meant so much.

AVA OPENED THE DOOR TO HER HOTEL SUITE, FEELING exhausted and exhilarated. Immediately after the show, she had met briefly with Carrie Song and her assistant, Laura Deng. Clark's designs had impressed them and — without making a commitment — Carrie said she had told Laura to start the process of assessing how the clothes might be acquired and introduced at Lane Crawford and Joyce. Ava said the PÖ contacts for Laura would be Gillian and Chi-Tze, and she took her backstage to meet them. Commitment or none, the fact that Lane Crawford was showing interest was enough to make everyone at PÖ dizzy. Their excitement about Lane Crawford and the *Vogue* photo shoot hyped an already electric environment at the after-show party at the sample factory, which had been organized by the factory ladies and the Pos' friends. Ava arrived there with May Ling in the late afternoon, and both of them got caught up in the excitement. Ava couldn't remember the last time she had drunk and danced so much. It was almost ten when she made her escape in a taxi, leaving May and the rest of team at the party.

She went directly to the hotel bed, looked at it lovingly, and was starting to step out of her dress when she saw the blinking red light on her hotel phone. She pulled her cellphone from her bag and saw two missed calls from Xu. She went to the hotel phone, guessing that any message would be from him.

"I'm in the car coming back from Nanjing," he said. "It's past nine o'clock, and we've got another hour or so before we're back in Shanghai. I'd like to see you tonight when I get back. Ring me and let me know if that's possible."

"Shit," Ava said. All she wanted to do was sleep. She contemplated calling him in the morning, but she knew she couldn't. He had sounded worried.

"Hey, it's Ava," she said when he answered her call.

"Where are you?"

"At the hotel. I just got back from the after-party at the sample factory in Pudong."

"I heard from Wu. He said the show was a huge success. He and Fan are thrilled that they'll have a chance to make some of the clothes."

"They're very nice people."

"Do you remember Auntie Grace?"

"Of course."

"Fan is her niece."

"Ah, that explains why you told me to be nice to her," she said. "And where are you?"

"About twenty minutes from the hotel. If you're up to it, I'll drop by and get you. We'll go to the house. Auntie Grace always has a pot of congee on the stove, and if you're really hungry she can make a plate of the best noodles in Shanghai."

"I'm stuffed. I ate all night. I couldn't eat a grain of rice."

"Then we'll just have a drink."

"I'm close to being drunk already. I don't think I can handle much more."

"Then you can drink tea and watch me drink Scotch."

"Xu, is everything okay?" she asked.

"No, it isn't," he said quietly.

"Tsai?"

"Yes, Tsai and his father and his whole fucking family. I need to talk it out."

"Sounds like it could be a long talk."

"Could be."

"Then I'd better shower and put on some fresh clothes. I'll come down to the lobby when I'm ready."

Ava knew that science said a shower would have no impact on her blood-alcohol level, wouldn't cure jet lag, and wouldn't make her any more alert, but she believed in the power of placebos; for her, warm, strong streams of water had somehow always worked. She stood in the shower for close to ten minutes and then quickly towelled herself dry. She threw on clean underwear, the PÖ T-shirt she'd got at the launch, and her Adidas training pants and jacket. She headed downstairs feeling, if not invigorated, at least refreshed.

She almost walked right into Xu's Mercedes when she exited the hotel. Suen was standing by the rear door. He opened it as soon as he saw her. She slid in and leaned over to kiss Xu on the cheek.

"You're lucky I checked my messages before going to bed," she said. "If I'd gotten between those sheets I don't know if anything could have wakened me."

"Are you okay?"

"I took a shower. It helped."

"To the house," Xu said to the driver.

"Were things that bad?" Ava asked as the car pulled away from the hotel.

"Let's not discuss that until we're home," Xu said.

Xu lived in the French Concession, a neighbourhood primarily west of the Bund. The land had initially been ceded to the French in 1849, and the territory was expanded around 1920. Its original street layout and architecture were mainly French with a touch of other European styles, but after the Communists took over in 1949, some buildings were torn down and parts of the area were badly redeveloped, until a public outcry ended the destruction. Xu's neighbourhood had escaped the Communist-style development and still had the aura of a European enclave. He lived in a cottage that was accessed through a narrow alleyway with brick walls on both sides.

She knew they were close to the house when the car slowed to a crawl and made a left turn down an alley with a fruit cart vendor at its entrance. The driver rolled down the window so Suen could talk to the vendor. Ava knew that at the other end of the alley was another fruit cart. They manned the alleyway twenty-four hours a day, and she was sure that under the piles of oranges and apples were a gun and an alarm.

As the car moved down the narrow alleyway, a gate swung open to the left. They turned into a courtyard that was big enough to park three cars alongside a fish pond and a patio. Just inside the courtyard, two men flanked the gate, while a third stood near the door to the house.

"I thought that after the issue with Guangzhou was resolved you wouldn't need this much security," Ava said.

"I don't think I'm in any particular danger, but security has become part of the structure, and Suen would be aggravated if I reduced it. Besides, I love it here and I don't want to move," Xu said.

They left the car and began to walk towards the house. The front door opened before they reached it, and Ava found herself looking at a tiny grey-haired woman.

"Auntie Grace," she said.

"Ava, I'm so happy to see you again."

"And I to see you," Ava said, knowing that she was looking at the one woman in Xu's life who could never be replaced. Auntie Grace had been Xu's nanny from the day he was born and his housekeeper from the day he became head of the family.

"I have congee," she said.

"I wish I could eat, but I'm stuffed."

"Noodles?"

"Auntie, I can't."

"Xu?" she said.

"I'll have noodles," he said. "But first, bring me that bottle of whisky I've been saving and let me get started on that."

Auntie Grace stepped back into the house so they could pass. "I don't like it when he needs that whisky," she said to Ava as if Xu wasn't standing next to her.

"We'll go to the kitchen," Xu said, pretending not to hear.

They walked through the living room and into the kitchen. The white-tiled floor was stained and chipped, and a folding table — the kind brought out for a game of

mah-jong — had been set up in the corner with two folding chairs. The appliances looked as if they were twenty
years old. On the stovetop was a pot of what Ava assumed
was congee. On the counter sat a hot-water Thermos and
a rice cooker.

Ava and Xu sat across from each other.

"Ava, do you want tea?" Auntie Grace said.

"Please."

The old woman took a teapot from the cupboard and
filled it with leaves and hot water from the Thermos. She
placed the pot with a cup in front of Ava. She then went to
another cupboard and took out a bottle of whisky and a
glass. She put those in front of Xu.

"Are you ready to eat?" she said to him.

"Not yet."

"Let me know when you are. I won't sleep," she said.

"Thank you."

Auntie Grace turned to Ava. "I spoke with my niece Fan
tonight. She was very excited about her day."

"She seems to be a very intelligent young woman."

"She was my only sister's only child, and she is my only
immediate family."

"I understand," Ava said softly.

Auntie Grace stared at Xu and then walked out of the
kitchen.

He filled his glass half-full with whisky. "Here's to family," he said.

"That sounds sarcastic."

"A day with Tsai will do that to you."

Ava sipped her tea while he took a gulp of the alcohol.
"So, what the hell happened?" she asked.

"I hardly know where to begin."

"Is it that complicated?"

"It's a fucking mess." Xu ran his fingers through his hair, pressing down on his scalp. "They're going to destroy me. They're going to destroy everything I've built and everything I want to build. What's making me crazy is that I don't think it's even deliberate. They just think they can do whatever they want and get away with it. I'm the one who sees the danger. But Tsai won't listen because his father doesn't listen and because his grandfather never had to listen. I'm dealing with three generations of people who have no idea what it's like to be denied anything."

Ava leaned across the table and touched the back of Xu's hand. "Why don't you start by telling me about the grandfather," she said.

XU WAS SIPPING THE EIGHTEEN-YEAR-OLD MACALLAN whisky with something close to respect.

"Tsai Da-Xia marched with Mao," he began.

"The Long March?"

"'The Long March of the Red Army' is how the Party people refer to it," Xu said. "Do you know much about it?"

"A little, but go on."

"In 1934 the Red Army was losing to Chiang Kai-shek and the Kuomintang in the struggle for control of China. The army was in Jiangxi Province and wasn't strong enough to take on the nationalists. So the soldiers withdrew. They retreated for more than a year, marching 9,000 kilometres. When they finally confronted Chiang, they had grown large enough and strong enough to beat him. The men who were on that march became legends. It vaulted Mao into his position. And the other senior officers all became office holders of the highest rank. Tsai Da-Xia was one of those men. He was eventually appointed to the Politburo Standing Committee."

"Standing committee? That doesn't sound like much of an appointment."

"It was the second most powerful group in the country. Only the chairman was superior to them. In fact, since Chairman Deng Xiaoping died in 1997, the committee has been the main seat of power. There have been no more chairmen since then."

"So Tsai survived the Cultural Revolution, he survived Mao's lunacies?"

"Yeah. The Tsais know how to keep their heads down."

"How long did Tsai Da-Xia serve?"

"He died in 1984, when he was seventy-nine. He was a member of the PSC until his last breath. He was one of eight men on the committee, and five of them were associated with the Long March. Tsai was ranked third. He had responsibility for government administration and the economy."

"How do you know all this?"

"My father and Uncle made it a point to know. We were already holding hands with some government officials and they wanted to know who we were doing business with and how they were connected further up the line. And, as they told me time and time again, there's always someone further up the line."

Ava poured more tea and then heard the gentle slap of slippers on tile. Auntie Grace appeared in the kitchen doorway.

"I think I'll start your noodles," she said. "They'll help reduce the effect of the alcohol."

Xu stared at her. "Do what you want. You will anyway," he said, and looked back at Ava. "Let's sit in the living room until the noodles are ready."

He picked up the bottle and glass. Ava took her cup but

left the pot on the table. As Xu walked past Auntie Grace, he stopped and bent down to kiss her on the forehead.

"Get going," she said, smiling.

The living room was furnished with carved wooden benches and chairs with thin, flat seat cushions. An old tea chest doubled as a coffee table, and two corners of the room were guarded by stone lions. The walls were decorated with traditional paintings of rushing waterfalls, rice paddies, and dragons. Xu sat on one of the benches. Ava took the chair across from him and put her cup on the glass top of the tea chest.

"You said to me yesterday that Tsai Men's father was the governor of Jiangsu," Ava said. "Can I assume that Tsai Da-Xia had something to do with making that happen?"

"Something?" Xu said. "He had everything to do with it."

"What's the governor's name?"

"Tsai Lian, and he's what's called a 'princeling,' or, as my father used to call them, 'the entitled ones.'"

"Neither term sounds particularly positive."

Xu shrugged. "They are the sons of the legends, and in this society, where for decades we tried to restrict the size of families, those sons were the most precious things imaginable. So they were pampered as children, given the best education possible as teenagers and young adults, and then immediately put into government positions. All the while, they were being guided by fathers who had the power to make sure they succeeded. Tsai Lian wasn't unique. I know of at least seven other sons of men who were on the PSC who today are running various parts of China. They're the closest thing we have to royalty. They certainly feel and act like they're part of a dynasty."

"How did he become governor?"

"He was appointed, like every governor in China, except he was given one of the largest and wealthiest provinces. There are eighty million people living in Jiangsu, and it has one of the highest per capita incomes among all of the provinces in the country."

"His father appointed him?"

"No, he was appointed by a committee in Beijing, but every member of the committee knew who his father was. And every member knew that sooner or later he might need Tsai Da-Xia's influence."

"*Guanxi.*"

"Now and forever. The Communists have turned it into an art form."

"How old was he when he was appointed?"

"Forty."

"And he's been in that position ever since?"

"He has, and so has the Communist Party secretary for the province. That's where Da-Xia was smarter than some of his colleagues."

"Why?"

"The secretary has, in theory, as much if not more power than the governor. Da-Xia arranged to have a nephew appointed. The nephew isn't an idiot, but he isn't nearly as smart or as tough as Tsai Lian, and Da-Xia let Tsai Lian call the shots. It's been that way for what seems like an eternity. Other governors and party secretaries come and go, but in Jiangsu the Tsai family rules the province."

"So why has it become so difficult all of a sudden?" Ava said. "From what I'm hearing, your father must have made some kind of arrangement with them."

"He did, and it lasted for years, but Tsai Men has decided he's going to change the way things are done, and his father is either letting it happen or is directing it. I'm not sure which. And it doesn't matter — the end result is the same."

"Do they really have that much power?"

"Yes," Xu said, reaching for his bottle of whisky.

Ava had emptied her teacup. Now she held it towards him. He half filled her cup and raised his glass. "To the Tsais."

"It sounds like you've given in to them."

"I haven't. Not yet, anyway."

"So what do they want?"

"Let's back up for a moment," Xu said. "I want you to understand how this has played out."

Ava nodded.

"When all my father ran were illegal activities — the underground gambling and prostitution and drug-dealing businesses — he didn't have to bother that much with the provincial government. Although he obviously knew who the Tsais were, it was enough that he paid off the Shanghai police and the mayor and his family. But when he started to move into production of knock-off designer clothes and the like, he had to move outside Shanghai to find land where he could build a factory. Jiangsu is Shanghai's immediate neighbour, and going there made sense. But the moment he did that, he ran into the Tsai family. He discovered that he wasn't going to get any land unless they approved the sale and transfer, and he wasn't going to build a factory unless they gave him the permit.

"The government in Beijing may control the military and foreign affairs and set the macroeconomic policies for the country, but it's the provinces that manage things like education, health, social security, and welfare. Those all require money, of course, and the provinces have the right to generate their own tax and revenue streams. They can also pass their own laws and regulations as long as they don't conflict with national laws. Since Beijing doesn't care about things like land rights, building permits, and tenders, those are left to the provinces as well. A lot of it is small stuff, but it all adds up."

"And the Tsais had their fingers in everything?"

"Of course. At first we paid for actual services rendered, like getting the rights to a piece of land and a building permit. Then they decided they wanted regular cash flow and demanded monthly payments from ongoing operations. My father gave ground grudgingly, but when all was said and done, he eventually didn't have any choice except to concede."

"How were they paid?"

"For years the money went through underground remittance shops in Hong Kong, and then they started using VIP junket operators in Macau to clean money. They finally opened some offshore accounts, but when two senior officials in other provinces were discovered to have bank accounts in Europe that had hundreds of millions of dollars in them, all hell broke loose. They were arrested, tried, and executed within a month. I don't know what the Tsais did with their offshore accounts, but we were told to stop sending money to them. Instead we found ourselves paying management and consultant fees to various companies."

"Did those companies do anything to earn the money?"

"No."

"How many are directly owned by the family?"

"The Governor owns nothing that we know of and has no formal association with any of them. Tsai Men is the managing director of one firm. We also send money to a company operated by a woman who is Men's sister. Then from time to time we're asked to pay a consulting fee to a third firm, run by a Hu Chi, who I was told is the sister's husband. So any way you look at it, all the money flows to someone who is a Tsai or related to the family. And you can be sure, one hundred percent sure, that the old man knows and ultimately controls everything."

"They aren't concerned about receiving money from your organization?"

"The payments come from our factories. They actually invoice them."

"Does Tsai Men have an official government position?"

"No, he's just an ordinary businessman whose father happens to be governor and whose cousin is party secretary for the province."

"How much have you been paying these companies?"

"When the monthly payments started, it was about half a million renminbi — about one hundred thousand U.S. dollars. It just keeps growing, and it seems like every month there's a new fee for something or other. And then those fees are always increased whenever we open a plant."

"And of course they would know when you expand."

"They issue the permits and the licences, so they sure as hell do know. Tsai says he likes to think of us as partners."

"And you don't?"

"They're leeches."

"How much do you pay them every month now?"

"In total, about five hundred thousand U.S. dollars."

"Is that the problem?"

"The monthly amount isn't the issue. As long as they provide us with services, protection, and a stable environment in which we can grow our business, they're worth the money."

"So what's changed?"

Xu reached for the whisky bottle and this time filled his glass. He took several sips and wiped his mouth with the back of his hand.

"They want us to build a new factory," he said.

"Is that what was being discussed in Nanjing?"

"Yes. They started talking to us about a month ago. They approached Feng first. He's my administrator. Their proposal worried him. He didn't like the idea that they were telling us what businesses we should be in. He said if we gave in to that, then next they'd be telling us how to run them. He sees it as a matter of principle."

"He has a point."

"Yeah, except arguing principles with the Tsais is a total waste of breath," Xu said. "When Feng came to me with their proposal, I met with Tsai Men. I told him right away and as bluntly as I could that I wasn't interested. He insisted. We reached an impasse. His trip to Shanghai was another attempt to resolve the matter, and we couldn't. That's why I went to Nanjing today. I met with him and his father. It's only the second time in the past ten years that I've seen or spoken to the Governor. The other time was at my father's funeral."

"He stays that much in the background?"

"He acts like he's invisible."

"But he met with you yesterday?"

"Yes, at the home of an elderly relative of his. They took me in through the back door."

"I can understand why he thinks he has to be discreet," Ava said. "What was important enough for him to meet with you?"

"He wanted to tell me how pleased he was about the number of jobs we'd created in Jiangsu, and he hoped that I would continue to work with Men to bring more jobs and prosperity to the province. Then he spent ten minutes drinking tea with me and reminiscing about my father."

"That was all?"

"That was enough. What he had to say didn't matter. The message was in the fact that he had bothered to meet with me at all. After he left, Men told me that I was being stubborn and stupid by refusing to build the plant. He told me that I had insulted his father and that the decision was no longer mine to make. They had selected the land and lined up the people we needed to operate the plant, and he was going to have a permit issued to one of my companies. Because I was being difficult, they'd also decided to partner with me. It would be a fifty-fifty arrangement. They'd be silent partners, of course. He said I should be pleased with the security that their involvement guaranteed. He gave me three months to get started."

"And if you don't meet that deadline?"

"He didn't say. He knew he didn't have to."

"What kind of plant is it?"

Xu took another sip of whisky, his eyes wandering away from Ava. She turned and saw Auntie Grace.

"Your noodles are ready," she said.

"I'll be right there," Xu replied.

"What kind of plant?" Ava asked again as they got up from their seats.

"The Tsais are determined to get me back into the drug business."

(7)

"ARE YOU SURE YOU DON'T WANT ANY NOODLES?"
Auntie Grace asked Ava in the kitchen.

"No, thanks," Ava said.

"There's a small plate on the table, just in case."

Xu sat at his place, and Auntie Grace filled his plate with fried noodles with thin slices of beef and chicken, slivers of green onion, and mushrooms.

"I'm going to bed now," Auntie Grace said. "If either of you need anything, let me know."

"We will," Xu said.

The older woman hovered for a few seconds as if there was something she wanted to say, but then she shrugged and left.

Xu dug into the noodles with his head down. Ava waited until he'd eaten about half, and then she couldn't wait anymore.

"What kind of drugs?" she said.

He sat back and picked up his glass of whisky. "They told me it was only synthetic drugs and that I shouldn't worry about it."

"Ecstasy?"

"And ketamine and methamphetamine."

"Meth is as addictive as heroin."

"I know. They said it was flooding into the province from places like Guangdong and they knew the profits were enormous. They said we should have control of our home market and not allow outsiders free rein. I said, 'What market? We're not in that business.' They reminded us that we had been, not so many years ago. I tried to explain why we got out of it, but their response was that we hadn't been so strongly connected to the Tsai family then, and if we had been, we'd still be in it."

"Is there any truth in that?"

"No," Xu snapped. "As powerful as they are, there are lines that can't be crossed."

"The police?"

"Eventually, but the more immediate problems would be with my triad colleagues in Guangdong and Guangzhou. They're in the business. I don't agree with it, but they have their reasons. If I tell them that I've started making meth, they'll think I'm trying to take over their markets. I mean, for the past few years all I've been talking about is how great it is to be out of that business. They'll think I'm a hypocrite, or worse, a liar. The trust I've been building among the gangs will start to deteriorate. I'll lose relationships and I'll lose business. And I'm telling you, Ava, once the trust is breached, even a friend like Lam in Guangzhou will be impossible to win back, and my chances of being re-elected chairman could disappear."

"What other risks are there?"

"The police and the military all have skin in the game.

The Tsais think they can shield us from them, provide security, but I know thinking like that is careless. How do you think K and meth are getting into Jiangsu and being so broadly distributed? Deals have been cut all the way down the line, from importer to street dealer. The cops are part of the system, and no one, including them, is going to sit back and let the new boys just stroll in and take over the market. They'll find out soon enough who we are, and then we'll be in their crosshairs."

"Wouldn't the Tsais be implicated as well?"

"Not very likely. This so-called partnership wouldn't be on paper; they'd just expect half the profits. And if the shit hit the fan, which I'm convinced it would eventually, they'd distance themselves as far from me as humanly possible. God, I can imagine them supplying the bullets to shoot me if it came down to it."

"I can tell you're frustrated, but I'm beginning to sense that you're maybe resigned to it as well."

He shrugged. "We have eight factories in Jiangsu that employ more than thirty thousand people. We could be China's largest manufacturer of cellphones, tablets, and other devices and software that isn't Apple, Samsung, or Microsoft. We make really good products. We have a great customer base. Profits are terrific. And the authorities leave us entirely alone. Life has never been better for my people."

"Thanks to knock-offs," Ava felt compelled to add.

"Yes, but we've still made huge investments and developed manufacturing expertise that is almost impossible for anyone else to acquire — especially quickly. So we have that market to ourselves for at least a while, and if we're careful and manage it properly we'll have it for years. It's a virtual monopoly. Why, I asked Tsai Men, would I put it all at risk by moving into a business like synthetic drugs, where the competition is ferocious and my presence will only piss off my customer base for software and devices?"

"What did he say?"

"The profit margins justify it."

"Do they?"

"Yes, if you don't care about the long term and don't give a shit about other consequences."

"So it's all about money in the here and now?"

"It's always about money in the here and now," Xu said, lifting the bottle. "You want another drink?"

"Sure. My head has suddenly cleared."

He poured her a stiff shot and then looked at his plate. "Auntie Grace does make the best noodles in Shanghai, and right now I can't taste a damn thing."

"Can you just say no to the Tsais?" she asked.

"In so many words, I've done that already. It's not an answer they're prepared to accept."

"What if you don't build the plant?"

"It wouldn't buy me any time, if that's what you're thinking," Xu said. "Once the permit is issued they'll expect to see results."

"No, I mean what would you expect to happen if you didn't build the plant? Surely they wouldn't be so short-sighted as to hurt your business when it's providing so much monthly cash to them."

"Hurt our business?" Xu said. "Ava, if they chose, they could shut us down in no time. Permits and licences could be cancelled and our plants closed for any number of contrived reasons."

"Including the non-contrived fact that you're actually breaking the law?"

"That too," he said with a tight smile. "But I'd be surprised if they wanted to call attention to that fact. It might raise questions they don't want to answer, like how it was possible factories that size could operate without the government knowing what they were doing."

"True enough."

"And anyway, they're too smart to do anything overly dramatic. I think they'd start by going after a couple of the smaller plants as their way of telling me they're serious. They might not shut them down, but they'd make life difficult. I imagine the parts and supplies we need to make our products might be tied up. We wouldn't get the clearances we need to export. They'd send in inspectors to comb through employment records and make us release some employees who aren't properly documented. And so on. It would be a mess."

"Is there anything you can do to deter them?"

"Aside from reasoning with them, nothing that I can think of. They've got the power and the means to use it. Uncle was always cautious, to the point of being paranoid, when it came to dealing with the politicians and bureaucrats in this country. He warned me more than once not to get too close. He said that no matter how much you pay them, you are always renting and never owning. He was right, but I got sucked in bit by bit."

"But they're taking money, right? They're taking bribes. They're corrupt as hell. What if that was known? Could you use that threat to make them back down?"

"Ava, that's dangerous even to think about, let alone say.

First, they've got their asses at least partially covered by all those supposedly independent companies that are issuing invoices for services rendered. There's no proof that they're taking bribes. Next, where are you going to take a half-baked accusation? There's no newspaper or media outlet in China that would touch it. The Tsais control the entire legal process in the province, and many of the people working in that system are on the take as well."

"What if you went outside the province? What if you went to Beijing?"

"That would be even riskier, and probably suicidal," Xu said. "Tsai Lian isn't just the governor of Jiangsu. He sits on the party's Politburo, and that gives him the same rank as a central government minister. He's one of the twenty-five most powerful people in the country. His fellow politicians will support him even if we have a strong case, because everyone has something to hide and one day they might need his support. No one is going to rock the boat. If we tried to make an issue of this, the entire political system from the top down would be focused on two things: protecting Tsai and killing the messenger."

Ava shook her head in frustration. "I can't believe there's nothing that can be done."

"I do have a short-term plan," Xu said.

"Yes?"

"It's not much of one, but it's all I have."

"I'm anxious to hear it."

"I'm going to build the plant."

"You're serious?"

"I am."

"Even though you think it will lead to disaster?"

"It will buy me the time you talked about earlier," he said. "I'll go to Guangdong and Guangzhou and tell Lam and Ming what's going on. I'll get one of them to help me put up the plant. We'll create enough problems that it will take a lot longer to finish than planned. So instead of three months, maybe I can get five or six."

"And then?"

"I either figure out a way to get around the Tsais or I'm back in drug production and will have to face the fallout."

8

IT WAS SOMEWHERE BETWEEN TWO AND THREE WHEN
Ava left the house in the French Concession and was driven
back down the alleyway past the fruit cart vendor. Suen sat
next to the driver in the front seat of the Mercedes. Xu was
in the back seat with Ava, his left hand gripping her right.

"You should stay the night," Auntie Grace had said to
Ava. "We have a spare room."

"No, I like my own bed, even when it's in a hotel."

The older woman burrowed her head into Ava's shoulder.
"It's been a long time since I've seen him this troubled," she
whispered. "Help him."

"I don't know what I can do."

"Figure something out," she said, kissing Ava on the cheek.

As soon as Ava got into her hotel room she threw off
her clothes and ran to the bed. At ten to nine, she woke
with the sun boring into her eyes. She closed the drapes
and retreated to bed. It was just after eleven when she woke
again, this time feeling alert.

She retrieved the newspapers from the door, made
a coffee, and sat in the easy chair by the window. The

international *New York Times* was crammed with stories about leaders under attack and governments under siege, in Thailand, Italy, Iraq, Syria, France, and Ukraine. The *Shanghai Daily News* didn't mention any of it. It was as if it didn't want to give its readers any ideas. Instead, the paper was full of economic data, including several charts showing how the twenty-two provinces were performing. Jiangsu was indeed among the leading provinces in the country in GDP per capita and GNP, and given that its population at eighty million was one of the largest, its economic performance was even more impressive. Among other things, it was China's number one exporter of textiles and electronics. Ava wondered if Xu's products were included in the data. Whether they were or not, Tsai Lian had clearly been an effective governor. She thought about Xu's dilemma and shivered. He obviously hadn't exaggerated Tsai's power and influence. If anything, he might have understated it.

Ava made another coffee and then turned to her electronic devices. There were no phone messages, but her mother had texted her twice. The first text, at five in the afternoon, Toronto time, said Jennie Lee had taken a break from the baccarat tables and was in Rama's Chinese restaurant. She was up $5,000. The next, at eight Toronto time, said her hot streak had continued and she was moving to the high-stakes room. That was three hours ago, Ava calculated — more than enough time for her mother to burn through any winnings she'd made. She texted back, Glad to hear you're doing well.

She turned on her computer and saw that both Amanda and May Ling had sent her emails. May Ling's had arrived at three thirty and Amanda's at four. Ava couldn't believe they'd been up that late. Both of them were already tipsy when she'd left Pudong.

Wanted you to know that we've given everyone the day off tomorrow so there's no rush to do anything, Amanda wrote. And wanted you to know how lucky I feel to have you as my sister and my partner. I love you, and the Pos love you, and Chi-Tze loves you. Your little sister, Amanda.

Good grief, Ava thought, *she must have been really drunk when she wrote that.*

May Ling wrote, We gave the factory workers the day off tomorrow, and I need it more than anyone. Can't remember the last time I drank like this. Suki wants to meet, but I've put her off until dinner. Did you get a chance to talk to Xu? Call me when you're up. You shouldn't have bailed on me so early. Love, May Ling.

She phoned May Ling's room.

"*Wei,*" May groaned.

"It's me."

"What time is it?"

"Close to noon."

"God, I feel awful."

"Drink some coffee, have a shower, and meet me downstairs in half an hour."

"It takes me longer than that to get my face on."

"Then forty-five minutes."

"An hour."

"Okay. Do you want to eat here or do you want to go out?"

"Who said anything about eating?"

"I'll meet you in Yi Long Court on the second floor," Ava said. "I'll try to eat before you get there."

"Good idea."

Ava went into the bathroom, looked at the shower, and then went to the sink. She brushed her teeth, washed her face, brushed her hair, and then returned to the bedroom. Five minutes later she was in the elevator, wearing a black Giordano T-shirt and her Adidas training pants. It was going to be that kind of day, she decided.

The hostess at Yi Long didn't give her a second glance before directing her to a table. She wasn't near a window, but the view of the Art Deco *objets d'art* scattered around the restaurant was pleasant enough. Ava glanced at the menu, and when the server arrived she was ready to order.

"Jasmine tea, hot and sour soup with shredded abalone, pan-fried bean curd with mushrooms, Shanghai fried rice, and the pan-fried sliced cod in soy," Ava said. "Bring whatever's ready first."

Half an hour later she was still working on the rice, but everything else had been consumed. She couldn't remember the last time she'd been so ravenous. There was something about wine and dancing that set off her appetite.

She heard May Ling before she saw her. Actually, she heard May Ling being fussed over by the staff before she saw her.

"I didn't realize you were such a celebrity," Ava said as May sat down.

"We just spent about half a million dollars here. If they hadn't known who I was, I would have been angry," May said.

"I've never seen you in sunglasses before."

"And I'm not taking them off. My eyes make me look like a fish."

"It was a great day and a great night," Ava said.

"I'm still on a bit of a high from the show, but I can't handle the nights like I used to."

Ava looked down at the table. "I have some rice left if you want it."

"Just tea."

Ava poured. "What time are you meeting Suki?"

"Five."

"Where?"

"I'm going to her office and then we're going out to dinner from there. Even though we don't have the money on hand, I think we need to get a final cost on what she wants to do and find out if there's any flexibility when it comes to timing. I just don't want to say no to her."

"Me neither."

"Will you join us?"

"I'd like to."

May downed her tea and then held out the cup for more. "You haven't mentioned Xu. I was hoping you had the chance to talk to him about the additional money."

"There was no opportunity at the reception. I saw him last night but it wasn't appropriate to bring it up."

"You saw him last night?"

"Yes."

"Where did you see him? You left Pudong rather late."

"I went to his house for a few hours."

"Oh."

Ava wasn't sure what emotion she had heard in May's voice. "May, do you mind if I ask you something very personal?"

"I don't think so, but then I haven't heard the question," she said carefully.

"It's about your business in Wuhan, in Hubei."

"Ask away."

"Well, I remember you talking more than once about how you handle provincial officials from a remuneration standpoint."

"You mean how we don't handle them?"

"Yes."

"It was Changxing who figured it out. He realized early on that giving them money or direct favours made both sides vulnerable. So he came up with the idea of providing jobs for their relatives. At first it was pretty basic work, but he made sure they were qualified and that they really worked. Then we started adding scholarships for their children — again making sure the kids were smart enough to earn them — and reserving entry-level positions for them when they graduated."

"So you never gave money directly to anyone?"

"Never, and if they asked for it, we didn't do business with them again."

"That's what I remember you telling me. I just wanted to make sure."

"Does this have something to do with Xu?" May asked.

"Yeah."

"I don't like hearing that."

"And I understand why. It isn't a good situation."

"Has he been paying someone?"

"His business has."

"Well, I may not think it's the wisest policy, but it can be effective. It all depends, of course, on who he's paying and how much he's paying and what he's paying them to do."

"Have you heard of the Tsai family?"

"It's a common enough name."

"This particular Tsai family runs Jiangsu."

May caught her breath. She adjusted her sunglasses and took a sip of tea. "I have trouble believing he's paying them."

"Why?"

"Maybe because I don't want to believe it."

"You think that highly of them?"

"Not especially, although they're a prominent family. We were taught about Tsai Da-Xia in school. He was on the Long March and served with Mao and Zhou Enlai in the government. His son has been governor of Jiangsu forever, it seems."

"I know about the history, and none of it excludes the possibility that they're corrupt."

"You should be cautious about how you use words like that," May said with a slight shake of her head. "People in government, especially those in high positions, have to do business with all kinds of people. Maybe they've dealt with Xu with the very best intentions."

"According to Xu, they've been taking money for years and it's now into the millions every year."

"Who's been taking it?"

"The family."

"Ava, you need to be specific. The governor's name is Tsai Lian, as I recall. Is the money going to him?"

"Not directly."

"What does that mean?"

"It's being funnelled through a number of companies that are controlled by his son, Tsai Men, and other family members."

"Xu is paying these companies?"

"Yes."

"Under what pretext?"

"They're supposedly management and consulting fees. It's all bogus."

"So no services are provided at all?"

"He gets all the permits and licences he needs, and the authorities turn a blind eye to his illegal factories. He doesn't have any problems either importing or exporting goods. I guess you'd call all those things services."

"So the money goes from Xu's companies to Men's?"

"I think so."

"Were contracts signed?"

"I don't know," Ava said, wishing she'd asked Xu that question.

"Is Tsai Lian directly connected to any of those companies?"

"Apparently not."

"So if there's any corruption going on, it could be orchestrated by his son acting on his own."

"No, Xu said his father had a long-standing relationship with Lian that's been passed down to Xu and Men."

"Does Xu ever have any contact with Lian?" May asked.

"He met with him yesterday in Nanjing."

"I have to say that's a bit shocking," May said. "What did they talk about?"

Ava closed her eyes and sighed. "Tsai Lian thanked him for helping to create so many jobs in Jiangsu, and asked him to keep working with Men to create more."

"That's it?"

"Yeah. I know it sounds weak, but Xu stressed that the fact Lian would meet with him at all is significant."

"This chat is starting to make my stomach feel upset. I

think I'll have some rice now," May said, reaching for the serving platter with her spoon.

Ava did the same and ate quietly while her mind raced.

"I'm not discounting anything you've told me," May finally said. "It's just delicate and complicated, and it's not something I'd rush to judge. It's risky enough accusing a senior official of being on the take even if you find him with a bag of cash. What you're telling me is a long way from that. It could be the son is milking his father's name and reputation."

Ava shrugged. "I understand that the link to Lian sounds tenuous, but Xu is insistent that it's real."

"Okay, but what does that matter and where does it lead? He's been paying them for years without any negative consequences that I can see. Why has it become a concern now?"

"They're not content with just taking money. They want to become his partner in a business and they're strong-arming him to get into it."

"What kind of business?"

"Drugs," Ava said without hesitation.

"You're not serious," May said.

"Drugs of the synthetic variety — ketamine, ecstasy, and meth. They want him to open a lab."

"That's insane."

"That's what Xu thinks, but they're not listening to him."

"Tell him to say no."

"He's tried to without actually saying so. He's afraid of the damage they can do to his existing businesses."

May shook her head. "I can't believe that Tsai Lian would condone that."

"Damaging Xu's businesses?"

"No, the drug lab."

"Maybe he hasn't. Maybe, as you say, it's Men acting on his own."

May poured tea for the two of them and took off her sunglasses. Her eyes were slightly puffy, but nowhere near as horrendous as she'd made out. "What's Xu going to do?"

"He doesn't know. He has a short-term plan to buy some time, but beyond that, nothing."

"Is he asking you for advice?"

"He's using me as a sounding board, that's all."

"When you get the chance, please tell him not to mess around with the Tsai family."

"If he doesn't do something he's going to be forced into building the lab, and if he does that he's going to make enemies of some triad gangs who are currently friends, and he thinks that inevitably the police and army will be all over him."

"That still might be easier than tangling with the Tsais."

9

"LET'S GO FOR A WALK," MAY SAID AS AVA SETTLED the lunch bill. "I could use some air, and it's almost a sin to come here and not experience the Bund on foot."

They left the hotel and crossed the street to the promenade. It was even more crowded than usual and their walk turned into a shuffle. That and the fact that the river view was blocked by a solid wall of people staring out onto the Huangpu and the Pearl Tower and skyscrapers that lined the riverbank in Pudong made the outing seem rather pointless to Ava.

"You surprised me when you made that remark about Xu tangling with the Tsais," Ava said. "I didn't think you'd put much credence into what I was telling you."

"Even if a quarter of it is true, that's still reason enough to tiptoe around that family. You don't want to give them the slightest indication that you might pose a problem. You don't get to Lian's status without being incredibly smart and superbly connected. And you don't survive for as long as he has without having a highly refined instinct for survival. He's the kind of man who can anticipate trouble before it has a chance of raising its head and is willing to chop off the head without waiting to see if his instincts were right."

"Why would Xu cause him trouble?"

"He doesn't have to; Tsai Lian just needs to think Xu's capable of it. Xu shouldn't mess with him or, by extension, with his son. Lian would regard any attempt to discredit his son or his family as a direct attack on himself."

"I understand."

"Good."

"But May, I've been thinking about what you said at lunch."

"I said a lot of things."

"Well, one thing you made clear was that I don't really know much about the deal between Xu and the Tsais."

"So?"

"You sparked my curiosity."

"That wasn't my intent."

"I know, but I wouldn't mind finding out how many companies the Tsai family actually has and who is running what, including which other relatives are in the mix."

"Ava!"

"Don't panic. I'm not going to run off half-cocked. But I am thinking about it and I am curious."

"What did I tell you about how sensitive this situation is?"

"May, I know how to be discreet, and I know how to keep my head down."

"Why bother with it at all?"

"Well, I'm thinking that if Xu is giving them money, then the likelihood is that they're doing deals with others."

"I'd say it's closer to a certainty than a likelihood."

"It would be interesting to know who they are."

"Why?"

"You never know what you might find," Ava said with a shrug.

"That's the potential problem," May said. "What if what you find is trouble?"

"All of the Tsai companies would have to be registered, wouldn't they?"

"You're not listening to me," May said.

"I'm listening. I'm just not agreeing."

"I don't want to talk about this anymore," May said.

"That won't stop me thinking about it."

"Ava, you just can't blunder about. You don't know the system here well enough."

"That's why I'm asking you questions."

"You're making me crazy is what you're doing."

"Look, given our relationship with Xu, we have a stake in this. And I think, like me, you still want us to be doing business with him a year or two from now. I don't want this drug thing to get him killed or thrown into a Chinese jail."

"You're being dramatic."

"Maybe, but don't forget what organization he's part of, and don't start minimizing the danger the Tsai family represents after you've just told me so much about it."

"Ava, I concede that Xu is in a difficult position, whichever way he turns. What I don't understand is what you think you can actually do about it."

"He needs to find some leverage that will persuade the Tsai family to back off on the lab."

"What kind of leverage?"

"I don't know. Maybe they've been careless somewhere. Maybe I can find a direct link between the Governor and the money. I won't know until I see it. That's why I want to take a close look at those companies."

"It sounds very iffy to me."

"So it should. I have no idea what I'll find, but I won't find anything unless I make the effort. If it turns out there's nothing, then Xu can deal with Tsai Men as best he can and we'll just hope it works out."

May stepped in front of Ava. "If I get involved, you have to actually listen to me and not just pretend to."

"I will."

"You would have to stay completely under the Tsai family's radar."

"I understand."

"That means no direct contact with any of them and no direct contact with anyone who's one of their partners or works for them. "

"May, I've spent my career following paper trails. They'll never know I'm looking."

"And I want you to tell me what you find when you find it. I don't want any surprises."

"So I assume you'll help?"

"Yes," May said slowly. "I only wish I felt as carefree about it as you sound."

Ava smiled. "Then can we go back to my original question about company registrations?"

"The companies would be registered," May said with a heavy sigh.

"Would the officers and shareholders be listed?"

"Of course, but that might not mean much. If they're intent on hiding the true identity of the shareholders they could have any number of people — including family and friends — listed instead. It's done all the time, and not always for sinister reasons. I mean, I know business-people who just don't want anyone to know what they're actually worth.

"The most important name attached to most of the companies is the designated legal representative. Every business in China, domestic and foreign, is required to have one. They're the people empowered to represent the company and enter into binding obligations on its behalf. They'll have full access to the company cash and capital. Their chop stamps — which are registered with the police — are as vital as any signature."

Pedestrian traffic had thinned and they were able to walk faster. As they did, Ava stretched her arms out in front and to the sides. Her morning languor was fading and she began to feel, if not invigorated, energetic. She knew that part of that energy spurt came from her decision to try to help Xu. What was odd was that she wasn't quite sure when she'd made it. She hadn't even thought about it until she'd started talking to May over lunch, and even then she hadn't been conscious of it. It was as if her mind was just pro-grammed to respond that way.

"I'm going to start with Feng," Ava said abruptly.

"Who's he?"

"Xu's administrator. He controls the records. I'll get him to provide me with all the information he has about the Tsai companies."

"Will he tell Xu that you asked?"

"I'll probably have to go through Xu to get Feng to do it."

"What will you say to him?"

"I'm information gathering, that's all," Ava said. "I want

to understand just how large the Tsai empire is and who else is affected by it."

"He'll want to know why."

"And I'll tell him the truth," Ava said. "I want to help Xu, but I don't have a clue what to do. So I'm doing what I would have done on any job with Uncle, and that's finding as much information as I can and hoping that somewhere there's a nugget or two that we can use to our advantage."

They reached the end of the Bund and reversed their course. As they did, Ava's phone rang.

"Hey," she said.

"How are you feeling?" Amanda asked.

"Surprisingly good. I'm out for a walk on the Bund with May. How about you?"

"I woke up about half an hour ago. I have a headache and I'm a bit nauseated, but the last time I felt this happy was on my wedding day. Yesterday was terrific."

"It was. You and Chi-Tze and Gillian did a wonderful job."

"It was Clark who did it."

"There's no doubt he's the star, but without your support it wouldn't have happened."

"Thanks, Ava. I'll tell the girls what you said."

"Do you have plans for today?"

"I'm meeting with Gillian and Chi-Tze later this afternoon. We're going to review the response to the show and figure out what needs to get done over the next few weeks. Tonight I'm having dinner with Elsa Ngan. Her photographer starts shooting tomorrow. I've arranged for him and Clark to spend most of the day together."

"I assume Lane Crawford will be part of your review," Ava said.

"Yes, it's at the top of the list. Carrie Song's assistant has already emailed us with a long list of questions. I forwarded some of them to Clark and he's promised to get back to me by tomorrow morning. She'll have to wait until then for answers, because I don't want to send her anything that's incomplete."

"Well, it has to be a positive sign that she contacted you so quickly."

"That's what we thought."

"I would join you for the meeting, but I'm tied up on another project right now and I could be for a few days."

"Do you need any help with that project?" Amanda asked. Ava detected disappointment in the question. She was going to have to be more sensitive with the girls. They should never feel that she was doing something for the business behind their backs.

"It has nothing to do with the Three Sisters. It's a carry-over from my old work. I'll be glad to get it out of way," Ava said. "I'm going to try to have dinner with Suki and May tonight."

"Suki's a force of nature."

"Like Clark, only different."

"They're not as different as they look," Amanda said. "Both are creative, focused, and driven."

"They are indeed."

"I should get going," Amanda said. "Good luck with your project."

Ava ended the call. "Gillian, Amanda, and Chi-Tze are getting together at the plant to plot the next steps."

"I wish I was joining them."

"It's better that we look after Suki. Amanda just called

her a force of nature, and she's right. But we don't want her out of control."

"That's exactly what I was going to say to you."

10

AVA CALLED XU'S CELL AS SOON AS SHE GOT BACK TO the hotel. When he didn't answer, she called the house.

"Auntie Grace, this is Ava."

"He's outside sitting by the fish pond. He's smoking and feeding his fish."

"Tell him to call me at the hotel or on my cell when he's back inside."

"No, wait. He's been out there too long anyway. I'll get him."

Before Ava could argue, the line went quiet. About a minute later she heard voices in the background. What Xu was saying was indistinct, but he sounded irritated.

"Ava, did you sleep well?" he said.

"Yes, not bad. I'm sorry if I'm disturbing you."

"Never. It's Auntie Grace. She's on a mission to get me to stop smoking."

"I've been thinking about our talk last night," she said.

"Me too, and I'm sorry I bothered you with it. You have enough on your plate with this new business. You don't need the distraction."

"What did you decide to do about your problem?"

"I called Lam this morning. I'm flying to Guangzhou tonight."

"Did you talk to Ming in Guangdong?"

"No, I decided against it. I don't have as good a relationship with him. Lam owes me — owes us — a lot. I'm hoping he'll be willing to help. If that falls flat, I'll go to Guangdong."

"Did you tell him what you wanted?"

"Not over the phone."

"Obviously face to face is preferable," Ava said, and then paused. "Xu, I'd like to do some research into the Tsai family. Would you ask Feng to give me absolutely all the information he has on the companies you're sending money to?"

"Why?"

The question was abrupt and caught her off guard. She started to frame a justification, and then stopped.

"Because I want it," she said.

"Okay," he said slowly.

"And while you're away, please tell him to give me whatever else I ask for."

"What are you up to?"

"Uncle and I always wanted to know as much as possible about the people we were dealing with."

"You aren't actually dealing with the Tsai family. I meant it when I said I was using you as a sounding board. You shouldn't get involved."

"I'm not really getting involved. I'm an interested spectator. I'll stay on the sidelines. You never know — I might find some information you could use to improve your situation."

"Like what?"

"I have no idea, and that's the way it always is until I stumble upon it. There's no guarantee, of course, that I'll find anything at all."

"Ava, I didn't tell you about this problem with the intention of pulling you into it."

"I know, and I'm really not getting pulled into it. I just want to poke around a bit. I mean, I'm in Shanghai and I have time on my hands, and I'm trained to do this kind of research. It can't hurt."

"Maybe not," he said slowly.

"So call Feng for me."

"If I do, I don't want anyone but him, me, and you to know what you're planning. We can't have your name dragged into this thing."

"I've actually told May what I'm thinking of doing."

Xu paused. "I wish you hadn't."

"She won't say anything to anyone. I trust her completely."

"I know, but you have to be careful," Xu said. "I'm not sure you understand. Tsai Men remembers your name. He mentioned it to me yesterday in Nanjing. So it would be a problem if it came up in connection with his companies or mine. He'd assume I put you up to it."

"Why would he mention me?" Ava asked.

"It isn't worth repeating."

"Pang Fai said he's a pig."

"Then you have some idea of what he said."

"Charming."

"That's the last thing he is," Xu said. "Ava, I still don't like this idea of yours, but I do see the possible benefits. You just need to be cautious."

"I will be very, very careful," Ava said.

"Okay, then I'll talk to Feng."

"Could you call him right away? Give him my cell number."

"I'll call him now."

"Thanks, and have a safe journey. Give my regards to Lam."

"He made a point of asking if you were coming with me. He has tremendous admiration for you."

"We did go to war together."

"And we won."

Ava ended the call and went to her computer, hoping to see an email from her mother. It was the middle of the night in Toronto, and she hadn't heard from her in what was now close to seven hours. She wrote: I'm worried about you. Hope you're home safely from Rama. There were a couple of ways to interpret the word "safely" and Ava knew Jennie Lee would pick up on them both.

She then turned to a Chinese search engine and entered the name Tsai Lian. Page after page of references emerged, and every page she looked at confirmed that he was indeed an important man from an important family who held an important position. *What are you doing asking Xu to open a drug factory?* she thought. Before she could answer her own question, she heard her cellphone.

"Ava Lee," she said.

"This is Feng."

"Where are you?"

"At the office."

"Did the boss tell you what I wanted?"

"He did."

"Good. Now, what are the three Tsai companies you're sending money to?"

He was quiet.

"There are three, correct?"

"Yes."

"And they are?" Ava asked, slightly annoyed that she had to prod him.

"Nanjing Hallmark Consulting Company Limited, Nanjing Evergreen Trading Company Limited, and Jiangsu Gold Star Investments."

"How is the money sent?"

"We remit monthly by wire transfer."

"Against an invoice?"

"Always."

"The same amounts to each?"

"Close enough."

"How many of your companies are remitting?"

"Just three. We designated one factory for each of their companies. It keeps things simpler. The invoices come directly to me and I tell the factories how much to send, although it hasn't varied in a while."

"How much do you know about the companies you're sending money to?"

"Not a lot. We have the company names and their bank account information. That's all we need to send the wires."

"Just a moment. Xu said that Tsai Men heads up one and that he has a sister who runs another, and her husband is with the third."

"That's right. They're listed as the legal representatives, although we never actually confirmed that the sister is married."

"Are there other individuals' names attached to these companies?"

"Not that I know of, although I haven't looked at the documents in a while."

Ava again sensed reluctance, or caution, emanating from the other end of the phone.

"Feng, tell me, are you having a problem with this conversation?" she said.

He hesitated. "No."

"Well, I think you are," Ava said. "I'm not going to explain to you who I am. It's enough that you know I've offered to help with this Tsai business and Xu has accepted my offer. If that's an issue for you, call Xu and explain it to him."

"I don't have to call him. He made it clear enough."

"So why are you behaving like this?"

"The truth is I'm scared."

"Are you saying you're afraid we're going to kick a hornets' nest?"

"No, I'm afraid you're going to."

"That's the third warning I've received. Let me tell you what I told the others: I know how to keep my head down and I know how to be discreet."

"I'm sorry if I sounded uncooperative."

"Okay, let's forget about it. How long will it take for you to get the names of all the people attached to those three companies?"

"I'll call the bank now."

"Speaking of our need to be cautious, do you trust the bank to keep your inquiry confidential?"

"My brother-in-law is my contact."

"Is he completely trustworthy?"

"He took the thirty-six oaths. His only loyalty is to Xu."

"Then please make your call and get back to me right away."

Ava took a new notebook from her bag and wrote *The Tsai Family* across the top of the first page. When she worked with Uncle, she had kept a separate notebook for every case they took on. It was a handwritten history of the people involved, the crime committed, and the trail she had followed. She found that writing detailed information in this manner helped her thought process and gave her a permanent record. It was a habit she couldn't break.

Ava started to write her impressions of the Tsai family on the first page of the new book. She turned back to the computer to glance at the Chinese website she'd accessed to glean information on them, and she saw that a text had finally arrived from Jennie Lee.

I'm in the car with Cindy on the way home with a big cheque from Casino Rama in my purse, Jennie wrote. I just sent a message to Marian saying I want to take her and the girls to Disneyland. How would you like to take a trip to Italy with me and Maria for your next birthday?

Ava blinked. Over the years her mother had had other big casino wins, and her immediate reaction was always to share. Ava knew no one as spontaneously and genuinely generous as Jennie, but even for her this was excessive. Just how much money had she won? Ava thought about asking and then dismissed the idea. Her birthday was months away, and no matter how much Jennie had won, it could likely all be lost by then. It was better not to know.

Italy sounds just wonderful, Ava wrote. I'll tell Maria when I get back.

As she sent the message, her phone rang.

"This is Feng. I just talked to my brother-in-law."

"Did you find out what I want to know?"

"I think so. There are different principals attached to each of the Tsai companies. Tsai Men is listed as the legal representative at Hallmark Consulting. His sister, Tsai Bik, has the same position at Evergreen Trading, and her husband, Hu Chi, at Gold Star."

"And we're sure they're married?"

"Like I said, we remit payment by wire transfer. When our bank created new templates a few years ago, they asked for two contact names in each company. Tsai Bik gave Hu Chi's name, and he gave hers. My brother-in-law, who doesn't know anything about the business arrangement, thought the cross-referencing was a bit odd and phoned their bank to see if a mistake had been made. He was told they were married and had shares in each other's companies."

"Does this mean they use the same bank?"

"Yes, the Founders' Bank of Nanjing."

"And Hallmark Consulting?"

"The same."

"Who were the contact names for Hallmark?"

"Tsai Men and someone named Wu Bo."

"What do we know about Wu?"

"Nothing, but I've already asked my brother-in-law to see what he can find."

"How would he do that?" Ava said.

"He is going to call his contact."

"At the Founders' Bank?"

"I'm not sure if it's someone who works at the bank or someone who knows someone who works there."

"Whoever it is, it would be invaluable if we could find someone at that bank who would be prepared to share information with us about the Tsai companies. Would your brother-in-law be willing to make an approach on our behalf, without using names?"

"Names?"

"Not our names obviously, but not the Tsai name or any of the company names either. We just need to establish, in general terms, that the person on the other end is prepared to answer questions and provide us with copies of documents about bank customers — any bank customers. We'd pay, of course."

"I'll ask him to feel them out."

"One last thing: what kind of information does a local bank require before it will open a company account?"

"Articles of incorporation, proof of registration, a tax number, the name of the legal representative, and some other minor stuff."

"Would it require the names of shareholders and company officers?"

"If they get copies of the incorporation and registration, that information will be there. And our banks are very big on paperwork."

"Good. I like it when things are well-documented."

"Anything else?"

"Not for now. Please call your brother-in-law and get back to me as soon as you're done talking to him."

Ava turned the first page of the notebook and on the second sketched a small chart.

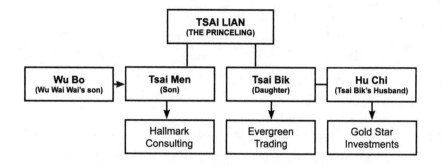

It took Feng less than an hour to get back to her, and when she heard excitement in his voice, she felt her own spirits rise.

"Huan spoke to his contact, and he thinks there's a deal to be done," Feng said.

"Who's Huan?"

"My brother-in-law."

"Sorry, I should have figured that out," Ava said. "Does his contact work at the bank?"

"No, but the guy's girlfriend does. His name is Zheng. I've met him a few times. I don't know the girlfriend."

"And she'll go along with this?"

"He thinks so."

"That sounds vague, and we can't afford to be vague."

"Huan says that she's prepared to help if the price is right."

"What kind of access to information does she have?"

"She's quite senior. He thinks she can get anything we want."

"Did Huan speak to her directly?"

"No, he worked through the contact."

"Did he mention names?"

"My brother-in-law kept us and the Tsai family completely out of the conversation."

"So what does she know?" Ava asked.

"He told her we want all the information she has on three accounts."

"She didn't ask which accounts?"

"According to her boyfriend, she doesn't seem to care. It's all about the money."

"How much money is she asking for?"

"She says that depends on the amount of detail we want, but Huan says that's bullshit. If it was a company owned by a nonentity she might charge ten thousand renminbi. Once she hears which companies they are and attaches the name Tsai to them, he guesses we're in the hundred thousand range, maybe higher."

"The money isn't an issue. I want to be assured that we're getting accurate information, and I want to be one hundred percent certain that she'll keep her mouth shut."

"The boyfriend will be the only name she knows. We'll be left entirely out of the conversation. She won't know who wants the information or where it's going."

"And you trust this boyfriend, Zheng?"

"He's affiliated, and he knows, without getting too specific, that this is triad business. Zheng understands the repercussions if things don't go as expected."

"How will we know what we're getting is real?"

"We'll ask for copies of original documents if you think that's necessary. We can also pay her half up front and withhold the balance until we can verify the facts."

"Do both," Ava said.

"Zheng says he's done this kind of business with her before. There's never been a problem. She has no curiosity."

"Then tell Huan to close the deal."

"What information do you want specifically?"

"I want copies of the registrations and incorporations. I want all of the personal information they have on file of the legal representatives, the shareholders, and the officers. I want to know the name of every company and individual who's put money into those accounts. I want to know every company and individual who's been sent money from the accounts. If money went in or out by wire transfer, I want copies of the transfers."

"That could be a lot of information."

"Let's hope it is."

"It might take a few days, or maybe even longer, for her to pull it together."

"Pay her more to work faster."

"How high are you prepared to go?"

"Feng, listen to me. Tell your brother-in-law what I want, and tell him I want it within twenty-four hours. However much she asks for, I'll pay."

"Okay."

Ava pushed the chair back from the desk and took a deep breath. She was getting caught up in this chase and the feeling surprised her. She had forgotten just how exciting it could be. The information from the Founders' Bank was going to open doors, and then, depending on how deeply the Tsai family wanted to bury its business secrets, those doors might lead to more doors and then more again. She knew that it all might add up to nothing, but that didn't dampen her sense of anticipation. It had also put her on edge. She knew she needed a distraction and reached for the phone.

"*Wei*," May Ling said.

"What time are you leaving for your meeting with Suki?"

"In about ten minutes."

"I've decided to come."

"That's perfect."

"I'm still dressed casually."

"You might want to put on a pair of slacks and a blouse. Suki just told me she has someone she wants us to meet at dinner. He's developed a carbon-fibre shipping container that she says will revolutionize the business."

"She didn't mention it at the reception, and it isn't in any of her proposals."

"Well, it's a new day and she's got a new idea."

11

THEY MET SUKI IN HER OFFICE AT THE MAIN SHANGHAI warehouse. She was surprised to see Ava and greeted her effusively. For two hours, they talked about her expansion plans and finally fixed on a three-month timeframe and a $100 million investment. There were contingencies attached, but despite that, Suki was satisfied. Ava imagined she wouldn't be so passive if in three months the $100 million they had earmarked wasn't available.

They met Wang, the man who had developed the carbon-fibre container, at a hot-pot restaurant that was a five-minute drive from the warehouse. He was already there when they arrived, a bottle of beer in front of him.

"These are my partners," Suki said.

Over the next two hours, between dipping oysters, shrimp, fish balls, mushrooms, tofu, lettuce, squid balls, and thinly sliced beef and pork into two boiling pots of chicken broth, Wang detailed the properties of carbon fibre and its use in sea and air transportation businesses. He lost Ava ten minutes into the scientific explanation. He regained her attention briefly when he started to talk about profit margins and market opportunity, but then her mind wandered to Feng. She had her phone on, hoping he'd call, and she kept checking it under the table in case he sent a text.

May noticed that Ava seemed distracted. "Anything wrong?" she asked.

"I'm waiting for a call, but it's nothing urgent, so don't worry about it."

When they finished dinner, May complimented Wang on his project and said they'd tell Suki if they had any interest in pursuing it further. He seemed discouraged, and Ava wondered what Suki had told him.

May started talking about the carbon-fibre containers as soon as they got into a taxi to go back to the Peninsula.

"I don't think I can handle this right now," Ava interrupted. "I'm jet-lagged and not processing very well."

"Are you thinking about Xu's problem?"

"A bit."

"Have you started looking into it?"

"We have a contact who might provide us with some information. I don't know yet what it is or what it's worth."

"You'll tell me if you find something useful?"

"Of course."

"Tomorrow I have to head back to Wuhan. There's business there that needs attending to."

"When does Amanda return to Hong Kong?"

"The day after tomorrow."

"I'll go to Pudong tomorrow and spend some time with her and the girls. I might even go to Hong Kong with her for a few days. There are some people I'd like to see."

"There are a lot of people there who'd be happy to see you."

"What time is your flight?"

"Early afternoon."

"Let's have breakfast before you leave."

When they got to the hotel, Ava dragged herself through the lobby and up to her suite. She glanced at the room phone and then quickly checked her email. No word from Feng. She showered, slipped into a clean T-shirt and underwear, and fell into bed.

She had barely fallen asleep when her cellphone rang. She cursed softly, but reached for it.

"Ava Lee."

"It's Mummy."

"Where are you?" Ava said, sitting up.

"At home. Did you get my text?"

"Yes, and thanks for the Italy offer."

"Aren't you going to ask me how much I won?"

"No," Ava said.

"Close to forty thousand dollars, and Cindy and Maggie each won about twenty. The casino was happy to see us leave."

"How many hours did you gamble?"

"Twelve or thirteen, but we took time out for dinner."

"I can't imagine sitting that long."

"I've gone for as long as thirty-six hours."

"I know," Ava sighed.

"Anyway, I just got off the phone with Marian. I'm going to fly to Ottawa in a few days to spend some time with the girls and to get the trip to Disneyland organized. She won't agree to anything without talking to Bruce, so I'll be there when she asks. That will make it harder for him to say no."

"I think that's the best way to handle it."

"And have you told Maria about Italy?"

"Mummy, with everything going on here, I've hardly had a chance to breathe."

"Well, tell her as soon as you can. I'm going to the bank today to deposit thirty thousand."

Ava started to ask about the other ten but then stopped herself. She had no doubts it would be reserved for mahjong or baccarat, or both.

"She'll be thrilled."

"Good. Now I'm going to head to bed and try to get some sleep."

Ava put down the phone with an enormous sense of relief. Her mother wasn't poor by any means, but she tended to push the outer edges of her monthly income. Ava had offered, several times, to give her mother a substantial amount of money, but Jennie had declined. She had a husband whose obligation it was to look after her. If her children wanted to spoil her now and again, that was okay, but it was Marcus Lee's responsibility to support her, and she wasn't going to give him any excuse to avoid it.

Ava fell asleep almost at once and entered a dream in which she was arriving at an old, grungy airport. She had to fight to retrieve her bag from the carousel and then get past a long customs line, where male officers were making passengers undress. She began to prepare herself to resist. She wasn't taking her clothes off for anyone, and if she had to fight she would. As she reached the first officer, two more appeared and the three of them stood side by side.

"Strip," the one in the middle said.

"No."

He turned his head and smiled at his colleagues. They started to move towards her, all of them grinning.

"Ava," a familiar voice said.

Behind the officers materialized a small man in a black suit, his white shirt buttoned to the collar.

"Uncle, what's going on here?"

"Nothing for you to concern yourself with," he said. "Come with me."

The middle officer swung around to face Uncle. Ava saw his fist clench and his arm coil. She was about to reach for it when it stopped in mid-air.

"Sir, I apologize," the officer said to Uncle.

"You need to talk to your superiors," Uncle said. "This young woman is with me."

A phone rang. Ava looked around the customs area and couldn't see where the ringing was coming from. She woke up, and it took her ages to realize it was her phone.

"Ms. Lee, this is Feng. I hope I'm not calling too late."

"No, it's okay."

"We reached an agreement with the woman at Founders' Bank. She's printing documents as we speak."

"Is she at the bank this late?"

"No, she's at home, but she can access everything from there. The plan is to meet her tomorrow morning just outside Shanghai. She wouldn't do half and half, but she has promised we can take all the time we want to go through the documents before paying her."

"She'll wait?"

"She took the day off work."

"How much are we giving her?"

"Two hundred thousand renminbi. I know that's more than Huan projected, but I didn't think you'd mind."

"No, it's fine. Who will be meeting with her?"

"Me and Zheng."

"The woman won't know who you are?"

"Nope."

"How much are we paying Zheng?"

"Twenty thousand RM."

"What time is the meeting?"

"It's at ten."

"I'll go to the bank in the morning to get her money."

"Ms. Lee, I've got the cash here. Xu wouldn't have it any other way."

"Call me Ava, and I wanted to pay for this myself."

"You can't. He'd kill me."

First Suen and now Feng, Ava thought.

"I won't argue," she said.

"Thank you."

"You said you're meeting her outside of Shanghai, but how far out?"

"In Nanqiao. It's a suburb only thirty to forty minutes from central Shanghai."

"And where in Nanqiao is the meeting being held?"

"I told Zheng to rent a hotel room. I figured we'd want privacy, and if we need to check any of the documents we have somewhere for her to stay while we do."

"What's her name?"

"He calls her Lanfen."

"Feng, I'm starting to think that I'd like to go to the meeting."

"I was going to suggest the same thing," Feng said slowly. "You may have some questions after you look at the documents, and she'll be there to answer them. When she gets her money, we'll want the transaction to be complete."

"How are you going to get there?"

"I'm going to drive. If you want, I'll pick you up at your hotel."

"That would be fine."

"I'll be there around nine fifteen. I drive a red Toyota Reiz."

"I'll be at the entrance."

Ava went to her computer and emailed May Ling. I have to leave the hotel early to go to a meeting that's related to the Xu affair. I think it's best if we skip breakfast. Call me when you get to Wuhan and I'll bring you up to speed.

Then she sent one to Amanda. I don't think I'll be able to go to Pudong tomorrow. That other business I'm trying to deal with has raised its ugly head. I'll call you when I get back, but my cell will be on in case you need me.

She started to get up and then saw that an email had arrived from Maria. She hesitated and then opened it.

I haven't heard anything formal about the appointment extension yet, but the Consul-General seems to think it's a done deal. And that's got me thinking about my house. If the extension is granted then I have to decide whether to renew my lease. The landlord has been making noises about selling it and I'm unsure about what to tell him or what to do. Do you have any ideas? Maria wrote.

Well, she is trying to be subtle, Ava thought, but the last thing she needed right now was any more pressure. She felt herself slipping back into her old job mode, and when that took a grip, her habit had been to shut out the entire outside world with the exception of Uncle and those directly related to the case.

Maria, I think it's premature to make a decision about

your lease. It's better to wait until you know for sure about the appointment extension. Now I'm involved in a project here that's going to keep me occupied, so you may not hear from me for a few days. There's nothing to worry about. I'll touch base when I can. Love, Ava.

She shut down the computer and went back to bed.

12

SHE WOKE AT EIGHT AFTER A PEACEFUL SLEEP, BREWED
some coffee, and collected the newspapers from the door
and quickly scanned them. It was nine o'clock by the time
she had showered and dressed. She checked her mobile
phone for voice messages and texts, and then went to her
inbox. Both Amanda and May had emailed telling her not
to worry about getting together and to just do whatever she
had to do.

Ava looked at herself in the mirror before leaving the
room. She had opted for a white Brooks Brothers button-
down shirt and a pair of black slacks. She wore no makeup
and her hair was tied back and fixed with her ivory chignon
pin. It was a serious look for a serious meeting. At nine
fifteen she exited the hotel carrying her Chanel bag. Inside
was the Moleskine notebook that she had designated for
the Tsai family.

The red Toyota Reiz was parked three cars down from
the hotel entrance. Feng stood by the driver's-side door
reading a newspaper and smoking. He didn't turn his head
until Ava said, "Hey."

He was wearing grey slacks and a navy blue blazer over a white polo shirt. He somehow looked younger than when she'd seen him at Capo. He was about five foot six and lean, and had a full head of grey hair.

"Ms. Lee."

"Ava."

"Yes, Ava, right on time."

"Let's go."

A doorman rushed to the car and opened the passenger door for Ava. She climbed in and then watched Feng give him a healthy tip.

"Please don't smoke in the car," she said to him as he got behind the wheel.

"I never do. My wife would kill me."

"Between Xu and your wife, your life sounds as if it's in constant danger," Ava said.

"That's true enough," he said, and laughed.

They left the Peninsula and started the drive towards Nanqiao. Ava lost all sense of direction within minutes. Unlike her mother, who was a slave to her GPS, Ava liked to know where she was going without having to depend on a computer. Parts of cities like downtown Boston and London defeated her. The most perplexing was Hamilton, Ontario, where north and south were inverted; Ava had once driven hours trying to get back to a highway. Shanghai had the same effect on her.

"Everything is on schedule," Feng said a few minutes after they left the Peninsula. "Zheng stayed at the hotel last night, and he's already heard from Lanfen. She said she'd be there by ten."

"Perfect. Does she have all the documents I asked for?"

"She told him she has lots of paper, but I can't speak to the contents."

The car was now on a highway and moving at a moderate speed. Ava saw a large sign for Fengxian and, underneath, a smaller one for Nanqiao. They were only twelve kilometres away.

"We'll be there in no time," she said.

"You can never predict traffic."

"I don't mind being early," Ava said, and then glanced sideways at Feng. His eyes were intently focused on the highway. "How long have you been dealing with the Tsai family?" she asked.

His expression didn't change. "Directly, for the past five years; indirectly, for another ten."

"Indirectly?"

"Before I became White Paper Fan — the gang's administrator — I helped my predecessor cope with them."

"It doesn't sound like you're too fond of the family."

"I've only met Tsai Men."

"What do you think of him?"

"He's a prick."

"That's blunt."

Feng shrugged. "Do you remember Ling, from the dinner the other night?"

"Tsai's man?"

"Yeah. He does for Men what I do for Xu. In private, I've never heard him say a kind or complimentary word about his boss. He calls him 'the greedy cocksucker,'" Feng said, and then looked at Ava. "I don't mean to offend you with my language, but that is exactly how he always refers to him."

"Nice."

"I can't blame Ling. You should hear the way Men talks to him. It's like he's shit on his shoe. When Xu isn't around, Men treats me the same way."

"Why doesn't Ling leave?"

"He only puts up with it for the money. I think he'd leave if he could."

"And he really thinks Tsai Men is that greedy?"

"Him and his entire family. According to Ling, the way they act, you would think the family owned Jiangsu."

"Does he know the other family members very well?"

"He works a bit like a Straw Sandal," Feng said and then paused. "Sorry, I don't know if you know that term."

"I think I do. It means he functions as a go-between?"

"Yeah, something like that. At one time he supposedly worked for the Governor's wife."

"Did he tell you that?"

"Not directly, but he hinted at it more than once over a few beers."

"In Indonesia they used to call the wife of President Sukarno 'Mrs. Ten Percent.'"

"I wish it was ten percent with the Tsais."

Ava thought about the drug lab and the 50 percent demand and wondered if that was what Feng was hinting at, but she didn't pursue the point. She didn't know exactly what Xu had told Feng about how much she knew, and it wasn't ground she wanted to test.

"Has he ever talked to you about who else is giving them money?"

"No."

"But you agree it makes sense that if they're taking money

from you, then they're taking it from a bunch of other people," Ava said.

"Yeah, but — and I don't mean to be rude — I'm still not sure where you think it leads. They're clever. Everything is disguised as a legitimate business transaction, and they're careful to keep the old man out of it. You never hear his name."

"And you've never met the sister or her husband?"

"No. Since I've been involved it's been only Men and Ling."

"Still, I figure they all have to be in on it."

"Maybe, but they're just taking advantage of the system. They didn't create it, but they sure as hell have figured out how to use it to their maximum advantage."

"From what I've heard, that doesn't make them unusual in China."

"No, but there have to be limits."

"What kind of limits can you put on someone who has so much power?" Ava said. "From what I've read, a governor has an almost unlimited amount as long as he doesn't step into Beijing's political territory, and as long as he keeps the provincial party secretary onside. Tsai Lian has obviously succeeded at doing both of those things."

"The secretary is his cousin," Feng said.

"So I was told."

"That makes it easy, no?"

"I guess."

"As for the other part, there's always someone in Beijing threatening to do something about corruption — except it never happens."

"I've read about senior officials being charged."

"It's always the low-level officials that they make an example of, or if it's anyone of any substance, then it's someone who's screwed up politically, and launching corruption charges is the easiest way to get at them. They're all corrupt, every last one of them. It's all about degree."

"Every system has its weaknesses," Ava said. "And in fact, the senior Communist Party leaders don't operate much differently than wealthy people in the West."

"Except they're not supposed to be capitalists," Feng said as he pulled off the highway.

He made two right-hand turns and came to a sudden stop in front of a shabby concrete building. Ava would never have thought it was a hotel, but the neon sign above the double glass doors read THE NANQIAO FRIENDSHIP HOTEL.

"We're fifteen minutes early," he said.

"I don't think that matters," Ava said, opening her car door.

Feng got out his cellphone as he led the way into the lobby, which had a dirty white tile floor and was furnished with two visibly worn leather couches and four chairs. "They're in 309," he said. "Lanfen is already there."

They waited five minutes for the elevator. When it finally reached the floor, they ran almost directly into a tall, thin, bald man. Ava moved to one side to let him pass, but Feng extended his hand. "Good to see you again," he said.

"You too," the man said. Ava assumed this was Zheng. He looked at her. "And this is?"

"My name is Jennie Kwong," Ava said, using a familiar alias. "I'm an accountant. I've been hired to examine the paperwork."

"Feng said he was bringing someone. I just didn't expect a woman."

"Does it make a difference?" Ava asked.

"Of course not," he said.

The door was open when they got to the room. Ava walked in first and saw a woman sitting at a small round table near the window. She was in her mid-forties, Ava guessed, and was heavily made up, with her hair piled high. The makeup and hair were in sharp contrast to the blue jeans and plain red cotton blouse she was wearing.

"Hi, I'm Jennie Kwong," Ava said. "I'm here to look at those documents."

The stack of files looked to be close to two feet high.

"All of them?" Lanfen said.

"As many as I think is necessary."

"That could take hours."

"I think that's a fair estimate," Ava said. She turned to Feng. "Why don't you take Zheng and Lanfen out for an early lunch? Come back in a couple of hours. If I need more time, I'll tell you then."

"Okay."

Ava looked again at the files. "How long did it take you to copy these?"

"I worked most of the night."

"Thank you," Ava said.

Half an hour later Ava couldn't help thinking that Lanfen had let them off incredibly cheaply.

13

SHE STARTED WITH THE HALLMARK CONSULTING FILE.
The first pages of the file were boilerplate copies of the company's registration and incorporation. There was nothing surprising. Tsai Men owned 70 percent of the shares and was legal representative and treasurer. Wu Bo held the balance of the shares and was-vice president and secretary. They both used the company address as their own.

Immediately following the incorporation documents were monthly bank statements. Lanfen had grouped them by year, starting with the most recent. Ava looked at the bottom stack and saw that the documents went back three years. Attached to each month's statement was a thick wad of copies of cheques, and all the incoming and outgoing wire transfers arranged by date. Ava began to work her way through the first statement and immediately felt almost overwhelmed by the level of activity in the account. She sat back and thought about how to structure the information she had in front of her so it would be easier to understand. Then she reached for her notebook.

On a clean page she began to record the names of the

companies that had made deposits, how often they'd made them, and the banks from which they'd originated. On another, she wrote down the names of companies and individuals who'd been sent money, how often they received it, and their banks. In both cases, she didn't focus on the amounts so much as the frequency. She would go back later and highlight any particularly large sums of money. Her immediate objective was to identify all the players.

As she worked through the file, the first page soon filled with names, and she moved to a second. When she finished recording Hallmark Consulting's latest year of activity, she had a list of eighteen companies, and she still had two years to go. The files for both Evergreen and Gold Star also went back three years and looked every bit as imposing.

The list of recipients of funds from Hallmark's account was thankfully much smaller. Tsai Men and Wu Bo were withdrawing the equivalent of about US$50,000 a month for themselves, but the bulk of the money was being sent on to Gold Star and two other companies: Shell Investments and Mother of Pearl Investments. Shell's money was sent to a different bank in Nanjing, and Mother of Pearl's to one in Shanghai. Ava had never heard of either of them. She riffled through the statements again and looked at the total of the monthly deposits and the outflow. Most months more than a million dollars was being deposited into the account and about $900,000 was being transferred out.

This is one hell of a business, she thought.

She checked the time. It had taken well over an hour just to work through one year of statements from Hallmark in the most cursory manner. She knew there was no way she would be able to finish the rest and assess the information in a meaningful and professional way all in one day. What was most logical was to start organizing the information in piles by company, but the table she was working at had barely room for the single stack of files.

As she waited for Feng and the others to come back from lunch, she leafed quickly through the Evergreen statements. The company had some of the same depositors and several new ones. The account wasn't quite as active as Hallmark's, but it was still raking in about $700,000 a month and most of that money was sent along to Gold Star, Shell, and Mother of Pearl. Ava looked at the Gold Star file on the table and sensed without even opening it that it was going to be more important than Evergreen or Hallmark. She went to pick it up and then stopped when she heard a gentle knock at the door.

"Come in," Ava called.

Feng led the two others into the room.

"Please sit," Ava said.

Feng sat at the table across from Ava. Lanfen and Zheng sat together on a brown leather sofa. Lanfen's knees were pressed tightly together and her hands were clasped in her lap.

"This is excellent information. You can give her the money," Ava said to Feng.

He reached into the right breast pocket of his blazer and took out a thick envelope; then he took another one out of the left breast pocket. He raised an eyebrow in Lanfen's direction, and she got up and walked to him with a smile tugging at the corners of her mouth.

"But don't leave," Ava said as Lanfen took the envelopes.

Lanfen settled back onto the couch, looking uncertain. Ava turned so she could face her directly. "Wu Bo is an officer in Hallmark Consulting. Do you know if he's related to Mr. Tsai?" Ava said.

"He's his cousin," Lanfen said.

"You sound sure about that."

"Mr. Wu told me. He's the one from the company who is always in and out of the bank. I've gotten to know him quite well. His mother is the Governor's sister."

"She's still alive?"

"So he says."

"Do you know her name?"

"Wu Wai Wai."

"Thanks for that information," Ava said. "Now, I may need you to do more work for us. Are you agreeable?"

"What kind of work?"

"I see that some of the other companies listed on the statements bank with you. If I need information on them, will you provide it? We'll pay, of course."

"I can do that."

"I'll leave it up to Zheng and my associate here to work out the numbers with you."

"That's fine."

"And your files go back only three years. If I need to go back further is that a problem?"

"No."

"Good. That's the easy part," Ava said. "Now, as I was going through the statements I saw the names of banks I've never heard of. Through Zheng, we'll provide you with a list. All I need to know is whether or not you have contacts at any of them who could provide the same service as you. We'd pay them well, and of course we'd pay you a healthy finder's fee."

"I would be happy to, but I have to tell you that I don't have many contacts in other banks who I would trust."

"As strange as it seems, that answer really pleases me," Ava said and then stood. "Thanks for all you've done thus far. Hopefully your work will continue to be as good."

Before Zheng or Lanfen could speak, Feng rose to his feet. "I'd like to add my thanks, and unless Ms. Kwong has anything else to say, I think you both can leave."

"They can go," Ava said.

When the door closed behind them, Feng said, "Was the information that good?"

"We won't know until we finish going through it, but there's lots of it, and from what I've seen it's more than we could have expected."

"What does it tell you?"

"The Tsai family has brought a great many people into a very large tent."

"And?"

"We need to find out who they are, what they paid to get inside, and what they expect to receive in return."

14

FENG CARRIED THE FILES DOWN TO THE CAR. AVA could see he was eager to talk about what she had found, but she waited until they were back on the highway before she spoke.

"I could use some help with those," she said, pointing at the files sitting on the back seat of the Toyota.

"What do you need?"

"All I went through was one year in the Hallmark file. Eighteen companies put money into their account, and there's still two more years to review. I'm making a list of everyone who gave Hallmark money, how much, and their banks. Then I'm recording how much money left the account and where it went. I'd like the same thing done with the Evergreen Trading statements and I'd like it done right away. Do you want to take it on?"

"I can do that. How about Gold Star?"

"I'll handle that one myself. It isn't as thick," she said. "When we're finished, we should cross-reference the information from all three files and put it on a spreadsheet."

"I have a couple of young accountants in the office who

could do that. I don't think it would be a challenge for either of them," he said, and paused. "And they both know how to keep their mouths shut."

"Would they be available tomorrow morning if we finish our work by tonight?"

"I'll make sure they will be."

"Then let's plan on getting everything done by tonight."

Feng nodded and turned his attention back to the road. After a while he said, "I'm thinking about all those companies that put money into the Hallmark account. What kind of businesses are we talking about?"

Ava's bag was at her feet. She reached down and took out her notebook. "Let me see," she said. "I recognized the names of some hotel chains and a restaurant chain, and there are a lot of companies obviously involved in real estate. There are a bunch of factories, including yours, I imagine. I counted three banks and at least two financial services companies."

"All making monthly payments?"

"No, some of them were one-time transfers, but they were substantial."

"I'm sure all very well supported by invoices."

"And probably contracts."

"They are careful. I suspect it's going to be very hard, if not impossible, to link Tsai Lian to any of those transactions."

"That could be true."

"And if we can't, then there's no leverage."

"Don't jump to conclusions," Ava said. "We have files to go through, companies and transactions to identify, and then we may have to chase down more details. Who knows what we'll find? In my old job, my approach was to go from

A to B and then B to C. I didn't believe in shortcuts and I wasn't a good enough fortune teller to forecast the future. I let the information I uncovered dictate my next step."

"Xu said you hunted down thieves and con men."

"I was in the business of finding and reclaiming money that had been stolen. The people who had taken it represented a wide spectrum."

"What kinds of sums were involved?"

"We — you know I partnered with Uncle, right?"

"I know."

"Well, we rarely went after anything less than two or three million, and one job went as high as eighty million."

"How often did you succeed?"

"Most often. We wouldn't have stayed in business as long as we did, or attracted the quality of clients we had, if that hadn't been the case."

"But all of your cases involved money that had been stolen?"

"They did."

"So far there's no indication that the Tsai family has stolen anything."

"There you go again, jumping to conclusions," Ava said with a smile.

Feng pulled up in the driveway of the Peninsula. Ava got out and opened the back door to retrieve the files. Feng joined her. She took the Evergreen files from the stack and passed them to him.

"Call me when you're finished," she said. "We can compare notes and then decide what we'll do next. But for sure, have your staff on standby."

"I'll organize that this afternoon."

"And Feng, how many banks do you do business with?"

"Three directly, and then probably another three or four indirectly, through some of our companies."

"The ones that you deal with indirectly, are they local or national or international?"

"Local."

"How many law firms do you retain?"

"There's one principal one in Shanghai, and then some of our companies have their own."

"All local firms?"

"Yes."

"Thanks," Ava said, putting the Hallmark and Gold Star files under her arm. "I'll talk to you tonight."

As she walked through the hotel lobby, she thought fleetingly about stopping to have lunch, but the files had a stronger grip on her. She was reminded again how much she enjoyed the hunt.

She glanced at the hotel phone when she entered the suite and was pleased when she saw no flashing red light. Her computer on the desk was closed, and she intended to leave it that way. Her cellphone hadn't rung all morning, and now she took it out of her bag and turned it off. She tossed the files onto the king-size bed.

By five o'clock, she was sitting in the desk chair by the side of the bed with her notebook in front of her. On the bed were more than thirty separate stacks of paper — some with only one sheet and several with substantially more. She had gone through both of the remaining years for Hallmark Consulting and found similar transaction records as in the first. The numbers were also consistent in magnitude from month to month and year to year. Over the last three years, Ava calculated that just over $36 million had gone into Hallmark from a wide range of companies. The funds had just as quickly left the account, in the form of monthly withdrawals by Tsai Men and Wu Bo and wire transfers made in almost equal amounts to Gold Star, Shell, and Mother of Pearl Investments.

Now she turned to the Gold Star file. She held it in her hand for a few seconds before opening it. It was thinner than Hallmark's, but she knew that weight meant nothing when it came to the importance of the contents. She felt a keen stab of anticipation as she opened it. An hour later, she picked up the notebook and reworked the chart she'd started the day before.

Then she circled the names Hallmark and Gold Star and wrote the word *conduit* next to them. She was sure she'd be doing the same when Feng gave her his summary of the Evergreen Trading File.

She turned back to the Gold Star file and her notes on its deposits and outflow. Over the past three years the company had received more than $80 million from Hallmark and Evergreen and directly from other companies, and just like Hallmark, it had emptied its bank account every month. The recipients were the now-familiar names of Shell Investments and Mother of Pearl Investments, but there were two new names: AKG Consulting and New Age Capital. The transfers to New Age totalled more than $40 million and were disproportionately and glaringly large.

In addition to adding two new companies to her chart, Ava also noted two new Jiangsu-based banks she had never heard of. New Age used one in Nantong; AKG used the Nanjing Founders' Bank. If the Tsai family wasn't deliberately trying to obfuscate the sources and the eventual homes of its money, Ava thought, as she looked at the growing list of companies and banks, they were accidentally doing one hell of a great job.

She rolled the chair to the desk and entered, in rapid succession, the names of each of the companies into a search engine on her computer. The result was identical each time. There wasn't a single mention of any of them. Maybe it was standard for private investment companies in China to keep a very low profile, Ava thought, but consulting companies?

She sat back in the chair, not knowing whether she should be pleased or frustrated by the day's work. They may have peeled away some layers, but she couldn't help but feel that she was even farther away from understanding what the Tsais were doing. She reached for her cellphone to call May, and then realized that she might not be back in Wuhan yet. Instead she sent a text: Call me when you get in.

She looked towards the window and realized it would be dark soon. Her stomach growled. She had been so absorbed in the Tsai files that she hadn't even thought about eating. Now hunger attacked. She thought about going to Sir Elly's or Yi Long Court but didn't relish sitting by herself in a restaurant. She reached for the room service menu.

Half an hour later she was eating jellyfish soaked in vinegar. When that appetizer was finished, her chopsticks flitted between pan-fried marbled beef and giant mushrooms in oyster sauce and Yangzhou-style fried rice with shrimp. She sipped a white Burgundy as she ate, but she drank almost absent-mindedly as her mind jumped from the Tsai family to Maria.

When she had emptied both plates, she pushed the serving trolley to the door and sat at the desk. Then she phoned Feng.

"How's it going?" she asked when he answered.

"I've just finished."

"And?"

"For the past three years an amount between four hundred thousand and nine hundred thousand has been deposited into the Evergreen account every month. Nearly all of it was just as quickly transferred to Gold Star, Shell, and Mother of Pearl Investments."

"How many companies contributed?"

"Twenty-three."

"How many did you recognize?"

"A lot of them are manufacturers. It seems they're paying in the same manner as us and probably for the same kind of services."

"Any oddities?"

"Not really, though I was surprised to see so many hotel chains."

"Any huge payments?"

"A couple close to half a million, both from real estate companies, that look like one-of-a-kind commissions tied to land acquisition. I'm sure that when the land is developed, those could turn into monthly fees," Feng said. "What did you come up with?"

"My results from the rest of the Hallmark files were similar to the first and like your Evergreen files. Lots of regular contributors and nearly all of the deposits sent on to Shell, Mother of Pearl, and Gold Star."

"How about the Gold Star statements?"

"They were more interesting," Ava said. "As well as getting money from Hallmark and Evergreen, the company was receiving payments from contributors like you. It added up to about eighty million over three years."

"What did they do with the money?"

"It was sent to Shell, Mother of Pearl, and two other players — New Age Capital and AKG Consulting."

"It seems that someone has gone to a lot of trouble to make it hard to track that money."

"Yes, it does. I think Gold Star is just a conduit. Now we need to find out if those other so-called investment companies are as well."

"I've never heard of any of them."

"And I went online and had a quick look and came up absolutely empty."

"They should be registered somewhere."

"I know, but I don't think we're the people who should be doing the looking."

"I agree. How about working through their banks?"

"No, I don't want to risk contacting any of them directly, or even through intermediaries. I know we did very well with Lanfen, but now there are five or six additional banks, and that brings too many people into the equation if we try to co-opt them. We'd never be sure about controlling them all."

"What are you thinking?"

"We have to go outside Jiangsu, and probably Shanghai as well."

"Go to whom?"

"We need to generate quiet, confidential, third-party inquiries about those companies from people who can't be connected to Xu in any way at all."

"Who would you use?"

"I'm not entirely sure. We have a law firm in Hong Kong — Burgess and Bowlby — that we think highly of. I want to talk to Richard Bowlby and see what he thinks. And I have banker friends outside China I can talk to as well to see if they have any ideas about how to make an approach."

"Do you still want my people to put together a spreadsheet of the information we have?"

"Yes, I think it would be a useful resource."

"Are you going to send me what you have?"

"I've made pages of notes that are quite well organized. I'll scan them and email them to you," Ava said. "I may make some preliminary phone calls tonight, and I may go to Hong Kong tomorrow."

"To work on this?"

"Yes."

"Then I'll get my people in here tonight to get that spreadsheet done. You might need it sooner rather than later."

"That's a good idea."

"Consider it done," Feng said, and then hesitated. "Ava, I have to say that when Xu first spoke to me about this, I was dubious about what it might accomplish. But after today, I can't help but think that if we dig deep enough we'll find something that's completely rotten."

"You mean more rotten than getting bribed by thirty or forty or more companies?"

"Yes. I do know that the bribes by themselves would be bad enough in most countries in the West, but they aren't China. We need something more sinister if we're going to get anyone's attention."

"Well, then, we'll keep digging."

"And by the way, I spoke to Xu a little while ago. He asked me how it was going and I told him about our success with the bank. He said he would call you later if his meeting with Lam didn't go on too long."

"Did he say how things were in Guangzhou?"

"Friendly enough, it seems."

"Good."

"But with the gangs, things always seem friendly until suddenly they aren't."

"So I discovered a few months ago."

"Yes, I heard about that."

"I hope the same isn't true about the Tsai family."

"It's safer to assume that it is," Feng said.

15

AFTER A QUICK TRIP TO THE BUSINESS CENTRE TO DIS-patch her notes to Feng, Ava sat down at the room desk with a list of phone numbers. Johnny Yan at the Toronto Commonwealth Bank was the first name she wrote down, but it was still too early in the morning there. She hoped that the second contact, Richard Bowlby, was working late in his Hong Kong office.

She got a recorded greeting and, as directed, dutifully punched in his extension number. The phone rang three times, and she was about to leave a message when a woman with an English accent said, "Good evening, this is the Burgess and Bowlby Law Offices."

"Hello, my name is Ava Lee. Our company, Three Sisters Investments, is a client of your firm."

"I know your company very well, and your name is quite familiar to me."

"I was calling to speak to Mr. Bowlby."

"He's in Europe for the next week."

"Oh."

"This is Brenda Burgess. Can I help you in any way?"

"I'm in Shanghai and I plan to fly to Hong Kong tomorrow. I should be there by mid-afternoon. Given Mr. Bowlby's absence, is it possible you could meet with me?"

"Concerning?"

"It's a delicate matter that's best explained in person."

"It involves Three Sisters?"

"Indirectly, but it has an impact nonetheless."

"Will May Ling be with you?"

"No, she's in Wuhan, but she's aware of the matter in question."

"I wasn't implying that we needed her permission to meet with you," Brenda Burgess said quickly.

"I didn't take your remark that way," Ava said, admiring Burgess's sensitivity.

"No. Well, that's good."

"So about tomorrow?"

"I'm available any time after three. I had another appointment scheduled for three thirty, but I'll rearrange it."

"That's very kind of you. I'll be there at three."

"See you then, Ms. Lee."

Ava hung up the phone and then immediately punched in May Ling's mobile number.

"Hi," May said breathlessly.

"Am I disturbing you?"

"No, I had to run to get the phone. I got your earlier message. I was going to call you back in a little while. What's going on?"

"Nothing terribly urgent. I wanted you to know that I'm flying to Hong Kong tomorrow to meet with Brenda Burgess."

"Why?"

"The Xu business we discussed before you left."

"You want to involve our law firm in it?"

"Not if you think it's unwise."

"I'm sure you have a good reason," May said.

"Let me explain," Ava said.

"You don't have to," May said quickly. "You know I trust your judgement."

"I want to explain anyway. I've involved you in this, and I don't want to do anything that has an impact on Three Sisters — even indirectly — without talking to you," Ava said. "As you and Xu said, we need to keep ourselves as far removed as possible from the Tsai family. My problem is that I've spent the day looking at bank documents that show the Tsais have built a network of businesses and bank connections for what I think looks like either a sophisticated money-laundering scheme or a way of disguising how they're accumulating assets. I need to do some deeper digging, but I can't do it myself."

"What assets?"

"I don't know. They're moving money around and through various companies, but if my hunch is correct, it's going to land in one or two places."

"How much money are you talking about?"

"More than a hundred million already, and that's only over the past three years. We've barely scratched the surface."

"That's aggressive of them, particularly given all the sensitivity in Beijing about money laundering."

"I have no indication it was laundered."

"So where is it?"

"I don't know, but that's what I intend to find out, which is why I contacted Brenda Burgess."

"How can they help?"

"I have the names of several companies that are linked directly to the family, and I have their basic banking information. I'm hoping that the lawyers can find out who owns them, what kind of business they're doing, and who they're doing it with."

"You said you spoke to Brenda, not Richard?"

"He's in Europe."

"Did you tell her what you wanted?"

"No."

"When you do, you'll obviously not mention the Xu connection."

"Of course not."

"The only reason I said that is because Brenda is always keen to get the entire picture."

"I'll fudge it."

"If she goes along with you, I would expect them to at least find out what you're looking for on the corporate side. The banking information will be trickier."

"I have some bank contacts I trust outside of the mainland. They're my backup, plan B. I'm going to phone them later. A bank-to-bank inquiry would probably be my best chance to get additional info."

"I agree."

"I'll make those calls tonight."

"Ava, if you need my help in any way, you know where I am."

"I know, May, and thanks. It's great to have you to talk to."

"How long do you think you'll be in Hong Kong?"

"At least a few days. I'll see Sonny, and if Amanda goes back tomorrow then I'll try to have dinner with her and Michael."

"And your father?"

"He's always easier one-on-one and at dim sum."

"Maybe you could also follow up with Carrie Song."

"May!"

"Don't sound so scandalized. It's just a suggestion."

"Her assistant has already communicated with Shanghai. I want to let that process run its course. I don't want the girls to think I'm second-guessing them."

"I've just come back to a situation where two deals were on the table ready to close and both went sideways. I'm second-guessing everyone, including my husband."

"I'm sorry, May."

"And what's more maddening is that he blames me. I know he could have finalized the deals, but he didn't bother. He can't come to grips with the Three Sisters and I think this was his way of punishing me for not being here."

"That's not good."

"He'll get over it."

"Is there anything I can do?"

"Keep Xu out of trouble."

The word "why" bounced on Ava's tongue and then quietly settled. "I'll do the best I can."

"Call me from Hong Kong," May said. "If things stay gloomy here I might join you."

Ava put down the phone feeling downcast. She wasn't accustomed to May's being negative. She checked the time. It was still too early to call Toronto. She was contemplating going outside for a walk when her cell rang.

"Yes."

"It's Xu."

"How did it go today?"

"Well enough. Lam understands my position and is willing to help, at least for the short term."

"That's great."

"Not really, but it gives us some time. How was your day?"

"It was productive."

"Feng told me that, but I wanted to hear it from you."

"He's a very good man."

"He's an accountant."

"So am I."

"Except I never think of you as one."

"You sound a little drunk," Ava said.

"I had a few drinks, but mainly I'm just tired. It was a long day."

"Here too."

"What did you find out?"

"The Tsai family is taking money from anyone who'll give it to them."

"I thought we knew that already."

"They also have a need to hide where it's going. Not where it's from, but where it's going."

"And do you have a plan to find out why and where?"

"I do."

"How?"

"Let me handle it."

"Do I have a choice?"

"Yes. You can always tell me to back off."

"What would that accomplish?"

"It would maintain the status quo."

"Which is the last thing I want, so go to it," Xu said.

"Thank you."

"No, thank you."

"It's way too soon to say that. We may end up with nothing."

"You have something already. What we don't know is what we can do with it that will make a difference."

"I concede to the truth of that," Ava said.

"I'm coming back to Shanghai tomorrow. Will you have dinner with me?"

"I'll be in Hong Kong."

"Hong Kong?"

"That's where your business takes me."

"I won't ask anything else."

"Better not to."

"Should I let Lop know you're there in case you need any help?"

Lop had been Xu's Red Pole, his main enforcer, in Shanghai. Now, in every way except title, he ran the triad gang in the Wanchai district of Hong Kong.

"I won't need that kind of assistance, and if I do, I have Sonny."

"Sonny's not a man to be taken lightly," Xu said. "He laid down his life more than once for Uncle."

"And for me."

"He's your man now."

"Yes, and my only problem is keeping him busy. He couldn't live anywhere else but Hong Kong, and I'm hardly there. So I've had him driving my father and my half-brother Michael. I'm sure he's bored, but it keeps him out of trouble, and Uncle warned me that he's a man who can fall into trouble easily if he's at loose ends."

"Well, say hello to him for me, and good luck in Hong Kong. I'm heading to dinner with Lam."

"Give him my regards."

"I already have, and he sends them right back."

Ava ended the call and glanced at her list. It was still a little too early to call Johnny Yan, so she called Amanda.

"Hey," Amanda said.

"How are you feeling? Still hungover?"

"I'm at the sample factory and I'm functioning. I threw up in the middle of the night and then took a couple of extra-strength painkillers. That helped."

"How about the others?"

"About the same, but I think we're all still on a bit of an adrenalin rush from the launch."

"It was fantastic."

"That's the collective opinion. We've had a raft of emails and texts today, and they've all been positive. We're in the middle of prioritizing who we need to talk to. There are a lot of options in terms of buyers. There's also some prime real estate that's been offered if we want to go with stand-alone boutiques."

"Work it through."

"We'll do what we can today, and then Chi-Tze, Gillian, and Clark can run with it."

"Are you still planning to fly back to Hong Kong to-morrow?"

"Yes. I've been gone for about two weeks and I'm sure there's a huge stack of work waiting for me."

"And a husband."

"Him too."

"What time is your flight?"

"Ten thirty on Cathay Pacific."

"I'll fly with you, if you don't mind."

"I'd love it, but what's taking you to Hong Kong?"

"I'm meeting with Brenda Burgess. I need her input on that non–Three Sisters business I mentioned to you the other day."

"You'll stay at the Mandarin Oriental?"

"If there's availability."

"Any idea how long you'll be there?"

"A couple of days, I would imagine."

"You'll have dinner with us?"

"Of course."

"Michael asked Sonny to meet me at the airport. Are you going to tell him you're flying in with me?"

"No, let's surprise him."

"That should be fun."

"What are you doing tonight?"

"I'm having dinner with Elsa Ngan again. I have to leave here in about half an hour. We're going to Sir Elly's."

"I'm sure it will go well."

"She's being tremendously supportive. And so, by the way, is Laura from Lane Crawford. She sent another email this afternoon with more questions and urged us to get back to her as soon as possible. She says they don't want to delay making a decision."

"Fingers crossed," Ava said.

"I know you don't like to make assumptions, but I have to say that the way Carrie Song reacted to you makes us all think it's almost a sure thing, unless something bizarre happens."

"I wish you hadn't said that."

"I know." Amanda laughed.

"Okay, I need to go before you say anything else," Ava said.

"If we leave the hotel at eight thirty tomorrow morning that should give us ample time to get to the airport."

"I'll meet you in the lobby."

She checked the time and finally decided to try Toronto. She had Johnny Yan's office and cell numbers and tried the mobile first. It went directly to voicemail. She called the office and, to her surprise, he answered.

"You're at work early," she said.

"Is this Ava?"

"It is."

"Where are you?"

"Shanghai."

"You're always somewhere I want to visit."

"All you need to do is buy a ticket."

"I have a wife and three kids."

"Then buy them tickets as well."

"I wish I could, but the bank business is long on pension benefits and short on immediate compensation. Nearly everyone else we went to York with is in the same position as me. They're working at banks or insurance companies or big accounting firms. You're one of the few who broke out."

"It wasn't entirely by choice," Ava said. "You know I went to Babson College after York, and when I left there I tried the corporate world. I didn't last six months. I quit before they tossed me out the door."

"Lucky for you."

"And maybe for you, Johnny. I need some help and I'd have no problem buying airplane tickets for you and your family, wherever it is you want to go."

"You know you don't have to do that," he said.

"I know, but I can afford it and you've been a terrific friend. Our York network of Chinese accountants has been completely supportive over the years, but I've taken more than I've given."

"You've thrown a lot of business my way. That's good enough."

"Thank you. So can I ask for another favour?"

"I was waiting for that." He laughed.

"I wish I wasn't so predictable, but since I am, there are some companies in China that I need to find out about."

"You're in Shanghai. I'm in Toronto. How does that work better from here?"

"Johnny, you work for a bank that has a huge international presence."

"True."

"And, as I remember, you have friends working in the international department."

"I have a few. Felix Lau is probably the best."

"So just tell him you have a client who has an interest in partnering with some Chinese-based companies and is looking for as much background information about them as possible before making an investment. He should be able to construct a reasonably simple bank-to-bank inquiry."

"How many companies do you want information on?"

"There are four, and I have account numbers, addresses, and whatever else Felix will need."

"Why am I not surprised?"

"Do you have a pen handy?"

"Go ahead."

She named AKG, Shell, Mother of Pearl, and New Age, and then provided their banking details.

"What do you want to know about them?" Johnny asked.

"The usual kind of thing. How long have they been bank customers? What types of business are they in? What's their creditworthiness? The names of company principals and signing authorities. And it would be great if we could get some business references."

"You want to know who they're doing business with?"

"Yes."

"That could be tough if you're looking for any real detail."

"I don't expect them to give us any confidential information. The name of a company would be enough. We'll take it from there."

"That could work," Johnny said.

"It will work."

"And I assume, as usual, that you want me to jump right on this?"

"Please."

"Just a second," he said, and his line went quiet as he put her on hold.

She waited several minutes and began to wonder what Johnny was up to.

"Felix is in his office already," Johnny finally said. "I'll pay him a visit in a while."

"I would like my name kept out of this," Ava said.

"He may ask which of our customers wants to do these bank checks."

"I'm sure you have lots of existing customers who are already doing business in Asia."

"Yeah. I'll find a name just in case he insists on one."

"And you'll get him to work fast?"

"He owes me a couple of favours."

"And I'll owe you another one."

"Do you have more business to send to me?"

"I'll find something," Ava said.

"You normally do," he said. "Now, how do you want to get this information?"

"You can email me."

"Given the time difference, he won't get a response from any of the Chinese banks for a minimum of twelve hours, and I expect it will be a lot longer than that."

"Just so it gets to me as soon as he has it."

"You're always in such a rush."

"My former partner used to say that people who are content to let life come to them never have a life worth mentioning."

16

AVA WENT ONLINE AND BOOKED A BUSINESS-CLASS
seat on the Cathay Pacific flight to Hong Kong and a
room at the Mandarin Oriental in Central. She couldn't
help but feel it was a bit like the old days, when the hunt
for money often sent her careering from city to city and
country to country.

She arranged for a wake-up call and then packed her
bags with everything except her travelling clothes and
toilet kit. She was about to take a shower when the room
phone rang.

"This is Feng."

"Hi. I was going to call you later. I'm leaving for Hong
Kong first thing tomorrow morning. Is there any chance you
could drop off two copies of the spreadsheet before eight?"

"I don't see why not. My people are working on it now."

"Great, and I'm trying to run down more information on
AKG, Shell, Mother of Pearl, and New Age through a law
firm in Hong Kong and a North American bank."

"That's the reason I'm calling."

"What do you mean?"

"Have you ever heard the term *gaizhi*?"

"No."

"It's the Chinese government's way of introducing capitalism, or at least private ownership, into the economic structure," he said. "The term is loosely translated as 'changing the system.' It's vague enough to mean just about anything, and that's the way they want it. No one wants to use the word 'capitalism.'"

"What does this have to do with our project?"

"One of my accountants was going through your notes and thought the name New Age looked familiar."

"In what way?"

"About two years ago, he was working as a trainee at one of the local Shanghai banks and became part of an internal team that was investigating the possibility of acquiring an appliance manufacturer."

"For New Age?"

"No, for themselves. The provincial government needed money at the time and was disposing of some non-essential and non-political assets that they thought — correctly — could do better in private hands. The bank was one of the bidders."

"And the bank lost?"

"It did."

"And New Age won?"

"Here's where it gets murky," Feng said. "As far as my guy remembers, the company that took over the manufacturer was set up just to make that acquisition. The appliance maker was named Kitchen Giant. The winning bidder was called KGS, and he thinks that meant Kitchen Giant Syndicate."

"Not exactly subtle."

"Maybe not, but it was effective."

"How much did they pay?"

"He doesn't know, but he remembers the bank was livid because they thought they'd been set up to lose."

"Why did they think that?"

"Because there were two rounds of bidding, with only the top three bids from the first round moving on to the second round. The bank bid one hundred and fifty million and made it through. The head of the bank then — according to my guy — got a phone call from a contact in Nanjing telling him that if they bid the same amount again, they'd win. They did and they lost. They were sure the process was rigged so that KGS would win."

"But Feng, I still don't see the connection to New Age."

"The bank looked into who was behind the syndicate and came up with a list of nondescript names. But two of them were listed as officers of New Age Capital. The bank then assumed KGS was a front for New Age."

"Was Tsai one of the officers?"

"No, my guy remembers that much. But there were rumours that a U.S. bank was aligned with New Age in the bid."

"Does he remember the name of the bank?"

"California something."

"Great," Ava sighed.

"I know, but it's the best he can do."

"It's still interesting."

"I thought so."

"What's the appliance manufacturer called now?"

"It's still Kitchen Giant. I looked it up before calling you.

I also looked at the list of officers and didn't see any names I recognized."

"It's still a private company?"

"Yes, so they don't have to publish financial reports or identify shareholders."

"And New Age seems to be private as well."

"It is."

"But a California bank probably won't be."

"You would know that better than me."

"It is worth investigating."

"My guy has offered to make some calls."

"We have to be discreet. I'll look into it and be in touch if I have something worth telling you," Ava said.

She went online as soon as she hung up. Kitchen Giant had an impressive website. Its products seemed to be available in every town in Jiangsu, and it had a decent presence in most of China's major cities.

She went to the contacts page. Under "Corporate Information" only the names of the marketing director and the finance director were listed. She wrote them down in her notebook and reached for the phone.

"Ava, I haven't even had a chance to leave my office yet," Johnny Yan said.

"Sorry, I'm not being pushy. I just have another detail I'd like explored when Felix is looking for information."

"I'm listening."

"I'm told that New Age Capital bought a Chinese appliance company called Kitchen Giant through a company named KGS. I'd like that confirmed, if possible. If they did, I'd like to know who the shareholders are in KGS."

"We can ask, but there's no guarantee we'll get answers."

"I know," Ava said. "And I was told there was a U.S. bank involved in the deal. I'd appreciate it if Felix would ask New Age's Chinese bank if the company has any existing Canadian or American bank ties."

"That's a pretty standard question for us to ask when we're looking for new business. I don't think it will be a problem."

"Great, and Johnny, although I gave you four company names, could you ask Felix to chase down New Age first? I want to know what he finds the moment he finds it. He needn't wait to get information on all the companies before giving it you."

"Will do."

Ava sat back and glanced at the computer screen again. She might have found where some of the Tsai money had settled. She began to write the name Kitchen Giant on her chart and then stopped. It was way too early to start making assumptions, no matter how strongly she felt the assumption was correct.

17

THE ENVELOPE FROM FENG SLID UNDER HER SUITE door at seven thirty the next morning. Ava was already dressed, had finished two coffees and read the *New York Times*, and had just opened her computer to check her email. She had hoped that Johnny Yan would have something for her, but the only messages from Toronto were from Maria and her mother.

Maria wrote that she was still waiting to hear about her extension and that she hoped Ava wasn't doing anything dangerous. Call me or email me as soon as you're able, she concluded.

There were two emails from Jennie Lee, both sent from her phone. The first said: I'm on my way to Fallsview Casino in Niagara Falls with Cindy. She talked me into it, though she didn't have to try that hard. I've banked the money for the trips, so don't worry about that. It's just that we're on a roll and it seemed a shame to waste it. Love, Mummy.

The second had been sent four hours later. It read: I'm up 15,000 and heading for dinner.

Ava replied: I'm leaving for Hong Kong in a few hours. I'll

be there for at least a few days. I'm travelling with Amanda and will see Michael. I'll also call Daddy and try to arrange a lunch. Do me a favour and don't email me again until you're at home. I don't need or want gambling updates. I find it very stressful. Love, Ava.

She hesitated and then sent it.

She retrieved the envelope from the door and opened it at the desk. Feng's people had done a very neat job of compressing and collating the information. She scanned the sheet quickly, looking for any mention of a company with the word "California" in it. She found it under Evergreen Trading. A firm called California Asian Trust had made two deposits of $100,000 more than two years ago, one month apart. She cross-referenced the money flowing from Evergreen. Fifteen days after each deposit had cleared at the bank, the entire amount had been sent to AKG Consulting. She blinked in surprise. She had expected to see the money move to New Age.

She entered California Asian Trust into a search engine. There were no results, and that sparked her curiosity even more. If access to the name was unavailable in China, there was a reason for it.

It was the middle of the evening in Toronto and Johnny Yan would be at home. Ava called his cell.

"Hello," he said, the noise of clattering dishes and voices in the background.

"Johnny, it's Ava. My apologies for disturbing you at home."

"I'm in a restaurant with my parents and my wife and kids, but the apology is accepted anyway," he said. "Felix doesn't have any information yet."

"That's not why I'm calling."

"Then what is it?"

"I mentioned to you that there might be a U.S. bank connected to New Age Capital. Well, I have a name — California Asian Trust — but it seems to be involved with one of the other companies, AKG Consulting. I don't know if California Trust is a U.S.-based business or one that's set up in China to do business here. Whichever it is, I can't find anything about it on the local Internet. Could you do a search for me, or ask Felix to?"

"Sure," Johnny said, and then paused. "Under one condition."

"What's that?"

"When this is over, you tell me what the hell this is about. I get involved in these cases of yours and never know what you're really up to."

"I promise I'll tell you," Ava said.

"Okay, I'll see what I can find tonight. Felix contacted all the Chinese banks, so one way or another you should hear from me when I get into the office tomorrow morning."

"I'll be in Hong Kong, but you can reach me by email or mobile phone."

"Do you ever stay in one place for more than a few days?"

"I had my butt parked in Toronto for months."

"And you never called me?"

"You know how it is when you're at home."

"I most certainly do. I didn't think you did."

Ava laughed. "I'll speak to you tomorrow."

Ava hung up and saw it was time to meet Amanda.

Both Amanda and Ava referred to each other as "sister-in-law," but the truth was a bit more complicated. Ava was the second child of the second wife of Marcus Lee. He had never divorced the first, Elizabeth, and in fact still lived with her. It was a common enough situation for wealthy men in Hong Kong, and Marcus had taken it one step further, with a third wife who now lived in Australia with two more of his children.

Amanda was married to Michael Lee, Marcus and Elizabeth Lee's oldest son. Ava had met Michael the previous year when his business ran into trouble and he needed her help. During that process, she had met Amanda and developed a relationship with her — aided by the fact that Ava and Uncle had twice assisted Amanda's father, Jack Yee, by recovering money that had been stolen from him. To outsiders, it all seemed very complicated. To Ava, this was normal life. Her father lived in Hong Kong with Wife Number One and their four sons. Her mother lived in Canada with Ava and her sister, Marian. Marcus called every day, visited once a year for two weeks, and paid all the bills. Ava was sure his third wife in Australia and her children received the same treatment.

The events that brought Ava into direct contact with Michael had been extraordinary. He had put the entire family's future at financial risk. Ava had extricated Michael from an attempted extortion and saved the family's fortune. Even Elizabeth Lee had willingly and gratefully acknowledged Ava's efforts, by publicly welcoming her at Amanda and Michael's wedding.

But even without the family connection, Ava would have been pleased to have Amanda as a friend. She was smart and witty, and during the crisis with Michael she had displayed tremendous loyalty and courage. Ava enjoyed her company almost as much as she did May Ling's, but she felt the age gap more keenly. Amanda was in her late twenties and had more in common with Chi-Tze and the Pos.

When Ava arrived in the hotel lobby, Amanda was standing near the entrance with an enormous Louis Vuitton suitcase by her side. She was dressed in blue jeans and a plain white cotton blouse, but Ava had no doubt that the clothes were from high-end designers. Ava walked over to her and they hugged. Amanda had her hair pulled back in a ponytail and wasn't wearing any makeup.

"You look like a teenager," Ava said.

"I wish I felt like one."

"Another late night?"

"Chi-Tze and Gillian joined Elsa and me for dinner last night, and then Gillian insisted we go to a club. Elsa was game and I felt obliged to go along."

"Has the photo shoot started?"

"Today."

"And did you answer all the questions that Lane Crawford had?"

"We did it late yesterday, although I ended up editing some of Clark's replies. He can go on forever about design elements and I thought some of it was way off topic."

"Who will follow up?"

"We asked Laura from Lane Crawford to email Gillian and Chi-Tze. They're the ones running the business."

"Together, it appears."

"It has evolved that way, and I have to say I couldn't be happier to see the way the two of them co-operate and support each other."

The doorman hailed a taxi and helped to load their luggage into the trunk.

"The traffic going in the direction of the airport is really bad this morning," the driver said.

"Are you suggesting a shortcut?" Amanda said.

"There isn't any. I just thought you should know."

"Thanks."

As the taxi eased into traffic, Ava turned on her cellphone and placed it on her lap.

They rode quietly for several minutes, the traffic not nearly as heavy as anticipated. As they left Shanghai and crossed the Huangpu River and entered Pudong, Amanda said, "Ava, would you mind telling me about Xu?"

"What?" Ava said, startled.

"I know he had something to do with helping us out in Borneo, and I heard from someone that he was a friend of Uncle's, but other than that I don't know much."

"Why do you ask?"

"When our people went to the factory where we're going to make our clothes, they were blown away by the reception they got."

"Was that so unusual?"

"They thought so. There wasn't a request they made that wasn't responded to positively, and some of those requests involved the factory making substantial investments in equipment."

"They sound eager to get our business."

"The plant manager went out of his way to tell Gillian that they'd do anything else we wanted, and on the way out of the building, he asked her to make sure that her bosses told Mr. Xu how co-operative they were."

Ava started to reply and then stopped. Amanda was still looking out the window, but Ava saw that her jaw was tightly set.

"Do you remember the rather large infusion of working capital we got a few months back?" Ava said.

"Of course. It financed Suki's expansion and the Po business."

"The money came from Xu."

"Oh. I thought it had come from you and May."

"It came from Xu. He was a friend to Uncle and now he's a friend to me," Ava said. "There are no strings attached to the money and no ownership participation. It's an investment that he hopes returns a profit. That's all. We should have told you sooner."

"I understand."

"Is there anything else you want to ask?"

Amanda hesitated, and Ava braced herself for a question about how Xu had acquired so much money.

"No," Amanda said.

"Good. Now let me ask you something," Ava said. "Has anything been going on between May and Xu?"

Amanda's eyebrows arched and her mouth flew open. "What do you mean?"

"He's single. He's handsome. She's on her own in Shanghai and is still damn attractive. And I couldn't help but notice that she was kind of flirting with him the other night at the reception."

"The only time I saw him was the other night. I didn't pick up on any flirting. And I've seen May every day since she's been here, and most nights too. She's always been alone."

"It must be my imagination," Ava said.

"Would it bother you if something was going on?"

"It would worry me rather than bother me," Ava said.

"They're both friends, and nothing can complicate a friendship quicker than sex."

"Or lack of it."

"What?"

Amanda reached for Ava's hand. "Michael and I have both been travelling a lot on business and, just speaking for myself, when I get home I'm tired and don't always feel like having sex. He doesn't like it when I'm not all eager. Living with someone isn't everything it's cracked up to be."

Ava pressed her head against the back of the seat. Amanda couldn't possibly know about her dilemma with Maria, could she?

"We're going at the speed limit," Amanda said. "We'll be at the airport in no time. I don't know why the driver was fussing."

"He was creating low expectations," Ava said, glad for the subject change. "That's often a smart thing to do, in business and in life."

18

AVA SAW SONNY STANDING UNDER A SIGN THAT READ
MEETING PLACE at Chek Lap Kok, Hong Kong's international airport. His eyes scanned the rush of people coming through the doorways. He was dressed, as Uncle and Xu always were, in a black suit with a white shirt. His thin black tie was loosened at the neck, and it looked to Ava as though he had put on weight and was having problems buttoning his shirt collar.

He had been a member of Uncle's gang in Fanling and then, in a relationship that spanned twenty years, he had become Uncle's personal bodyguard and driver. It was only in that capacity that Ava had known him. He was a big man, only a few inches shorter than Suen, and he was thick and broad across the shoulders and chest. Despite his size, he had incredible agility that, combined with raw power and natural ferocity, made him a terrifying opponent. Ava had never seen anyone come close to besting him in hand-to-hand combat. She had doubts that even she would be able to take him down, despite her years of bak mei training. Not that she would ever have to. Sonny had completely transferred his loyalty to Uncle to her. She knew there wasn't a single thing he wouldn't do for her.

"Sonny," she said, as they emerged from the crowd.

"Boss," he said, stepping forward with a grin. He stopped just short of her and Amanda and bowed his head, clenching his hands in front of his chest and moving them slowly up and down.

"Don't be so formal," Ava said as she reached him.

"You should have told me you were coming."

"It was last minute. Besides, I wanted to surprise you," she said as she stood up on her toes and kissed him on both cheeks.

"How long are you staying?"

"I have no idea."

"I like the sound of that," he said. "Does Lop know you're here?"

"No, and why should he?"

"No reason," Sonny said, reaching for her bag and Amanda's suitcase. "The car is parked outside in the VIP area."

"How have you managed to retain that privilege?" Ava asked.

"They know it was Uncle's car," he said.

Ava and Amanda walked in Sonny's wake as he forged a path through the crowded arrivals hall to the main exit. Within ten steps they were standing in front of the silver Mercedes S-Class. Sonny opened the back door for them and then placed their bags in the trunk. When he slid into the driver's seat, he turned towards them. "Amanda, are you going to the office or the apartment?"

"Apartment."

"Boss?"

"The Mandarin Oriental in Central."

"Do you have any plans after you check in?" he asked.

"I have a meeting at a lawyer's office in Central at three."

"I'll drive you?"

Burgess and Bowlby was a fifteen-minute walk from the Mandarin Oriental, but Ava knew that meant nothing to Sonny. "Of course. You can pick me up at quarter to three."

He eased the car into traffic. "I drove Michael and Simon to Shenzhen this morning," he said. "They're taking the train back. Michael said to tell you he'll be home before seven and asked if you could wait for him for dinner."

"Thanks," Amanda said.

Sonny began the drive along Route 8 that would take them along the northeastern coastline of Lantau Island towards the New Territories and into Kowloon. From there, Ava knew he'd probably take the Western Harbour Crossing to get to Hong Kong Island and into Central. She looked at the passing countryside without much interest, but when the Mercedes drove onto Tsing Ma Bridge, she sat upright and stared intently at the scene below.

Tsing Ma was more than two kilometres long and was one of the largest and longest suspension bridges in the world. It had six traffic lanes, three in each direction, and beneath them were two sets of train tracks. Two hundred metres below was the Ma Wan Channel, the major shipping lane in and out of Hong Kong, Asia's busiest commercial port. From the bridge, Ava had a spectacular view of an armada of ships and boats of all sizes and shapes, ferrying goods and people in and out of Hong Kong to and from every part of the world. The sight always generated a touch of emotion in her, a feeling that she was now officially back in Hong Kong, her second home.

She turned on her phone and saw that she hadn't received any texts or emails from Johnny, and all was quiet on the Maria and Jennie fronts. She wasn't sure that hearing nothing from Jennie was a good thing. She had a vision of her mother sitting at a baccarat table playing black hundred-dollar chips. If all she lost was the $15,000 she'd been up, it would be a good night.

Amanda was listening to some voicemails and then checked for texts. "The girls have been active," she said to Ava. "I'll forward you these texts if you want to see them."

"No thanks. I trust them, and you," Ava said.

"Oh," Amanda said quietly, looking down at her phone. Ava was wondering if she'd offended her when Amanda turned to her and yelled, "Yippee!" A huge smile broke across her face.

"Listen to this. Chi-Tze just forwarded it to me," Amanda said. "'Hello, everyone, this is Laura. I received your information yesterday, thank you. I reviewed it with a few of my colleagues and then met with Ms. Song this morning. We would like to organize a conference call with you tomorrow. Clark should most definitely be a party to the conversation, as well as your in-house people who look after marketing plans and costings.'"

"That's great. Will you take part?" Ava asked.

"No, I think it's better to let Chi-Tze, Gillian, and Clark handle it. They're the team in Shanghai. I don't want them to think we're looking over their shoulders all the time."

"That's very smart of you," Ava said. "And that email is very encouraging. Not quite a commitment, but it sounds like a positive start to the process."

"You're not kidding. The fact that we're communicating

with Lane Crawford is cause enough to celebrate," Amanda said. "Ava, speaking of Lane Crawford and Hong Kong, do you ever think about living here?"

"Pardon?"

"I'm sorry if that sounds nosy, but it's something that May and I, and Michael and I, have talked about. We'd all love it if you were closer, and we aren't the only ones," Amanda said, nodding towards Sonny.

"It's something I've never thought about."

"Not even when you were in business with Uncle?"

"No. The most time I've spent here was when he was dying, and my life was rather restricted to making sure he was looked after."

"Would you think about it now that the business is centred and growing here in Asia?"

"I'm not sure that's actually a consideration," Ava said. "May can keep her eye on our investments from Wuhan. You're running the business very well here in Hong Kong. The Chiks seem to have things under control in Borneo. Chi-Tze and Gillian will manage PÖ. And Suki Chan doesn't need my guidance or presence. So what would I do? Interfere?"

"You have no idea how much you're respected, how much you're loved."

"That's all very nice, but what does that have to do with my moving to Hong Kong?"

"So much of your life is here."

"A part of it is here, but I'm not sure it's the biggest part," Ava said, and then paused. "You've met my mother."

"How could I forget? She is an incredible woman."

"And you met my girlfriend, Maria?"

"I did, and I found her incredibly sweet."

"Well, they're the two most important people in my life."

"Ava, I'm sorry. I wasn't trying to pry."

"It's okay. I know you and I have a relationship that goes beyond Michael, but all of it is based here in Asia. No one here understands what it's like to live in a country like Canada. My mother can do and be anyone she wants. Maria and I can walk hand in hand on the street. We can kiss and hug in public and no one will say a word against us. In fact, many people will applaud us. Can you imagine that happening in Hong Kong, or anywhere else in Asia?"

"Ava, I'm sorry."

"No, no, no," Ava said. "I don't want you to be sorry. I want you to understand. My mother built a life and a future for my sister and me in Canada. She made sure that we both had educations and would never have to be dependent on anyone. Now my sister is married to a *gweilo* and has a life that could be described as domestic, but I'm convinced that if the need arose, she'd be able to look after herself. I am a different case. I never needed anyone to look after me. Not even Uncle. That frame of mind came from my mother, but it was reinforced by my day-to-day experiences living in Canada. I've never had to apologize for who I am, or explain why I am who I am.

"There, I have my mother, a woman who's devoted her life to me and my sister and who would step in front of a speeding truck to protect us if that was necessary. And I have the only woman who has ever loved me so unconditionally that it almost makes me cry thinking about how devoted she is. How could I leave either of them or ask them to come to live in Hong Kong, where everything they represent is considered either an abhorrence or second-class?"

"Ava, I'm sorry I asked that question," Amanda said, her voice cracking. "It only came from good intentions."

Ava sat back. Her torrent of words had surprised her. "I know it did, and I'm sorry for overreacting," she said. "It's just that I'm struggling with my own feelings about some things right now."

"We do love you."

"I know, and I love all of you too. I'm just tired and jet-lagged," she said, squeezing Amanda's hand.

Throughout the women's conversation, Sonny's eyes had been locked on the road, his body rigid. Now his shoulders relaxed and he turned towards the back and said, "The Western Harbour Crossing is moving well today. We'll be in Central in a few minutes. I was planning to drop Amanda off at her apartment first, if that's okay."

"That's fine," Ava said.

Amanda and Michael lived in an 800-square-foot apartment on Queen's Road in the Mid-Levels. The streets to that area ran from Victoria Harbour through Central and up the mountain towards Victoria Peak, or "the Peak," as it was commonly known. The higher the real estate, the greater the cost. The Mid-Levels, as the name implied, was halfway between the harbour and the Peak. The neighbourhood was mainly residential, nearly entirely apartment buildings, and home to comfortably retired senior managers and a younger crowd who aspired to eventually buy on higher ground. Michael and Amanda's apartment was just high enough to get a sliver of a Victoria Harbour view from the window.

The Mercedes traversed Victoria Harbour and exited onto Connaught Road. If Sonny had kept going straight he would have reached the Mandarin Oriental. Instead, he made a right turn and started the climb to Queen's Road.

"Do you want to join us for dinner?" Amanda asked Ava.

"You haven't seen your husband in two weeks. I think he might prefer having you to himself," Ava said.

"Tomorrow night, then?"

"Yes, that'll be great," Ava said. "But do me a favour — when you see Michael tonight, ask him not to tell my father I'm in Hong Kong. I'll meet up with him for dim sum in the next day or two, but I'd like to initiate the contact myself."

"*Momentai.*"

"Thanks."

They came to a stop in front of an older apartment building with red brick walls and small windows. Sonny climbed out of the driver's seat and went to the trunk to retrieve Amanda's suitcase.

"Give me a hug," Ava said to Amanda.

As they embraced, Amanda said, "I'm sorry if what I said about you moving to Hong Kong triggered something unpleasant."

"Don't be. It's nice that I'm wanted here as well as in Toronto," Ava said. "The truth is that my relationship with Maria is on my mind. I need to make a decision about the future and I'm not finding it easy."

"I'm sure you'll sort it out. You always do."

"I wish I was that sure," Ava said.

Sonny stood on the sidewalk with Amanda's suitcase.

"I'd better go," Amanda said. "I'll touch base with you tomorrow."

Ava watched her sister-in-law enter the building, and then she climbed back into the car. Sonny did an awkward

U-turn before heading down the mountain towards the harbour.

Five minutes later, the Mercedes stopped in front of the Mandarin Oriental, and Ava was greeted by the doorman with a loud and cheery, "Welcome back, Ms. Lee."

It had been her hotel of choice in Hong Kong for years. She loved the location, which was close to the harbour and surrounded by great shops and restaurants. It was within walking distance of the Star Ferry, which could take her to Tsim Sha Tsui, the southern edge of Kowloon, and then further into the New Territories. An MTR station was only a few blocks from the hotel, and she used the subway system to get to places like Victoria Park, near Causeway Bay.

"I'll be back downstairs at about a quarter to three," she said to Sonny. "The lawyer's office is in the Bond Building."

"A ten-minute drive at most," Sonny said.

After checking in, she hurried to her room. It was already well past two o'clock and she didn't have a lot of time to get ready for her meeting with Brenda Burgess. She brushed her teeth and hair, then put on a clean pair of black linen slacks and a blue button-down shirt. She thought about checking her email and decided to wait. It was the middle of the night in Toronto and she was sure Johnny Yan didn't have anything for her yet.

Ava took the Tsai files from her bag and set them on the desk. Then she opened her notebook and reviewed the items she wanted Burgess to pursue. Some of them would duplicate the work that Johnny and Felix were doing, but she wasn't concerned about getting back similar information from two different sources. She appreciated certainty and confirmation.

At twenty to three she left the room and headed for the lobby. Sonny wasn't in sight, but she knew the car would be near the hotel entrance and he'd be standing by it. When she walked out of the hotel, he was parked right in front, chatting amiably with the doorman and a policeman.

As Ava climbed into the car, Sonny said, "Uncle Fong called me a few minutes ago. I mentioned that you were in Hong Kong. I hope that's okay."

"That's fine."

Sonny opened the driver's door and slid behind the wheel. "He wondered if you would be available for dinner sometime."

The question surprised her. "Does he have a problem?"

"No, he'd just like to see you. Truthfully, he doesn't have many friends left since Uncle died. I try to get together with him every week or so," Sonny said. "I think he'd also like to thank you for continuing to support him financially."

"If he's going to thank me, then I won't have dinner with him," Ava said. "He's Uncle's oldest and dearest ally and friend, and you know it was Uncle who asked me to look after him."

"You would have anyway."

"That's beside the point."

"No, it's not."

"Well, anyway, whatever he gets from me he's earned, both from his days with Uncle and from the help he's given me since Uncle died. We would never have been able to resolve the conflict with the gang in Guangzhou if he hadn't helped us set up those meetings."

"That is true," Sonny said.

"So please tell Uncle Fong I'll be happy to have dinner

with him, as a friend. In fact, I'm free tonight, so ask him if he wants to join me somewhere," Ava said.

"I'll do that."

"And Sonny, I'd like you to join us, as a friend to both of us."

He twisted his head in her direction and she saw a rare smile cross his face. "I'd like that," he said.

"What do you think he'd like best? There's that noodle place near here that Uncle liked. Or how about Man Wah, the Chinese restaurant in the Mandarin?"

"There's that hot pot restaurant near the Landmark Hotel. The two of them used to go there a lot."

"Then tell him to meet us there at seven."

"I'll do it as soon as I drop you off," Sonny said as he eased the car through the heavy Central traffic.

They reached the entrance to the Bond Building at five to three. "I can't park on the street here," Sonny said. "There's an underground lot nearby. Call me when you're finished the meeting."

Ava nodded and then turned and walked through double glass doors into a spacious, marble-floored lobby. She took the elevator to the thirty-first floor and stepped out into a circular reception area.

"I'm Ava Lee and I'm here to see Ms. Burgess," she said to the young woman at the reception desk.

"Yes, Ms. Lee, she's expecting you. Let me show you the way to the boardroom."

Ava was led into a room with a long wooden table surrounded by close to twenty leather and steel chairs. The table was made of a dark, dense wood that was scarred in several places, and it had eight thick legs that were carved from top to bottom. It wasn't until Ava drew close that she saw the carvings were stylized dragons, their mouths agape near the tabletop, their tails wrapped around the feet.

"You're admiring our table?" a voice said from the doorway.

Ava turned and saw a middle-aged Western woman in a light blue sweater set and a dark blue skirt cut below the knee. She was a bit taller than Ava, and thicker through the waist and shoulders. Her hair was cut into a loose bob with short bangs.

"Hello, Ms. Burgess."

"Brenda."

"The table looks like an antique."

"It's one of my husband's most prized possessions. His great-great-grandfather was the first Bowlby to come to Hong Kong. He joined the Jardine Matheson trading company in 1845, just one year after it set up shop in Hong Kong and about fifteen years after it arrived in China. He eventually ran their Canton office. His son and his grandson after him worked for the firm. It was Richard's father who broke the tradition by going into law, but he still maintained ties with the company. When Richard's grandfather died, Richard's father asked Jardine if he could buy something as a memento of his family's time with the company. They allowed him to purchase this table. It dates back to the 1850s."

"It's fantastic, a combination of Western and Eastern."

Brenda Burgess smiled and walked towards Ava with an outstretched hand. "While I'm glad to meet you, my husband was quite disappointed he couldn't be here. He's beginning to wonder if you really exist."

Ava shrugged apologetically. "The last time I was in Hong Kong I was forced to cancel two meetings with him."

"He told me it was three."

"Maybe it was," Ava said.

"And now that you're finally here, he's in the U.K. watching rugby."

"Perhaps we're not fated to meet."

Brenda Burgess motioned to the table. "Let's sit, shall we? Can I offer you anything to drink?"

"No, thank you," Ava said.

Burgess went to the opposite side of the table so she was facing her. She pointed at the file Ava had in front of her. "Is that the purpose of this meeting?"

"It is indeed."

"And you mentioned that it's only indirectly connected to the Three Sisters."

"That's true."

"Well, I'm here to listen."

Ava opened her notebook and looked at the notes she'd made. "May Ling told me that you like to know everything about the work you're asked to do."

"Only because it usually helps us work more efficiently, and ultimately benefits the client."

"I don't think I can provide full details where this matter is concerned."

"I see," Burgess said slowly.

"It has nothing to do with trust. May has tremendous respect for you and your husband and the manner in which you operate," Ava said. "My problem is that I gave my word to one of the parties involved that I would keep his name out of it."

"Does May Ling know the party?"

"She does, but no one else."

"That normally would be sufficient assurance, but I do have to ask you if this matter is in any way illegal."

"No," Ava said, finding the question a touch irregular.

"Then, as I said, I'm here to listen."

"Thank you," Ava said, opening her file. "Tell me, have you heard of the Tsai family?"

"From Nanjing?"

"The same."

"I've certainly heard of them, and I have a rudimentary understanding of their background and standing."

"Tsai Lian is the governor of Jiangsu Province. He's a princeling, the son of Tsai Da-Xia, who was on the Long March with Mao and later was a member of the Politburo Standing Committee."

"Yes, Chinese royalty."

"Exactly," Ava said.

"And doesn't Tsai Lian's cousin also hold a senior position in the province?"

"He's the provincial secretary of the Communist Party."

"What's his name?"

Ava glanced at her notebook. "Ying Fa."

"I should have remembered. I had a client who was trying to do business with the province and he ran afoul of Ying."

"How so?"

"I can't give you any details other than that money was expected to change hands and didn't."

"And the business came to nothing?"

Brenda just shrugged and smiled.

"We haven't run into Ying yet, but it is early days," Ava said.

"Do I take from that remark that Tsai Lian has had his hand out?"

Ava removed the spreadsheet from the file and passed it to Brenda. "This will help explain, but I haven't made any copies yet."

"Why don't I get that done now."

"That's a good idea, and while you're at it, could you have this page of my notebook copied as well?" Ava said, turning to the page where she'd drawn her last chart.

Brenda took the documents and then turned and picked up a phone that was on the credenza behind the table. "Vanessa, could you come into the boardroom, please?"

In less than a minute a tall young woman strode into the boardroom.

"Vanessa, this is Ava Lee. I think you know the name. She's a partner with May Ling Wong and Amanda Yee in the Three Sisters," Brenda said. "And Ava, this is Vanessa Ogg. She's one of our best young lawyers, and she has in fact handled most of the due diligence and paperwork related to your company's acquisitions."

Ava looked up at a long, angular face that was more striking than pretty. The young lawyer's sleek black hair was shoulder length and her eyes were a dark brown. "Ogg is a name I've never heard," Ava said.

"It's Scottish."

"Ah."

"The name originated around Aberdeen and is a sept of the Clan MacGregor. When James the First of England outlawed the MacGregors, he also banned any use of their name. The Oggs got caught up in that and the name fell into disuse."

"How interesting," Ava said. "It's strange that a name should generate such a strong reaction. Mind you, I was in Indonesia on business not that long ago and met the members of a Chinese family who, like every other Chinese family in the country, were forced to change their name to an Indonesian one because Sukarno banned the use of their Chinese one."

"Did it make them any less Chinese?" Brenda asked.

"Not in the least."

"Unfortunately, there's very little that's Scottish about my father except for his name," Vanessa said. "He was born in Hong Kong. My grandfather worked for the Swire Group and my grandmother was Chinese. As is my mother."

Brenda held up the spreadsheet. "Vanessa, I hate to interrupt, but could you have this copied, along with this page of Ms. Lee's notebook?"

"Of course."

"And then come back and join us for the rest of the meeting."

"Okay."

When she left, Brenda said to Ava, "Vanessa is a rising star in the firm. That's why I had her handle the Three Sisters business. Whatever it is you want done, I'll most likely assign it to her, so it makes sense for her to sit in with us."

"That's not a problem."

"*Do jeh.*"

"You speak Cantonese?"

"I try. Richard is fluent, but then he has his Hong Kong roots and was raised by an amah who spoke only Cantonese to him."

Vanessa returned to the boardroom with Ava's originals and two copies. She took a chair next to Brenda.

"Ms. Lee was starting to outline a problem she has with the Tsai family of Nanjing," Brenda said, looking down at the spreadsheet. "You said this would help explain things," she said to Ava.

"You'll see I have identified a number of companies. The spreadsheet shows how much money has been going to some of them, where the money came from, and where the money was sent on to."

"Do you mind if I ask you where you got this information?" Brenda asked. "It is quite specific and remarkably detailed."

"I had access to company bank accounts. This is a summary. I have more information if it's needed."

"Can I ask how you came by that access?"

"I would rather you didn't."

Brenda nodded.

"There are individuals' names attached to some of the companies on your chart," Vanessa said.

"Yes."

"Is there any connection between them, other than corporate?"

"They're all linked to the Tsai family."

"I see."

"My hope is that when you find out more about the companies that don't have names attached, that same link will be a constant."

"New Age Capital, AKG Consulting, Shell Investments, and Mother of Pearl Investments," Vanessa said.

"And KGS, which stands for Kitchen Giant Syndicate. There's also another company called California Asian Trust.

I'm not sure if they're American or Chinese and they're not on the chart," Ava said.

"What exactly is it that you want to know?" Brenda asked.

"All I have right now are the company names and their banks. I'd like to see where and when they were incorporated. I'd like to know who they're doing business with and what kind of businesses they actually are, because I don't have a clue. A list of shareholders, including as much information as you can get on them individually, would be very helpful. And if there's any way of finding out what assets these companies own or control, I would appreciate knowing."

"That's a fair amount of work," Brenda said.

"Well, it could be even more, because I'd like the same information on every company you can link to those on my chart."

"Can I use our Beijing people?" Vanessa asked her boss.

Brenda looked at Ava. "We have a law firm in Beijing we often call upon to assist us in this kind of search. They have better access to some records."

Ava started to say no and then stopped. "You trust them completely?"

"We do."

"They can't know who the client is."

"Well, actually, aside from you, I don't know who the client is," Brenda said.

"It's me, personally. This has nothing to do with the Three Sisters."

"All right."

"And there also can't be any mention of the name Tsai coming from your office in any of the inquiries. Just stick to the company names, and if Beijing notices the connections, put it down to coincidence."

Brenda turned to Vanessa. "That seems clear enough. Will it be an issue with Beijing?"

"No."

"Now, Ms. Lee, as I said before, this is quite a bit of work. How soon do you want to see results?"

"Tomorrow?"

"You're joking, right?"

"Testing, and please call me Ava."

"Vanessa, if I clear your workload, how soon can you get this information pulled together for Ava?"

"Three or four days, depending on Beijing."

"What's your hourly billable rate?" Ava asked.

The question seemed to catch both women off guard, and Vanessa looked at Brenda to answer.

"Our normal rate is six thousand Hong Kong dollars an hour, but we give a discount of ten percent to valued customers, and Three Sisters is valued," Brenda said.

"I'm the client, not Three Sisters, so I don't expect a discount," Ava said. "And I appreciate that speed sometimes costs more. So, I'll pay you ten thousand an hour if I can get a preliminary report by this time tomorrow."

"How preliminary?" Brenda asked.

"I'll want everything that Vanessa and your people in Beijing have been able to uncover after working full-time on this project from the time I leave your office. I don't have any other conditions."

"And after you get the report?"

"I'll pay ten thousand an hour for follow-up on anything that I deem necessary."

"I wasn't referring to the rate. I was asking if you are going to be satisfied with a preliminary report."

"I won't know until I see it, but my instinct is telling me that I won't be."

"Good, because we don't like to leave jobs only half done."

"That's a trait I share."

"Vanessa, how soon can you start?" Brenda asked.

"If I can put the Consul file aside, I'll get on it tonight."

"Take as many trainee lawyers as you need, and call Beijing and get them started too."

"Yes, Brenda."

Brenda stared across the table at Ava. "You'll get a report tomorrow. I'm not sure what will be in it, but we'll do the best we can."

"Thank you very much. Should I come here around the same time?"

"Why not."

"If I have any questions, who do I contact?" Vanessa asked as she stood.

"Call me," Brenda said. "I'll reach out to Ava."

Ava watched the young lawyer leave the room. "She seems very capable."

"She is, but then all of our people are."

"May Ling has said that many times. She has tremendous respect for your firm."

"We hold her in the same regard. She is a remarkable woman, and your young Ms. Yee has the makings of one as well. You were the only partner I'd never met, although I do have to say that the way your partners, and others, speak about you, I felt I knew you already."

"Pardon?" Ava said, surprised by the reference to "others."

"Excuse me, I didn't mean to get personal," Brenda said, shaking her head. "I'm just happy to finally meet you and to be able to tell my husband that you are not a phantom."

19

IT WAS NEARLY NINE O'CLOCK WHEN SONNY DROPPED Ava off at the entrance to the Mandarin Oriental. They had just spent close to two hours together with Uncle Fong, exploring the wonders of hot pot at a favourite restaurant of Uncle's.

The dinner didn't start very well. After exchanging greetings, Sonny asked Uncle Fong if he had taken the hydrofoil ferry back from Macau. It was an innocent question, but Fong blanched and suddenly looked quite angry.

Ava knew he didn't want to her to know he'd been in Macau, and she would have thought Sonny would know that as well, but obviously he didn't. The main reason that Ava was supporting Uncle Fong financially was because of his addiction to roulette and, to a lesser extent, other table games. He had made millions during his career and lost it all. Uncle had willed him a substantial amount of money, but he'd burned through it in a few months. When Ava found out about this loss from Andy, another ex-colleague of Uncle's and a friend of Ava's, she had called Uncle Fong to confirm that it was true. He admitted it was. Ava asked him how much money he needed every month to maintain a respectable lifestyle. When he told her, she doubled the amount and then set up a regular monthly payment. If he lost it gambling, she thought, the pain would at least be short-term. And not once had she remonstrated with him about his problem. He needed her respect and support — he didn't need to be scolded by a young woman.

"And how was Macau?" she asked lightly. "The last time I was there I could hardly believe the changes. I can't imagine that Stanley Ho is thrilled about all the new competition from the Las Vegas big boys."

"I almost preferred the old days," Fong said, his mood softening. "When I went into the Lisboa, I was treated like an emperor. Now everything is corporate, and the players are just numbers on a card. And the mainland Chinese dominate the place. Some of them lose more money in a day than I've ever lost in a month."

Like many Hong Kongers, Fong regarded the mainland Chinese with some suspicion. It was an attitude that Ava was used to, because she'd seen it expressed not just in Hong Kong but in Singapore and even in cities like Shanghai and Beijing. Westerners looked at China and saw a monolith. They had no understanding of the differences in language, culture, history, and cuisine that existed within China and the diaspora. It was like China looking at Europe and assuming everyone there was the same.

A server appeared at their table, and right behind her was the man Ava remembered was the owner.

"It's so good to see you back here," the owner said to Uncle Fong. "And you, young woman, I remember you being here with Uncle Chow."

"Yes, this was one of his favourite restaurants," Ava said.

"And he was one of our most valued customers."

"You used to serve us some very large shrimp that Uncle said you saved for special customers."

"I have some for you."

Ava looked at Sonny and Fong. "What else would you like?"

"Beef and fish balls and oysters," Sonny said.

"Some greens and mushrooms and shrimp dumplings," Fong added.

"That will get us started," Ava said. "I see that Uncle Fong already has a beer. I'll have a glass of white wine. Sonny?"

"Tsingtao."

"And I'll have another," Fong said.

The owner turned on the element set into the table. Another server appeared with a large stainless steel bowl that he placed on the flames. The bowl was divided in two. One side held plain chicken broth and the other had a spicy broth.

Over the next hour and a half, platters of raw food arrived at their table, and just as quickly this food was put into the broths. Ava wasn't surprised by how much Sonny could consume, but Fong almost matched him, and Ava did her best to keep up. They ate all of the initial order and then had seconds of shrimp, beef, and fish balls.

When the time came to settle, Ava reached for her wallet. Sonny's hand shot out and took the bill from the tray. "I'm paying for this," he said.

"Sonny!"

"No, you have to let me do this."

She heard determination in his voice. "Yes, of course I should. Thank you."

While Sonny was paying the bill, Uncle Fong said quietly to her, "I want you to know that I was in Macau for something other than gambling."

"You don't have to explain yourself to me."

He shrugged. "Well, over the years I made a fool of myself and Uncle had to bail me out a few times. I thought he might have told you, because I know he told you just about everything."

"He never said a word," Ava said.

"Anyway, now you know."

"Thank you for sharing that."

He nodded.

"Do you want Sonny to drive you home?"

"No, I live close enough to walk. That's one reason I like this place."

"I'm so happy you could join us."

"I know this sounds strange," Fong said, "but I almost felt that Uncle was at the table with us. I mean, I know he wasn't, but I could picture him sitting there next to you, plucking a shrimp from the bowl and then peeling it for you."

"Yes, he often did that." Ava laughed and reached out to touch Fong's arm. "Now, I want you to stay in touch, and I promise you that we'll have dinner every time I'm in Hong Kong."

Fong nodded. He gave her a smile and then began walking away from the restaurant.

"I wish I hadn't said anything about him going to Macau," Sonny said when he was out of earshot.

"I know."

"I didn't mean to embarrass him. I know he's a gambler and he can't help it."

"I know someone else like that," Ava said, thinking about her mother. "I don't think we should talk about it anymore."

They climbed into the car for the short trip to the Mandarin. After a few minutes, Sonny said, "I told Michael this afternoon that since you're in Hong Kong I won't be available to drive for him until you leave."

"I may not have a lot of driving for you to do."

"I'd rather be on call and know for certain that I'm there if you need me."

"That's best, I think," Ava said, knowing he wouldn't be happy with any other answer.

When they stopped in front of the hotel, she started to open her door but saw Sonny coming around the car. She sat back until he opened it for her, and then she climbed out and looked up at the big man. "I have missed you. It's great to be with you again, even if it's just for a few days. I also want to say how much I appreciate your looking after my brother and Amanda. It takes a great weight off me," she said, and then got on her toes and kissed him lightly on both cheeks.

"You will call if you need me?"

"You know I will."

She checked her phone as she took the elevator to her floor. She hadn't received any calls or texts during dinner. She had hoped to hear from Johnny but realized it was still quite early in the morning in Toronto. And despite herself, she wanted to know how her mother was doing. Uncle Fong's travails in Macau had triggered Ava's concern about Jennie Lee. In Ava's mind, the problem was less about the money than about her mother's psychological well-being. Bad casino losses took a toll on Jennie emotionally, and as much as Ava hated casino gambling, she hated what it did to her mother more. She thought about phoning the house to see if she was there, but then decided against it. Jennie wasn't an early riser on any occasion and Ava didn't want her to think she was checking in on her.

She spent fifteen minutes getting ready for bed and then turned on her computer to see if Johnny had emailed. He hadn't. She debated about what to do. *Surely they've heard something from the Chinese banks,* she thought. *What the hell.* She called Johnny's cell.

"Ava?" he said.

"Yes."

"You're so impatient."

"I can't help it."

"I just finished talking to Felix a minute ago. I was organizing my notes before I called you."

"He found something?"

"Yes, some of the banks answered his queries, but I don't know what his information is worth."

"Tell me what you have."

"Give me a moment. I have to figure out where to begin."

"I'll wait."

"He didn't hear back from the bank that handles Shell Investments," he mumbled as if he was talking to himself. "He couldn't find anything about that KGS company or California Asian Trust, but he discovered quite a bit about this Mother of Pearl, and it is interesting . . ."

"Johnny!"

"Sorry. Now let me see," he said and paused. "Okay, Mother of Pearl appears to be a holding company. It maintains an average balance in the low to mid eight figures."

"Ten to fifty million?"

"That's about right."

"Dollars?"

"All the numbers are in dollars."

"That's a lot of cash."

"We don't know the account fluctuations. That fifty million could have been one time last year."

"You said it was a holding company?"

"Yeah, according to its bank it has one major asset: it's the biggest shareholder in a company called Jiangsu Trust and Insurance Corporation. Felix looked into that company. Four years ago it was a small provincial operation and then it got taken over by Mother of Pearl and a minority partner from the U.S."

"Who is the American?"

"Patriot General Insurance, out of Hartford."

"What percentage does it own?"

"Forty."

"How much did they pay for it?"

"Well, the company sold for just under a hundred million, so you have to figure they put up at least forty million."

"Which means Mother of Pearl paid the balance."

"No matter who paid what, it seems to have been a really good deal."

"Why do you say that?"

"A well-run insurance company will generate a return on equity of ten percent and up. Jiangsu was returning nine when they bought it. The price they paid indicates that the company had a book value assessed at around one hundred million dollars. Insurance companies are typically sold at a price equal to their book value. If in fact, as we think is the case, the book value was understated, the selling price wasn't a reflection of the company's actual worth or its potential profitability," Johnny said. "Last year, Jiangsu's return on equity was twelve percent, and according to Felix its book-value is now close to five billion dollars."

"That's an incredible increase in book value."

"Felix attached a comment saying that the company's sales skyrocketed right after it was bought. He also said that the original book-value price of one hundred million could have been misleading."

"Is there any explanation for the rise in sales?"

"Yeah. According to the annual report, the company became the insurer of choice for Jiangsu Province."

"I see. How about the misleading book value?"

"Felix wasn't precise but he said that, looking back at the company's sales four years ago and its ROE, he would have expected a book value of closer to five hundred million."

"Johnny, is Jiangsu a private company?"

"Yeah."

"Then how did Felix get those numbers?"

"Because Jiangsu is in the insurance business, it has to file mandatory reports to the Chinese government so they can make sure the customers are covered. And Patriot is a public company, so he was able to confirm some numbers through their annual reports."

"Could I find those reports?"

"They're available online."

"Good, I'll have a look at them. Now, one last thing, what personal names are attached to Mother of Pearl?"

"Just one."

"And?"

"Wu Wai Wai."

Ava gasped. Wu Wai Wai was Tsai Lian's sister.

"You sound surprised," Johnny said.

"Only in the nicest possible way," Ava said.

"Do you want me to go on?"

"I sure do."

"Okay, he also found some data on AKG Consulting. The principle shareholder and legal representative is someone named Ying Jie. Average account balance is in the low seven-figure range, but that's going back only a year."

"Is she the only person listed?"

"She is."

"Did the bank provide any customer names for this consulting business?"

"I have to pull up a separate email. Felix was sending me information as he came across it, so it's quite disjointed. Give me a second."

Ava pulled out her chart while Johnny searched. The name Ying Jie went next to AKG, and Wu Wai Wai next to Mother of Pearl.

"Holy shit," Johnny finally said.

"What?"

"That California Asian Trust you mentioned, Kitchen Giant and Kitchen Giant Syndicate, New Age Capital, and the Patriot insurance company are all listed as clients of AKG."

"Isn't that interesting. I'd love to get into those AKG bank records."

"I can't help you there."

"No, I understand. So let me see, that leaves New Age Capital. Did Felix find anything on them?"

"He did. A guy named Zhu Huan is the legal representative, and there's a Hu Chi listed as CFO. The monthly balance is in the low to medium seven-figure range. The only two customers mentioned are Kitchen Giant and AKG."

"Do you sense that we're starting to connect dots?" Ava said.

"You'd know better than me."

"Yes, I guess I would," Ava said as she circled the name Zhu Huan and drew a straight line that connected AKG Consulting and New Age Capital.

"That's about all Felix got back from the banks he contacted. Do you want him to keep digging?"

Ava stared at the notes she'd made. "No, he's already given me enough to work on. I need some time to absorb it before I start asking more questions."

"Okay. You know where I am."

"I do, and I'll make sure that we send more business your way."

"It's all appreciated."

Ava hung up the phone and looked at the changes she'd made in the chart.

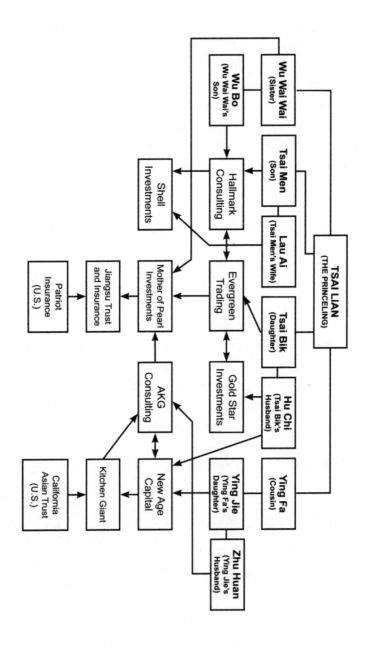

Money was moving in every direction. Assets were being acquired at cents on the dollar of their real value. It was all very clever, and it was beginning to feel to her like a complicated and well-orchestrated shell game with more to it than simple bribes and payoffs. It was already bigger financially than she had expected, and who knew what the lawyers would uncover. There were increasingly more people involved, but they had — thankfully — one thing in common: every one of them was connected in some way to Tsai Lian. Her problem was that she still had no direct link between him and the money the family was accumulating.

20

IT TOOK AVA AN HOUR TO SORT THROUGH HER NOTES from her chat with Johnny and then fit them into the ones she'd made previously. Hopefully the lawyers would provide more clarity and not more clutter when she met with them the next day.

She reached for the phone to call Feng.

"This is Ava," she said.

"How is Hong Kong?"

"We're making progress."

"Really?"

"I think so, and I need you to do something for me that will push things along even further."

"What is it?"

"I see from my notes that AKG Consulting banks with the Nanjing Founders' Bank. I know that I told you I didn't want to go back to Lanfen, but I don't think I've got any choice. So talk to Zheng and arrange it. Pay what it takes for Lanfen to get me the bank information on AKG by noon tomorrow. I want the same kind of detail she provided before, except I want her to go back five years, not three."

"Okay."

"Also, have you heard the name Ying Jie?"

"She's the daughter of Ying Fa. Have you heard of him?"

"I have, and I thought she would be related. Who's Zhu Huan?"

"Her husband. They're involved as well?"

"Probably."

"This thing keeps mushrooming."

"And the stakes keep getting higher. I'm beginning to suspect that the money you've been putting into Hallmark, Evergreen, and Gold Star is a pittance compared to some of the other deals the family has done."

"Like what?"

"I don't have any hard facts," Ava said quickly. "And I probably shouldn't have mentioned it at all. It's just a hunch."

"I spoke to Xu again. He asked me how we were doing. I told him I didn't know, and that's the truth."

"Did he tell you how things ended up with Lam?"

"Evidently well enough, because if we are pushed into drug production, Lam may partner with us."

"I don't think that's particularly good news."

"Xu doesn't think so either, but it may be the only choice we have unless we come up with some dirt on the Tsais that could make a difference."

"We have dirt, and I'm sure we'll find more, but its making any difference to the situation is the challenge — our only real challenge," Ava said.

"So what now?"

"I have a meeting later in the day tomorrow, so I'd appreciate getting that information from Lanfen on time. Email me when you get it."

Ava sighed as she put the phone down. A lot of people were now involved in this investigation. It wasn't her normal method of operation; she preferred to keep information tightly held. But she didn't know what other options she had. She was in unfamiliar territory dealing with a myriad of companies, and she didn't have enough time to assemble all of the information herself. Like it or not, she needed help.

She turned on her computer. It was now late morning in Toronto. Her mother should — she hoped — be home from Fallsview Casino, but there wasn't a word from her. *She's angry at me*, Ava thought.

She emailed her friend Mimi: I'm in Hong Kong and I need a favour. Could you call my mother's house and see if she's home? If she is, just tell her you were wondering where I was and leave it at that. But let me know if she's there or not.

Half an hour later, Mimi sent a reply. Your mother isn't answering her phone.

Where is she? Ava thought.

21

AVA WOKE JUST AFTER SEVEN WITH A SENSE OF PUR- pose. She checked her emails and her cellphone. Feng hadn't sent her anything overnight. And still not a word from her mother. *She can't still be at Fallsview,* Ava thought, her anxiety ramping up again.

She thought about going for a run in Victoria Park, but she knew that this early in the morning it would be crammed full of tai chi practitioners, walkers, joggers, and people just enjoying some fresh air. Still, she wanted to run, and if she couldn't run in the park, she'd run to the park.

She turned right onto Connaught Road and headed towards the Hong Kong Convention and Exhibition Centre. Stores were closed and the sidewalks were negotiable. It was a familiar route. Before she began staying at the Mandarin Oriental, she had often stayed at the Grand Hyatt, which was only a two-kilometre run from the park.

Ava followed Hung Hing Road past the Royal Hong Kong Yacht Club and the Noonday Gun, which had been fired every day at noon for more than 150 years. If she had kept going she would have encountered the Causeway Bay Typhoon Shelter, where sampans, filled with families who had never known what it was like to live on land, still moored. But she stopped short of the park, turned, and headed back to the hotel the same way she'd come.

She figured she had run about fifteen kilometres in less than an hour and a half. Whatever residual physical kinks remained from the flight had disappeared, and her mind felt clear and focused.

Back in her room, she went directly to her computer. Feng had been busy. His message had four attachments. Here's the info on AKG. I perused it myself. There's some serious shit going on here. I just hope you can do something with it, he wrote.

She took her time reading through the attachments and then went back and read them again, this time making notes. When she was finished, she looked at the chart she'd drawn the night before. None of the assumptions she'd made were wrong. In fact, if anything, she'd underestimated just how deeply enmeshed the Tsai family companies were with one another.

And then there was the money.

As significant as the monthly payments were that Xu and others were making into Evergreen, Hallmark, and Gold Star, they looked minuscule compared to the amount of money being deposited into AKG. And Ava guessed that if she ever got her hands on more detailed banking information for New Age and Mother of Pearl she'd find a similar pattern.

Over the past five years the AKG deposits came to more than $400 million. A steady inflow came from Evergreen and Hallmark, but those amounts were dwarfed by two huge deposits.

Four years ago, Patriot General Insurance had sent a single wire transfer of more than $105 million to the account. Three weeks later, AKG sent the exact same amount to Mother of Pearl Investments. That money, Ava was certain, had been for the purchase of Jiangsu Trust and Insurance.

A year later, the bank records showed that California Asian Trust had wire-transferred $120 million to AKG. Less than thirty days after the money reached the account, AKG sent the exact same amount to New Age Capital. Ava was certain that the money had been used in the Kitchen Giant acquisition.

Despite her opinion about where the monies had ended up, there were some obvious gaps in the paper trails. The most glaring was that she didn't have access to the Mother of Pearl or New Age bank accounts, and she knew that unless she could confirm the transactions, her conclusions were just speculation.

She paused and then reached for the phone. She tried May Ling's cellphone first, but it went directly to voicemail. Then she called May's private office line.

"Can you talk?" Ava asked when May answered.

"Yes, I'm alone."

"Are you getting your problems sorted?"

"Bit by bit. How about you?"

"I have no idea."

"It's not like you to be so uncertain."

"Well, the Tsai family — the entire extended family, as it turns out — is frustrating me and fascinating me at the same time."

"So you obviously have more information than you started with."

"Yes, and that's one reason I'm struggling."

"Why?"

"I've got almost too much. There are tens of companies from all over the world paying money into about a dozen companies that the family controls, and when you toss in all the banks, all the inter-company transfers, and some foreign partners who might be subsidiaries of larger corporations, it does get complicated."

"But everything ends up with the Tsais?"

"Well, the Tsais and the Wus and the Yings and some other in-laws."

"Who are the Wus?"

"Wu Wai Wai is Tsai Lian's sister."

"I see, and the Yings? Are you saying Ying Fa is involved as well?"

"His daughter Ying Jie and her husband are major players, but what I don't know is if they're being directed by her father or by Tsai Lian."

"Tsai Lian heads the family," May said abruptly. "If the Yings are involved, it's because he's approved it."

"You're certain?"

"Absolutely."

"That does add some clarity."

"Have you found anything that directly links Tsai Lian to any of the companies?"

"Only his entire family."

"Even if that came out, he would claim that they were acting on their own as independent businesspeople."

"I know."

"How much money do you think they've accumulated?"

"I'm not sure."

"You must have some idea."

Ava looked down at her notebook. "A billion for sure, and maybe as much as two or three billion."

"Good god."

"And I haven't stopped looking yet. Who knows what else I'll find. I have a meeting scheduled with Brenda Burgess and her team this afternoon, and they may have more information to throw at me."

"Did Brenda grill you about why you are looking at the Tsais?"

"No."

"She may."

"I can handle it."

"Ava, don't be defensive with her," May said. "She and Richard know how to keep a confidence, and they're both incredibly smart and connected. She may be more help than you can imagine."

"There are a lot of people involved already, although I've managed to maintain what I think is sufficient control."

"Well, it is a big project. We're talking about the governor of the richest province in China, his large family, dozens of companies, and billions of dollars."

"All the more reason to try to keep it close."

"That's going to be impossible if you want to bring down the Tsai family."

"May, that's never been my objective," Ava said sharply. "All I want to do is get them to back off on their demands to Xu."

"I know, but I've been thinking that you may not be able to achieve one without the other."

Ava hesitated, taken aback by May's comment. "Well, I'm going to try," she finally said. "This doesn't have to be an all-or-nothing situation."

"Assuming you're right, you still need leverage. What do you have?"

"I don't know yet."

"You have no idea at all?"

"There's one lead that has some promise and another that could work out," Ava said slowly. "But I haven't wrapped my head around either of them sufficiently. I'm still in data-gathering mode. Hopefully by the end of the day, I'll be able to sit back and take some time to digest it all."

"Let me know when you think you're ready to act," May said.

"Are you worried about fallout in Wuhan?"

"No, I'm worried about you and Xu."

Ava paused, a question about Xu buzzing in her head. She left it there. "I'll let you know, assuming there is anything to know. It may all come to nothing."

"Knowing you, I don't believe that's possible."

"I think you mean that as a compliment, so I'll say thank you."

"I did, and you're welcome," May said. "Now, what's up with Lane Crawford? I haven't had a chance to talk to any of the girls today."

"Chi-Tze, Gillian, and Clark have a conference call sched-uled for some time today with Laura and, I presume, Carrie Song. It's all sounding very positive."

"No Amanda?"

"She thinks it's best for the Shanghai team to handle it. She thinks our job is done, and now it's up to them to close the deal and start putting together an implementation plan."

"For someone so young, she seems very secure. When I was that age, I would have been afraid to let anyone else negotiate something that important without my involvement."

"When you're given responsibility, you have to learn to handle it or you sink. From my first day working with Uncle, he insisted that I make decisions on my own. I was always afraid of disappointing him, and that made me work that much harder. I think we'll see the same reaction from Shanghai. They'll do everything possible to make this company a success, and I think Amanda understands that very well."

"Yes, they do want her approval. And she wants ours. The question is, who is our higher power?"

"I'm afraid of Suki Chan," Ava said with a laugh.

"Who isn't?" May said. "There is something so incredibly fierce about such naked ambition and drive."

"Speaking of naked, I came back from a run ages ago and haven't showered yet. I'll be in touch, okay?"

Ava took her time in the bathroom. She had thought about calling her father and asking him to meet her for dim sum, but she wasn't sure she would be good company. She also didn't want to get into a discussion about her mother. She was beginning to really worry about her and she didn't want Marcus Lee to see her concern. Though she had spent very little actual time with her father, he had an uncanny ability to see right into her heart.

She left the room with her notebook in her Chanel bag and went to the Man Wah restaurant on the twenty-fifth floor. It was past lunch and the crowd had thinned. She got a table by a window overlooking Victoria Harbour. As the waiter poured jasmine tea, Ava set her notebook and phone on the table. After a quick glance at a menu she almost knew from memory, she ordered hot and sour soup, Alaska king crab dumplings, beef tenderloin puffs with black pepper sauce, and mushroom dumplings with black truffles.

As she waited for her order, she looked out onto the harbour. As always, it was busy with ferries, sailboats and powerboats, and freighters winding their way in and out of the harbour and across the bay. She even saw a junk and a couple of sampans. The British had wanted Hong Kong for its harbour and acquired the territory through cession in 1842. They took complete control of it in 1860, when Kowloon was also ceded to them. Since then, everything around the harbour had obviously changed in ways beyond anyone's imagination, but the harbour itself was almost timeless. When people went to sea, they still went in ships, and the basic laws of navigation hadn't changed. If she could blot out the wall of skyscrapers, she could almost see in the waters the Hong Kong of 150 years ago.

Her phone rang as the bowl of hot and sour soup was placed in front of her. She hesitated to answer, but saw it was Amanda calling.

"Hey," she said.

"Where are you?"

"In Man Wah."

"Michael wanted to take you there tonight."

"I'm having dim sum. I don't mind returning for dinner," Ava said. "Is that the reason you're calling?"

"Partially, but not really. I just heard from Chi-Tze."

"About Lane Crawford?"

"Yes, they just got off the phone with them about half an hour ago."

"Was it good news?"

"They said they want to bring in three looks," Amanda said. "That means three different design concepts executed as trousers, jackets, blouses, skirts, and coats. So about fifteen pieces in total."

"The fact that they want to take three is terrific. How many stores are they giving us?"

"All of Lane Crawford and half of Joyce."

"That's wonderful."

"Not entirely. There are a few requests attached to their offer."

"Requests or conditions?"

"They're framed as requests, but we're treating them like conditions."

"Like?"

"They want an exclusive for six months — starting after they get the first shipment — in Hong Kong and a long list of major cities in China."

"What do the girls and Clark think about that?"

"They're okay with Hong Kong, but they don't want to give up China. We've had a lot of interest from some mainland retailers and real estate operators. They're afraid that if we don't move fast, those retailers will lose interest and move on."

"May Ling will probably feel that way as well. She brought a lot of contacts with her and I'm quite sure she doesn't want to put them off. It would also seem rather rude to ask them to come to Shanghai and then tell them we've decided not to do business with them."

"I'm thinking that we could offer Hong Kong, Kowloon, the New Territories, and Macau as exclusive territory, and maybe extend it for a year instead of six months."

"I like that approach. Those are Lane Crawford's strongest markets."

"They've also made some marketing and merchandising requests that could add up to a lot of money," Amanda said.

"Such as?"

"At least one dedicated salesperson in every store that carries the PÖ line. Financial support for the catalogues and advertising that feature PÖ. They'd also like us to create our own advertising and marketing program to support their efforts. They want to have splashy in-store launches. And they want us to put a structured discount program in place in case our products don't sell that well."

"All things we expected, yes?"

"Yes, only bigger and more expensive."

"What do Gillian and Chi-Tze say about it?"

"They're for it."

"And you?"

"Absolutely."

"Then why are we talking about it? You and the girls can make the decision on your own."

"I know that, and so do they. But given the Carrie Song connection, we all feel it's best to keep you well informed. I'm sure once we're past the early stages that will pass."

Ava drew a deep breath. "It's exciting, isn't it?"

"It sure is."

"When you talk to Shanghai, tell them how proud we are of the work they've done. My connection wouldn't mean a thing if Clark's clothes were less than brilliant."

"I'll tell them."

"And how about May Ling — does she know?"

"Chi-Tze was calling her as I was phoning you. In fact, I just got a text from Chi-Tze," Amanda said, and then paused. "May said almost exactly the same things you did."

"So now it's up to Lane Crawford."

"The girls will be onto them today."

"I'm going to be in a meeting with the lawyers most of the afternoon," Ava said. "You and I can discuss it over dinner tonight."

"Seven?"

"Perfect."

"Man Wah?"

"Also perfect."

"Great. Michael has already made a reservation."

"Just the three of us, right?"

"Ava, Michael would never invite Marcus without consulting you."

"I thought so, but I still needed to ask."

AT A QUARTER TO THREE, AVA LEFT THE MANDARIN Oriental and began the short climb to Bond Street and the offices of Burgess and Bowlby. She reached the lobby at almost exactly three and was led directly to the same boardroom she'd occupied the day before.

Brenda Burgess and Vanessa Ogg sat with their backs to the window, a stack of files in front of them. They both rose and walked around the table to shake Ava's hand.

"You've been busy," Ava said.

"There's a lot that's kept us busy," Brenda said.

"I've been doing some more looking on my own," Ava said. "I have some names to add to the chart I gave you yesterday."

Vanessa glanced sideways at her boss, and Ava thought she detected some uncertainty in her manner.

"Before you do that, would you object if we talked this through a bit?" Brenda said.

"Talked what through?"

"This project."

"I thought I made it clear yesterday that I don't want to do that," Ava said.

"It's true that you did, but as Vanessa and the Beijing law-yers dug into the companies whose names you provided, it quickly became evident that your project is bigger than we anticipated, and possibly far more sensitive."

"I'm not surprised that it expanded in size," Ava said. "But I have no idea why you refer to it as sensitive."

"Vanessa, why don't you explain," Brenda said.

Vanessa opened the file in front of her. "We briefed the Beijing firm as soon as you left yesterday, and they went right to work. I had two interns start from this end. There was some duplication of effort, which I expected, but I thought it would help us cross-reference and confirm the information we found."

"That makes sense," Ava said.

"The incorporated companies left a paper trail, but in some cases the shareholder structure was vague, so we tried to go deeper. We made phone calls to other law firms, to some individuals, and to some banks. That's when it became sensitive."

"They wouldn't talk to you?"

"Not all of them refused, and some were actually forth-coming at first, but then around noon today all co-operation ended," Vanessa said. "When our trainees and the Beijing firm followed up on some calls they'd made earlier, they were told rather bluntly that no further information would be provided. They were then asked who they were work-ing for and if we had any links to a bank called Toronto Commonwealth."

"Given your Canadian roots, we thought this might involve you," Brenda said.

"Shit," Ava said.

"So you know the bank."

"I had them do some bank-to-bank inquiries."

"How productive was it?"

"Quite."

"It was also disruptive."

"Evidently."

"Well, it put at least a temporary end to the work you wanted us to do, but we are prepared to share with you the information we did manage to acquire," Brenda said. "But before we do, I have a question to ask."

"I'm listening."

"Is it your intention to use the information in some way to damage the Tsai family?"

"No, not directly."

"What does that mean?"

"It means you're getting into areas that I don't want to discuss."

Brenda leaned across the table, her eyes focused tightly on Ava. "As a law firm, we represent our clients to the very best of our ability. We aren't afraid of challenges and we don't back away from fights, but that doesn't mean we run blindly into situations that we don't understand. We also take lawyer–client confidentiality very seriously. What I would like to happen is that you explain why you want this information. There are things we may be able to do that you haven't considered. We've spent many years doing business in China and we have some knowledge of how things operate. Poking around in Tsai family affairs is not something we recommend unless there is a very clear objective."

"And if the objective is clear?"

"Then we'll work with you to create a strategy to accomplish it, as long as we stay within the law."

The look on Brenda's face was grim, but out of the corner of her eye Ava saw Vanessa smiling encouragingly at her.

"May Ling thinks highly of you," Ava said.

Brenda nodded.

"It is an odd situation," Ava said carefully.

"A circumstance to which we're not unaccustomed."

"Me neither. I'm just not that accustomed to sharing these kinds of confidences."

Brenda leaned in even closer. "Ava, you were partners with Uncle Chow, weren't you?"

"Yes," she said, not hiding her surprise at the question.

"Our law firm was well aware of the two of you and the kind of business you ran. In fact, there weren't many law firms in Hong Kong that didn't know about you. It was hard not to, when so many clients who weren't happy with the results we got for them turned to you. There was a lot of gossip about him and you, and about your business. But we never pay attention to gossip, and more than once we quietly referred clients to you."

"I had no idea."

"We were discreet about it, and we were equally discreet when May Ling Wong came to us and asked us to incorporate the Three Sisters. Not once, not even obliquely, did we hint to her that we knew of you and your past. Like I said, we don't gossip and we know how to keep a confidence."

Ava nodded as Brenda sat back.

"So, what do you want to do?" Brenda asked.

Here it was again, Ava thought, the eternal question of whether or not to trust. Uncle had maintained that it was a question that couldn't be quantified or justified rationally. He said it came down to instinct. She wasn't sure her instincts were as sharp and refined as his had been, but it was one of his lessons that she had taken to heart. She looked across the table at Brenda, who returned her steady gaze. Vanessa sat calmly, waiting for Ava to answer her boss's question.

"I have a friend in Shanghai who is being pressed by the Tsai family to go into a business that he wants nothing to do with," Ava said, speaking deliberately. "But he's already enmeshed with them through other businesses and they have leverage over him."

"Is the business he's currently doing with them legal?"

"I'm beginning to understand that the word 'legal' doesn't have the same application in China as it does in other parts of the world."

"I have an opinion on that, but I would like to hear yours."

"His current businesses are a bit shady but they are condoned by the Jiangsu government. In fact, they gave him the licences and permits he needed and they continue to support his companies."

"And their leverage is that they can revoke the licences and permits?"

"Partially, but by itself that is enough."

"When you say he's 'enmeshed,' are you saying they're partners?"

"No, he simply pays them bribes disguised as commissions and management fees."

"That's not uncommon."

"So I'm discovering."

"Does he want to stop paying them?"

"No, he considers it the cost of doing business with some semblance of quid pro quo."

"So it is this proposed new venture that's causing the problem?"

"It is."

"Is he afraid that if he doesn't play along they'll shut down his present businesses?"

"Exactly."

"What is this new venture?"

"They want him to start manufacturing synthetic drugs."

Brenda turned to Vanessa, shook her head in disbelief, and then turned back to Ava. "I wasn't expecting anything that venal."

"Well, there you are."

"I can certainly understand his reluctance."

"To say he is reluctant is an understatement. There are other consequences — in addition to and beyond what the Tsai family might do — that worry him as much if not more. Those consequences disappear if he doesn't go ahead with the factory."

"I'm not going to ask what those are specifically," Brenda said. "What interests me more is what you thought you could do to help your friend."

"I wasn't sure I could do anything. I was simply trying to gather information, hoping that somewhere in the mix there was something I could use to put pressure on the Tsais."

"To accomplish what?"

"Get them to back off."

"Not bring them down?"

"Of course not. I'm not completely naive. I understand

that the family is above the law. I was just hoping to find something that would persuade them that being circumspect was better than being identified as the crooked, money-sucking vampires they are."

"Persuade them how, through embarrassment?"

"I don't know if they're capable of being embarrassed," Ava said. "My instincts are telling me that if they become the focus of considerable publicity, they might want to pull in their horns and not risk getting involved in any new ventures that could be messy and have a negative impact on their current business."

Vanessa smiled. "How interesting."

"What does that mean?" Ava asked.

Vanessa tapped one of the files that sat in front of her. "When one of the interns came to me with this information, the very first thought that crossed my mind was that it wasn't something the Tsai family would want publicly broadcast."

"Why? What did you find?"

Vanessa glanced at Brenda.

"Go ahead," Brenda said.

Vanessa opened the file. Ava saw *SHELL* written in capital letters on the front cover.

"We thought we were initially looking at a shell company," Vanessa said. "We thought the name was a tease, a play on words, because we couldn't find anything it actually did. But the intern did a lot of research, got Beijing involved, and we quite suddenly found ourselves looking at a very substantial business."

"How large?"

"By our estimates, the companies owned by and affiliated

with Shell did over four billion U.S. dollars' worth of sales last year and turned a profit of close to four hundred million."

"Wow."

"That's what I said when I first heard the numbers, but when I reviewed the details, the amounts seemed real enough."

"What kind of business?" Ava asked.

"Shell is an umbrella company for the importation, marketing, and distribution of a lot of steel, copper, and other metals used in construction. It doesn't do any of this work directly, but it owns fifty-one percent of a company called Mega Metals, which in turns owns at least eight companies that do. Those companies engage in quite a bit of trading among themselves, and our intern took great pains to separate those transactions from those that were actual sales to end users. The four billion is the end-user number."

"How did the intern find out what Shell did?"

"Her father is in that business. She mentioned the name to him last night and he got very angry. He told her that several years ago he had a modest sales volume in Jiangsu, but then along came Shell and Mega Metals and he got blown away."

"How did they manage that?"

"According to him, no construction company got a government contract unless they bought metal through a Mega Metals affiliate. And when it came to non-government construction, it was hard to get a permit to build unless a Mega company was going to be a supplier."

"Could you confirm his allegations?" Burgess asked.

"A friend of the father, who is also in the business, verified how things operated. Then we lucked out with the bank and got some valuable information from them. We were scheduled to speak to the bank again when they slammed that door shut."

"Starting a business that size takes a lot of money," Ava said.

"From what we've seen and been told, it was all put up by a British partner."

"British?"

"Calhoun Metals, in Newcastle."

"How was it structured?" Ava asked, sensing she already knew the answer.

"Mega and all the affiliates were set up at the same time. Calhoun put five million U.S. dollars into Mega as working capital, and then provided all of the inventory on ridiculous terms — payment wasn't due after the delivery date for 120 to 180 days. In essence, the inventory was as good as cash, and the company started with two hundred million dollars' worth. Mega eventually parcelled out the inventory to the subsidiaries."

"How much money and goods did the Chinese partner put in?"

"It looks like nothing."

"And you say that Calhoun got what, a forty-nine percent stake for being so generous?"

"Yes."

"And Shell got the rest?"

"It did."

"What name is attached to Shell?"

"A woman named Lau Ai."

"And she is?" Ava asked.

"Tsai Men's wife."

AVA SAT QUIETLY FOR A MOMENT, HER HEAD LOWERED and her eyes on her notebook. She wasn't completely taken aback by anything Vanessa had related, but the immensity of the Tsai family empire was beginning to sink in, and there were almost too many questions bouncing around in her head.

"Are you all right?" Brenda asked.

"I'm fine," Ava said, raising her head. "I'm just trying to come to grips with the complexity of it all."

"The family has been in power for a long time, so they've had the opportunity to accumulate assets," Brenda said.

"I know. It's just bigger than I ever imagined, and then there are the international elements. I wouldn't have thought the family would be trusting enough to have foreign partners."

"Why not?" Brenda said. "As far as any one of them is concerned, they're doing perfectly legal business together, and the Tsais do retain a majority position in the company."

"Mega Metals isn't the only company that they used partners to finance," Ava said.

"There are more?"

"At least one. Mother of Pearl is the majority shareholder in Jiangsu Insurance. Its junior partner is Patriot General Insurance, out of Connecticut."

"Jiangsu is a private or public company?" Vanessa asked.

"Private, but Patriot isn't, and the investment is reflected in their financial reports. That's where we found the details."

"How was the investment structured?"

"From what I can see, Patriot was the only one to put any money into the business. It provided all the cash that allowed Mother of Pearl to buy Jiangsu."

"And, like Calhoun, it was content with a minority position?" Brenda asked.

"Yes, it got forty percent, but within a year of the acquisition, Jiangsu's sales exploded, thanks to a flood of business from the provincial government, and Patriot's initial investment more than quadrupled in value."

"The same kind of thing happened with Calhoun," Vanessa said. "Mega Metals became highly profitable almost instantly, and Calhoun's U.K. stock price has more than tripled since it partnered with the Tsai family."

"There's another company that I hoped you would find more about as well: California Asian Trust."

Vanessa reached for another file. "It is a wholly owned subsidiary of the California Technical Trust Bank, out of San Francisco."

"That's good work," Ava said. "The California bank is a public company?"

"Yes."

"What else did you discover?"

"Not much. We didn't have time."

"That doesn't matter. You've given me a lead I can pursue."

"According to your chart, this California Asian Trust is a part owner of Kitchen Giant," Brenda said.

"It is."

"I know of Kitchen Giant. It's a big operation that has to be worth four or five billion."

"It's a private company, and we haven't been able to access its sales numbers and profits yet, but we should be able to come up with an estimate now that we know who the U.S. partner is. They'll have numbers on their books."

As Ava was speaking, Brenda had started writing on a foolscap pad.

"Going back to Mega and Calhoun," Ava said to Vanessa, "how do the Chinese company and the affiliates operate?"

"What do you mean?"

"Who runs them?"

"Each of the affiliates seems to have its own management, but they all report to Mega Metals, which is run by a Chinese Brit, Vincent Yin. He's been there from the start, and I imagine he was put in place by Calhoun, with the Tsai family's blessing. He may actually be the one who put together the deal with the family in the first place."

"Where does Yin live?"

"Nanjing."

"How active is Lau Ai in the business?"

"She seems to be a figurehead."

"An expensive one."

"Not if you look at what she was able to deliver to Calhoun through the family."

"I was just putting together some rough numbers," Brenda Burgess said, putting down her pen. "From my calculations, the Tsai family has at least ten billion dollars in assets."

"Assets that we've found," Ava said. "There's tons of cash that's not accounted for — the money that's been flowing into Hallmark Consulting, Evergreen Trading, Gold Star Investments, and AKG. Much of it was transferred to Mother of Pearl and New Age Capital and Shell, but I thought it had been used to make acquisitions. Evidently it hasn't been, since Calhoun Metals and Patriot Insurance and California Asian Trust seemed to have funded them all. Where's that cash?"

"It could be offshore or it could have been used to make other acquisitions."

"Either way, I think even your ten billion could be a modest estimate," Ava said.

"Either way," Brenda said mildly, "I don't think we should be searching for those missing dollars right now. We've put the family on alert and it might be wise to step back for a while."

"I don't know if I can. My friend needs help rather quickly."

"We may have enough information already."

"All we know is that the Tsai family is probably one of the wealthiest in China," Ava said.

"There are a few individuals and families who are richer, but not many of them are in government, and that may be the pressure point you're looking for," Brenda said.

"Tsai Lian isn't attached directly to any of those companies," Ava said. "There's a wall around him."

"That's the same game that his fellow governors, the mayors of the major cities, and the members of the Politburo Standing Committee in Beijing all play. I daresay there isn't one of them who isn't looking after his family's interests before the state's interests. They're all trying to accumulate wealth and they're doing it the same way — at arm's length."

"So how do you get through, around, or over the wall?"

"Even the rich and the powerful can get jealous, and when they do, they have the means to create havoc," Brenda said.

"What are you saying?"

"I doubt that many of his friends in Beijing are playing the money game as well as Tsai Lian, and I doubt that they know what kind of wealth he's accumulated. If the information were made public, it might cause a stink," Brenda said. "At the very least, Tsai Lian might find himself having to answer some questions that he doesn't want asked. And who knows — some of his colleagues might resent his success enough that they would try to generate more serious repercussions."

"I was told it's a waste of time trying to get any of the Chinese media to report on corrupt officials unless they have the approval of the government to do it."

"It is."

"So what are you thinking? Releasing it in Hong Kong?"

"An equal waste of time."

"Then where?"

"I'm not really sure, but the Tsai name is known outside of Asia, and there is growing foreign interest in what goes on inside China, especially when there's scandal involved. There has to be someone who would be interested."

"Scandal?"

"Aside from the money, laws have been broken."

"What laws? I've been told that Chinese law doesn't apply to men like Tsai Lian."

"That's true enough in most cases, but there are times when it is to the state's benefit to apply the law. They always lie about the real reason, of course. Instead they use corruption as a vehicle because it's popular with the public. It normally happens when someone becomes dangerous politically. They usually go after a young person, and in China that means someone in their forties or fifties who's threatening the status quo. It's also inevitably true that the person has been corrupt, because they all are."

"But Tsai Lian is part of the establishment. He's no radical and no threat."

"We have to make him such an embarrassment that they won't want him in the club anymore," Brenda said.

"Is the money that he's accumulated enough to do that?"

"Perhaps, but I think some of his family members have broken several laws, and that would discredit them."

"Are we back to talking about Chinese law?" Ava said.

"No. Vanessa believes that they and their partners have broken British laws, and I agree with her assessment."

"The U.K. has a bribery act," Vanessa said. "It is against the law for British companies or individuals to bribe foreign nationals to acquire business. The law is quite severe, and those found guilty face substantial fines and even jail terms."

"How does it apply in this case?" Ava asked.

Vanessa shrugged. "From what we know, the family was given a fifty-one percent stake in Mega Metals without putting in a dollar of their own. Their partner put in more than two hundred million dollars in cash and inventory for a forty-nine percent stake. The family then ensured that the partner was compensated by forcefully compelling any company doing construction in Jiangsu to buy metals from the new venture. It seems to me that quite a few legal terms could describe that kind of behaviour, and the words 'bribery' and 'coercion' would be among them."

"As I said before, a similar pattern was used with Jiangsu Insurance," Ava said. "The Tsais got a majority share in a viable insurance company for absolutely nothing because they most certainly promised to direct the province's insurance business to the company. There's no other reason why Patriot would simply hand over forty million dollars for a minority position in a company that was valued at only a hundred million."

"That brings the American Foreign Corrupt Practices Act into play as well," Vanessa said. "It can be as tough as the U.K. law."

"Who would the laws target?"

"Calhoun Metals and Patriot Insurance. They can't touch the Tsai family directly."

"Well, assuming that both American and British laws have been violated, it seems the Tsai family's partners could be in some trouble," Ava said. "Although I'm not sure what impact this would have on the family. They may not care about problems that their partners have."

"Then we have to find a way to make them more vulnerable," Burgess said.

Ava smiled. "Do you have some ideas?"

"We do."

"I think I may have some as well," Ava said.

24

AMANDA AND MICHAEL WERE ALREADY SEATED IN Man Wah when Ava arrived at ten past seven. She apologized for being late and was forgiven in a flurry of hugs and kisses.

"I was at the lawyer's office and lost all track of time," she said.

"Is everything okay?" Amanda asked.

"It's better than it was this morning."

"You're so mysterious."

"That's her style," Michael said. "She kept me in the dark even when it was my case she was working on."

"There's nothing mysterious about what I'm doing, and it isn't a case," Ava said. "I'm doing something for a friend and I promised him I would keep it quiet."

"Speaking of which," Michael said, "are you going to call our father? I talked to him this morning and your name came up. I didn't feel quite right not telling him you're in Hong Kong."

"I'll call him tomorrow morning."

"Great. Now let's decide what we're going to eat."

"I'll leave that to you," Amanda said.

"Me too," Ava said.

As Michael looked over the menu, Ava turned to Amanda. "Any word from Lane Crawford?"

"No. Chi-Tze and Gillian sent them our offer late this afternoon and we haven't heard back. The girls agreed to just about everything they wanted except complete territorial exclusivity."

"Money?"

"We told them we'd spend whatever it took to market the brand properly."

"Good. At this point money should be the last of our concerns. We're in so deep now that another million or so is irrelevant."

"What do we do if they insist on having such a widespread exclusive?"

"What do you suggest?"

"We want the business, but I'm worried about how May Ling might react if we give in to them. As we discussed, she feels at least a moral obligation to the people she convinced to go to Shanghai."

"If it comes down to that, I'll make the phone call," Ava said.

"To May?"

"No, to Carrie Song," Ava said.

A waiter had arrived at the table and stood patiently while Michael continued to read the menu. Finally he put it down. "Do you mind if I go heavy on seafood?" he asked.

"We told you to decide," Amanda said.

He nodded. "Okay, then we'll have double-boiled fish maw soup, stir-fried lobster with caviar and scallop mousse, the stewed Japanese sea cucumber, fried rice with prawns and conpoy, and the wok-fried wagyu beef."

"And to drink, sir?" the waiter asked.

"The Roche de Bellene Meursault."

"How is your business doing?" Ava asked Michael when the waiter had left.

Ten minutes later he was still describing the growth of the noodle restaurant chain he and Simon To had started. They had more than forty locations now and had sold off the 7-Eleven franchises they owned to generate more capital for restaurant expansion.

As he spoke, Ava couldn't help thinking of her father. Michael looked like him — tall and sturdy, with chiselled features and a full head of hair combed straight back — and he spoke in the same slow, measured way. It was Marcus Lee's wish now that his three families become closer, but Ava was the only one who had actually bridged the gap between herself and the first family, and it had taken a crisis to make that happen. Now she was comfortable, if not that close, with Michael and his brothers. Truthfully, her relationship with Amanda was deeper and more enjoyable. Ava knew there would always be a distance between her and her half-brothers. Their loyalty was to Marcus and his wife, their mother, Elizabeth. Ava's was to Jennie Lee. She might love her father and feel kinship towards her half-brothers, but she knew they would never come close to touching her emotionally in the way her mother could and did. And that thought brought Jennie Lee front-of-mind again. It was almost seven thirty in the morning in Toronto. Her mother should be home from Niagara Falls by now. Even an extreme round of gambling should have ended hours ago. Ava looked at her phone and felt the urge to call. As she pondered whether to do it, the phone rang.

"Hello," she said, half expecting it to be Jennie.

"It's Xu. I hope I'm not disturbing you."

"Well, I'm having dinner with Michael and Amanda," Ava said.

"Feng seemed excited about what you were uncovering when I talked to him earlier, and that's not like him."

"He's reading too much into things."

"So no progress?"

"Some, but there's still a lot of work to do. Is that why you're calling?"

"No, I wish it was."

"What's happened?"

"I just got off the phone with Tsai Men. He wants to meet. I tried to put him off, but he was insistent to the point of being insulting."

"What does he want?"

"All he said was that we have to meet and that I have to come to Nanjing."

"Did you agree?"

"Not entirely, because I hadn't spoken to you."

"What do I have to do with it?"

"He wants you there as well."

"Why?"

"I asked, but he waffled."

"Xu, this is too strange."

"All I can think of is that Pang will be there and he wants to balance dinner."

"In Nanjing? She's his Shanghai woman," Ava said, and then noticed Michael and Amanda staring at her.

"Ava, I don't know more than I've told you."

"Okay, I understand that. The thing is, what do you want me to do?"

"Fly to Nanjing tomorrow."

"What time is dinner?"

"Eight. I had one of my people check and there's a Dragonair flight that leaves Hong Kong at four. It would get you into Nanjing at six thirty."

"Did you book it for me?" Ava asked, a touch of annoyance in her voice.

"No, I'm not that presumptuous."

Ava realized she'd overreacted, and sighed. "Well, that still leaves me part of the day to work here tomorrow."

"So you will come?"

"I guess so."

"Do you want me to book the Dragonair flight?"

"Sure."

"And I should reserve some hotel rooms for us. There isn't a Mandarin Oriental or Peninsula Hotel in Nanjing. I usually stay at the InterContinental."

"That's fine."

"I'll send Suen to the airport to meet you."

"That's not necessary."

"I know, but it would make me feel more comfortable."

"Okay, book the flight and the hotel and send Suen to meet me. In the meantime, could you try to find out why he wants us to go there?"

"I have already put out feelers."

"I didn't mean to sound bossy."

"I can't fault you for being curious."

"And you're not?"

"I am. I just don't vocalize it."

"Xu, we are finding out things that could be very useful to you when it comes to dealing with the Tsai family, but if you want me to stop, I will."

"There's no reason for that. Keep going."

"Okay, I will," Ava said as a tureen arrived at their table. "I should go now."

"Fine. I'll call if I find out anything. If I don't, then I'll see you tomorrow," he said.

Ava put down her phone as the fish maw soup was ladled into their bowls. Both Amanda and Michael were looking at her and she could feel questions lurking. "That was my friend Xu," she said. "He has an investment opportunity that he wants me to see in Nanjing."

"You're going there?" Amanda asked.

"Yes," Ava said, noting the concern in her sister-in-law's voice.

"But you'll still be able to meet with Dad tomorrow?" Michael said.

"That shouldn't be a problem," Ava said, wondering how he could be so tone-deaf. "I won't leave until late afternoon."

The dinner was superb, but Ava struggled to eat. The phone call from Xu had unsettled her more than she had let on, and she was worried about her mother. She passed on dessert and coffee and used jet lag as an excuse to make an early exit.

It was just past nine when Ava said goodbye to them at the elevator. "Call me as soon as you hear about Lane Crawford," she said as she hugged Amanda.

"I will."

"And don't worry," she said to Michael. "I'll email Daddy tonight about getting together tomorrow."

Ava opened the door to her room and stepped inside with a feeling of relief. She had silenced her phone after Xu's call. Now she checked it for messages and saw there were none. She went to the computer and opened her email account. Xu had sent her the flight information and confirmation.

Without much thought she called her mother's mobile. It went directly to voicemail. Ava said, "It's me, Mummy. I'm in Hong Kong. I'll be seeing Daddy sometime tomorrow. Hope you're well. Call me when you can."

She then phoned the house. Five rings later it also went to call answering and Ava repeated her message. *Where are you?* she thought. She had the number for Jennie's friend Cindy, and for a second contemplated trying to reach her, but then she put aside the idea. Her mother would consider it meddling, and she had no tolerance for shifts in the normal balance of power between mother and daughter: the mother could meddle all she wished and the daughter's only response should be silent respect.

She returned to the computer and wrote to her father. I arrived in Hong Kong today, but I have to leave tomorrow for Nanjing. Can you meet me for breakfast or an early lunch? Love, Ava.

When that was sent, she opened her notebook and began to review the notes she'd made at the meeting with Brenda Burgess and Vanessa Ogg. At its conclusion they had assigned tasks, but there wasn't anything for Ava to do until she heard from the lawyers. Then she saw a remark she had underlined and picked up the phone again to call Toronto.

"Are you still in Shanghai?" Johnny Yan asked.

"Hong Kong."

"What's up?"

"I was wondering if Felix has heard more from any of the banks he contacted."

"Not in any way that would please you."

"What do you mean?"

"I talked to him an hour ago. He said he tried to follow up with one or two banks that hadn't replied to his initial information requests, and he fired off a couple of additional questions to those that had given us something."

"Let me guess. None of them would co-operate?"

"It was worse than that."

"How?" Ava said.

"Not only would they not give him anything, they grilled him about why he was asking questions and they wanted to know who our client is."

"What did he say?"

"Not much. He said he stumbled around a bit," Johnny said. "I believe him. Felix was never too quick on his feet."

"Are you sure?"

"Absolutely, but that doesn't mean I'm not concerned. I told him, if anyone else calls, to refer them directly to me. I'll handle it."

"What will you say?"

"I'll come up with something."

"Johnny, I'm sorry. I didn't expect this to happen."

"I'll manage," he said.

"I wish you didn't have to, but it is important that you keep a lid on this."

"Speaking of which, Ava, why did we get so much blowback? I can't remember the last time one bank, let alone several banks, confronted us like this. What the hell are you involved in?"

"Nothing dramatic."

"I'd like to believe that."

"You can. And in time I'll be able to tell you more."

"Okay. Now let me go and calm Felix," he said. "And if someone from here wants to talk to you?"

"Give them my cell number."

"Thanks."

"No, thank *you*, and Johnny, when this is over, I will send you a serious chunk of business."

"*Momentai*," he said.

Ava pushed her chair back from the desk. Vanessa and her people had run into a brick wall. Johnny and Felix had run into another. Had she pressed too hard? Was the Tsai family's influence that pervasive?

She checked the bedside clock. It was almost nine thirty and Brenda had promised to call her at ten. She had time to shower and get dressed for bed, but if Brenda had had any luck, Ava knew she wouldn't be sleeping for several hours.

25

AVA WAS ON THE BED WHEN HER CELLPHONE RANG.
She leapt at it.

"Brenda?"

"I just finished talking to Richard."

"How did it go?"

"Well enough, I think. He has a lawyer friend who is very politically connected and prominent in the London legal community. According to him, all the trouble in the Middle East has caused the government to fixate on corruption. They don't want U.K. corporations being the vendors of choice for dictators and despots."

"Tsai Lian is hardly that."

"When it comes to foreign governments, the lines do become blurred."

"I guess in this case that's a good thing."

"We'll find out soon enough. I sent Richard the Mega-Calhoun files we compiled. He's going to pass them along to his friend, who in turn has promised to pass them along to some senior government people. I sent him a larger package on the Tsai family empire separately, to share with a few journalists that he trusts."

"How long will this process take?"

"I stressed the urgency."

"I think it just got even more urgent. My Canadian banking friends got some pushback from the Chinese banks they were talking to, and I've been invited to go to Nanjing to meet with some members of the Tsai family."

"I'm not surprised about the banks, but that Tsai family invitation is decidedly strange. Do you have any idea what they want?"

"No."

"You aren't going to go?"

"I don't know how to get out of it."

"Just say no."

"I can't."

"So what should we do?"

"Have you heard from Vanessa?"

"She was going to wait until ten before calling her friend in Washington and the other one in New York."

"The lawyer is in Washington?"

"Yes, and the reporter is in New York."

"I am starting to think that we don't have enough time for the legal processes to work their way through the two systems," Ava said.

"I thought we agreed that getting charges laid would be the perfect vehicle for generating publicity."

"I'm not sure we can wait that long. We might need another angle."

"Like what?"

"I don't know. I've just started to think about it. Perhaps if we tried to do something privately?"

"Blackmail them into doing what you want?"

"I'd prefer to think of it as persuading them to do the right thing for the wrong reason."

"My experience in dealing with people in China who have their kind of power is that they would take your attempt at 'persuasion' as a direct attack. They have the entire state apparatus behind them. Your attempt to construct a private deal would last only for as long as it took them to set the police on you and make you and your information disappear. The least risky option for all of us is to have someone else firing our bullets."

"I guess you're right."

"Ava, my husband has just called in a very large favour, and Vanessa is doing the same. We can't ask them to go back and say, 'Sorry, but we've changed our minds.'"

"No, I agree with you, but is there any reason why we can't push one of the pieces we have in play a bit faster than the other?"

"You mean publicity?"

"Why not? Even without corruption charges being laid against the Tsais or their partners, it's a fascinating story. I mean, who in the Western world thinks of the word 'multibillionaire' when they picture a government official in China?"

"More people than you can imagine. And there is nothing particularly remarkable about Tsai that would cause him to stand out."

"He is a princeling. There is that connection to Mao through his father."

"Ava, you're stretching."

"I might be, but I find it interesting all the same how a

diehard Communist family can evolve from being peasant revolutionaries to billionaire establishment politicians in one generation," she said.

"Have you ever worked in advertising or public relations?" Brenda asked with a laugh. "You do know how to spin things."

"I just have an active imagination."

"Well, let's keep it in reserve until we see what Richard's friend can do, and let's hear what Vanessa has to say after she's talked to her friends. Right now we're operating from a limited information base."

"That's true enough."

"Will you come by the office in the morning? We should know more by then."

"What time is good?"

"How's ten?"

"That's fine."

"Good. See you then."

Ava put down the phone with a sigh and began to regret involving the lawyers. Burgess hadn't said anything that was particularly wrong, but Ava felt constrained nevertheless. In her old life, speed had been of the essence. It was all about creating and maintaining momentum and then striking before the target knew what was happening. Approaching the justice departments in the U.K. and the U.S. to try to initiate legal action against Calhoun Metals and Patriot Insurance had seemed a good enough idea in the boardroom, but the phone conversations with Xu and Johnny Yan had jolted her.

Something was going on in Nanjing. She didn't know what, but she wasn't programmed to be passive.

Ava decided she was going to give it twenty-four hours. She would talk to the lawyers in the morning and she'd go to Nanjing for dinner. If she still felt the same way afterwards, then she would do something. She didn't know what, but something would come to her.

It always had.

26

WHEN SHE WOKE, THE FIRST THING SHE WONDERED was where she was. It was just past seven o'clock and she'd slept for more than eight uninterrupted hours. The room was almost pitch-black. Ava slid from the bed and stumbled towards the window. She pushed the curtains open and looked out on a wet, dreary morning.

She searched for her cellphone and called her mother's home phone. Again it went to voicemail. Annoyed, frustrated, and now getting seriously worried, she tried her cell. After it had rung twice, Ava began to feel her anxiety rising.

"*Wei*," Jennie Lee said. Ava could hear women laughing in the background.

"Where are you?" Ava blurted.

"I'm at dinner with Cindy and Tamara. We're in a new noodle restaurant in Markham that's supposed to be terrific."

"Did you get my messages?"

"Of course I did."

"Why didn't you call me back?"

"Ava, it would have been the middle of the night in Hong Kong."

Ava heard the calmness in her mother's voice and realized that she must be sounding frantic.

"I was worried about you."

"Why?"

"You went to Niagara Falls and then it was like you disappeared into a sinkhole."

"You told me not to bother you from there."

"I know."

"So I didn't."

"When do you ever do what I ask?"

"You're being silly," Jennie Lee said.

"I can't help it. I woke up with a feeling that something awful had happened."

"Nothing horrible has happened here, so you can put me out of your mind, at least for now."

"Thank goodness you're well."

"I'm actually more than well. The girls and I are having a bit of a celebration."

Ava heard a touch of eagerness in her mother's voice, and then she heard Cindy yell, "Tell her how we did."

"How did you do?" Ava asked, rolling her eyes.

"Eighty-five thousand," Jennie said, every word clipped.

"In total?"

"What do you mean?"

"Your Rama winnings plus your Niagara winnings?"

"No, I won another eighty-five thousand in Niagara."

"I don't believe it," Ava said.

"What's so hard to believe?" Jennie said. "I went to the bank this afternoon and deposited it. So start thinking about Italy."

"That's wonderful."

"I think so too. Now tell me, what are you up to and why are you in Hong Kong? I thought the trip was supposed to be to Shanghai."

"It was, but some business brought me here."

"And you said you'll be meeting Daddy?"

"I emailed him last night to ask if he could get together this morning, but I haven't checked yet to see if he replied."

"I'm sure if the morning doesn't work you can find some other time."

"Not necessarily. I'm leaving here late this afternoon for Nanjing and I don't expect I'll be back here on this trip."

"My god, you're getting around. I thought those days were behind you."

"Me too."

"Well, if you do get together with him, give him a kiss for me."

"I will."

"And Ava, please don't mention my windfall. He doesn't like it when I gamble, even when I win."

"I won't say a word."

When Ava put the phone down, her spirits felt considerably lighter. She walked to the window to confirm that it was still pelting rain, made herself a cup of coffee, and then settled in at the computer.

Her father had emailed to say he was going to be in meetings all day and asked when she was leaving Hong Kong. She told him about her plans to go to Nanjing and said she'd touch base once the rest of her schedule was set.

There was a raft of emails from Richard Bowlby that Brenda had forwarded. Some had been sent to and from someone named David Katz. Katz, it became apparent, was Bowlby's London legal contact. The emails were rather general in nature and touched more on the various applications of the U.K. Bribery Act than on Calhoun Metals specifically, and even then they were loaded with ifs, ands, and buts. Katz did refer to a justice ministry lawyer he knew personally and offered to set up a meeting between him and Richard. The old boys' network seemed to be in play. She was pleased to have it on her side for a change.

Richard had also had some preliminary communication with a Michael Dillman. He worked at the *Economic Herald* and also seemed to be an acquaintance. The two men had agreed to meet for a drink, but nothing beyond that. Still, Ava thought, it was a start.

There were no emails from Vanessa. Had she come up dry or was she just keeping Brenda informed? Ava left the computer and went to the bathroom to shower. Before she could turn on the water, her mobile phone rang again. She glanced at it and saw an unfamiliar Chinese number. Almost hesitantly, she said, "This is Ava Lee."

"I called the Peninsula and they told me you'd checked out," a woman's voice said. "So I thought I'd try the cell number you gave me."

"Who is this?"

"Fai."

"Fai who?"

"Pang Fai."

"I'm so sorry, I didn't recognize your voice."

"It's early for me to be up," she said. "I woke to call you."

"Why?"

"Tsai Men phoned me yesterday."

"Is that unusual?"

"It is when all he wanted to talk about was you."

"That's odd," Ava said uneasily.

"I meant to call you last night, but I got caught up in some things."

"It was nice of you to remember and to make the effort," Ava said, not wanting to know what Fai had been caught up in.

"It isn't a big deal. I liked you when I met you and I thought I owed you a heads-up."

"Why, what did he say that warranted it?"

"He was quite sneaky — for him, I mean, because he's normally blunt to the point of being rude," Fai said. "He started off by talking about our dinner the other night and asking if you and I had gotten along. I said yes, and then he asked me if you'd discussed the nature of your relationship with Xu. I told him I didn't know what he meant. Then he laughed and said that Xu had described you as his girlfriend. He wanted to know if you were getting paid."

"What did you say?"

"I said no, you were a businesswoman, a real businesswoman."

"Thanks for that."

"I figured it was true enough."

"Was that all he wanted to know?"

"No, he asked me what kind of business you were in, where you lived, and did I know how to contact you."

"Did you give him my phone number?"

"I'm not that stupid," Fai said. "But I did tell him you're a Canadian from Toronto and that's all I knew."

"I see," Ava said, her heart sinking a little.

"He said he remembered my saying that to him the night we had dinner."

"Did you?"

"I can't recall, but it is possible."

Ava felt her heart sink further. Was he smart enough, or paranoid enough, to use that broad a coincidence to connect her to the Toronto Commonwealth Bank?

"How did he react to it?" Ava asked.

"When I told him at dinner, he just sort of shrugged as if he didn't care. Yesterday he was certainly more interested."

"He's invited Xu and me to Nanjing," she said.

"Where are you now?"

Ava hesitated and then realized she was being paranoid herself. "I'm in Hong Kong."

"I would stay there if I were you."

"I can't. I promised Xu I'd go with him."

"I told you the other night that he's no friend of Xu's. Well, I think you can also assume he's no friend of yours. I wouldn't go anywhere near Nanjing."

"I'll think about it a bit more," Ava said, not wanting to argue.

"Do that."

"Fai, I want to thank you again for calling. It was very considerate of you."

"Girls who work with men like Tsai and Xu need to look after each other. I hope you'd do the same for me if it came down to it."

"You can count on that," Ava said. "Call me if you ever need anything."

"And you should feel free to call me. Did my number show on your phone?"

"Yes."

"It's my personal line. Not many people have it. The only thing I ask is that you not share it."

"I wouldn't think of it."

"Good luck with whatever decision you make," Fai said.

Ava was about to end the call when a thought came to her. "Fai, would you ever consider doing some work for one of my companies?"

"I'm hardly trained to do anything but act."

"We've launched a new fashion line with a brilliant young Chinese designer named Clark Po, and I think it's going to go very well. It would be a privilege to have someone like you associated with it."

"You want me to wear his clothes?"

"I'm thinking along bigger lines."

"Such as?"

"You could be our spokesperson in Asia. You could be the face of the brand here and elsewhere."

"I'd have to like the clothes before I agreed to anything."

"Of course."

"And I would have to be well paid."

"Of course."

"When you have something concrete to offer, call me."

"Not your agent?"

"He's a man. He'd only get in the way."

27

AT HALF PAST NINE SHE WALKED INTO THE HOTEL
lobby with her bags. Sonny was already lingering by the
door. She had called to tell him that she was checking out,
going to a meeting with the lawyers, and then heading to
the airport. He grunted when she told him she was leaving
Hong Kong so soon, but he didn't ask any questions.

She was early getting to the law office but was shown
into the boardroom. Within a minute Brenda and Vanessa
walked through the door.

"How was your evening?" Ava asked.

"Long," Vanessa replied.

The two women sat down across from Ava, and then
Vanessa pulled several long sheets of foolscap from a file,
passed one to Brenda and slid another to Ava.

"I reworked your chart based on the additional information we've uncovered," Vanessa said. "I needed something to send to my contacts in the U.S. I hope you don't
mind."

Ava looked down at it and blinked.

"When you add in all the companies kicking in money

to Evergreen, Gold Star, and Hallmark, we must be up to more than forty," Ava said.

"That's true," Vanessa said. "I couldn't fit them all on the page so I created an addendum that lists them alphabetically."

"And you sent all of this to your contacts?"

"I did, and then I followed up with phone calls."

"What was their reaction?"

"Disbelief."

"They disputed the facts?"

"No, they were shocked by the sheer extent of it all."

"By the number of companies that are paying off the family?"

"Yes, and by the amount of money the family seems to have accumulated."

"That's good to hear."

"Actually it is, and I think we have to give a lot of credit to Vanessa and the way she's handled this," Brenda said. "She stayed up most of the night going back and forth between New York and Washington. Initially there was a lot of skepticism on the other end."

"The people I was talking to are friends, so I think the correct word to use is 'caution' when it comes to describing their first reaction," Vanessa said.

"They still had to be persuaded."

Vanessa shrugged and a slight, satisfied smile crossed her face. Ava then noticed the dark circles under her eyes and knew it was true that she'd stayed up most of the night.

"Do you mind if I ask who these friends are?" Ava asked.

"Felicia is a lawyer in the Department of Justice. She's Chinese American and gets an emotional reaction — though she would deny it — to this particular kind of corruption. The other, Sam Curry, writes for the *Wall Street Tribune*."

"So what happens now?"

"Felicia will press to have an investigatory file opened on the Jiangsu–Patriot Insurance deal."

"That will take time."

"Yes, it will, and regardless of the information we have, the Department of Justice will move at its own pace."

"How about Sam Curry?"

"He has to check the facts before he does anything else."

"But he's interested?"

"Truthfully, he wasn't terribly keen at first, but he started to warm to the idea when he saw we had actual bank records. And then I used a line that Brenda said came from you."

"I told Vanessa about your mentioning the single-generation evolution from idealistic peasant revolutionary to corrupt billionaire businessman," Brenda said.

"Sam loved it."

"I'm sure he loved the bank records more," Ava said. "So now he's fact-checking?"

"Yes."

"How long will that take?"

"Given the bank records and the fact that some of the information is in the public domain, not as long as I imagined. He thought it would be a day or two, and if he's satisfied with what he finds, he'll go to his editor with the story suggestion."

"How about in London? Did you hear anything more from Richard?" Ava asked Brenda.

Brenda looked at her watch. "He's going to call us in about ten minutes with an update."

"It's three o'clock in the morning there," Ava said.

"I don't really care," Brenda said, and then put her hand to her mouth. "That sounded so bitchy."

"My boyfriend took off for two weeks last year to watch soccer games in Europe," Vanessa said. "I felt the same way."

"I don't have that problem," Ava said with a shrug.

Brenda started to say something and then stopped.

Vanessa stretched her arms skyward and yawned.

When the phone rang, Brenda answered. She listened for a moment and then said, "Wait a second. I'm with Ava and Vanessa and I want to put this on speaker."

"Hello, ladies," Richard Bowlby said. "What an interesting day and night this has been."

"Sorry to take you away from your sports," Ava said.

"Not at all. It was nice to get a break from rugby. My team has been doing badly and I couldn't stand much more of it."

"Richard, none of us really wants to hear about your rugby team," Brenda said.

"Are you still upset over my love of the game?" he said.

"No, I'm just trying to conduct business, since our client is here and the clock is running."

"Then turn off the clock, because we've created a bit of a stir here and we need to take time to digest it."

"With David Katz?" Brenda asked, her voice rising.

"Yes, to a degree, but more with Michael Dillman at the *Economic Herald*. Our quick drink turned into a three-hour meeting. He left with copies of all the documents that you sent. Two hours later he called me back and we met for dinner and several nightcaps."

"What generated so much interest?" Brenda asked.

"Dennis Calhoun."

"I don't know of anyone by that name. Can I assume he

is involved in Calhoun Metals?" Ava asked.

"He's the company founder, long-time CEO, and currently its chairman," Richard said. "He also happens to be the chairman of the Conservative Party in the U.K."

"Oh," Ava said.

"'Oh' indeed. He's a man of considerable power and influence with friends in high places. Luckily, he has also made as many, if not more, enemies, and they aren't without their own clout. The bottom line is that he's a man who a great many people know and have an interest in."

"Richard, as I remember, party chairmen are internal appointments and not elected," Brenda said.

"That's true."

"And the position is almost honorary."

"Also true."

"So while Calhoun's political affiliation is interesting, I can't see its having any direct bearing on the business practices or the success of his company."

"That was my initial reaction, and it's essentially true, but according to Michael Dillman — and hence his interest — Dennis Calhoun has muddied the waters. Apparently, he's been a relentless self-promoter for many years, and since assuming the party chairmanship nine months ago, that's only intensified."

"Self-promotion is not an unusual trait in a businessman or a quasi-politician," Ava said.

"Except that Calhoun presents himself as the man who has shown the U.K. business community how to successfully do business with the Chinese."

"How interesting," Ava said, a large smile breaking across her face.

"According to Dillman, Calhoun maxed out his growth potential here years ago. He was evidently quite the terror, a real predator. I have a list of companies he destroyed and lawsuits he fought off. With the U.K. market saturated, he turned his attention to Asia. He had a few bumps along the road in Singapore and Malaysia, but then he discovered China. He has been bragging about Mega Metals for years. He says it's the ideal model for other U.K. companies to emulate if they want to succeed in China. Dillman said that Calhoun has been a regular contributor to the business press and a guest on a horde of TV and radio shows. Dillman thinks that high profile helped him get the chairmanship."

"Mega Metals as a model — how hypocritical is that?" Vanessa said.

"And the Calhoun message has only been getting stronger," Richard said. "Since he's become chairman of the party, the government has been trying to turn him into a poster boy."

"A what?" Brenda said.

"He was the leader of the last major trade mission that the government organized to go to China. Then they organized a series of seminars aimed at educating small to medium-sized firms on how to do business in China. Calhoun doesn't conduct them, but his name is attached to them."

"So Calhoun and his business are linked with the government?" Ava asked.

"Exactly."

"That's fascinating," she said.

"Dillman thinks so too."

"Is he going to do a story?"

"Well, he was spouting possible headlines as he left the bar. One was 'Calhoun's Secret Key to Success in China — Bribe the Buggers.' My favourite was 'Chairman Calhoun Pays Chairman Mao.' Although knowing the *Economic Herald*, I'm sure if they do a piece, the headline will be less tabloid and far more serious."

"If they do a piece?" Ava said. "Is there any doubt they will?"

"Dillman still has to talk to his editor. If he gets the green light, then they'll obviously have to confirm the information we've given them, and he said they would have to speak to Calhoun. It could take several days, maybe longer."

"I know the *Herald* has a tremendous reputation, but how many readers does it have?" Brenda asked.

"There are about a million and a half subscribers, but the total readership is larger than that," Richard said. "And you are correct about it being a very serious and respected publication. Anything it publishes will have instant credibility worldwide, and you can expect that other media will pick up the story and run it as well."

"I have to confess that this is more than I ever hoped for," Ava said softly.

"It isn't a sure thing yet," Richard said.

"I understand that, but it's a very large leap forward from where I was twenty-four hours ago," she said.

"Richard, did you make any promises to Mr. Dillman?" Brenda asked.

"Like what?"

"An exclusive."

"No, although he asked me who else I was talking to and I told him no one."

"Vanessa has spoken to a friend who works at the *Wall Street Tribune*. They might have an interest as well, although I imagine it might be more focused on the Tsai family and their American interests."

"Given its English roots, I expect the *Herald* would be all over the Calhoun–government angle."

"We wouldn't want them to downplay the Tsais," Brenda said.

"That's not a thing we can control. It's Calhoun's stature and position that are most important here."

"I just want the story published," Ava said. "It can be ninety-nine percent about Calhoun and one percent about the Tsais. It doesn't matter. I'll still find a way to make it work."

"That's the right approach to take," Richard said.

"It's the only approach, but there is one thing I am concerned about," Ava said, turning to Vanessa. "I don't want us to lose the chance to have the *Tribune* run the story as well. I would hate it if the *Herald* got it out first and your friend felt blindsided. I think it might be wise if you gave him a heads-up."

"I think Ava is right," Brenda said.

"And Richard," Ava continued, "is there any chance that the *Herald* might run the chart we've been assembling?"

"Truthfully, Dillman didn't have much interest in it."

"Well, when you speak to Sam Curry," Ava said to Vanessa, "make sure you tell him that. It might encourage him to use it."

28

THE DRAGONAIR FLIGHT LEFT HONG KONG FIFTEEN minutes late and was parked on the runway at Lukou International Airport in Nanjing for another fifteen while it waited for another plane to vacate the arrivals gate. Ava phoned Xu from the plane.

"I've landed, but it will be past seven o'clock by the time I get out of the terminal."

"I'm glad you're here, but we're cutting it really close. The restaurant is in the Yihe Mansions, and that's a fifty-kilometre drive from the airport. Even in good traffic it will take close to an hour to get there. I'm still at the InterContinental, which is close to the Mansions, so I'll go directly to the restaurant and wait for you there."

"Who's meeting me here?"

"Suen is already in the arrivals hall. We brought our driver from Shanghai with us, so the car will be at the curb when the two of you leave the terminal. With any luck you'll make it on time for eight."

"Did you find out why Tsai Men wants to see us?"

"No."

"Well, I have a hunch."

"What?"

"I had a friend from a Canadian bank making bank-to-bank inquiries about several Tsai businesses, and I had our Hong Kong law firm doing the same. It appears that the Chinese banks may have become suspicious about the interest being shown. They may have said something to Tsai Men."

"The bank and the lawyers were discreet?"

"Completely. All of the communication was of a normal commercial variety."

"And no names were mentioned?"

"If you mean mine and yours, absolutely not."

"Then we should have nothing to worry about."

"I felt the same until Pang Fai called me."

"What did she want?"

"To tell me that Tsai Men had contacted her to ask about me. He wanted to know if I was a kept woman, and when she said no, he grilled her about my business and where I was from."

"I think it's because he's attracted to you. That's the impression I got when he spoke to me the day after the dinner."

"I have trouble believing that."

"I think you're being overly modest," Xu said.

"Maybe, but I had hoped that dinner in Shanghai was the last time I would have to meet the man."

"We'll get past it," he said. "Did the bank and law firm inquiries provide any useful information?"

"Lots, but I don't want to discuss it over the phone. It's quite complicated," Ava said. "I spent the morning with the lawyers and then two hours on the plane making notes. My notebook is filling up, and I can't remember the last time that happened."

"Then I'll wait until we can really talk."

"That's best. And now my plane is finally moving towards the terminal," Ava said. "See you in about an hour."

Ten minutes after reaching the gate, Ava walked into the arrivals hall and saw Suen. He gave a respectful nod and reached for her bag.

"I'm told I have to hurry," she said.

"The car is waiting for us outside."

When Ava walked through the exit, she was immediately assaulted by a wall of thick, odorous steam. She stopped and looked for the Mercedes. It was parked about fifty metres away.

"What's that smell?" she said to Suen.

"They tell me it's a bad pollution day. They closed all the city schools, but luckily they let the highways stay open. Last year, they had to shut down almost the entire city for close to a week."

"And it's so humid."

"That's typical for Nanjing — hot and muggy in the summer, cold and damp in the winter. We're lucky it isn't monsoon season."

"I don't feel that lucky," Ava said, putting a hand over her mouth and nose.

"He's seen us," Suen said, pointing to the car that was crawling towards them.

Ava climbed into the back seat as Suen put her bag in the trunk. He then sat next to the driver and reached for his phone.

"I have to call the boss," he said.

"Be my guest."

He punched in a number. "It's me. Ava is in the car and we're headed for Yihe Mansions," he said, and then paused. "Okay, I'll do that."

He put his phone away and sat staring straight ahead. The car pulled onto a highway signed S55 North.

"What does he want you to do?" Ava asked.

Suen turned halfway towards her. "Nothing to do with your dinner," he said.

Ava thought she saw some tension in his shoulders.

"I've never been to Nanjing," she said, looking out at the hilly terrain.

"It's the ancient capital."

"That much I do know."

"I grew up in a village close by," Suen said. "When I was a child, we came here every summer to visit Xuanwu Lake, which is in the middle of the city. I always found it strange that a lake was there."

"How big is it?"

Suen shrugged. "All I remember is that there were five islands in it, all interconnected by bridges, and it used to take us more than half the day to walk from one to another around the water. My mother was religious and stopped at various temples. My father was more interested in the teahouses and restaurants."

"It sounds lovely. I'd like to see it."

"The Yihe Mansions are just to the west of it, but it will be dark by the time we get there."

"Maybe tomorrow."

"Maybe," Suen said.

Ava closed her eyes and let her head fall back against the seat. She had worn black linen slacks and a plain white button-down shirt to the meeting with the lawyers in Hong Kong and hadn't had a chance to change. If there were other women at the dinner and it was anything like Shanghai, she was decidedly underdressed.

"I might nap," she said to Suen. "If I do, wake me at least ten minutes before we reach our destination."

She did sleep, and woke with a start when Suen's hand gently pushed her knee.

"Almost there," he said.

She sat upright. Her lips were dry and her hair was mussed. She reached into her bag for a brush and lipstick. By the time she was finished with them, the car was pulling into what looked like a complex of townhouses.

"Xu said you are to join them in a private dining room in the Yuanxia-Dongyin Restaurant. You can get there through the hotel entrance," Suen said. "We can't leave the car here. There's a lot about fifty metres away. Someone should call me when you're ready to leave."

She stepped out of the car and climbed five levels into the lobby. She walked across a thick, richly coloured rug towards a young woman who sat at a large antique desk.

"I'm meeting Mr. Tsai and Mr. Xu for dinner," she said.

The young woman leapt to her feet. "They've been waiting for you. Let me show you the way."

She led Ava through a long corridor lined with traditional paintings of dragons and waterfalls, and then cut right and left before stopping before a door. She knocked.

"Come in," the familiar voice of Tsai Men said.

The woman opened the door and stepped to one side.

Ava walked into a room that had a single empty table with sixteen chairs. Only three were occupied. Xu stood and walked over to Ava. He held out his arms and she stepped into them. Then he pulled back and turned towards the table.

"You know Tsai Men," he said. "And I'm pleased to say that his wife, Lau Ai, has joined us."

Ava smiled at Tsai, who was dressed in a grey suit, and Lau Ai, who was heavily made up and had a grim look on her face. She was probably in her forties, Ava guessed, and was thin, with delicate features. She was wearing a powder-blue Chanel jacket with pink trim over a white silk blouse, her neck adorned with a string of pearls. One hand rested on the table, showing off a five-carat diamond ring and a diamond-encrusted bracelet.

"You look quite different from the last time I saw you," Tsai said.

Ava glanced down at her white cotton button-down shirt and black linen slacks. "Is this inappropriate?"

"Not at all. Have a seat."

She took the chair to the right of Xu. Tsai sat across from him and Lau Ai was to her husband's left.

"We've ordered wine and tea," Tsai said.

"We won't be staying for dinner," Xu said. "I misunderstood the initial invitation. Men and Ai have a function that they have to attend elsewhere." He said it deliberately, and Ava thought she heard some tension in his voice.

"I'm sure we can find food somewhere in Nanjing," she said, and smiled.

Tsai shifted in his chair, his eyes drifting upward. Lau continued to glare at her.

"Xu said you weren't in Shanghai when we asked you to meet us here," Tsai said. "Where were you?"

"I was in Hong Kong," Ava said, surprised at his rudeness.

"And what took you to Hong Kong?"

"I have family there. I was visiting my father and brothers."

"And you came all the way from Hong Kong to Nanjing for what you thought was a dinner?"

"Xu asked me to come as a favour."

"A favour?"

"He's a friend."

"Still . . ."

"He's a special friend."

There was a knock at the door and then it swung open. A server stood in the entrance with a large tray held chest high. Tsai motioned for him to come in. The room went quiet as he placed the tray on the table and then set a cup and glass in front of each of them.

"We'll pour," Tsai said to the server as he took a bottle of white burgundy from an ice bucket. He offered it to Ava, who shook her head. So did Xu and Lau Ai. Tsai shrugged and filled his glass.

Lau lifted the teapot and reached over the table to pour the pale gold liquid into Xu and Ava's cups.

Ava tapped the table with her middle finger.

"*Xie xie*," Xu said.

"To friends, old and new," Tsai said, lifting his glass.

"To your health," Xu responded.

As Ava sipped her tea she felt Lau's eyes on her. She raised her head and offered the older woman a tentative smile.

"What do you do for a living?" Lau asked in a tone so soft it was almost a whisper. "My husband was quite vague about it."

"I'm an accountant by training, and I'm a partner in an investment business with two other women."

"That's not what I expected," she said.

"How so?"

"All I was told was that you are Xu's girlfriend and absolutely stunning. I thought you were maybe a model or an aspiring actress."

"When I met your husband that one time, I was dressed for a reception to launch a new fashion line," Ava said, ignoring the innuendo. "This is my more normal style. It's mundane and rather boring, like my life."

"We have known Xu for many, many years," Lau said.

"So I understand."

"You are the first woman of his we've ever met, so you'll understand if we're a little curious."

"We didn't know if he actually liked women," Tsai said with a grin.

"I can assure you he does," Ava said.

"And your life can't be all that boring," Tsai continued. "Evidently you travel quite a bit."

"Not particularly."

"You are a Canadian?" he asked.

"I'm Hong Kong–born, Canadian-raised," she said without hesitation.

"But where is home?"

"Canada."

"Which city?"

"Toronto," she said carefully, remembering Pang Fai's warning.

"Where did you meet Xu?"

"In Hong Kong."

"How did that happen?"

"We had a mutual friend who brought us together."

"Men, that's enough," Lau Ai said. "You're making Ms. Lee uncomfortable with all your questions."

Tsai sipped his wine, his eyes darting between Ava and Xu. "Let's you and I go out for a smoke," he said to Xu. "There are some business issues we need to discuss."

"Excuse me," Xu said to the women as he stood.

When the door closed behind the two men, Ava felt her shoulders relax and realized she'd been tensed up. Lau seemed distracted, her attention flitting around the room. Ava started to speak and then opted for silence. Five minutes passed, and then another five, and she felt her tension rise again. Finally, as lightly as she could, she said, "The men left us rather quickly."

"I apologize for my husband," Lau said. "He can be abrupt."

"I understand," Ava said, glad for the conversation.

"We're having dinner later with his uncle and his father and some other relatives. That sometimes makes him anxious."

"I'm told that his uncle, Ying Fa, is the Communist Party secretary in Jiangsu."

"He is."

"And his father is governor."

"He is."

"They must be the two most powerful and influential men in the province."

"They are."

"I heard they are in their seventies. Is either of them thinking of retiring?"

"Why do you ask?" Lau said, her attention keener.

"In Canada it's common for men of that age to step aside. I was simply wondering."

Lau shook her head. "Neither of them will retire voluntarily. They love what they're doing too much."

"Do you mean that they love the exercise of power?"

"Probably," she said, reaching for the teapot. "That isn't necessarily a bad thing."

"Of course not, and I'm sure they've done wonderful things for Jiangsu and its people."

Lau poured tea for both of them.

"*Xie xie*," Ava said. "Now tell me a bit about you. Xu said that, like me, you're involved in your own business, with an English partner."

"He told you that?"

"Yes, but he didn't provide me with any details."

"Because there aren't many details to share. My name is on the company letterhead and from time to time I have documents to sign. Besides that, I know very little about the business other than that we seem to be providing materials to the construction industry."

"You must have a very capable manager."

"We do. He's with the English."

"That's very trusting, to leave your business in the hands of a foreigner."

"He's actually Chinese-Anglo. Besides, my husband does keep his eye on the business."

"How about your father-in-law?" Ava asked, as casually as possible.

Lau shot her a questioning glance.

"I'm sorry, I don't mean to pry," Ava said. "It's just that

there is so much about China that I don't understand."

"My father-in-law is head of the family before he is governor of the province," Lau said. "Does that answer your question?"

"Perfectly."

Lau looked down at her hands and fiddled with the diamond ring, turning it around her finger. "Since you felt free to ask a personal question, I'd like to ask one in return," she said.

"Certainly," Ava said.

Lau took a deep breath. "When you had dinner with Xu and my husband in Shanghai, was that woman with him?"

"What woman?"

"The actress."

"Which actress?" Ava asked, not taking the bait.

"Pang Fai."

"Yes, she was."

Lau turned her head away from Ava. "Thank you for being direct."

"No thanks are needed."

"What was she like?"

"I don't think I should answer that question."

"Please," Lau said. "My husband has been involved with her for some time, and all I know about her is what I've read in magazines and seen on the screen. I'd like to know more than that."

"I didn't spend much time with her."

"But you formed an opinion?"

"Of course."

"Share it with me, please."

"Well, he pays her to keep him company," Ava said carefully. "And I don't think he's the only one who does."

"My husband thought that you and Xu had the same kind of relationship."

"I can't think of any man who'd pay to spend time with me," Ava said with a laugh. "And if one made me that offer, I can assure you that I would take it the wrong way."

"You are a beautiful young woman."

"That's not true, but I am completely monogamous."

"Me too, but not by choice. This may be the modern China, but a married man can still do what he wants while a married woman is bound by age-old convention."

"It's the same in Europe or North America."

Lau toyed with her ring again and then sighed. "Tell me what she's like."

"I did."

"No, you only told me what was obvious."

Lau was trying to appear calm, but Ava heard some desperation in her voice. She thought back to the few minutes she'd spent alone with Pang Fai, and then about her phone call to Ava. Ava had been drawn to Pang's magnetism and was impressed by her candour and her understanding that Tsai Men's questions about Ava could mean trouble. She was, in fact, a woman Ava would like to know better. Should she tell Lau what she actually thought of Pang or what she guessed she'd like to hear? "She is rather crude and mercenary. I doubt she has any real feelings for your husband. It's all business," Ava finally said.

"What leads you to think that?"

"Five minutes of conversation going to and coming from the bathroom."

"What did she say?"

"What does it matter?"

"It matters. Please tell me."

"It wasn't anything specific," Ava said hesitantly. "She was simply disparaging about the men who pay for her services, and then she told me something that I'm sure your husband didn't want shared. I found that particularly disrespectful."

Lau was about to say something when the door opened.

Two men dressed in black stood in the doorway. Ava glanced at them. She thought they were waiters and turned back to Lau, but when she did, she saw that the other woman's mouth was agape.

"What do you want?" Lau said.

"We were told to get this woman."

29

AVA'S HEAD SWIVELLED TOWARDS THE DOOR. TWO men stood poised, staring her down. They were both of medium height, dressed in black running shoes, pants, and cotton turtleneck sweaters that showed off muscular shoulders and arms. One had a pair of handcuffs looped through one side of his belt and a nightstick on the other. His partner had what looked like a Taser in a long holster hanging down his right leg. There was nothing particularly sinister about them. They had none of the scars and tattoos that Ava associated with gangsters. Instead, they displayed a quiet, confident, and determined reserve.

"What do you want with her?" Lau said.

"There are people who have questions for her," the man on the left said.

"We weren't informed about this," Lau said.

"We're just following orders," he said.

"Why don't we leave now," the other man said to Ava, taking several steps forward and extending his hand towards her.

"I'm not going anywhere," she said.

"You don't have a choice."

"Maybe it's better if you do go," Lau said softly.

Ava stood and moved so she was closer to the wall. Her position didn't afford the two men much of an angle to come at her.

"I don't want to hurt you," the man with the handcuffs said.

"I appreciate that, but I'm still not going with you."

He looked at his partner as if to say, *Do you want to take her or should I?*

The partner answered by taking three or four rapid steps towards Ava. The suddenness and speed of his move surprised her and she fell back a step. He reached for her left arm, caught it around the biceps, and squeezed hard enough to make her grunt in pain.

"Now, come quietly or I will really hurt you," he said.

"Okay," Ava said.

His grip relaxed, and as it did her right hand shot forward and grasped the elbow of the arm that held her. Her fingers held tight while her thumb searched for the nerve it was looking for. She dug into it until he screamed. She kept digging until she was sure the pain was the only thing he was conscious of. When she let go, his arm fell uselessly to his side and his body lurched in the same direction. He tried to his swing his other arm at her, but it was a listless effort and she sidestepped it easily, driving the knuckle of her middle finger into his ear. He collapsed onto the floor, and she knew it would be a while before he would be able to get to his feet.

The other man stood almost transfixed, and it wasn't until his partner hit the ground that he started to reach for the Taser. By the time it had left the holster, Ava was on him. She jumped over the body of the man on the floor and landed with her right foot poised. She propelled herself forward and sunk her foot into his groin, with her heel leading the way. He groaned but didn't keel. Ava's fist, clenched in the traditional and lethal phoenix-eye position, carved its way into his belly, striking the cluster of nerves gathered just below the middle of his rib cage. He fell back and then sideways, already beginning to vomit.

"What's going on in there?" a voice yelled.

From where she stood, Ava could see Xu and Tsai approaching the room. They both looked agitated.

"They wanted to take me somewhere for questioning," Ava shouted. "Who are they?"

Xu and Tsai stopped when they reached the doorway.

"What the fuck?" Xu said, looking at the men on the ground.

"I had nothing to do with this," Tsai Men said.

"I told her that," his wife said.

"But you know who did," Xu said.

"It's a mistake," Tsai said.

Xu shook his head. "I think we should be leaving," he said to Ava.

Ava nodded and turned towards Lau. "It was lovely chatting with you, at least until those men arrived."

"I'm sorry."

"There's no need."

"I didn't know," Tsai repeated.

"You and I will talk later," Xu said.

Tsai looked blankly at him.

Ava stepped out of the room and slipped an arm through

Xu's. Side by side, they left the restaurant, Ava glancing in all directions in case there were more men outside.

"I called Suen a few minutes ago," Xu said. "He'll be waiting."

"Are we going to the hotel?"

"Not a chance."

"Why not?" Ava asked.

"It isn't safe for us anywhere in Nanjing."

30

THE MERCEDES WAS SITTING IN THE SAME SPOT WHERE Suen had dropped Ava off. He leapt from the car as soon as he saw them and opened the back door.

"The InterContinental?" he asked.

"No, we're going directly back to Shanghai," Xu said.

"You have a bag at the hotel."

"Send someone to get it later. I'll give you my room key."

Ava saw a question form on Suen's lips and then disappear.

"Call Shanghai and let them know we're coming back tonight. I want extra men posted around the neighbourhood and at both ends of the street. They should be on the lookout for police or military vehicles."

"Yes, boss."

As the car pulled away from the Yihe Mansions, Xu hit a number on his cellphone.

"Auntie Grace, it's me," he said. "I'm not staying over in Nanjing. I'm driving back to Shanghai tonight with Ava. Could you please prepare the guest room for her, and have some food ready? We haven't eaten."

The housekeeper's voice was muffled, but Ava thought she heard concern in it.

"Yes, there is a small problem," Xu said. "And I don't want you to answer the house phone again unless you see it's my number."

They were driving through Nanjing now, negotiating heavy traffic, visibility made difficult by air dense with fog.

"Do you want us to take the main highway or side roads?" Suen asked.

"The main highway should be okay for now."

The car veered left and started to climb an on-ramp. Ava saw a sign for Shanghai.

"Who were those men?" she asked.

"Probably military, but what's strange is that they sent only two men. Normally they would have sent in a fully armed unit. They don't do things in half measure. They must have thought a couple of their men could take one woman, or they're trying to keep this low-key."

"Whatever the rationale, those two men were professional. Do you think the Governor ordered them to pick me up?"

"Or his cousin did. Or both of them."

"But not Tsai Men?"

"I honestly don't think he knew. This meeting was all about confirming what Pang Fai had told him. By the way, it was wise that you didn't lie to him," Xu said. "He still could be our only lifeline."

"What caused him to call her in the first place?"

"He's shrewd. According to Men, the family — including his father and uncle — started getting phone calls yesterday from some of the banks and their business partners, telling them that someone was looking into their affairs. Their initial reaction was that some rival in Beijing was trying to cause mischief. But when Hong Kong and Toronto kept coming up, they thought it had to be an outsider. Men remembered an offhand remark Pang Fai had made about you and phoned her. She confirmed the Toronto connection."

"Toronto is a large city."

"In their minds, it was you."

"That's a very selective process of elimination."

"That's how they think."

"Shit."

"They already know the name of the bank in Toronto and of the law firm in Hong Kong. Another firm in Beijing also made contact, but they think it's connected to the one in Hong Kong. They're now using intermediaries to confirm who initiated the requests for information."

"Men told you this?"

"Yes."

"What else do they know?"

"Just what I told you."

"Xu, I don't have an account with the bank in Toronto, and my contact there would never reveal me. The law firm was hired by May Ling. She's the client of record. They're tight-lipped as well and wouldn't disclose her name or mine. So the Tsais can try all they want, but they'll never be able to connect me to the inquiries."

"The problem is that it doesn't matter if they can or not," Xu said. "They don't need proof of anything in order to believe that something is true."

"What is it that they believe?"

"They think it was me who instigated the inquiries. They think I hired you. Men told me that point-blank, and then he said they knew I wasn't happy about the drug proposal and that maybe I was trying to find a way to throw the deal back in their face."

"They thought it through to that extent?"

Xu nodded.

"That is smart," Ava said. "I've underestimated them."

"I always knew they were smart," Xu said. "What I didn't really grasp was just how paranoid they are. All it took was the mention of Toronto and you went from being a pleasant dinner companion to the mysterious girlfriend who had appeared out of nowhere to cause trouble. They leapt to a great many conclusions, none of which favour us."

"And you denied them?"

"Forcefully and rather angrily. Men backed down a bit when he saw how furious I was. He then said that whether I had hired you or not, the family thought you were the one digging into their affairs. That's a problem for them. A problem that he said had to be dealt with."

"Dealt with how?"

Xu reached for Ava's hand. "He told me to get rid of you. He didn't specify how, but he made it clear that they were open to a wide range of options. They just want you gone from their lives."

"And taking me from the restaurant tonight was the first step?"

"It could have been, although I still think he knew nothing about it."

"What did you say to Men when he asked you to get rid of me?"

"I told him that you're my girlfriend and have been for the past year," Xu said. "I told him that you know nothing about my business and wouldn't dare interfere even if you did. I said the Toronto and Hong Kong connections were coincidental, and that there was nothing abnormal about either banks or law firms doing due diligence and running credit checks on Chinese companies."

"How did he react?"

"Guardedly, but then I told him I've just returned from Guangzhou and have cemented a deal with the triad head there to build the designer drug factory. I explained to him that any reluctance I'd had was based on my worries about how that colleague would react to the factory initiative. I told him that colleague is now going to be a partner. At that point he asked if they were expected to give up part of their shares to him. I said no, and he started to relax."

"I know this may be repetitive, but did he also let go of the idea of getting rid of me?"

"He agreed that might have been an overreaction. He said he is meeting with his father and uncle later tonight and will explain things to them."

"What are the chances he'll be successful?"

"Before I saw the two men on the floor I would have said not bad, but now I think he'll have to be extremely persuasive."

"So where does that leave us?"

"On the highway heading back to Shanghai."

"Okay, I get that, but do you think it's really necessary to place extra men at the house?"

"The Tsais are going to get together for dinner tonight, and they're going to talk about you and about me. They'll feed off each other's paranoia, and by the end of the evening they'll likely have decided that you're going to be an even bigger problem and I'm going to be one as well, because no matter what Tsai Men says, I'm defending you, and they'll be convinced that proves I put you up to it. We've done them no harm, but that won't matter. They see the potential for harm. They don't take any chances. One way or another, they'll find an excuse to set the cops or the military on us."

"Do they know where you live?"

"No, very few people do. Not even Feng. It's the safest place I can think of, and even though I don't think they'd try to do anything in Shanghai, it would be foolish not to take extra precautions. I don't want to be surprised in the middle of the night. Even a ten-minute warning would give us time to prepare."

"But how?"

"Don't worry about that."

Ava shook her head. "May warned me about the family. She told me that the old man will strike at shadows. I should have listened to her."

"She was right," Xu said.

"This is getting out of control."

"That's my sense of it as well, but the problem is that I'm not sure there's anything we can do to get them to back off. Once you become a target, you are forever one, until you're gone."

"We have to respond. We can't sit back and let this happen."

"You say that like you have something in mind."

"We have to move faster than them."

"What do you mean?"

"We need to give them something else to worry about, something that diminishes our significance," Ava said. "Are you prepared to go public with some of the information we've uncovered?"

"Through those newspapers you've been talking to?"

"Yes. We've laid the groundwork. Maybe we can find a way to speed the process."

"Can the papers be connected directly to you?"

"I haven't communicated with any of them. It's all been done through our lawyers, and I trust them completely."

"It would be good to get out in front instead of being chased."

"Is that a yes?"

"Go ahead."

"Great. Let me make some phone calls."

"Before you do, I have one that I need to make," Xu said. "I want to brief Lop on everything that's going on with the Tsai family."

Ava blinked in surprise. "What can he do from Wanchai? Unless of course you're thinking of bringing him back here to fight."

"I don't want to bring him back or to fight — although he would gladly do both if it came down to it," Xu said. "I don't know if you remember, but he was a captain in the Special Forces of the PLA, and he's still well connected enough to get inside information. So if something is going down, he's our best chance to get an advance warning."

While Xu called Lop, Ava looked out the window at the passing apartment buildings and office complexes. He was completely matter-of-fact, almost abnormally calm, as he described the situation to Lop. Ava's one encounter with the ex-military man had been in Wanchai, when he flew into Hong Kong with Suen to take down Sammy Wing, the triad leader in the district. It had been a quick and brutal skirmish, and Lop's emotions were barely held in check. Ava wondered if that was why Xu was taking such care to speak calmly about the Tsais.

"He'll make some phone calls to some senior people on the inside who he trusts," Xu said when he had finished the conversation.

"That's great. I'm only sorry that it's necessary."

He glanced at her. "Is that your way of trying to say you think this is your fault?"

"In hindsight, I involved too many other people. Maybe I wasn't careless, but I sure wasn't cautious enough."

"The only way you could have exercised greater caution would be to have done nothing at all."

She started to respond and then stopped. Mistakes had been made and they were on her. She'd not only involved too many people, she'd also sent them off in too many directions. She had been uncharacteristically undisciplined, something that Uncle would never have allowed. There were times when she sorely missed his judgement, and this was one of them. But there wasn't much point in rehashing errors. The only thing that mattered now was getting to a different place, and that was going to take some work.

She reached for her phone.

31

JOHNNY YAN WAS QUICK TO PICK UP THE LINE.

"I was hoping you'd call," he said.

"What's going on?"

"We've been getting bombarded with requests from the Chinese banks we contacted, and some of the companies that you wanted us to look into have come at us as well, all of them wanting to know who requested the bank-to-bank inquiries."

"They communicated with Felix?"

"Yeah."

"What is he telling them?"

"Nothing right now. He's referring all their emails directly to me, as I asked, but he sure as hell is nervous that this is going to find its way up the corporate ladder here."

"What are you saying?"

"I've been telling them the information is confidential."

"I can't imagine that's working very well."

"You guessed right."

"And I imagine you're getting as worried as Felix about them going over your head."

"The thought doesn't thrill me."

"You need a plausible story."

"And I don't have one."

"Johnny, does your bank have customers in Hong Kong?"

"Yes."

"Good. So what you say is that one of your Hong Kong–based customers is considering expanding their business in China and sent you a list of more than a hundred companies they wanted some basic information about. Tell them it was a laundry list of companies; that way they won't feel so targeted."

"And if that doesn't satisfy them?"

"Tell them you'll give them the name of the customer if they agree to sign a non-disclosure agreement."

"And if they agree to do that, where the fuck am I going to find that agreement?"

"You're not, because you won't have to. I'll give you the name of a large trading company in Hong Kong you can send to them, and I'll arrange for the company to back up your story."

"Jesus, Ava, this is getting too complicated."

"Johnny, all we're doing is buying time. Given the time difference, it will take at least two days before you get anywhere near having to send them a name. By then, no one should care."

He sighed.

"I owe you another one, and I know this one is particularly big," Ava said.

"If I need to contact you, I can use your cell number or email address?"

"You can, and I'll get right back to you. I won't leave you hanging out to dry."

"Okay. Let the stalling begin," he said.

She looked at Xu as she ended the call. His eyes were closed and his head was resting against the back of the seat. He was either trying to sleep or creating space for her to feel unrestricted about what she had to say during her conversation with Johnny. Whichever it was, she appreciated it.

It was the middle of the evening and the only number she had for Brenda Burgess was at the office. Predictably, she was greeted by an automated receptionist, and accessing Brenda's line didn't get her any closer to making contact. A call to directory services was next, and she was given a home number. To her surprise, Brenda answered it.

"I'm sorry for calling you at home and so late," Ava said.

"I assume there's a reason."

"The Tsai family."

"What else?"

"Our Canadian bank is under siege from the Chinese banks and some of the Chinese companies. They're trying to find out who's been asking questions," Ava said.

"We've had more calls ourselves."

"Sorry for that."

"It isn't anything we can't handle."

"The thing is, the family has been doing some digging on their own and they've decided I'm the culprit."

"How did they arrive at that conclusion?"

"It was a stretch, but however limited the facts, we can't ignore the end result."

"Is that why they invited you to Nanjing?"

"Yes."

"Did they threaten you?"

"They did. I believe I was supposed to have been taken into custody."

"But you weren't?"

"No."

"Are you still there?"

"I'm in a car heading out of Nanjing. My friend thinks we need to lie low for a little while."

"I can't say he's wrong."

"The thing is, Brenda, we also think we need to be proactive. Staying out of sight isn't the answer. We need to blunt their aggression."

"How?"

"I want to speed up the process with Richard and Michael Dillman, and with Vanessa and her man in New York. Could you get in touch with them for me and find out where we're at, and if there's anything we can do to move things along more quickly?"

"It's early afternoon in London, and Richard was going to a rugby match during the day, but I'll see if I can get hold of him," she said. "And I'll have Vanessa call New York. It's morning there, so we have an entire day."

"One more thing," Ava said.

"Yes?" Brenda said cautiously.

"Could you ask Richard and Vanessa if they would mind if I dealt directly with the journalists?"

"Why do you think that's a good idea?"

"Events are moving faster than I anticipated and are becoming increasingly messy," Ava said. "I'm not sure that having all these people in the middle serves our purpose that well, and I don't want your firm being fingered by the Tsai family if things go badly."

"I don't care about the Tsai family," Brenda said. "You are correct, though, that communications are rather complicated right now and could benefit from being stream-lined."

"Thank you."

"It's too soon for that. I have to call Richard and Vanessa, and they'll have to call their contacts and confirm that they're willing to take this approach. I assume I can reach you on your cell?"

"You can."

"I'll get back to you when I have some answers."

The car was on the outskirts of Shanghai when an hour later Ava's phone rang. Xu was still sleeping.

"This is Brenda."

"Hi."

"Richard hasn't been able to reach Michael Dillman, but he's left messages and will make himself available when-ever Dillman calls back," Brenda said. "Vanessa did speak to Sam Curry at the *Tribune*. He's prepared to talk to you, but he's still doing fact-checking and has asked if he can get actual copies of the bank records instead of just summaries of the transactions."

"He'll want electronic copies?"

"I assume so."

"I only have paper. I'll have to convert them."

"Obviously the sooner the better."

"Where do I send them when I'm done?"

"I'll ask Vanessa to send you Sam's contact info. She's already given him your coordinates. I'm sure he'll be in touch with you at some point."

"Sooner rather than later, I hope."

"Vanessa did stress the need for speed."

"Thank her for me."

"And I'll stay on top of things with Richard."

Ava saw Xu stirring. They were in the city now, nearing the French Concession.

"Hey," she said, nudging his arm.

"Hey yourself," he said, opening his eyes.

"I've been working on the newspaper stories."

"I know, I heard some of your conversation. How much progress do you think you made?"

"Not much, but it's early and I'm still waiting for some people to call me back," she said. "In the meantime, I have to scan a raft of documents and email them to New York. Do you have what I need at the house?"

"No, all I have is a computer. Does Feng have copies of the documents?"

"Yes."

"Then we'll have him do it."

"Perfect," Ava said, turning to her phone again to find Feng's number.

"Hello," he answered.

"This is Ava. I have something I need you to do for me."

"Yes?"

"I want you to scan all the Tsai company bank records and email them to me," she said.

"Okay."

"Can you do it right away?"

"The records are at the office. I'm at home right now, so it will take about an hour."

"That's not a problem, as long as it's done tonight."

"I'll leave right way."

Ten minutes later, the car turned into an alleyway and drove past a fruit vendor. Ava knew they were almost home.

32

AUNTIE GRACE WAS STANDING IN THE DOORWAY WHEN the car pulled into the courtyard. Ava wondered how she had known they were arriving, and then realized that the fruit vendor must have alerted the house.

The housekeeper was all smiles, and if Xu's phone call had alarmed her she showed absolutely no sign of it. "Ava's room is ready and the food can be served whenever you want to eat."

"I'll eat now. I'm starving," Xu said.

"Leave your travel bag here. You can bring it in later," Auntie Grace said to Ava. "Xu, where is yours?"

"I had to leave it in Nanjing. Someone will get it for me."

"No matter. Let's go to the kitchen."

Ava had smelled a faint aroma coming from the doorway, but in the kitchen the scent was powerful, a combination of black bean sauce, garlic, and at least one other flavour she couldn't identify. She sat at the table and looked at the two woks on the stove. Next to them was a platter of scallions, sliced cucumber, small translucent pancakes, and a bowl of hoisin sauce.

"Peking duck," Ava said.

"Yes," Auntie Grace replied. She opened the oven door and took out a baking sheet covered in thin slivers of golden brown skin. She placed the sheet on the table and then turned back to the stove. "I also made *dou miao* and scallops steamed in black bean sauce with noodles. I know Xu will eat both. How about you?"

"Please."

"And what do you want to drink?"

"Tea for me."

"I'll start with that as well," Xu said.

As Auntie Grace prepared their plates, Xu glanced at Ava. "Is your phone with you?" he asked.

Ava reached behind her and took it from her Chanel bag. She put it on the table next to her plate. "There it is. I wasn't going to miss any calls."

She ate slowly, relishing the food. Xu was a fast eater, a trait he shared with Uncle. It had always seemed to Ava that the way Uncle ate was a clue to his character. He was always calm and in control on the surface, but she guessed that fires were raging underneath. She wondered if Xu hid his tensions as well as Uncle had. Or maybe she was overthinking things and both men simply liked to eat quickly.

Auntie Grace's *dou miao* was especially good. *Dou miao* — snow pea shoots fried in garlic with chicken stock — had been a particular favourite of Uncle's until he was diagnosed with stomach cancer.

"Did you ever make this for Uncle?" Ava asked.

"I did a few times, but it became too much for him."

"I've eaten it many times, but there's something different about yours," Ava said.

The old woman smiled. "Guess."

"I can't."

"I use duck fat instead of oil."

"So you made the Peking duck yourself as well?"

"Where do you think I got the fat?"

"Now you know why I like to eat at home," Xu said.

"I have to confess, Auntie Grace, that if I didn't already have a girlfriend, I might ask you to marry me."

"You don't have to do that to eat my food." Auntie Grace laughed. "All you have to do is move to Shanghai."

They were interrupted by Ava's cellphone. Both she and Xu looked at it for a second before she picked it up.

"This is Feng."

"Yes?"

"I'm at the office and I've just emailed the bank records."

"Thanks. If I need anything else, I'll call," she said.

She turned to Xu. "That was Feng —" she began, only to be interrupted by another incoming call. She didn't recognize the number but saw a familiar country code.

"This is Ava Lee. Is this Richard?"

"No, this is Michael Dillman at the *Economic Herald*."

"Mr. Dillman, thank you so much for calling," Ava said in a rush.

"Please call me Michael."

"And I'm Ava."

"I've just left Richard, and he explained your desire to communicate directly with us."

"I thought it would save us all some time and eliminate any confusion."

"I have to say I agree with you."

"Great, but there's one thing I'd like to make clear before

we continue," Ava said. "I don't want to be named or quoted in any story."

Dillman paused and then said carefully, "My understanding from Richard is that you're the direct source for all of this."

"I gathered the information and I'm prepared to verify that it is genuine, but I don't want to become part of the story. I like to think that the information speaks for itself."

"It is impressive. We are, of course, particularly taken with the possible involvement of Dennis Calhoun."

"The deal he struck to create Mega Metals and the manner in which that company operates are as corrupt as it gets."

"Apparently so."

"You say that as if there is some doubt."

"It's one thing to believe something and another thing entirely to prove it."

"You aren't satisfied with the information you have?"

"Truthfully, I am, but I have a slew of editors and lawyers looking over my shoulder. As it stands, the paper isn't prepared to run the story based on the facts we have on hand. That doesn't mean they're discounting it. They've simply told me to put the story on hold until we — and that means you, I guess — can provide them with more details."

"What details?" Ava asked, trying to hide her disappointment.

"There are two problems as we see it," Dillman said. "The first is that we have nothing that directly connects Tsai Lian or Dennis Calhoun to any of these business dealings, and in Tsai's case proof of any links is especially lacking. He appears to own nothing. He's a director of nothing. My editors would love evidence of how he uses his power and position to enrich himself and his family."

"I can provide you with complete bank records instead of just summaries."

"Will they directly implicate either of them?"

"No," Ava said reluctantly. "They will only reconfirm that the family has extensive business holdings and that Calhoun put money into Mega Metals."

"And that brings us to the second problem," Dillman said. "It's obvious that some of their dealings have to be a bit shady. But there's no hook. What we need is something or someone to directly link Calhoun and Tsai Lian. We need a detailed understanding of how the corrupt practices — assuming they are as corrupt as you claim — actually take place."

"I see."

"Do you think it's possible to uncover that kind of information?"

"I don't know."

"Ms. Lee, you sound a bit discouraged right now. I can only encourage you not to be," Dillman said. "None of us here is impatient or negative. We think the story has enormous potential and I'd like nothing more than to write it. Dennis Calhoun is a loud-mouthed buffoon and I'd love to stick a pin in him, and your Mr. Tsai seems to be the worst sort of thief. But, as I said, I have editors and lawyers I have to convince. We need to give them what they want."

"I understand."

"Are you talking to any other newspapers?"

Ava hesitated. "One in the United States."

"A serious one?"

"The *Wall Street Tribune*."

"A very serious one. Good for you, and I'm sure they don't give a rip about Calhoun."

"But we really like the U.K. connection, and your paper has a reputation that can't be easily dismissed."

"You know, I met with Richard, who's an old friend, out of courtesy, but the story intrigues me and I'd like to see it in print in our paper. You are correct about our reputation. We don't publish anything without doing everything we can to ensure it is accurate. Everyone knows that. If you want to make an impact, then the combination of the *Tribune* and us will be hard to beat."

"I don't know if the *Tribune* is going to publish either."

"Well, hang in there and keep digging. Contact me when you have something. You have my number now?"

"It's on the screen."

"That's the best one to reach me at."

Ava closed her eyes and sat back in her chair, the phone face down on the table. She took a deep breath, savouring the lingering aroma of duck. Then, quite abruptly, she sat forward.

"What's going on? That didn't sound very positive," Xu said.

"They don't think we've given them enough information to warrant publishing the story," Ava said, and then related in detail Dillman's misgivings.

Xu listened without saying a word or showing any emotion. When she finished, he said, "But you don't know the *Tribune*'s reaction?"

"They're still fact-checking, and God knows how long that will take."

"And the *Herald* didn't say no."

"Unless we give them what they want, it is a no."

"There are other British newspapers."

"But this one is the best. Anything they publish is taken seriously," she said. "I don't want to give up on it."

"Then we need to find the information they want."

"I know. I've been thinking that maybe we can find someone inside the Tsai family business who can give us what we want, or at least point us in the right direction."

"Like who?"

"I was thinking about that man Ling, the one who was with Tsai Men at Capo. Feng told me that Men treats him badly. Maybe, for a price, he'd be willing to help."

"He certainly knows where the bodies are buried. He may not make decisions but he attends a lot of meetings, sees a lot of correspondence, and certainly manages the inflow of money."

"So he knows things?"

"He certainly does."

"That's ideal, assuming of course that Feng wasn't exaggerating his treatment by the family."

"Feng doesn't exaggerate, and I've seen Men humiliate Ling in public more than once."

"Well?"

"It is risky. He could run directly to Men."

"Do we have any other options?"

Xu pursed his lips and gently rolled his shoulders. "I need a smoke," he said, and stood. "I'll be back in a few minutes."

His sudden departure caught Ava off guard. She was thinking about following him outside when Auntie Grace reappeared.

"Have you had enough to eat?" she asked.

"Yes, and it was wonderful."

"Would you like something to drink?"

Ava was about to say no and then stopped. "I'd like a glass of Xu's very expensive Scotch."

"I'll bring the bottle and two glasses," Auntie Grace said.

Xu was gone longer than Ava thought one smoke should take, and she had sipped her way through half a glass of Scotch by the time he re-entered the kitchen.

He smiled as he sat down and poured himself a stiff shot. "I was thinking about Ling," he said.

"Yes?"

"We'll make an approach."

"When? How?"

"Feng is calling him at home right now. It isn't unusual for the two of them to meet. Feng will request that they meet early tomorrow morning somewhere neutral, and that isn't unusual either. I'm going to send Suen with him. He won't have anything to say but his presence will be enough to discourage Ling from acting rashly if he decides not to co-operate."

"What are we offering him?"

"Money — lots and lots of money — and a promise that we'll cover his back, keep our agreement secret, and act as a lifeboat for him if anything happens to the Tsai family."

"I'd like to be there."

"I thought about that, but it's too soon. We don't want to rattle Ling. He's comfortable with Feng. Let the two of them try to reach an agreement," Xu said.

33

SHE DREAMT THAT SHE WAS WITH MAY LING, AMANDA,
and Chi-Tze. They were by the sea, walking along a boardwalk near dusk. Ava realized they were back in Borneo, in
Kota Kinabalu.

The boardwalk was nearly deserted but for a few women
who were leaning over the guardrail and looking out at the
beach. The sun was setting on their right and Ava held up
a hand to shield her eyes from its glare. They were chatting and laughing when Ava saw a group of men walking
towards them. They edged towards the railing to give them
room to pass. The men moved in the same direction. Ava
began to feel nervous but stayed on course, her eyes fixed
straight ahead.

The men barged into May, knocking her into Amanda.
They stopped and moved so they circled the women.

"Watch where you're going, you fucking bitches," one said.

There were six of them, all with thick arms and broad
chests.

Amanda reached out to steady May. As she did, one of
the men pushed her so hard she fell. Amanda began to cry,

and then Chi-Tze took several steps back until she was pressed against the railing.

"I think you should leave these ladies alone," a man's calm voice said.

The men turned and Ava saw Uncle standing behind them. He was wearing his black suit and white shirt buttoned to the collar. He had a lit cigarette burning between his fingers.

"Fuck off, old man," one of them said.

"I've chewed up more men like you than I can count," Uncle said.

Two men moved towards him. Ava watched in horror as the larger of the two threw Uncle to the ground. She took a tentative step forward, then she saw both men standing over him with their feet poised to kick. She leapt at them.

Her attack was mindless frenzy. She had no sense of where she was, of who they were, of how many there were. She just wanted to destroy them. Her phoenix-eye fist drilled into eardrums, noses, throats. Her long, sharp nails gouged eyeballs. And when the men hit the ground, the pointed toe of her crocodile-leather high heels cut into their groins. There was blood everywhere, and the men were crying and moaning and begging her to stop. She was poised to finish them off when Uncle stepped in front of her.

"No more, my girl," he said. "You've done enough."

She looked down at the carpet of bodies. "I want to kill them."

"I know, but we're better than that."

Ava woke with a start. Her mouth was dry but there was sweat on her upper lip and brow. She heard water running and thought of the sea she'd just left. She was in a small room, big enough for a double bed, a chair, and a dresser. Through the lead-paned window she could see the first signs of morning. She looked at the bedside clock and saw that it was just past seven thirty.

I'm in Xu's house in the French Concession. It was only a dream, she thought. *But what kind of dream was that?* She couldn't ever remember bak mei entering her nighttime wanderings in such a violent way. The ancient martial art — which she'd learned as a teenager on a one-to-one basis with Master Tang — wasn't particularly acrobatic and was never pretty. It was designed to inflict the maximum amount of pain and damage by concentrating the entire body's power into a small focused point such as the knuckle of the middle finger. She had used the art often, but always in self-defence, with the intention of incapacitating the enemy. This dream had been different.

Ava slid from the bed and kneeled by its side. She placed her hands in front of her face and began to pray. She prayed to Saint Jude, the patron saint of lost causes. He was her last attachment to the Catholic Church, a church she had turned her back on when, in her mind, it had turned its back on her with its position on homosexuality. Still, she found comfort in prayer, and Saint Jude had been a constant and faithful companion over the years.

She stood and realized she was in her underwear and a T-shirt. She reached into her bag, took out her Adidas training pants, slipped them on, and left the room.

Auntie Grace was already up, standing over the stove. "Good morning, Ava. I'm making congee. Do you want some?"

"I'm still full from last night."

"Tea or coffee?"

"Coffee, please."

"I only have instant."

"Perfect," Ava said. She turned her head towards the bathroom as she heard the taps being turned off. "Is that Xu?"

Auntie Grace filled a cup with water from the Thermos and put it on the table. "He's been up for a couple of hours."

"Is that normal?"

"He's a morning person, but this was unusually early. He's been on the phone with Feng."

"I'm pleased to hear that," Ava said, and sipped her coffee.

"I thought you might be. I heard the two of you talking last night."

"And is Feng in the meeting we wanted him to have?"

"I think so."

"What a nice way to start my day."

"Ava, you are a very different kind of young woman."

"Thank you, I think."

"I wasn't being critical. If anything, I'm jealous. I always wanted to be in control of my own life."

"Auntie Grace," Ava said with a laugh, "do you know how silly that sounds? Who has more control than you?"

"Only within these walls."

"What else do you care about?"

"Truthfully, not much else," the housekeeper said, pursing her lips. "If I were younger, it might be different."

"Auntie, we can't pick our time and place. We can only do the best we can with what we've been given."

"Aren't you philosophical this morning," Xu said from the doorway.

Ava turned. Xu was dressed in a white shirt and black

slacks, his wet hair glistening in the overhead lights.

"I had a bad dream," Ava said. "I have them more often than I'd like, but they do make me think."

Xu walked to the kitchen table with his phone in his hand, stopped, leaned over, and kissed Ava on the forehead. "Good morning, *mei mei.*"

"Good morning. Auntie Grace just told me that you've been up for hours."

"Feng is with Ling. We've been going back and forth."

Xu sat down. Almost instantly the housekeeper had a cup of tea and a bowl of congee in front of him. He took a sip of tea, then delicately put the tip of the spoon into the rice porridge and raised it to his lips. "This is wonderful," he said.

"Why wouldn't it be?" Auntie Grace said.

He nodded, and smiled at Ava. "Ling is being co-operative."

"Was it difficult?"

"Ask Feng yourself. He's on my phone," Xu said, handing it to her.

"I heard your question," Feng said. "Ling leapt at the chance to stick it to the family. It cost us some money, but not as much as I expected."

"That's great."

"We've been talking since six thirty. Ling has gone over our summaries of payments and cash movement and says they're accurate. He confirmed that the fix was in on that Kitchen Giant purchase, and said that the Jiangsu Insurance deal was totally dependent on the province sending their business to the new company."

"So the American insurance company knew what was going on?"

"They insisted on what went on."

"Can he get us anything that would prove it?"

"He says he was copied on some emails that are pretty damning."

"Did you ask to see them?"

"We'll have them as soon as he gets to his office."

"Do the emails implicate the Governor?"

"We won't know until we see them, but I have to say that Ling has made no mention of him, and even when I press, he makes it clear that his dealings were strictly with Men and the rest of the family. Tsai Lian seems to have stayed well above the clouds."

"That is still terrific work, Feng," Ava said. "Now, how about Mega Metals?"

"He says he can't help very much. He had no involvement."

"Feng, that's in some ways the most important deal to understand."

"Sorry."

"He knows absolutely nothing?"

"He can confirm the amount of money they're making because he's the one who goes in with Lau Ai to check the books, but he claims he knows nothing about the way the business actually operates. He says an English-Chinese guy, Vincent Yin, runs things."

"He's the one that Lau mentioned to me," Ava said. "How about the way the deal was originally put together?"

"He says he was involved only in the early stages."

"So who finalized things?"

"He thinks it was the Governor himself, with the Englishman."

"He thinks?"

"That's what he's heard. He can't confirm it."

"And what Englishman is he referring to? Yin?"

"No, Calhoun."

"He knows this or he thinks this as well?"

"Well, he said that one night he was with Men and his wife and they started to talk about the money that Mega Metals was making. They were happy about it, of course, but Men couldn't help mentioning that the Englishman, Calhoun, had been so difficult during the negotiations that it was a wonder the deal had ever gotten done."

"Did Men pass along any other details?"

"No."

"Shit."

"Ling is still here. I can ask him again."

"No, don't bother."

"Is there anything else you want besides the insurance emails?"

"No. Just tell him to keep his eyes and ears open and to report to you if he hears anything unusual concerning me."

"He already told me that they're all bent out of shape about you."

"We know."

"And that they sent two off-duty military men to pick you up."

"I was there."

"Lau Ai was impressed with the way you handled them."

"A lot of good that does me."

Feng hesitated. "Ava, I'm sorry about Mega Metals."

"It isn't your fault," Ava said. "But listen, what you can do is ask Ling where I can find this Vincent Yin. And ask him what kind of man he is."

"Do you want to wait a minute? He's next door."

"Sure."

Xu was looking at her from across the table. "It doesn't sound like we're making as much headway as you wanted with Mega Metals."

"We're not done yet."

"Ling can't help?"

"Not much, but there's an English-Chinese guy named Vincent Yin who might be able to."

"Are you sure about that?"

"No, but he's all we've got right now."

"Ava," Feng said.

"Yes, I'm here."

"Mega Metals' office is in the southern outskirts of Nanjing. I'll text you the address and phone number."

"Thanks."

"And Ling says that Yin is in his mid to late thirties and is sort of a nonentity. He's listed as the legal representative of Mega Metals, but he acts more like a bookkeeper."

"But he does run the business?"

"He does in name, but he doesn't make any real decisions. The company was set up to operate in a very structured way. He works strictly within a system."

"There's nothing I like more than a man who does what he is told," Ava said.

34

AVA SAT QUIETLY AT THE KITCHEN TABLE MULLING over everything she'd just learned. Xu took back his phone, checked his messages, and took a sip of tea.

"I have to make a few calls," he said. "I'll be back shortly."

"No problem."

When he left, Ava picked up her own cell and punched in May Ling's number.

"How is it going?" May said.

"Have you heard something?" Ava replied, sensing concern in her friend's voice.

"Nothing specific, but I was talking to Brenda about an hour ago and when I asked how your project was coming along, she was evasive. That's not like her, so I figured something had happened."

"Well, things are heating up," Ava said. "The Tsai family is onto me. Last night they tried to have me picked up by some paramilitary men."

"They obviously didn't succeed."

"The fact that they tried was alarming enough."

"What are you going to do?"

"Go after them."

"How?"

"I'm still working on it but I'm making some progress."

"Is there anything I can do to help?"

"Yes, there are a few things," Ava said. "First, I don't have the time or the will to worry about Lane Crawford and PÖ. Could you please take control with Amanda? You have my complete trust. Do whatever you think is right."

"Okay, that's easy enough."

"Next, could you start thinking about friends and contacts you have in China who might have some influence in Beijing?"

"Why?"

"We might need to create a firestorm around the Tsai family, and we may have some information we want you to feed to your people. The information will be accurate, but it could be controversial."

"The more controversial the better," May said with a laugh.

"What's so funny?"

"Most of them like to gossip."

"That's good to hear."

May drew a deep breath. "Seriously, though, you need to be careful. I know I keep saying it, but that doesn't make it any less true."

"I should have listened more closely to you before," Ava said.

"Hey, you'll find a way out of this. You always do. And this time, you're not so alone. You've got quite a few of us standing behind you."

"Thanks."

"Stay in touch."

"Count on it," Ava said.

She checked the time and figured that the Mega Metals head office had to be open by now.

"Mega Metals," a receptionist answered.

"Good morning. My name is Jennie Kwong and I'm calling to speak to Vincent Yin."

"He's not in the office at present."

"Are you expecting him shortly?"

"No, he's out of the office on business matters."

"Will he be checking in for messages?"

"Yes."

"Then could you tell him that Jennie Kwong called? I represent a Hong Kong–based construction consortium that will be starting some projects in Jiangsu, and I'm told he's the man to speak to."

"I could connect you with our vice-president of sales. He's in the office today."

"Actually, I was told to speak directly to Mr. Yin. The senior partner in our firm is an old colleague of Mr. Dennis Calhoun. Mr. Calhoun was quite insistent that Mr. Yin be our point of contact."

"I see. Well, I will pass that message along to Mr. Yin."

"Please tell him I'm in the vicinity of Nanjing and that I'm hoping we can set up a meeting."

"I'll pass that information along as well."

Xu returned to the kitchen and sat at the table. "I have to head out in a while. I have some meetings scheduled that I shouldn't postpone, although God knows I'd like to," he said.

"Before you go, could you do something for me?"

"What?"

"I'm trying to get together with Vincent Yin from Mega Metals today. I've put in a call to him, and if I'm lucky he'll agree to see me. What I need is a meeting space that is businesslike but secure at the same time."

"You could use the boardroom at the Xin Fang Fa Co-operative."

"That's the business you used to funnel money to the Three Sisters."

"Yes. The office is about half an hour from here towards Nanjing. It isn't fancy, but it is a real business environment."

"Could you make an arrangement with the co-op for me to have the boardroom for at least a few hours, assuming I get Yin to agree to meet?"

"Sure, I'll call them before I leave."

"And could you lend Suen to me? I don't want Yin to feel threatened in any way, but in case he reacts badly or decides to bolt, I want to have some backup."

"I can do that," Xu said. "Anything else?"

"I may need a videographer."

"I'll talk to the people at the co-operative about that," he said, a slight smile crossing his face. "I'll tell them to have one on standby."

"Great. Now I need to get ready just in case he calls back and is willing to meet."

"I'm here for another half-hour or so. I'll contact Suen and the co-operative before I leave."

Ava went to the bathroom to shower, carrying her phone with her. She turned up the volume and placed the cell on top of the toilet, next to the shower stall. She washed quickly, fearful the phone would ring. When it did, she was already leaving the bathroom with a towel wrapped around her.

"Hello," she said.

"Jennie Kwong?"

"Yes."

"This is Vincent Yin from Mega Metals. I understand you want to talk to me."

She walked into her bedroom and sat on the bed. "I'd like to meet. Today actually, if that's possible."

"This is very short notice."

"I apologize for that. I didn't expect to be in Shanghai today, but my plans changed at the last minute and here I am," Ava said. "I realize my timing could be inconvenient, but I thought I'd take the chance that you might be available. My boss was quite insistent that I should speak to you. He was talking to Mr. Calhoun — who is an old friend of his — about our projects, and Mr. Calhoun said your company could be of real assistance to us. He also said you were the man we had to deal with. He seems to really admire everything you've done with the business."

"You're with a construction company?"

"A consortium of companies that, among other things, do construction," Ava said. "We are considering some large projects in this region and we would be grateful for the opportunity to go over them with you. My boss said you might be able to give us some strategic advice, as well as, of course, be one of our major suppliers."

"You're in Shanghai?"

"Yes, but we have offices in Qinjin, on Harvest Street, number 338. Would meeting there work for you?"

"It would, actually — I'm only twenty minutes from Qinjin."

Ava checked the time. "I can't get there until about noon."

"One is better for me."

"Then one it is. Just ask for me when you get there. We can use our boardroom."

"Do you need me to bring any information about our company?"

"No, just bring yourself."

"I'm looking forward to it," he said.

Ava opened the bedroom door and stuck her head out. "Xu, I'm meeting Vincent Yin at one," she called.

"Okay, I'll have Suen ready with the car at twelve. That should get you there in lots of time. I've already spoken to the co-op and they're expecting you."

"Fantastic."

"Now I have to get going. I won't be back until late today and I may be hard to reach."

"Hopefully I won't need to talk to you."

Ava closed the door and stepped back into the room, filled with a sense of anticipation. She had her man. She would have his undivided attention. It was an opportunity she had to exploit. Standing in the shower, she had already begun to create a question-and-answer scenario, one that would lead Vincent Yin to the inescapable conclusion that doing what Ava wanted was the only sensible option he had.

From her travel bag she took out clean underwear, a white shirt with a modified Italian collar and French cuffs, and a clean pair of black linen slacks. She slipped on the underwear and shirt, and to secure the cuffs she fastened the blue enamel links she had bought at Shanghai Tang in Hong Kong. She pulled back her hair and clasped it with her ivory chignon pin. She hung her crucifix around her neck and then slipped on her Cartier Tank Française watch. She hoped it wouldn't be too much. Makeup was out. She wanted to look as plain and sincere as possible.

Xu was still sitting in the living room when Ava left her room. He had put on a black jacket and black tie. He sat in a chair, leaning forward, his eyes focused on the front door. An unlit cigarette dangled in his right hand. Ava blinked. For a moment she thought she was looking at Uncle. The profiles were almost identical, and the way Xu was positioned was as familiar to her as Uncle's voice.

He heard her and turned and smiled. "I thought I'd wait for a few extra minutes. Suen just phoned. He said the co-op has a videographer on standby."

35

TWO HOURS LATER, AVA WALKED INTO THE COURT- yard to find a black BMW X6 with a driver Ava had never seen behind the wheel. Suen leaned against the back door. When he saw Ava, he stood up and opened it for her. She climbed in. He sat next to the driver.

"Traffic is good," Suen said. "We should be there by quarter to one at the latest."

Ava took out her notebook and began to review the notes she'd been making. She lost all sense of time and direction as the BMW worked its way through the city, and was surprised when it came to a stop and Suen said, "We're here."

She looked out the window at an unmarked four-storey brown brick building. She started to open the door, but before she could, Suen opened it for her. As she climbed out of the car, a man and a woman rushed out of the building and headed for Suen. He held out his hand and said something that Ava couldn't quite hear, but which generated huge smiles.

"We can go inside," Suen said to Ava. "The boardroom is available to us now, and we have it for as long as you need."

The couple led Suen and Ava into the building. It was as plain inside as out — brown tile floors, beige walls, and a white tile ceiling. They walked past an unstaffed reception desk and down a corridor lined with closed doors. At the end of the hall, the man opened a set of double doors. The boardroom was large and had four long tables forming a square and twenty plastic chairs. The walls were covered with whiteboards.

"We need everything erased from the boards," Ava said. "He doesn't need to know anything about the co-op's business. Besides, I think it could be visually distracting."

"Xing, will you look after that please," Suen said to the man who had led them into the boardroom.

"Sure," he replied and went immediately to work on the boards.

"Is this room okay?" Suen asked.

"It'll do fine."

"Most of the offices on this floor are empty, so you don't have to worry about being overheard."

"Are you going to stay when I talk to him?"

"Do you need me to?"

"I think I'd rather have you sitting just outside."

"No problem. What else will you need?"

"Some water, and eventually I hope I'll need that videographer. How close is he?"

"Fifteen minutes, and he's been told to be on standby."

Suen's phone rang. He answered it, nodded, and said to Ava, "Your man is here."

"He's a bit early. That's good," Ava said. "Could you bring him here?"

"Sure."

"I'll get organized," she said, taking her notebook from her bag.

"How much time do you think you'll need with this guy?"

"I have no idea. It depends on how smart he is."

"Smart or scared?"

"A bit of both isn't bad, but I prefer smart. It always goes faster when the other party really understands what kind of situation they're in and how limited their options are."

36

SHE HEARD THEM FIRST, FOOTSTEPS ON TILE. THEN THE door opened and Suen filled its frame. Looking slightly uncomfortable in the big man's wake was a man who looked to be in his mid-thirties, thin, about five foot nine, his hair stylishly shaved along both sides and spiked on top. He wore a smart slim-cut grey tailored suit and a blue and gold Hermès tie.

"What a pleasure to meet you," Ava said, extending her hand. "I meant to ask you before what language you prefer to speak — English or Chinese?" she asked him in Chinese, and as he stumbled over an answer she added in English, "I'm a Hong Konger and went only to English schools there."

"Then English will be fine," he said. "It will be nice for a change."

"Your accent is quite distinctive."

"I was raised and educated in Newcastle. I have a bit of a Geordie accent, although it isn't as broad as most you'll hear."

"Have a seat. Can I offer you some water or another beverage?"

"No, I'm fine," he said.

"How did you get here? Do you have a car and driver?"

"No, I came by taxi."

"Well, thank you for taking the time to see me," Ava said, opening her notebook.

"What company did you say you were with?" Yin asked.

"I didn't say."

"And which one is it?"

"Well, this is where things start to become a little complicated, Mr. Yin."

"Call me Vincent, and I don't understand what you mean by 'complicated.'"

"For starters, there isn't any company."

"What?"

"I can explain."

"How about Mr. Calhoun's friend?"

"I'm sure Mr. Calhoun has many. I just don't know or work for one of them."

"This is absurd," Yin said, starting to rise.

"Don't do that," Ava said. "The large man who brought you here is sitting outside. He won't let you leave until we've finished talking. So please sit down."

He flinched, and she saw a trace of fear in his eyes.

"You have to tell me what this is about," he said, now standing.

"In the very broadest sense, it is about the rest of your life," she said.

"That's crazy."

"No, it really isn't," Ava said. "Because by the time we've finished talking, you're going to have to make some important and difficult decisions that will affect the rest of your life. I know what I want you to do, and I know what I think is best for you to do, but ultimately we're going to find out how practical and sensible you are."

"I have no idea what you're talking about."

"Mega Metals."

"What about it?"

"It's a business created out of corruption and run in a corrupt manner."

He looked towards the doorway, then back at Ava.

"Who are you?" he asked as he slid back into the chair. "What do you want? Is this some feeble attempt at blackmail?"

"A week from now, I doubt that Mega Metals will still exist," Ava said. "Dennis Calhoun will be disgraced, and instead of bragging about his business acumen he's going to be fighting to stay out of jail. The Tsai family will be looking over its shoulder, wondering what the powers in Beijing will do to them. It's going to be complete chaos."

Yin shook his head. Ava noticed he was having trouble looking her in the eye.

"The main question you have to ask yourself is whether you want to go down with them."

"How can you possibly make those kinds of assertions?" he said.

"I have the facts to support them. It's going to go under, you can count on that. Calhoun and Tsai have only one chance to avoid getting swamped themselves," Ava said, and then leaned towards Yin. "And that's if they pin the blame entirely on you."

"I'm an employee."

"You're managing the business. If Tsai and Calhoun say they knew nothing about the deals and it was all your doing, then who are the authorities in the U.K. and China going to believe?"

"They wouldn't do that."

"Don't be so naive," Ava said. "They would do it in a heartbeat and without a second thought. They'd throw you to the wolves, and the Chinese wolves have shown a tendency to kill whoever they sink their teeth into."

"I'm a British citizen."

"You were born in China and you live and work in China. The Chinese government won't care what passport you carry or what citizenship you claim. They'll come and get you, and once they have you, they won't let you go until you're on your knees and they're putting a bullet in the back of your head."

Yin shook his head. Ava could see panic and confusion on his face.

"You know Mr. Calhoun quite well, I imagine, and you've seen how the Tsai family operates. You know the kind of power they have," Ava said. "Neither Calhoun nor the Tsais are what you would call warm and considerate. Can you imagine them not doing whatever is necessary to protect themselves and their reputations?"

"Still . . ."

"Look, you have a chance to get out of this situation intact, but you need to realize that I'm your only lifeline."

"In what way?"

"I'll come to that," Ava said. "But before I do, let's you and I just talk. I want to verify and expand on some facts. And, if you don't mind, I'd like to start at the beginning."

"I'm not sure I have any interest in doing that."

"Then you can try to run past the big man outside, but I

have to warn you that he's surprisingly fast."

"And if I agree?"

"When we're finished and if you want to leave, I promise you that we won't prevent it. And when we're finished, if you decide you want our help, you'll have it."

He took a deep breath. "Are you with the government?"

"No, but we've opened up lines of communication with more than one government and they have an interest in our efforts. It's safe to assume they will become directly involved sooner rather than later, and charges will be brought against Mr. Calhoun in the U.K. God knows what the Chinese government will choose to do with the Tsai family, and with you — if you're still here."

"Then who are you with?"

"Does that matter?"

"Someone trying to settle a score with Mr. Calhoun?"

"You could say that."

"Then why do I have to get dragged into it?"

"Vincent, you're running a company that was founded on the basis of a corrupt agreement, an agreement you were a party to. The agreement is going to be exposed and all hell is going to break loose. Now, I repeat, do you want to co-operate with me and get out of here in once piece with your wealth intact, or do you want to end up in a British jail, a Chinese jail, or a Chinese grave?"

"How do you expect me to respond to a question like that?"

"Does that mean you're going to co-operate?"

Yin hesitated and looked towards the door, then back at Ava. "I'll tell you what I can," he said. "But I may not know as much as you think I do."

"I can accept that, and I'm not going to be unreasonable.

So, let's start with an easy question: do you run a company called Mega Metals?"

"You know I do."

"What's your title?"

"Managing director."

"Are you also the legal representative?"

"Yes."

"Is your boss Dennis Calhoun?"

"My immediate boss is Rory Taggert, the CEO in the U.K. Mr. Calhoun is the company chairman."

"And you have a partner named Lau Ai?"

He hesitated.

"Let me rephrase that," Ava said. "The majority owner of your business is a company called Shell Investments. Shell is owned by the Tsai family, and they're using Lau Ai as the person of record."

"You could put it that way." He licked his lips. There was white residue in the corners of his mouth.

"There's water on the table if you want some," she said.

He reached for a glass and filled it.

"How did you know about Lau's role?" Yin asked.

"I'm asking, not answering questions. So just answer, please, and please be direct," Ava said. "Now, when was Mega Metals established?"

He hesitated, his eyes flitting around the room. Ava knew he was looking for a way out.

"Vincent, you're making this much more difficult than it needs to be."

"Close to five years ago," Yin said.

"Have you been with the company since the outset?"

"Yes," he said.

"Where were you before that?"

"Calhoun Metals."

"In the U.K?"

"Yes, I worked in the Newcastle office. I joined them right out of Northumbria University."

"Doing what?"

"Sales and marketing."

"You obviously did well."

"I did okay."

"Did you work for Dennis Calhoun?"

"Not at first, but it was his business, and it wasn't so big then that he didn't know who most of us were."

"Your importance must have increased when he decided to expand into Asia."

He nodded. "There wasn't anyone else in the office who spoke Mandarin."

"Were you born in China?"

"Beijing. My parents emigrated when I was eight."

"So you didn't know anyone in Nanjing?"

"No one."

"Then how did Mr. Calhoun hook up with the Tsai family?"

"He had a friend in Manchester who was doing business with them. He recommended that Mr. Calhoun contact them to see if he could work out his own arrangement. At the time, Mr. Calhoun was quite discouraged about our prospects in Asia. He'd set up businesses in Singapore and Kuala Lumpur, but neither of them did very well. This friend told him that the Tsais made doing business very easy."

"This friend was a Westerner?"

"Yes."

"What kind of deal did he have?"

"He had a factory that was making cheap housewares. He said he paid a monthly fee to make sure he had no problems getting raw materials, managing his labour force, or shipping goods out of the province."

"How do you know that?"

"Mr. Calhoun told me."

"When?"

"Later, after we had started our discussions with Tsai Men."

"What was the name of the friend's company?"

"I think it was called Phillips Trading."

Ava flipped back to the front of her notebook and her first list of people paying the Tsais. Phillips Trading was contributing $5,000 a month.

"How did Calhoun Metals initially contact the Tsais?"

"Mr. Calhoun's friend told Tsai Men about our company and then arranged a conference call."

"Did you take part in it?"

"I took part in all of them, and in all of the meetings that followed."

"Obviously Mr. Calhoun speaks no Mandarin."

"And I don't think that Tsai Men speaks English, or at least I never heard him speak it."

"So you interpreted?"

"For Mr. Calhoun. Tsai Men had his own person."

"What was his name?"

"Wang."

"Not Ling?"

"Ling was only there for the first few meetings and then he was replaced."

"Why?"

"I don't know."

"How many meetings were there in total?"

"A lot. They went on for several months. I think we made four trips to Nanjing."

"It sounds like things were complicated."

"The basic structure of the deal was in place very quickly, but sorting out the numbers was the hard part."

"By 'basic structure' you mean that it would be a fifty-one, forty-nine split in the Tsai family's favour? Calhoun Metals would front all the cash and inventory, and the Tsai family would make sure that business came to the new company?"

"How do you know that?"

"Never mind. Is what I described accurate?"

Yin squirmed in his chair.

"Vincent, I asked you a question and I want an answer."

"Yes."

"So what was making people uncomfortable about the deal?"

"It wasn't so much people as it was Mr. Calhoun."

"What was bothering him?"

"Tsai Men wanted Mr. Calhoun to commit to a far larger inventory than he thought prudent, and Mr. Calhoun was looking for guarantees that the business would operate the way Tsai Men promised. Truthfully, there was quite a bit of mistrust from our side at the beginning."

"What was Calhoun's reluctance about the inventory?"

"He was being asked to put two hundred million dollars in cash and goods into a company that we owned only forty-nine percent of. He was afraid that two months down the road the majority owner would scrap the business and scoop the inventory."

"That's a legitimate concern. What prompted him to take the plunge?"

"He met the Governor."

Ava fought back a smile. "And were you there at the meeting?"

"Yes."

"Who else?"

"Tsai Men and his wife."

"What did they discuss?"

"The business."

"Specifically."

"Well, Men outlined the deal to the Governor and then explained that Mr. Calhoun was looking for assurances that the inventory would be turned over quickly and that the profit margins would be healthy."

"How did Tsai Lian respond?"

"He asked Mr. Calhoun if he was financially stable enough to provide a five-hundred-million-dollar inventory if it was required."

"And Calhoun said?"

"He could provide an inventory of any size as long as it was turning and the margins were there."

"And the Governor was satisfied with that?"

"He seemed to be, because he immediately told Mr. Calhoun that he would never have to worry about the inventory turning."

Ava looked down at her notebook and took some small breaths. "Did he give any reasons why Mr. Calhoun should believe him?"

"He said that any company that didn't commit to buying from Mega Metals wouldn't get a dollar of government business and would find it difficult to get a building permit for any private project. He emphasized how much construction the government undertook. He finished by saying that any company that reneged on a commitment to Mega Metals would get their permit revoked."

"Are those the words that came directly out of Tsai Lian's mouth?"

"As best as I can remember."

"This is important, Vincent, so think back. Was it the Governor himself who told Mr. Calhoun he would ensure that anyone who didn't buy from Mega Metals would have a difficult time getting building permits?"

"It was."

"Did you put those guarantees on paper? Did you write them into the agreement?"

"Of course not. It was a handshake deal as far as those details were concerned. What was funny was that the Governor commented on that. He said to Mr. Calhoun that this was the way Chinese preferred to do business — friend to friend."

"*Guanxi*?"

"Exactly."

"How about protecting the profit margins? Did the Governor comment on that?"

"All he said was that it was up to us to make sure the company was profitable, but given that the customers had to buy from us, he couldn't foresee that ever being a problem."

"That made your sales and marketing job kind of easy, didn't it."

He smiled tentatively. "There was never any problem with turning inventory or making a profit, if that's what you mean. My job is mainly inventory control and margin management."

"So the company has operated along the lines that Tsai Lian established from the start?"

"Yes."

"And you've been running it since day one?"

"It was Mr. Calhoun's idea that I do it. He wanted someone who knew our end of the business and someone he felt he could trust. It was a huge advantage that I could speak both languages."

"What does Lau Ai do?"

"She comes to the office every quarter with an accountant — actually that Ling you mentioned — to check the books. That's about it."

"Vincent, talk to me a bit about the money side of the business."

"What exactly do you want to know?"

"What are your sales?"

"The company has grown every year since we started, and this year we were on schedule to do close to four billion dollars."

"That's huge. What about your profit margins?"

"Twenty percent, on average."

"And what do you net?"

"Ten percent."

"So about four hundred million dollars in profit this year, split almost evenly between the partners."

"Yeah, that's about right."

"If you didn't have the deal with the Tsais, where would those numbers be?"

"Mr. Calhoun was operating at around seven to ten percent gross profit margin in Singapore and Malaysia and was lucky when he broke even. I imagine it would have been much the same here without the arrangement with the Tsais."

"So basically the Governor is now putting four hundred million a year into your company coffers."

"I wouldn't put it that way," Yin said.

Ava shrugged. "Where does the profit go? Do you put some of it back into inventory? Have you invested in other businesses?"

"Obviously we've had to keep expanding our inventory, and there's an allocation for that. Some money goes back to the U.K. parent company and the balance goes into an account in Cyprus."

"Whose account?"

"I don't know. It's just a number."

"Is it logical to think it's Mr. Calhoun's?"

"I guess."

"How about the Tsai family profits?"

"Lau Ai looks after those."

"What do you mean?"

"She issues her own instructions to our bank. It's her business. I don't interfere."

Ava pushed her chair back from the table. Yin recoiled and she saw he was startled.

"I have to make a trip to the ladies' room," she said. "When I get back, I'm going to ask you many of the same questions again, just to make sure you haven't forgotten anything. But I have to tell you that so far I think it's gone very well."

"Can I leave when we're done?"

"Not quite so fast. I'll explain that part later," Ava said. "Oh, and give me your cellphone. I'll hold on to it until I come back."

37

SUEN WAS SITTING IN A CHAIR JUST OUTSIDE THE boardroom. He looked tired and bored.

"It's going very well," Ava said. "I need to make some phone calls, and I'd appreciate it if you could contact your videographer and tell him to come here."

"Yin stays in the room alone?"

"Yes. I have his phone, so there isn't much he can do. Check in on him once in a while just to keep him on edge. I'll be back soon. And look, I know you had a long night. If you want to get a replacement, I don't mind."

"I'll manage," he said.

The building's lobby was empty and the front desk was still unoccupied. Ava sat down and took out her phone. She checked the time and saw it was just past seven a.m. in the U.K. She hoped that Michael Dillman was an early riser.

"Dillman," he said after two rings, his voice sharp and clear.

"This is Ava Lee."

"Ms. Lee, it is early."

"Well, I have what you want and I was eager to tell you."

"I beg your pardon?"

"You told me last night that you didn't have anything that directly connected Dennis Calhoun to Governor Tsai, and that you didn't have anything that detailed how Mega Metals actually operates. Well, I've found both of those things."

"How is that possible? When we spoke last night, my understanding was that you were dead-ended. What could you possibly have found so quickly?"

"I found Vincent Yin."

"The name sounds vaguely familiar."

"He's the managing director of Mega Metals in Nanjing. He's a Brit, a graduate of Northumbria University, and was an employee of Calhoun in Newcastle before being appointed to this position."

"Oh yes, I remember seeing his name on one of your charts."

"I have just finished having an initial discussion with Mr. Yin."

"When?"

"Five minutes ago."

"By phone?"

"In person."

"Where?"

"Here in Shanghai."

"What's he doing in Shanghai?"

"He came here to meet with me."

"Why?"

"I invited him."

"I see, but then why would he tell you these things?"

"I was persuasive."

Dillman paused, and Ava waited for him to ask the question she wasn't going to answer. Instead he said, "What did he tell you?"

"He admitted that Calhoun put up all the money and gave the family fifty-one percent of the business in exchange for the family strong-arming construction companies into buying from Mega Metals. I think that fits the definition of 'bribe' under the U.K. Bribery Act."

"Yes, it does, and if that is correct then the Tsais are equally guilty of accepting bribes."

"And of coercion, although I'm not sure how that would play out under Chinese law."

"You said you've found a link between Calhoun and the Governor. So far, I haven't heard anything about that. All we have — on paper — is proof of a relationship between Mr. Yin and Tsai Men's wife."

"The deal was negotiated between Dennis Calhoun and Tsai Men, and then closed by Tsai Lian himself in a meeting with Calhoun and Men."

"Yin told you this?"

"Yes."

"How does he know?"

"He was at every meeting between Calhoun and Men, and he was at the meeting where the Governor committed to the deal and promised to uphold the Tsais' end of it," Ava said.

"Let's back up for a second," Dillman said. "You've made some assumptions about how the family persuades companies to buy from Mega Metals. How does Yin say pressure would be applied?"

"If a company didn't agree to buy from Mega, it wouldn't

get any government business and it would find getting building permits of any kind very difficult."

"Those were his exact words?"

"Yes."

"And he claims he heard those same words come from the mouth of Tsai Lian?"

"Yes."

"And you believe him?"

"He has absolutely no reason to lie. Besides, he is confirming much of what we guessed."

"That is true," Dillman said slowly. "Ava, can I ask you why Yin was so willing to share this information with you?"

"The usual reason people do things like this: a combination of self-preservation and self-interest."

"Was he coerced in any way?"

"I assure you he is in wonderful health — in mind and body — and I'm confident that I can persuade him to put everything he's told me in writing, with names, places, and dates. I've also made an arrangement to videotape him."

"Could we interview him?"

"I'm not so sure that's a good idea."

"It would add tremendous credibility and make it an easier sell to my editor and the lawyers."

Ava thought of the man she'd just left in the boardroom. How much pressure could he sustain? What assurances would he need? What would make him feel safe? What did she have that she could offer besides his freedom and, if the Chinese authorities were in a nasty mood, his life? If he truly believed what she'd said about the Chinese police, then his life was a strong starting point, she thought.

"I'm not going to say no," she finally said. "But I'd like

to videotape him first. I'll send you a copy of the video as soon as it's done. Review it and let me know if you think an interview is necessary."

"How soon can I expect to see the video?"

"In a couple of hours."

"Can I brief my editor in the interim?"

"Of course."

"And tell her that an interview is a possibility?"

"Yes."

"Will you call me or will I call you?"

"I'll have to call you."

"That's fine," Dillman said.

"Michael, how big will the Calhoun-Tsai deal actually play in the U.K.?"

"It's incredibly juicy. It will be a front-page story for us, and once we run it, every tabloid in the country will have a field day with it. There's nothing they like more than skewering the rich and the powerful. Calhoun also happens to be pompous, self-important, and a hypocrite."

"That's satisfying to hear," she said. "Okay, I'll be in touch as soon as we're done."

She ended the call and did a quick check through her emails. Feng had sent her one with the subject line "Jiangsu Insurance Correspondence." It simply read, Here are some emails between Patriot Insurance in the U.S. and Wu Wai Wai. She opened the attachments and quickly scanned them. There was nothing subtle about the content. In the first, an Alan Jefferson, senior vice-president of international business development, asked Wu to confirm when and how much of the province's insurance business would be transferred to the new company. She had replied that the transfer would be done within three months of their deal closing and that it would amount to at least $200 million. He responded by asking her how she could be so sure about the timing and amounts. She wrote back that she had discussed the matter with her brother and her nephew. Tsai Men was copied on that email but Tsai Lian wasn't. Ava looked at the list of people copied on the previous emails. For each there were at least five Patriot Insurance executives and Ling. Tsai Men was named on only the one, but it was important. The rest of the emails were about boiler-plating the deal, arranging for its signing, and transferring the money.

Ava could hardly believe how blatant both parties had been in their collusion. She could only conclude that the Patriot employees had no idea they were breaking the law. As for Wu, she probably felt she was above the law.

She phoned Feng. "I've just read the emails that Ling sent to you. They're fantastic."

"I know."

"I'm just about to forward them to my contact in the U.S. You should give Ling a heads-up that some of this could become public in a few days."

"He's a careful man. He sent them to me from a computer in a hotel business centre. And when I spoke to him after I got them, he said he was leaving tonight for a holiday in Japan."

"Good."

"Is there anything else you want me to do?" Feng asked.

"Not right now, but don't stray too far from your phone."

Ava reread the emails and smiled as she wrote to Sam Curry at the *Wall Street Tribune*. Here, I think, is everything you need to tie Patriot Insurance directly to the Tsai family, and to some business practices that seem to fall afoul of the Foreign Corrupt Practices Act. Let me know that you received this email, and tell me what time is good for me to phone you.

She checked the time. It was three a.m. in New York, and Curry wouldn't see the message for hours yet. She imagined she wouldn't hear from him until about eight. She felt like she was on a roll, and the idea of waiting that long irritated her, but she had no choice. She turned her attention back to what she had on hand: Vincent Yin.

38

AVA WAS IN THE LOBBY FOR CLOSE TO HALF AN HOUR
thinking about Yin. She reviewed the questions she'd asked,
the answers Yin had given, and tried to identify holes. Then
she thought about the pitch she was going to make to convince him to put his recollections of the Calhoun-Tsai deal
on paper and on video. What was left, and what perplexed
her, was what she would do with Yin when he complied,
and she had no doubt at all that he would comply. Getting
him to talk in the first place had been much easier than she
had thought it would be, and she couldn't imagine that he
would offer resistance now.

He seemed to be a decent enough man, a company hack
who'd become caught up in the demands of a boss he wanted
to please. He probably never once thought that what they
were doing was illegal or immoral, and his admission had
been equally naive. But after the matter became public she
knew he could find himself accused of managing a criminal enterprise. She didn't know how he would react once
the story was out, but denial wasn't an option as long as
she had him on the record. The problem, she thought again,

was what to do with him until the story did become public. She couldn't let him go back to his office. She couldn't let him communicate with Calhoun or Tsai Men. So that left two choices — keep him under lock and key in Shanghai, or scare him so much that he would voluntarily go into hiding. The advantage to scaring him was that it would give him a realistic dose of what he could expect in the coming days and weeks, and it would give him the chance to get prepared. She felt she owed him that much.

She walked back to the boardroom. Suen was still in the same spot. "The guy with the camera should be here soon," he said.

"Keep him here. I'll come and get him when I need him," Ava said.

She opened the door and saw Yin standing by a window. He turned when he heard her and she saw a sheepish look on his face. She wondered if he was having second thoughts about co-operating.

"I think you should sit again," she said.

When he had settled into the same chair, Ava slid several sheets of paper to him and handed him a pen.

"I'm going to dictate a statement and you're going to write it down," she said. "If anything I say is inaccurate or incomplete, I want you to tell me and we'll discuss it."

"Why are you asking me to do this?"

"Vincent, this little deal that Mr. Calhoun and Mr. Tsai concocted just happens to break British law and Chinese law. One is going to be charged with bribing a public official, and the other with accepting bribes and corruption. You are a key figure in all of it. What you have to say corroborates what we know and distances you from any blame."

Yin stiffened. "I heard all that, but I still don't know why I should help you any more than I already have."

"The U.K. Ministry of Justice is already aware of the scam, and the Chinese government soon will be. Things are going to get very nasty for everyone concerned. You need to cover your ass," Ava said, her frustration building. "Mega Metals is going to blow up. You can be collateral damage or you can stand safely on the sidelines getting credit for having done the right thing."

"I'm a British citizen," he said stubbornly.

"As I said before, you're a Chinese resident doing business in China. The government here won't care what passport you carry. As far as they'll be concerned, you're Chinese and will be treated accordingly."

"But Mr. Tsai *is* the government."

"He's the provincial government, and a long way removed from Beijing. When the shit hits the fan, there's nothing he'll be able to do to protect you even if he wanted to, and he won't, because the only chance he'll have to cover his back is to make you the scapegoat."

Yin paled and Ava saw that his hands were shaking.

"How can you be certain about what's going to happen?" he said.

"You were correct earlier when you said the people I work for have a grudge against Mr. Calhoun," Ava said. "They've been trying to find something to use against him, and then this came to their attention. It is unfortunate that you and the Tsai family have to get dragged into it, but that's the way it is.

"As for what's going to happen, in a few days some very reputable international newspapers are going to publish a story that will outline Mr. Calhoun's crimes. Given his position in the Conservative Party, you can expect that every media outlet in the U.K. will run the story as well."

"He has a lot of powerful friends."

"Not in the media, and you can bet that when the stories break, his friends will be nowhere to be found."

"He'll deny everything."

"I have no doubt that he'll bob and weave, and that's when your name will likely get thrown into the fire," Ava said. "But if you're smart, you'll get out in front of this thing. You do have a decided advantage. You know what's coming down. He doesn't."

"How do I get in front?"

"Tell your side of the story first. Tell the truth. I'm sure it could only help you with the authorities," Ava said.

"I wouldn't know who to talk to."

"I'll help connect you and I'll help prepare you."

He hesitated, but Ava saw she had him bending in the right direction.

"One more thing. You should get out of China as quickly as you can. Being here when the story is released is too dangerous. When we're finished here, I'll have our man drive you back to Nanjing to get your passport and whatever personal items you want to take with you. You should get out of the country tonight if you can."

"This is all so rushed and so crazy," he said, shaking his head.

"Hey, it's out of your control. The story is going to be published with you or without you. If it's without, then you're completely on your own, and I don't fancy your chances."

He filled his glass with water and drained it. He wiped

his mouth with the back of his hand and closed his eyes.

"Do you need some time alone to think this through?" Ava asked.

"No. Tell me what you want me to do," he said.

"I want you to do some writing," she said.

"Write what?"

She opened her notebook. "Write exactly what I read and try to do it neatly. If I go too fast, let me know. I'll read it through one time so you get the gist, and then you can start."

"Okay."

"My name is Vincent Yin. I am a British citizen and an employee of Calhoun Metals, a U.K. firm. I manage Mega Metals in Nanjing, a joint venture between Mr. Dennis Calhoun and the Tsai family. I was personally present and involved in all of the negotiations leading to the creation of the joint venture about five years ago, and I was present when Mr. Dennis Calhoun and Mr. Tsai Lian finalized the details. I wish to repeat and emphasize that it was those two gentlemen — and not anyone else — who concluded the deal and agreed to its financial structure. Those arrangements consisted of Mr. Calhoun bribing Mr. Tsai to deliver provincial government construction business at a fixed and inflated rate. The two men shared the illicit profits almost equally, and in recent years those profits were as much as four hundred million U.S. dollars per year.

"At the time the agreement was reached, I was acting as an interpreter and had no input into its contents. I had some reservations, but I never voiced them directly. I did make mention to Mr. Calhoun that business was certainly done differently in China. His response was, 'When in Rome do as the Romans do,' and that passing money under the table in China was a common and standard business practice and we'd be fools not to do it," Ava said, and then stopped.

"I obviously made up that comment by Calhoun," she said. "I thought it might fit."

"It fits perfectly," Yin said, his eyes widening. "In fact, so well I can hardly believe it. Mr. Calhoun did actually use that line about the Romans at the time."

Ava smiled. There was something tiresomely predictable about the clichés thrown about by crooks and thieves when the time came for them to justify their actions.

39

SHE READ THE STATEMENT AGAIN AND THEN HAD YIN read it back to her.

"That's really good," she said. "Now I'd like you to sign it and date it."

"You knew I was going to do this, didn't you," he said as he signed the document.

"I knew that agreeing with me was the intelligent thing to do. Was I wrong to make that assumption?"

"Obviously you weren't," he said. "And tell me, what would you have done if I hadn't?"

"Vincent, you would have been allowed to leave, but I believed that, once you fully understood the situation you were in, your conscience and good sense would take over," Ava said. "It did, so let's move on to the next step."

"What, I'm not done?"

"Not quite. I want to make a video of you reading what you just signed."

"Why?"

"I think if you can read the statement in a calm and measured way for the camera, it will add that much more depth and credibility to your story. You certainly will come across as a sympathetic, serious professional."

"Who'll see the video?"

"Some lawyers and journalists, for starters."

"I'm not sure I like that idea."

"Vincent, it's time for you to accept your new reality. Like it or not, you are up to your neck in this thing, and if I was in your position I'd rather be the aggressor than the prey."

"Is that how you see me, as the prey?"

"If you choose to sit idly by, that's exactly what you will be."

He shook his head in resignation.

Ava opened the door and saw that someone had joined Suen.

"This is Chan," Suen said, motioning at a young man in jeans and a white T-shirt.

"Are you ready to work?" Ava said.

He picked up the bag at his feet. "Point the way."

"Mr. Yin has a statement he's going to read," she said as they entered the boardroom. "It has to be taken seriously, but I don't want it to be formal or stiff."

Chan looked at Yin. "How does he read?"

"Well enough, I think."

"I could do it in close-up. If he's sincere, it will come across that way."

"That's fine."

"Mr. Yin, when you're reading, look up at the camera as much as you can. Don't smile, but stare directly at me."

"Okay," Yin said without any enthusiasm.

"Now, before you begin, I have a couple of questions," Ava said to Chan.

"Go ahead."

"You do understand that everything that is said in here is confidential?"

"Suen was quite clear about that."

"One more thing. He's going to read in English. Is that a problem?"

"I don't speak English, but I'm filming, not translating."

"Then let's get started."

Despite Chan's professionalism and Yin's willingness, it took more than an hour before they had a reading that satisfied Ava. Yin was understandably nervous at the beginning and flubbed words. Then he read too quickly, and then too slowly. Ava stopped him before he got too far along, so they didn't waste too much time with each try, but the attempts added up. Finally he got through one that was passable, and that seemed to give him confidence. His final effort even had Chan nodding in approval.

"Very nice work," Ava said to Yin, and then turned to Chan. "Let's go outside."

Suen was slumped over in his chair. He looked like he was napping, but the second they drew near he sat bolt upright, looking alert.

"Who's paying Mr. Chan?" she asked.

"I am."

"Give him a nice bonus."

"Sure."

She handed Chan a slip of paper with her email address on it. "Could you send that video to me right now?"

"Sure," he said, and a moment later added, "Done."

"If there are any problems, how do I contact you?"

"Suen knows how to reach me."

"Thank you for your help," Ava said and turned to Suen. "I need to use a computer for a few minutes."

"Follow me."

He led her upstairs to an office occupied by Xing. "Ava needs to use your computer for a few moments," Suen said to him.

Xing nodded and got up from the desk. She took his chair, accessed her email, opened the video, and watched it. Yin seemed calm and credible. *It couldn't have gone much better*, Ava thought as she sent it to Michael Dillman.

When she returned to the boardroom, Yin was in his seat with his head resting on the table.

"You were wonderful," Ava said to him.

He looked at her, and she saw he was pleased by the compliment. "It was exhausting."

"But worth the effort to get it right."

"If you say so."

Ava reached for her phone and called Michael Dillman.

He answered before the first ring ended.

"Hello, Michael. I just emailed you a video of Vincent Yin talking about Mega Metals and Dennis Calhoun. Mr. Yin has been very co-operative. Take a look at what he has to say and get back to me as soon as you can," Ava said.

"We're anxious to see what you have."

"Who is 'we'?"

"My editor, Tamara Klinger, and our in-house lawyer, Charlotte Field."

"I think they should both be satisfied with the content."

"Nevertheless, do you think an interview is possible?"

"Watch the video. If you still think an interview is necessary, I'll do what I can to make it happen."

"Okay, I'll call you in a while."

As Ava ended the call, she could see that Yin had been following her conversation. "That was a journalist in London," she said. "I should warn you that his newspaper will probably want to interview you."

"I don't like that idea."

"I don't either, but it may come to that. And if it does, we need you to be credible."

"Are you saying I'm not?"

"No, I believe you, I believe you entirely, but for sure one of the questions a journalist will ask is why you decided to make this information public. You need to have an answer other than that I lured you into a meeting under false pretenses," Ava said and then paused. "And Vincent, let me be clear, if you ever tried to say anything like that I would not be pleased."

"How about if I say my conscience was bothering me?" he said, ignoring her veiled threat.

"Why did it kick in after five years of making huge amounts of money?"

"Maybe it was gradual."

"That could be, but it's still kind of weak," Ava said. "What are your politics?"

"What do you mean?"

"In the U.K., are you or your parents Conservatives?"

"We're not affiliated with any party."

"Well, that just changed," Ava said. "You just became lifelong supporters of the Labour Party."

"What?"

"That is your motive. You became upset when Calhoun used his success in China to become chairman of the

Conservative Party. Did you know he was chairman?"

"Yes."

"And as chairman he used Mega Metals to promote the party and himself. Did you know that he has been advertising himself as the man who set the standard for how to do business with the Chinese? He's led trade missions here. The party is running seminars for British businessmen using Calhoun as a model to emulate."

"That I didn't know."

"It made you angry. It got to the point where you couldn't stomach the lies and the hypocrisy anymore and decided the British people deserved to know the truth."

"Where do you come up with this stuff?"

"You could be a hero," she said, ignoring his question. "A martyr, willing to sacrifice personal financial gain in order to guard the integrity of the British political system."

"Good god, that's a stretch."

"But it is one that might play, as long as you don't say anything about being a martyr or personal sacrifices. Let the people make the inference. One thing is certain: it would provide you with an extra layer of protection, and you're going to need it. Once the Tsai family and Calhoun know that you're speaking to the media, they'll do whatever they can to shut you up — and they have the capacity to do a great many things."

"Do you think being identified in a newspaper can help shield me?"

"Somewhat."

Yin stood and walked back to the window. Ava gave him time to let his new reality sink in. He was still looking out the window when finally he said, "If you're right about the newspapers running those stories, then I have to get out of China as soon as I can."

"I know. We'll try to get you out tonight, or at the latest tomorrow."

"But I have so many things here — my condo, furniture, bank accounts."

"I'm sure you can make all kinds of arrangements from London or Newcastle or wherever, and what you can't do yourself, we'll look after. You won't lose a dollar, Vincent, I promise you that."

"I should contact my office," he said abruptly.

"Why?"

"It's been hours since I texted them. I've never been out of touch that long. I don't want anyone getting suspicious."

She took his phone from her bag and turned it on. "Come here," she said.

When he reached the table, she handed him the phone. "Put in your password and then sit next to me so I can see what you're looking at and what you're sending."

He sat down and punched in the code. When the phone activated, he tapped in a number and accessed his email. Ava could see there were more than twenty messages, but none were from Calhoun or one of the Tsais, and none looked especially urgent.

"It doesn't look as though they miss you," Ava said.

"The company is well run. That's how it should be," he said.

"Send them a text anyway," Ava said. "Say that you have a dinner meeting tonight and that you won't be in the office until later tomorrow morning. Then tell them you won't get back to the office today and you have an early morning meeting tomorrow. That should buy us some time."

She watched as he did what she asked.

When it was done, he passed her the phone. "How long do we have to wait to hear from the lawyer or the Brits?"

"I'm not sure. Maybe an hour or so."

"I'm starving."

"Me too, but why don't I call the U.K. first and see what the paper wants to do."

"All right."

She phoned Dillman. He wasn't as quick to pick up, and he sounded out of breath when he did.

"I just came out of a meeting with the editor and the lawyer, going over the video," he said. "I left my phone at my desk and had to run to get it."

"What's the consensus?"

"The lawyer just arrived and we've had only one viewing. They want to watch it again and then chat. Can I call you back?"

"Sure."

Ava ended the call and shook her head. "I'll send someone to get food. What do you feel like?"

"Anything."

Ava opened the boardroom door. "Suen, could you ask Xing to fetch some food? Fried noodles, steamed vegetables, some barbecued pork or duck, and rice should be enough."

"How much longer are we going to be here?" he asked.

"I won't know until London calls me back."

"Then I'll get some food for myself too."

Yin was at the window again when Ava returned. She sat at the table and took out her phone. There was a flurry of text messages among Amanda, Chi-Tze, Gillian, and May Ling. Chi-Tze and Gillian had been in conversation with Laura Deng at Lane Crawford that morning in an attempt to finalize the arrangements for the PÖ line. They hadn't been successful, primarily because Deng said she wasn't prepared to budge on the exclusivity demand. There were a few other minor points about promotional money and discounts, but the girls thought those could be sorted out.

The texts were initially being sent by Chi-Tze and Gillian to Amanda, who then brought May and Ava into the loop. It was clear the girls thought they should give in to Laura Deng, but they didn't want to do it without May and Ava's approval. Ava grimaced. There was nothing wrong with the proposal except for the fact that it put May in a very difficult and unfair position. If they said no, then the deal might fall apart. If they said yes, May ran the risk of alienating some friends and business associates.

Ava phoned Amanda.

"Hey, I was hoping you'd call," Amanda answered.

"Look, I'm tied up in meetings and I've asked May to take over for me when it comes to Lane Crawford. You and she can make the decisions. I'll go along with whatever you decide."

"Is everything okay?"

"Everything's fine, but go and talk to May, okay?" Ava said. "Just one thing, don't let her be so completely unselfish. You know that she personally persuaded about thirty people to be at the launch. If we do the deal, she's going to have to tell those of them who are interested in doing something with PÖ that they're out of luck and they wasted their time going to Shanghai. I don't want her to lose any friends over this."

"She also understands what a phenomenal opportunity Lane Crawford is offering us. A month ago we would have walked on nails and chewed glass if we thought it would help us get a deal like this."

"I know, but no deal is worth losing friends over. So Amanda, please, find a way to make this work."

There was a knock at the boardroom door. Xing walked in carrying two large paper bags. Suen followed.

"I have to go," Ava said. "I'll be in touch."

Suen sat at the table and watched as Xing emptied the bags. The four of them ate without speaking. Then Xing said to Yin, "And what is it that you do?"

Ava laughed at how casual the question was. It was as if her commandeering his boardroom and bringing in a videographer were everyday occurrences. There was something about eating dinner among the Chinese that fostered sociability and broke down cultural and economic barriers. Countless times she had seen her mother start a conversation with someone sitting at the next table in restaurants all over the world. Invariably, by the time dinner was over her mother would know most of their life story. Ava wasn't going to let that happen with Xing and Yin.

"Mr. Xing, our guest has been talking all afternoon. Perhaps we should give him a rest," she said.

They went back to eating in silence. Xing and Yin put down their chopsticks first, but Ava and Suen kept going, the big man glancing sideways at her, showing surprise at her appetite. They were finishing the last of the noodles when her phone rang. She saw Dillman's number on the screen.

"Suen, I think that you and Xing should leave now," she said. "I have to take this call."

Xing began to clean up, and Ava was about to tell him not to bother when Suen caught her eye. "Let him help," he said.

"Michael, it's me. I'll be right with you," Ava said, and then sat back until the paper plates and cartons were all packed up and Suen and Xing had left the room. "Okay, I can talk now."

"That was the longest short wait of my life," Dillman blurted.

"Why, what's going on?"

"That video has caused a bloody sensation."

"I was hoping it would have a positive reaction."

"Tamara and Charlotte have watched it four times now."

"And?"

"We need to interview Vincent Yin."

"We have some conditions," Ava said.

"Such as?"

"The timing of the story's release will be important to him."

"You want to know when the story will run?"

"We'll need a bit more information than that."

"Such as?"

"Am I wrong in assuming that you will want to interview Vincent so you can confirm that he did record the video and that it is an accurate rendering?"

"That's part of it, but we'll also want to make sure that Vincent is who he says he is."

"Of course, and I'm expecting that when his bona fides are established, you will approach Dennis Calhoun to get his side of the story."

"Of course."

"We have to know precisely when you intend to contact Calhoun."

"Why?"

"We have to get Vincent out of China. In fact, ideally, we should have him physically back in England before you call Calhoun. Because when you do, you can bet that the first phone call Calhoun makes will be to Tsai Men or Tsai Lian, and the first thing they'll do is try to find Vincent. If he's in China, they'll probably be able to do just that," Ava said. "Whistleblowers in the West are provided some level of protection by the law and public opinion. In the East, they end up in jail or dead and no one is around to object."

"It isn't my decision to give you the kind of information you want. I'll have to talk to our people here."

"Then put it to them."

"If they say no?"

"Then tell them we're going directly to Plan B."

"Which is?"

"You'll find out when we launch it," Ava said. "The thing you need to stress is that we don't have a lot of time. I want to hear back from you within the hour."

"I'm at the office and everyone I need to talk to is here. It won't take that long."

"I'll be waiting," Ava said.

She put down the phone and saw Vincent Yin staring at her.

"You're scaring me with all this talk about my safety," he said.

"Would you rather I lied?"

"No."

"Good, because I would find it most difficult to do so under these circumstances."

"But what's this Plan B?"

"I have no idea," Ava said.

AVA SAT QUIETLY AT THE TABLE, WAITING FOR Dillman's call. She looked out the window, trying to ignore Vincent Yin's sudden hyperactivity. He paced around the table, sat for a few seconds, and then paced some more, all the while throwing anxious glances in her direction. Finally, she'd had enough.

"Sit down and stay down," she said. "Things are getting resolved and there's not a damn thing all that pacing will accomplish."

He almost collapsed into his chair. "I was just thinking that it was only this morning that I got out of bed, showered, dressed, and left for work like I have done a thousand times before. Now look at me. Now look at the situation I'm in. My whole life has been turned upside down."

"Vincent, you've done a magnificent job up until now. We need you to stay brave," Ava said.

"The last thing I feel is brave," he said.

"Let me tell you what I've learned," Ava said. "Life is completely random. None of us can truly control our fate, and those who think they can are always the biggest losers.

The secret to having a long and happy life is to be prepared for anything and to be willing to roll with it.

"Think about Calhoun. He's the chairman of the Conservative Party. He's making more money than he ever imagined possible," she said and looked at her watch. "It's just past breakfast time in England. He's just eaten his bacon and eggs with potato scones. He is perhaps about to leave his mansion in Newcastle to travel down to London for a meeting with the party executive, and then maybe he has an early dinner with the prime minister. The PM might be asking him if he would consider accepting a cabinet position, and Calhoun is hesitating because, truthfully, what could possibly be better than the situation he's in? I mean, he has everything. Do you think for an instant he imagines it could all disappear? Do you think he considers it even remotely possible that his entire life's work, his reputation, and maybe a lot of his wealth might evaporate overnight?

"But I guarantee that when the headline story on the front page of the *Economic Herald* links Calhoun with bribes and corruption, everyone but his lawyer will stop taking his calls. That is how random life is.

"The reality is that if you do what we've discussed, your life is going to be better than you've ever imagined, and Calhoun's is going to be a living hell. Did you think about that when you were brushing your teeth this morning?"

"Are you always this confident?"

"I don't know how else to be, and so far it has worked out quite well for me."

"I'm always thinking about how things could go wrong."

"I'm not irresponsible. I do weigh my options," Ava said.

"The most important thing, though, is to act. The moment you hesitate, someone else makes your decision for you, and that never works out."

"You are incredible," Yin said.

"Hardly," she said. She was about to continue when her phone rang. "Hello."

"Ava, this is Michael and I have Tamara Klinger on the line with me."

"You said Tamara is your editor?"

"Yes, she's a senior editor at the paper," Dillman said. "She's reviewed all of the material you gave me, and she's seen the video several times."

"Before anyone starts to answer questions I need you to confirm that it's the paper's plan to contact Calhoun before the story is published," Ava asked.

"It is," Dillman said.

"And do we have an agreement that you won't do that until we feel Vincent is safe?"

"We do. Do you need something in writing?"

"No, I trust you."

"Thanks for that," a woman's voice said.

"Ms. Klinger?"

"The same."

"How do you want to do this?"

"We want to talk to Mr. Yin."

"Can I put him on speakerphone?"

"Do you have Skype?"

"No."

"Then speakerphone will have to do. I'm sure we'll recognize his voice from the video."

Ava put her phone in front of Yin.

"He's here and ready to go," she said.

"Mr. Yin, could you please tell us where you were born, who your parents are, when you moved to the U.K., and where you lived?"

He looked at Ava with panic in his eyes. She reached out and touched the top of his hand. "Don't rush," she whispered. "Tell them everything they asked as slowly as you want. They aren't trying to trick you. They just want to confirm that you are who you say you are."

He nodded, and then said, "My name is Vincent Yin. I was born in Beijing and moved to the U.K. with my parents in 1987, when I was eight years old. We lived on Hunter Street in Newcastle."

"What was your house number?" Dillman asked.

"One hundred and one."

"And where did you go to school?"

"Burnside Elementary and then Northend Secondary."

"Do you have any siblings?"

"No."

"Excellent. Now we can move on to the reason we're having this talk," Dillman said.

"Before we get into the details surrounding the business and the business arrangements that were made in China, would anyone object if I asked Mr. Yin a personal question?" Tamara Klinger asked.

"That depends entirely on how personal it is," Ava said.

"I'd like to know what motivated him to come forward with the information at this time. He is managing a very successful and profitable company. Has his job security been threatened?"

"Are you asking if he thought he was going to be fired?" Ava said.

"Yes."

"I can assure you that this is not the case."

"Then why do this now?"

Ava looked at Yin.

"I became disenchanted by the way that our success here was being used for political gain," he said. "It made me rethink the basis for the business's existence, and that made me more keenly aware that we might be breaking several laws."

"You had never thought about that before?"

"Not in any depth, but please remember I was much younger and less experienced when we started Mega Metals. Also, I had the chairman of my company telling me that what we were doing was perfectly fine, that we were simply following local practices. And, on the other side, we were dealing with the governor of the entire province and his family. How was I supposed to think anything was wrong?"

"Did you raise any of these new concerns with your chairman?"

"No. After the company was set up here I didn't have a chance to talk to him very much. My main contact is Rory Taggert, who runs the day-to-day business."

"Did you raise your concerns with him?"

"No, I wasn't secure enough, confident enough to do that. What I did do was talk to a friend of mine in the U.K. who's a lawyer. I explained to him how things were set up and operating and asked him if he thought there was a problem."

"What is your friend's name?"

"I won't say. I don't want him getting dragged into this."

The English side of the conversation became quiet. Ava nudged Yin's knee to get his attention. *Did you talk to a lawyer?* she mouthed.

He shook his head, and then covered the microphone on the phone. "What laws were we actually breaking? I forget," he whispered.

"The U.K. Bribery Act."

"What did your friend say about the way Mega Metals was being run?" Klinger finally asked.

"He said that in all probability we had broken the U.K. Bribery Act, and he guessed we'd broken several Chinese laws as well, though he couldn't be specific about them."

"What did you do after he informed you of that?" Dillman asked.

"Nothing at first. Like I said, I was scared, but I couldn't get it out of my mind," Yin said. "Then when Mr. Calhoun became chairman of the Conservative Party and started promoting himself as the model for how to do business in China, my fear started to give way to anger. I thought it was all so dishonest and hypocritical."

"Are you a political person, Mr. Yin?" Dillman asked.

"Not officially."

"What does that mean?"

"I've never carried a party card."

"But you do have some leanings?"

"Who doesn't?"

"And in which direction do you lean?"

"I won't deny it," Yin said. "I am further to the left than most of my colleagues."

"You are a supporter of the Labour Party?"

"I certainly prefer them to the Conservatives."

"Could part of your motivation for coming forward at this time be construed as political?"

"Are you asking me if I hope that the Conservative Party

is embarrassed and maybe damaged by what I have to say?"

"Yes."

"It would be a welcome bonus," Yin said.

The line went silent again. Ava shook her head at Yin. He raised his eyebrows in question.

"You are brilliant," she whispered.

"Okay," Dillman said. "We'd now like to change course and talk specifically about Mega Metals and its operations in China."

"And when we're finished with that, I would appreciate it if one of you would answer some questions I have about the extent of the Tsai family's holdings and influence," Klinger said. "Among other things, I'm curious to know if the way they do business with Calhoun extends to others."

"I can answer those questions but whatever I say has to be completely off the record," Ava said.

"I'm not sure —"

"Ms. Klinger, unlike Mr. Yin, I can't avoid being in China. I don't want to be the object of retribution — not now and not in the future. If you want to know what I know — and what I know is substantial — there can be zero attribution. The best thing for all of us might be for you to create the impression that the newspaper did its own research into the matter."

"We can agree to that," Klinger said quickly.

So she's the boss, Ava thought. "In that case, you can ask whatever you want."

41

THE INTERVIEWS LASTED INTO THE SHANGHAI EVENING.
Surprisingly, to Ava, the *Herald* people were finished with
Yin quite quickly and spent more time focusing on the Tsai
family business interests. At one point Ava said, "I thought
your major interest was in Dennis Calhoun."

"The Calhoun story is quite straightforward and is for
our U.K. market, and you can bet it has the possibility of
being the front-page headline," Klinger said. "But the tan-
gled web that the Tsai family has spun is fascinating, and
there are so many recognizable names among the companies paying them that we're sure there will be a big readership for this larger story as well. We were going to make it
a sidebar to the Calhoun story, but it could be a separate
feature."

"I am curious, though," Dillman said. "How did you ever
accumulate such a level of detail?"

"My training is as a forensic accountant. I had a solid
starting point with one organization that was paying into
four different Tsai companies, and from there it was all
about connecting dots."

"You have bank records. How did you get those?"

"I can't say," Ava said.

"Well, can you tell us what prompted you to start this investigation in the first place?" Klinger asked.

"I have a friend who has run into some problems doing business with the Tsai family. They're trying to put him under. We decided to see if there was a way for us to take them down first."

"And we are the chosen vehicle?"

"Yes," Ava said, and then hesitated, unsure whether she should mention the *Wall Street Tribune*.

"How much do you think the family is worth?" Klinger asked.

"I'm not entirely sure now that the value of their Mega Metals asset is probably going to disintegrate."

"Take a guess, and include Mega Metals as it exists today."

"Well, the public companies Kitchen Giant, Jiangsu Insurance, and Mega Metals combined have to be in the ten-to-sixteen-billion-dollar range. Then there are seven other companies they own privately that are either sitting on huge stacks of cash or have invested heavily in things like real estate. I would think they might be worth another five billion."

"One thing that interests me is that you didn't unearth that much information about Wu Wai Wai."

"Tsai Lian's sister?"

"Yes. In your notes she's listed as the CEO of a company called Mother of Pearl, but one of my colleagues here has told me that she's one of the largest gold and silver traders in Asia."

"Through which business?"

"Golden Tomorrow."

"That name didn't come up during any of my searches."

"Well, the company shares are tightly held, and she's supposed to be highly secretive."

"How much money is she worth?"

"My colleague thinks that Golden Tomorrow must have a value of at least ten billion."

"You know, I haven't been able to find out where all the cash from these businesses was sent," Ava said. "Golden Tomorrow might have been the recipient of at least some of it."

"And that brings the Tsai family's wealth to something more than twenty billion dollars," he said.

"You say that number as though it means something important."

"I can see it in a headline."

The conversation was becoming repetitive and Ava started to fidget. "Can we wrap this up soon?" she asked.

"I have only a few more questions," Dillman said. "When do you expect Mr. Yin will be leaving China?"

"Tonight if possible, but most probably tomorrow."

"So how long before we can contact Calhoun for his comments?"

"Forty-eight hours."

"That works well enough," Klinger said.

"What if for any reason we need an extension?" Ava asked.

"Contact me," Klinger said. "Thank you all for your time. We'll be in touch soon."

Ava ended the call and looked at Vincent Yin. His eyes were closed and he was taking deep, gulping breaths. "Are you okay?" she said.

"I'm exhausted," he said, opening his eyes. "I'm exhausted and exhilarated and scared out of my mind all at the same time. I can't believe what we've done. I mean, I can't believe what I've just done. I've thrown away my entire career."

"What you've done is found a way to stay out of jail or a grave."

"So you keep saying."

"Well, when they take Calhoun and maybe some of the Tsais into custody, you can call me and say thank you."

"I have to say," Yin said softly, "I almost feel sorry for Mr. Calhoun. He's always been good to me."

"Your sympathy is misplaced. He put you in charge of what was essentially a criminal enterprise, and if things had come unstuck I have no doubt he would have found a way to leave you holding the bag."

"I know you're probably right," he said. "The other thing that's bothering me is that I've never been out of a job."

"Think of this as a novel way of resigning from one. Tell yourself it was time to move on, and that the story in the *Herald* and elsewhere is one hell of a way to jump-start a job search."

He shook his head, and Ava couldn't figure out if he was agreeing with her or not. "What do we do now?" he asked.

"We need to get you on a plane from here to the U.K. You can go back to Nanjing and pick up your passport and some personal effects, or we can send someone to get them for you. Either way, I think you're better off leaving Shanghai."

"I need to call my driver."

"I thought you came here in a taxi."

"I did, but my driver's brother lives in Shanghai and he's

visiting him. He dropped me off at my first meeting this morning. That's where I caught the cab."

"I think it might be wise to avoid your driver. We don't want him or anyone else asking any questions. I'll get our car to drive you to Nanjing. I'll send Suen with you as security. And it's security for me as much as for you," Ava said. "I can't take the chance that you'll have a sudden change of heart, maybe feel sorry for Calhoun again and make some ill-advised phone calls. Suen will be your constant companion until you get on the airplane tomorrow, and I might actually arrange for him to fly with you."

"Do I have a choice?"

"No," Ava said, standing up. She opened the boardroom door and saw Suen talking to Xing. "Are you okay to drive to Nanjing with Yin, get his passport and a suitcase, and return here tonight?"

"Absolutely."

"I don't want him left by himself. I have his phone. Keep him away from any others."

"Okay."

"And I'm going to book a flight to London for him. I'd like you to be his companion."

Suen nodded.

"Good. Under what name do I book your seat?"

"Suen Wah."

"I'll leave the return open. I want you to stay with him until I tell you otherwise. It should only be a day, two at the most. Take a holiday after that if you want."

"Thanks, but that's not necessary," Suen said. "Oh, Xu phoned me. He asked if you could call him when you have the chance."

"I will," Ava said. "You stay in touch with me, though. I want to be sure that there are no issues in Nanjing."

"No problem," Suen said. "Where do I take him when I get back here?"

"I'll book a double room for the two of you at the Peninsula, under your name."

"My wife might get jealous if she finds out where I'll be spending the night."

"I doubt that." Ava laughed.

"The other car is still outside waiting for you. It will take you wherever you want to go, but Xu thinks his house is still the best option."

"I can't say he's wrong."

42

AVA SAT QUIETLY AT THE BOARDROOM TABLE TRYING
to gather her thoughts. She wasn't sure how long she had
been sitting there, but when the door opened she jumped,
startled by the intrusion.

"Excuse me, but how much longer will you need the
room?" Xing asked.

"Are you leaving?"

"Not until you do."

She looked at her watch. "I have one more phone call to
make."

"We'll wait."

She picked up the mobile and weighed her options.
There were a lot of balls in the air, more than she liked and
more than she thought she could control. She shivered as a
fleeting sense of anxiety attacked her, and then she dialled
Xu's number.

"Where are you?" Xu answered.

"Still at the building. I've just sent Suen back to Nanjing
with Vincent Yin to collect his passport. Could you book
them into a suite at the Peninsula tonight, and then put

them both on the first flight from Shanghai to London?"

"So it went well with Yin?"

"It couldn't have gone much better. That's why we need to get him out of here."

"But Suen has to go with him?"

"It's a precaution."

"I'll get someone to look after the bookings right away."

"Could you also give Suen a call and just remind him that we don't want Yin out of his sight until they land in London?"

"Didn't you tell him that already?"

"I did, but even though he does what I ask, I think it's stronger when it comes from you."

"I'll tell him, though I don't have to. He understands how things operate," Xu said. "How much longer are you going to be there?"

"I'm ready to leave. How are things at the house?"

"So quiet it's almost worrisome, but that's just me taking my turn to be paranoid."

"We'll talk tonight," Ava said. "I'll tell you how the day went and what we can expect in the next day or two."

"See you then."

Ava sat back. Xu was calm and in control. Even his talk about paranoia was low-key and jokey. She found that her own emotions had ramped down, the anxiety gone. Uncle used to have the same effect on her. No matter what difficulty she was in, talking to him always grounded her. He made her feel that she was never alone, and the sense of security that knowledge generated was something she'd tried to carry over into the rest of her life. As long as she had friends like May, Amanda, Mimi, and Maria, there wasn't much she couldn't withstand. It was loneliness that made people weak and desperate. Strength came in numbers, and pain that could be shared was diluted and dulled.

She had started to rise from her seat when her cellphone rang. *Now what?* she thought.

"Is this Ava Lee?" a man's voice said.

"Yes."

"This is Sam Curry."

She looked at her watch. "It's the middle of the night in New York."

"More like early in the morning, but either way I couldn't sleep thinking about this story, and then I got your email. That did it as far as sleep was concerned," Curry said. "When I opened the attachments and saw the correspondence between Patriot and Jiangsu, my first thought was that they couldn't have been so stupid as to put that kind of understanding in writing."

"I can't speak for Patriot, but I know that the Tsai family is supremely confident. They probably didn't care if someone saw their emails or not."

"The Patriot people were probably a touch naive, or maybe just careless," Curry said. "I spoke to several of their representatives yesterday and that's how they came across."

"You spoke about this, about their dealings with the Tsai family?" Ava asked, feeling a touch of panic.

"Only in the most general kind of way," Curry said. "I told them I was doing an article on mid-sized American companies that were successful doing business in Asia. I told them they were one of ten or so success stories that we were looking at. I asked them what advice they could give to other companies."

"And they said?"

"They stumbled a bit and then finally said it was all about finding the right partners."

"Did they say who their partner is?"

"A Nanjing-based company called Mother of Pearl Investments that is run by a remarkably talented businesswoman named Wu Wai Wai."

"But no mention that she's a member of the Tsai family, the sister of the governor of Jiangsu?"

"No. I guess they didn't think that was important," Curry said.

"Such honesty," Ava said and laughed.

Curry laughed in turn, and then said, "More seriously, the emails are terrific. They're the icing on the cake. They confirm everything you told us and everything we've been able to find out from this end. Patriot's investment in Jiangsu is on their books and the returns are highlighted in their quarterly financials and annual reports. There isn't a lot they can deny."

"Are you saying your story will focus on Patriot?"

"It will be the hook, but the overall focus is going to be on the Tsai family and the nature of doing business in China with the power elite. I loved the peasant-revolutionary-to-billionaire-politician line."

"I wish I was always so clever," Ava said.

"I've reworked your chart a bit, and I'd like you to review it and make sure it's accurate."

"You'll send it to me?"

"Of course," Curry said.

"I'll tell you in advance that I'm going to add a company called Golden Tomorrow. It's worth — according to the

Economic Herald — at least ten billion dollars. It's a gold-trading outfit, and I suspect that's where a lot of the Tsai family cash went."

"It gets more interesting by the moment."

"Or abhorrent, anyway. Can you hold off running your story until I approve the chart?"

"As long as you are expeditious."

"I normally am."

Curry went quiet for a second and then said, "Ms. Lee, my understanding is that the *Economic Herald* is going to run some variation of this story too."

"Ideally, both papers will break their stories the same day."

"We're almost ready to go. Are they?"

"I don't know."

"You know, I don't think it matters if one story breaks first. If both appear at the same time, one might detract from the other. Whichever one runs first is going to cause a stir. Then *boom*, a different kind of story is going to hit. I think that one-two punch will be more impactful."

"What do you mean by 'different kind of story'?"

Curry hesitated, and then said, "I hope I'm not breaching a confidence, but my friend Vanessa Ogg insinuated that the British paper would be focused on Dennis Calhoun and his Mega Metals business."

"That's true, and it was perfectly all right for Vanessa to tell you that."

"Good. She's been very professional and circumspect throughout."

"Let's just hope we can bring it all to a satisfactory conclusion."

There was a pause, and then Curry said, "You have a rather distinctive accent. Canadian perhaps?"

"It is."

"Do you live in Canada?"

"Most of the time."

"Then I'm terribly curious to know what drew you to the Tsai family. They're hardly known outside of China."

"I have a client who became tired of being extorted by them. He asked me to find some ammunition he could use to fight back."

"A Canadian client?"

"What does that matter?"

"It doesn't, I guess," he said. "He must be very pleased with what you've uncovered."

"He seems to be."

"How did you do it?" he asked abruptly.

"I was a forensic accountant for many years. I started with the information my client gave me and built structure around it. The only problem I had was that every time I unearthed one layer, there was another, or maybe two, underneath it."

"Where did you go to school?"

"York University in Toronto and Babson College in Wellesley."

"My mother went to Wellesley College."

"Those girls were a bit too grand for us at Babson."

"My mother was hardly grand. She was there on a scholarship — but that's off the point," he said. "Getting back to your information, some of it was highly detailed and confidential. I'm curious about how you got your hands on it."

"Is this for publication?"

"Of course not. I know we're off the record. I'm simply curious."

"I traced bank records. The Tsais tried to get fancy. They funnelled money through a family holding company called AKG to another family company, Mother of Pearl. Mother of Pearl supposedly invested in Jiangsu Insurance. It was all Patriot Insurance money."

"How did you get the bank records?"

"I paid for them."

"How do you know they're genuine?"

"I had a source inside one of the banks involved whom I trusted. The source accessed and printed the records. Any doubts I had about them being genuine disappeared as soon as I saw that everything we found on the public record matched what had been given to us."

"It was a nice piece of work."

"Thanks, and now could you answer a question for me?"

"I hope so."

"I have concerns about the Tsai family being warned by one of their partners that an investigation is going on. Do you think Patriot might do that?"

"I would be very surprised. They seemed flattered rather than alarmed by our attention."

"I was told you spoke to some other companies as well."

"We used the same pretext and got the same kinds of answers."

"That's comforting to know," Ava said.

"And I have another question for you. It's one that my editors have been rather persistent about," Curry said. "What do you have that ties Tsai Lian directly to any of these businesses?"

"Do they doubt for a second that he isn't pulling all the strings?"

"No, they don't, and I'm quite sure in Asian culture it is completely understood who is the mastermind, but here in the West — as you know — we don't have your refined sense of family structure and loyalty. My editors would like to have something beyond supposition. The story is still going to run without it, but it would make it even stronger."

"We have a video of Vincent Yin, the general manager of Mega Metals, explaining how Dennis Calhoun and Tsai Lian put their deal together."

"Does it specifically implicate Lian?"

"It does."

"Fantastic. Can we see it?"

"Under one condition."

"Which is?"

"We're concerned about Yin's safety. The *Herald* has agreed not to approach Dennis Calhoun in the U.K. until Yin is out of China. That will take at least twenty-four hours. I would need the same assurances from you."

"I can't imagine we'd approach Calhoun in any event."

"I still need your word."

"You have it."

"Then I'll send you the video. And I might have something else you can use," Ava said. "I personally met with Lau Ai, Tsai Lian's daughter-in-law. We chatted a bit about him and I asked her about his roles as governor and senior member of the family. She said — and I'm quoting almost verbatim, I think — 'My father-in-law is head of the family before he is governor of the province.'"

"I have no way of verifying if that quote is accurate."

"I know that."

"And I can't use your name in reference to it?"

"No."

"It's quite self-serving, isn't it?"

"Yes, I guess it is."

"I may use it anyway. Anonymous sources are not totally frowned upon," he said and then paused again. Ava thought she heard pages turning.

"Ms. Lee, we've been hearing about corruption in China for years. What makes this so special?"

You must know the answer to that or you wouldn't be talking to me, Ava thought, and then caught herself. He did deserve a serious answer.

"The size of it, for one thing, makes it stand out. We're talking about at least ten billion dollars. That makes the Tsai family one of the wealthiest in Asia, and all of their money has been accumulated because of his public position, but of course completely out of public view and scrutiny.

"Then there's the question of his stature. Tsai Lian is a true princeling. He is one of the chosen ones. It's like being a Rockefeller or a Kennedy in the U.S., or anyone in the U.K. who is born into royalty. The chosen ones always look after each other. They understand their interdependence. They feel it is their right to have power and to get rich in the process, and by protecting their colleagues' rights to do that, they're protecting themselves. The Chinese government at the highest levels is filled with people like them."

"So why will anyone in the government care about what the Tsai family has done?"

"As China expands its role in the world, even members of the elite have become sensitive to how they are perceived. It has become the case of a larger political issue overcoming some personal loyalties. Those loyalties are easier to maintain when things are kept under cover; when they hit the light of day, they can't be ignored. And, hopefully, problems of this nature have to be acted upon if the government wants to maintain any semblance of being credible and respectable.

"But you can't ignore the personal side of it entirely. As one of my friends said, even someone wealthy can be jealous of someone who has more wealth. My hope is that the scope of the Tsai family's empire will anger some of his colleagues. They may think he's gone too far with his greed. They may feel the need to rein him in and to send a message to others."

"You should talk to my editor sometime when this is over," Curry said. "He and you are on the same page."

"My opinions are hardly original."

"He actually wants to title our piece 'The New Chinese Royalty.'"

"How perfect."

"I think so too," he said. "One last question. What do you think will actually happen to the Tsai family?"

"As a result of this information becoming public?"

"Yes."

"At the end of the day, I expect it will come down to a combination of politics and personal animus," Ava said. "If their elite colleagues feel threatened in any way or see some benefit to punishing the Tsai family, then they'll do it. If the Tsai family has enough dirt on them to make them think twice about retribution, then they might wait and hope the scandal passes."

"That is very cynical."

"No, it's completely practical, and the Chinese are nothing if not practical."

43

AUNTIE GRACE OPENED THE DOOR TO THE HOUSE WITH a huge grin.

"Welcome home," she said. "Are you hungry?"

"No, not really. Maybe in a while."

The diminutive woman looked up at Ava with a trace of disappointment on her face. "Well, whenever you're ready," she said. "He's in the kitchen. He's been waiting for you."

Ava went to the bedroom first to drop off her bag, and then made a bathroom visit to freshen up. It seemed like a lifetime ago since she'd showered there.

Xu sat at the kitchen table, an empty glass and a bottle of Scotch sitting in front of him. "*Mei mei*," he said, rising.

He was in a shirt and slacks. His tie hung loose around his neck and his black suit jacket was draped over the back of the chair. They hugged, and she felt some extra tension in his body.

"Are you okay?" she asked.

"The landscape is ever changing," he said and then smiled. "Sit and tell me about your day. Auntie says you're not going to eat right away, but how about a drink?"

"Do you have cognac?"

"I have a fifty-year-old bottle of Martell VSOP."

"That might do," Ava said.

"I'll get it," he said and left the kitchen.

"It's better when he has someone to drink with," Auntie Grace said from the stove, where she was stirring something in a wok.

"Yes, I'll keep him company that way, but truthfully I do need it for myself."

"Did you get that man from Nanjing?"

"We did."

"And did you get what you wanted from him?"

"We did."

"Was it hard?"

"Not so much."

"Xu says that you can get a stone to talk."

"That's an exaggeration."

"It's a compliment."

"I know."

"One day I'll get you to accept one."

"Auntie —" Ava began, only to be interrupted by Xu's arrival with a bottle of cognac and two snifters in his hands.

"I decided to drink Martell as well," he said, taking his seat. He pulled the stopper from the bottle, took a long, deep smell and sighed. "Wonderful."

"Just a bit," Ava said.

He ignored her request as he filled each glass to almost the halfway mark.

"*Gambei*," he said.

Their glasses touched and their eyes met. Ava shivered; it was dawning on her how close they were getting. He made her feel comfortable in a way that no man except Uncle and her friend Derek ever had. With Derek there wasn't any doubt that she was the boss; with Uncle, she often felt like a child. This was something else, and she was beginning to value it.

"Tell me about your day," he said again.

She talked for close to half an hour, with the only interruption a reminder from Auntie that Xu's duck fried rice was ready whenever he wanted to eat. He had her serve him a bowl, but his eyes hardly left Ava as he dug his chopsticks into the rice.

"The hotel and flights are booked for Suen and that man Yin," he said when she finished.

"Have you heard from Suen?"

"No. He'll call me when they're on their way back from Nanjing."

"I hope it goes smoothly."

"There's no reason it shouldn't."

"Xu, when I arrived home tonight, you seemed preoccupied. Why?"

He smiled.

"What's so funny?" she asked.

"You said 'when I arrived home.' It was nice to hear that."

Ava felt herself blush. "You're avoiding my question."

"I am, but one has nothing to do with the other."

Ava heard Auntie Grace cackle and turned her head towards the stove. The old woman was still bent over the wok.

"I spoke with Men about half an hour before you got here," Xu said.

"What did he want?"

"He wants to meet with us again."

"Us?"

"Yes."

"In Nanjing?"

"He's prepared to come to Shanghai."

"Why does he want to meet?"

"He wasn't specific."

"What did you tell him?"

"I told him we would think about it."

"Why would we do that?"

"He sounded different."

"What is that supposed to mean?"

Xu leaned forward, the snifter nestled between the palms of his hands. "I've known him for many, many years. He is an arrogant son of a bitch. He understands the power he has and he's never been afraid to threaten to use it. This is the first time I can remember a meeting request from him that wasn't a demand."

"It could be a trap."

"I changed my mind about leaving Lop in Hong Kong. He's here. He flew in a few hours ago."

"What are you saying?"

"If we decide to go, he'll organize a defence. I've already spoken to him about it. I won't meet anywhere that isn't public, and he will infiltrate the area, surrounding the meeting place with about twenty men. There's no way I'm going to let either of us be taken."

"Why take the risk at all?"

"The thing is, if we refuse to meet it's only going to make them more suspicious and fuel their paranoia. I'd rather have them calm until it's too late for them to take the initiative."

"Do you think it's possible he actually knows what we're trying to do?"

"I can't discount it entirely."

"He can't know the details. I'm sure of that."

"I am too."

"So why go?"

"If for nothing else, to pretend that everything is normal."

"I still don't like it."

"I'm not too crazy about it myself, but I think, given everything else we have going on, it will buy us some time."

"God."

"Does that mean you won't go, or that you will go but very reluctantly?"

"I'll go," Ava said.

He reached across the table and took her hands. "I can't begin to tell you how appreciative I am of everything you've done so far."

"I haven't been doing it alone."

"No, but you're the force behind it."

"Let's just pray that it works out even remotely close to the way we want it to."

"I have a sense we'll know more about that after we meet Men," Xu said, and then looked at his watch. "Speaking of whom, I need to call him to fix a time and place."

"Where's Lop?"

"In a house three doors down. We own most of the street."

"And the men he needs?"

"As close."

"You never fail to surprise me."

While Xu called Tsai Men, Ava went to her bedroom. She turned on her computer and glanced at the highly stylized chart that Sam Curry had sent. They had placed Tsai Lian in the middle of it, with the other family members and businesses extending from him like the spokes on a bicycle wheel. They had even found photos of most of the family, although Lian's looked as though it had been taken years ago — his hair was thick and black, his face unlined, and he wore rather large aviator glasses that dated the image to the 1970s.

She checked the lines connecting the various members and businesses against the chart in her notebook. The *Tribune*'s was completely accurate. They had even added Golden Tomorrow.

This is exactly right. Nice job, she wrote, and then sent the email to Curry.

When she re-entered the kitchen, Xu was eating another bowl of fried rice.

"Did you talk to Tsai Men?" she asked.

He nodded. "We meet him tomorrow morning at ten in the restaurant at the Le Sun Chine Hotel."

"Was that his suggestion?"

"No, he told me to pick somewhere central. Lop suggested Le Sun Chine. It's on Huashan Road in the Changning District, right on the edge of the Concession. The hotel is walled and has a fair-sized courtyard."

"How is Lop?"

"Eager, as usual. The man loves to fight, and the only thing that makes him happier than fighting is the prospect of it."

"He won't do anything rash?"

"You saw him in action in Wanchai. He may have a tendency to be vicious, but he follows orders and he is highly disciplined. My orders are for him not to do anything unless he is one hundred percent certain we are in danger."

"I'm still uneasy about this meeting," Ava said.

"We'll have men positioned as sentries on all the streets leading to the hotel. We'll have men in the courtyard, in the hotel, and in the lounge. We're going in one car that will be left at the front entrance, and another car will be waiting at the rear in case we have to leave that way."

She shook her head. "I just wish this wasn't necessary."

"What are the other options?"

"I can't think of any. I know avoiding Men can only make things worse."

"It will be over soon enough."

"This day has already been very long and stressful, and tomorrow doesn't sound like it's going to be any easier," Ava said. "I think I'm going to lie down for a while."

"Yes, you do look tired," Xu said. "I have to go out, but I'll be back in a few hours."

"If I fall asleep, don't worry about waking me."

She went into the bedroom, stripped down to her underwear, pulled on a T-shirt, and crawled under the duvet. She lay on her back with her hands folded across her chest. Over the years she had developed an ability to sleep just about anywhere at any time. It had been useful when she was on jobs that bounced her from place to place and time zone to time zone. This trip to Shanghai, she thought, was turning into the same kind of circus. She tried to clear her mind and relax, but there were just too many things going on with the Tsai family, as well as with the PÖ negotiations and with her mother and Maria at home. The only comfort she could find was that all of them were bound to be resolved in a day or two. Whether they would be resolved to her satisfaction was entirely another matter.

44

SHE WOKE TWICE DURING THE NIGHT, THE FIRST TIME feeling thirsty and the second time needing to pee. She made quick and quiet trips to the kitchen for a glass of water and to the bathroom. Both times, as soon as she snuggled under the warm covers, she fell right back to sleep.

The third time she woke, it was because Auntie Grace was gently shaking her knee while whispering her name. It startled Ava, and she struggled for a second trying to remember where she was.

"It's just past eight o'clock. You've slept for about twelve hours. Xu said I should wake you."

"I can't believe I slept this long," Ava said, feeling groggy.

"I have congee on the stove."

"I can't eat yet, but I'll have coffee."

"I brought you one," Auntie Grace said, pointing to the dresser, where a steaming cup sat.

"Thank you."

"Even though I woke you, there's no need to rush. Xu has gone to meet with Lop. He said he'd be back to get you at about a quarter to ten."

Ava waited until the old woman had left the bedroom before pulling back the covers and swinging her legs over the side of the bed. She slid to the floor and then kneeled to pray. She invoked Saint Jude, asking him to protect her and everyone close to her during the day ahead.

She then took the cup from the dresser, sat on the bed, and spent five minutes sipping coffee and clearing her head. Normally before any meeting she would review notes and get her train of thought organized. But in this case, she had no idea what to expect. All she could do was make herself look professionally presentable and keep her emotions under control.

She finished the coffee, took the cup into the kitchen, and made herself another that she took into the bathroom. Half an hour later she emerged shiny and clean. She fussed in the bedroom for a while, unsure about what to wear, but finally opted for her ever-reliable black slacks and a blue button-down shirt with French cuffs. Then, unlike the day before, she put on red lipstick and black mascara, slid her Tank Française watch over her wrist, fastened the shirt cuffs with green jade links, and pulled her hair back and fixed it with the ivory chignon pin.

Auntie Grace was standing at the stove when Ava sat down at the kitchen table with her computer and phone. "Are you ready to eat now?" she asked.

"No, thank you, but I'll have another coffee while I do some work," Ava said, turning on her devices.

A moment later a new cup was placed in front of Ava.

"I have to tell you that I've never seen anyone who dresses so plainly look so beautiful."

Ava started to wave off the compliment and then caught

herself. "You are very kind to me, and I appreciate it."

"Just do something for me, will you?"

"What?"

"Try to stay out of trouble. I can't help but notice that whenever you and Xu are together, something dangerous always seems to be going on."

"It isn't anything I plan."

"It's his life. It doesn't have to be yours."

Ava shot a glance at the old woman. Auntie Grace was back at the stove, stirring the congee.

"Does he tell you everything?" Ava asked.

"He lets me hear everything. That's almost the same if you're clever enough to piece things together."

"And you obviously are."

"I've been with the family and with him for so many years that there aren't many things I haven't heard before."

"Auntie, I have no interest in trouble, dangerous or otherwise."

"I believe you, but that won't stop me from worrying."

Ava pushed her chair back from the table and stood. Auntie Grace's back was turned to her. In five steps Ava was at the stove. She wrapped her arms around the other woman's waist and pressed her face into her neck. "You have become my favourite auntie. I promise I'll try not to give you any reason to worry."

"Hey," Xu said from the kitchen doorway.

Both women turned towards him and began to laugh.

"The two of you are starting to make me jealous," he said.

"Poor you," Auntie Grace said. "It serves you right for bringing such a wonderful young woman into my house."

"You slept well," Xu said.

"Very."

"I just finished talking to Lop. He's on his way to the hotel. His men have been there for a while."

"Any signs of strange activity?"

"Not yet."

"Good."

"I also spoke to Suen. He's at the airport with Vincent Yin. Everything went well last night and this morning, and they're checked in now for the flight."

"I should let the journalists know," Ava said, looking at her computer.

"I told him to text the moment the plane took off. Maybe you should wait until then."

"Okay. Did he have anything to say about Yin other than it's going well?"

"No."

"Does he mind having to fly to London?"

"Actually, he seemed excited at the prospect. He's never been anywhere outside of Asia."

"Have you heard anything else from Tsai Men?"

"Not a word."

Ava sat down at the table again. She signed into her email and saw she had been copied on a myriad of correspondence going back and forth between May Ling and Amanda on the PÖ negotiations with Lane Crawford. She couldn't help perusing the most recent. It seemed as though a deal was imminent.

Sam Curry had also emailed to thank her for signing off on his chart, and then, almost as an afterthought, wrote, I expect our story will break in tomorrow's edition, which means that the online version could be up as soon as dinnertime in Shanghai.

The reality of it almost shocked her. It was what she had wanted, but realizing it was going to happen filled her head with doubts. She took a deep breath. There wasn't any way she could stop it now, she thought as she wrote, Please send me a copy as soon as you can. I don't want to be blindsided.

"I think we should get going," Xu said from the doorway.

"It's early yet."

"We'll circle the area for a while before actually going to the hotel," he said. "That's one of Lop's requests."

Ava closed the computer. "Okay, let's go."

There were six men instead of the usual three in the house courtyard. The Mercedes and the BMW were there as well. Xu and Ava climbed into the Benz and were joined by the driver who had met her at the Nanjing airport and another man. Two men got into the BMW. When the gate opened, the BMW was the first to leave, with the Mercedes following closely behind.

"I just got an email from Sam Curry at the *Tribune*," Ava said as the cars started along the alley. "He thinks their story may appear in tomorrow's paper. If it does, it will be available online by tonight, our time."

"I thought they were going to hold off until you told them it was a go," Xu said.

"No, I never had that understanding with the American paper."

They pulled out onto a main street and Xu's attention was immediately drawn to a black Toyota SUV. "Is that a military vehicle?" he asked the man sitting next to the driver.

"No, it's not."

The BMW turned right and then left, with the Mercedes trailing. After five minutes Ava had no idea where they were anymore. Xu was quiet, his focus on the surroundings. Ava leaned back in her seat and let her mind wander. She was jolted back to the present when the car slammed on its brakes at an intersection. She checked her watch.

"It's five minutes to ten," she said to Xu.

"I know, but we're only two blocks away. I don't want to be the first ones there. We have men at the hotel entrance, more in the lobby, and Lop is outside the lounge. He's going to text me when Tsai arrives."

Ava nodded and then heard his phone buzz.

He reached into his shirt pocket and took it out. He checked the screen and then turned it towards her.

She read, Plane has left the gate and is on the runway ready for takeoff. No problems. I'll text you when we get to London. Suen.

"That's good news," she said.

As Xu closed the message, his phone rang. He looked at the incoming number and seemed surprised. "You were going to text," he said.

Ava could hear a muffled voice coming through the phone. She assumed it was Lop.

Xu leaned forward and tapped the driver on the shoulder. "You can go to the hotel now," he said, putting the phone back into his pocket.

"You said Lop was going to text."

"Something came up."

"What?"

"Lop wanted me to know that Tsai isn't alone. He came with three other men in two cars."

"Military? The police?"

"He thinks that two of them are bodyguards."

"And the third?"

"He thinks it's the Governor."

45

THE MERCEDES DROVE THROUGH A LARGE GATEWAY
into a brick courtyard. The four-storey boutique hotel had
red brick walls, white trim, lead-paned windows framed in
wood, and a curved white overhang. Two black Bentleys
were parked in front of lead-paned wood double doors. Lop
stood near the cars talking to a man in a black suit. When
the Mercedes stopped about ten metres away, he walked
rapidly towards it.

Xu and Ava stepped into the courtyard.

"You remember Ava," Xu said to Lop.

"How could I forget her?"

Ava held out her hand. He took it and squeezed harder
than she thought necessary, but entirely in keeping with a
personality who seemed permanently on edge. When she'd
met him in Hong Kong, she had been surprised by how
small — about five feet nine inches — he was for a Red
Pole, although there was the hint of real power in his ropey
physique. But it was his energy level that was the key to his
character. He was wired, his body always in some kind of
motion, and his eyes darted everywhere, constantly alert.

He looked like the kind of man you'd have to kill if you got in a fight with him. There wasn't any quit in Lop.

"Who is the guy you were talking to?" Xu said.

"One of the Governor's bodyguards."

"So it is him."

"Absolutely."

"Then I guess we should go inside," Xu said.

"Just a minute, boss," Lop said. "They don't want to meet in the lounge. They've gone to the library. They think it's more private."

"Privacy doesn't enter into it. What they want is to show who's making the decisions," Xu said.

"Do you want me to —"

"No, forget about it," Xu interrupted. "We're too far along to be bothered by these games. We're going in. Where's the other bodyguard?"

"Outside the library."

"Come with us, and then stay with him in the hallway."

Lop led them into the hotel, through the lobby, and down a corridor to the library. The bodyguard outside nodded at them as they walked past. They paused in the doorway, Xu's body blocking Ava's view.

"Governor, this is a surprise," Xu said, stepping inside.

Ava followed him into a small room lined with wooden bookshelves. There were two couches covered in white linen and a long wooden coffee table between them. Tsai Men stood to greet Ava and Xu, but the small man wearing large aviator glasses stayed seated.

"It was a last-minute decision, and I wish it hadn't been necessary," Tsai Men said.

"And why was it?" Xu said.

"Why don't you sit before we start this conversation," Tsai Lian said.

Xu stood to one side so Ava could pass. She felt Lian's eyes on her as she walked to the couch. His thick hair was still coal black and his face had only a few lines across the forehead and down the sides of his mouth. If Ava hadn't known he was in his seventies, she would have guessed he was about sixty. She remembered the aviator glasses from the photo that Sam Curry had sent her. She had assumed it was an old picture. Maybe it wasn't. Maybe the glasses were Lian's trademark.

She sat directly across from him. "My name is Ava Lee," she said and held out her hand.

"I know who you are," he said, his hands folded in his lap.

Xu sat next to her and Tsai Men sank into the couch beside his father.

"Do you want anything to drink?" Men said.

"We're fine," Xu said.

"Good, then we can start." Men glanced at his father and then leaned towards Xu. "My main reason for meeting with you is to mend the relationship we've had for so many years, first with your father and then with you."

"I appreciate that."

"After our unfortunate meeting in Nanjing, I saw my father and my uncle. They had already been told about what happened between the woman and the men they had sent, and they weren't happy with the outcome."

"By 'woman,' you mean Ava?" Xu said.

Tsai Men nodded.

"Then respect her by using her name."

"Of course," he said.

"And please explain why those men were sent there in the first place."

"There was no sinister intent," Men said. "They just wanted to clarify why she had such a keen interest in our family and our businesses."

"I told you that she had no interest."

"Yes, and you did so quite forcefully. When I explained that to my father, he said it was stupid of me to confront you so directly. In hindsight, I think he's right."

"Was he being critical of your approach or of the reasoning behind it?"

Men shrugged, and shook his head as if he was frustrated or confused. "Look, our two families have been friends and allies for many years. It's obvious to us that this current unpleasantness started with my request that you get into that new business. I think that request was mistimed, and maybe misjudged."

"It was."

"But your reaction wasn't that of a friend. You could have reasoned with me. Instead, you chose to stall and dig in your heels. I knew you weren't being honest with me. I knew you didn't want to do it and were trying to find a way around it."

"I can't deny that."

"My father told me that I should never have pushed you so hard," Men said. "He said I should have laid it out as a business proposition and then let you decide if you wanted to pursue it."

"That would have saved us all a lot of time and trouble."

"Would it have stopped the woman from prying?" The question came from Tsai Lian.

"I'm not sure what it is that I'm supposed to have done that has caused so much offence," Ava said.

"Some of our banks and businesses were quite suddenly being pestered about things that should concern only our family," Men said.

"When we met in Nanjing, you said you thought I was responsible for that," Xu said.

"I meant that I thought you had asked her to do it, or she was doing it in some misguided effort to help you. Either way, I didn't have much doubt that she was the perpetrator."

"Based on what facts?" Ava said.

"The calls originated from Toronto and Hong Kong."

"That leaves you with only several million candidates," she said.

"Don't treat us like fools," Men said sharply. "We don't believe in coincidence, and you were too much of one. We did some further checking and found out about the old business you had with the man named Chow. We also discovered that you are an accountant with the kind of special skills that can direct the types of inquiries that were being made."

"Are you going to tell us you didn't know of her background?" Lian said to Xu.

"Ava has been a friend for some time, and she and I shared the friendship of the man you call Chow for more than ten years. Of course I knew what she did for a living, but that's not why she was in Shanghai."

"Maybe not initially," Men said.

"Look, we can go around in circles, but you can't prove anything and we can't disprove such broad suppositions," Xu said.

"And there is one more supposition, one more develop-ment, that we haven't discussed yet," Men said, glancing sideways at his father.

"I wasn't going to come here today. My plan was to leave it to my son to repair the relationship that you and he have built over so many years," Lian said, slowly and deliberately. "That changed early this morning, when my sister called me. Do you know her, Wu Wai Wai?"

"I certainly know the name, but we've never met," Xu said.

"She is a remarkable woman — well-educated, smart, and strong in every way. She owns and manages several large businesses, none of which have anything to do with you."

"I'm sure she is formidable."

"Yes, that's a good word to describe her," Lian said. "She isn't a woman given to panic, but when she called me this morning, she wasn't quite herself. I wouldn't go so far as to say she was alarmed, but she certainly was concerned — concerned enough to phone me."

"You have me at a complete disadvantage," Xu said. "I have no idea what you're talking about."

"I'm talking about the *Wall Street Tribune*," Lian said.

46

AVA FELT HER FACE FLUSH, BUT SHE DIDN'T REACT IN any other way that might indicate surprise. Beside her, Xu was completely still.

"Again, I have no idea what you're talking about," Xu said.

"My sister received a phone call late last night from one of her partners, Patriot Insurance in the United States. They told her they had been contacted by a reporter at the *Tribune* who asked a number of questions about their business relationships in China. According to them, none of it was particularly specific or threatening. Still, they thought they should give her a heads-up in case the same paper tried to contact her."

"Did it?"

"No, not yet."

"So why is she concerned?"

"She's as cautious as I am, maybe even more so, and she is very sensitive to changes in her environment. I had told her about the inquiries made about our banks and businesses. She thinks the *Tribune* article could somehow be related."

"If her American partner isn't worried about the article

in the *Tribune*, why should she be? And why should you?" Xu said.

"We can be overly sensitive, but that's what's helped keep me in office for so many years, and it's what has helped her build a business," Lian said. "When we see shadows, we assume the worst. There are a lot of shadows following you and your friend sitting next to you. My son has tried to minimize how bad the relations between us are right now and has kept reminding me of how many years our two families have been interdependent. I told him that is the only reason I am still prepared to talk to you."

"This is ridiculous," Xu said.

"Not to me. The threat is very real," Lian said. "If the woman isn't snooping, then someone else is. Find them and deal with them."

"And if I can't find that someone?"

"Then, unfortunately, I'm going to assume it's her," Lian said, and then shifted his gaze from Xu to Ava. "Young woman, you have to stop your meddling. If it persists, you will regret it, and there is nothing that Xu can do to prevent what might happen."

"I have done nothing," Ava said, returning his gaze.

"I won't believe that until my entire world becomes quiet and peaceful again."

"If it does?" she said.

Lian shrugged.

"In the meantime," Men interceded, "let's forget any plans to get into that new business."

"Thank you," Xu said.

"I just hope it isn't a wasted concession on our part," Lian said as he started to rise.

Everyone else stood too. Lian stared at Ava again, his eyes blinking behind the large glasses. He was even shorter than she had thought, only an inch or two taller than her, and his torso was so thick he looked almost square. He would have seemed comical if he didn't radiate such power.

With a shake of his head, he walked past them and out of the library. Men lingered for a moment, his attention on Xu.

"My father means what he says," Men said.

"I believe you."

"He won't be easily placated."

"I believe that too."

"In the car on the way here, he was angrier. I think I calmed him a little, but it won't take much to set him off again. Don't give him any reason."

"We'll make every effort not to," Xu said.

Men turned to Ava. "He thinks you're the problem. He said to me in the car, 'What's one woman more or less? Xu can always find himself another.'"

"I won't let myself be held responsible for his active imagination," she said. "And I'm not intimidated by your threats."

Men reached out to Xu and they shook hands. "I have to go. Don't say you haven't been warned."

Xu and Ava stood side by side. After a minute, Xu went to the door and looked out into the hallway. "They're gone," he said.

Ava collapsed onto the couch.

Xu had his back turned to Ava. She couldn't remember a heavier silence. It lasted only five seconds, or maybe ten, but it felt like someone was sitting on her chest and she could hardly breathe.

"If they had dropped their demand that we get into the drug business two days ago, we wouldn't be in this situation," he finally said.

"It's too late to turn back," Ava said, sensing a question in Xu's comment.

He walked to the couches and sat in the seat Men had occupied. When she looked across the table, she saw a trace of doubt on his face. There had been times with Uncle — not many, but some — when she and he had reached a crossroads where decisions had to be made that were a test of their trust and loyalty. What would one sacrifice for the other? What value did each place on their relationship? Neither of them had ever failed the other; neither of them had come even remotely close to doing that.

"I know," Xu said, his voice low and calm. "So what we have to do now is plan for the fallout from the newspaper stories."

"How bad do you think it could be?"

"I expect he's capable of closing down all my businesses and putting me in jail, or worse. As for you, I don't think you would have much chance of getting out of China."

"That's assuming he retains the power to do all those things."

"I suspect you're thinking along the same lines as I am."

"We need to damage him so badly that he can't come after us," Ava blurted.

"And extend that thinking to the entire family. We need them under siege. The attack has to be so forceful that they'll be preoccupied with surviving and they'll forget about us for a while," Xu said. "How big and ugly are those newspaper stories going to be?"

"I'm confident that the Calhoun story will be huge, and it won't be restricted to the *Herald*. Once it breaks, every media outlet in the U.K. is going to pick it up."

"And New York?"

"I don't know, although Sam Curry did indicate we'd be front page."

"You said they might publish as early as tonight?"

"Yes."

"But you asked the *Herald* to hold off until Yin was back in the U.K."

"I did."

"Can you ask them to speed things up?"

"I don't see why not. The plane has left and the Tsais don't know he's on it," she said, looking at her watch. "It's four in the morning in London. I'll call my contact in a few hours and urge him to move at full speed. I'll tell him the *Tribune* is going to go with a story tonight."

Xu sat back and closed his eyes for a few seconds. "That fucking family is so hard to stay ahead of," he mumbled.

"Yes, you're right. They are a handful."

"That sounded negative on my part," he said, sitting upright. "Don't take it that way."

"I didn't. I'm just thinking about something else."

"What?"

"How many high-level political contacts do you have here and in Beijing?"

"Quite a few."

"So does May Ling, in Wuhan and Beijing."

"Why does that matter?"

"Well, your remark about making an impact made an impact on me," Ava said. "I've been so busy trying to

orchestrate these stories that I may have forgotten something crucial."

"What?"

"People have to read them — people who matter, and
people who live in China, not just in the U.K. and the U.S.
That's the only way they'll have any effect."

"How do you propose to make that happen?"

"We have to prime the pump. We need to hype the stories
before they come out so that the power brokers in Beijing
and in other provinces are desperate to read them."

"That would warn the family in advance. I'm not sure
that's wise."

"We don't have to name the Tsais. In fact, it would generate more interest if we didn't."

"What are you thinking?"

"Well, how many senior government officials are corrupt?"

"Most of them. It's all a matter of degree."

"So, what if we let it be known that two major international English-language newspapers are about to name one
of them as the world's most corrupt and wealthiest public
servant?"

"We let it be known?"

"Yes, one by one, confidential phone call by confidential
phone call. You and May contact your friends to tell them
to be wary, that this story is coming. You tell them you
don't know who's going to be identified, but they had better
be prepared just in case they have some connection to the
person who is. Do you think that might grab their interest?"

"Heads would definitely reel."

"And how much gossip and buzz would it generate before
the story broke?"

"I can imagine that everyone we'd contact would make a ton of phone calls themselves. It wouldn't take long before every governor of every province, every provincial party secretary, and every member of the standing committee would be anxious, maybe even frantic, to find out who's going to be named," Xu said, and then hesitated. "We have to assume that someone would contact the Tsais or a person close to them."

"I know, but what choice do we have? I think it's a risk we have to take," Ava said. "It's crucial that we catch the interest of as many people as possible. The more we can engage, the safer we'll be, and the more vulnerable the Tsais should be."

"We will certainly generate interest," Xu said.

"And how will that interest be transformed when the people you contact see that it's Tsai Lian who's named and the deals he's cut and the money he's made?"

"They'll be relieved at first, but I can imagine that for some of them, relief will turn into anger."

"And not just anger because of what he did, but anger in part because, for at least a few hours, they were made to feel vulnerable."

"There's also the chance that some of them might be afraid of ending up in the glare of the spotlight that's being shone on the Tsais," Xu said. "They won't want that to linger. Taking down the Tsais as fast as possible could be in many people's self-interest."

"And it can be done under the legitimate guise of weeding out corruption."

"Which some of them might actually care about," Xu said. "Not that that matters."

"Not in the least."

"I need to talk to Lop," Xu said suddenly.

"Did something happen that I didn't notice?" Ava said, looking towards the door.

"No, but he has a wide range of contacts in the PLA and security forces. It might be useful to fill them in too. They have their own interests to serve."

"I think we need to start making some phone calls," Ava said.

47

LOP RODE WITH THEM FROM THE HOTEL BACK TO THE house. He sat in the front, but his head was turned towards the back seat for the entire trip as Xu explained to him what he wanted him to do. Lop responded with an enthusiasm that, from anyone else, Ava would have considered over the top, but she was beginning to realize that this was his normal state.

"I'll start making calls as soon as our defensive perimeter is set," Lop said. "I know five or six senior officers who are fed up with this level of corruption. They'll pass the word."

"But make sure not to mention the Tsai family," Xu said.

"I understand."

"And what's this about a defensive perimeter?" Ava asked.

"We're going to have men posted around the broader neighbourhood. We don't want to be caught off guard, and if there is any action, we want to be prepared for it," Xu said.

"I see."

"Don't be alarmed. I'm not expecting them to do anything stupid, but it would be careless of us not to accept it as a possibility — however far-fetched."

When they reached the alley, Ava saw that the fruit vendor was now accompanied by two other men. They sat on stools on either side of the cart. They didn't look armed, but Ava assumed that weapons weren't far away.

Lop got out of the car at the cart, and as the Mercedes crawled along the alley, Ava saw him talking to the men.

"I know he's a bit manic," Ava said, "but having him on our side does provide a sense of comfort."

"I've been lucky to have him and Suen," Xu said. "They're both loyal to an almost irrational degree."

"It takes a special kind of person to inspire that kind of loyalty."

Xu glanced in her direction and smiled.

For once there was no sign of Auntie Grace when the car turned into the courtyard.

"Where's Auntie?" Ava asked.

"This is her shopping day," Xu said. "I'll work from the kitchen until she comes back."

"I'm going to my room."

Ava closed the bedroom door and sat on the bed. The morning had rattled her and she had had to struggle to appear calm. There were just too many people involved and too many unknowns for her to feel that she had any kind of control. She took several deep breaths. What made the situation even more worrying was that the number of people was about to dramatically expand. What were the other options? None she could readily think of, and she didn't have the time to ponder. She retrieved her phone and called May Ling.

Her friend answered at once. "Where are you and what's going on? I've been worried," May said.

"Are you still in Wuhan?"

"Yes."

"Are you free to talk?"

"I'm alone in the office."

"Good. I need some help. Do you have you time available in the next hour or two?"

"What's going on?" May said, her voice rising.

"Things have been getting more complicated with the Tsai family."

"How is that possible?"

Ava sighed and lay on the bed. "I should have listened to you. I should have stayed away from them. I think if I had, it's quite possible that Xu and the Tsais would have worked out a compromise."

"Why can't they still do that?"

"I just left a meeting that Xu and I had with Tsai Men and his father."

"The Governor?"

"Himself."

"Shit."

"Yeah, and he is every bit as smart and paranoid and menacing as you said. I haven't met many people who scare me, and he did."

"Is that why they met with you, to frighten you?"

"No, the Governor wanted to tell me and Xu in person that he knew I was the one who was looking into his business affairs. He doesn't have any real facts, of course, but he believes it all the same, and he wasn't about to be persuaded otherwise. He made it clear that it has to stop at once or there will be consequences."

May remained quiet.

"I'm waiting," Ava said.

"For what?"

"For you to say, 'I told you so.'"

"Just stop pestering the lion," May said, ignoring Ava's invitation. "If that's what he wants, do it."

"It's too late."

"Why?"

"The *Wall Street Tribune* is going to publish a story tonight that details the Tsai empire and says God knows what about how he built it. The *Economic Herald* won't be far behind, except they're going to highlight Dennis Calhoun and his corrupt partnership with the family. Tsai Lian is going to go absolutely nuts."

"That prospect hasn't bothered you up to now."

"Yes, but I thought he wouldn't be able to identify the source of the stories. Now I know he will. He may have no real proof, but that's not going to matter. It will fall on me and Xu."

"Can you get the papers to back off?"

"I've been the one urging them to go forward and providing them with nearly all of their information. And I've involved Brenda Burgess, Richard Bowlby, Vanessa Ogg, and a whole bunch of other people, including Vincent Yin, the MD at Mega Metals. I've actually convinced Yin to pack in his job and take off for England," Ava said. "I can't ask the papers not to run the stories without all those people finding out about it. It would look like I'd been using them for my own selfish purposes, and if the papers said no and ran the stories anyway, I'd look even worse."

"This is complicated," May said.

"Well, we have to come up with a plan, and that's why I need your help."

"I'm all ears."

"Given that the stories are going to run regardless of what we do, our feeling is that we need to make sure they reach the widest and most influential audience possible. If we can create enough of a stink about the family and the whole issue of corruption at the most senior levels of government in China, we think we might be able to paralyze the Tsais for at least a while."

"Not everyone reads English-language newspapers, and even if they do, they might discount what they read."

"We want to try to make sure they do read the papers."

"And you say you have a plan?"

"I'm at Xu's house. He's in another room making phone calls. His man Lop, the ex–Special Forces officer, has flown in from Hong Kong and is a few houses away. Both of them are making calls to every person of influence they know here and in other parts of China, particularly Beijing. They're telling everyone that two prominent English-language newspapers are about to publish stories that name a senior Chinese government official as the most corrupt and wealthiest public servant in the world. They're going to say they don't know who's going to be identified, but they thought they should give their friends some advance warning, just in case they might have some connection to any official they think could be a candidate."

"That's very clever," May said with a chuckle.

"May!"

"No, I mean it. It is clever. I'm quite sure some of the people they call will think it could be them. I'm more sure that most of them can think of someone else who they're connected to."

"Our objective is to get them talking among themselves and desperate to read the newspapers."

"You're also going to cause a lot of people a lot of anxiety."

"We're more interested in getting them to focus on the Tsai family story when it breaks."

"Oh, they will. Believe me, they will."

"So, could you make some phone calls as well?"

"It will be a pleasure. There are more than a few of our friends and business acquaintances who I don't mind making uncomfortable for a while."

"Get back to me later in the day?"

"Of course."

"I can hardly wait to put this behind me."

"And Amanda and the girls can hardly wait to have you back in the loop again."

"I feel bad that I've been so distracted."

"There's no reason to feel that way — and besides, it's forced them to make their own decisions. I have to say they've been doing a very good job."

"I love them all," Ava said.

"I feel the same way. Now let me make some calls."

Ava ended the call and checked the time again. It was almost six a.m. in England. *If Michael Dillman isn't awake and out of bed, he should be*, she thought as she pressed his number. It rang five times and went to voicemail.

"This is Ava Lee. Please call me as soon as you can. It's urgent," she said.

She heard Xu's voice through the door. The words were muffled, although she could make out "corrupt" more than once. His voice level was rising and falling. She guessed he was walking back and forth as he made his calls.

She checked the emails on her phone. There was a multitude from the girls and May, one was from Carrie Song, and the most recent was from Maria. She debated opening them and then decided against it. Her mind was too preoccupied. She reached into her suitcase and took out a clean T-shirt and her Adidas track pants. As she slipped the T-shirt over her head, the phone rang. She almost jumped at it.

"This is Michael Dillman."

"Thanks for calling me back so promptly."

"What's so urgent?"

"Vincent Yin is on a plane headed to London. We've decided that it might be better for all concerned if you contact Dennis Calhoun right away."

"Does that mean you're prepared to let us publish when we're ready?"

"It does, and in fact it would please us if you could publish today — I mean, today in your time zone."

"I have to ask, what caused this change in attitude?"

"Vincent is safe now and that was our main worry. In hindsight, there is really no reason to wait until he lands."

"I see. Well, I'll have to talk to Tamara, but I can't imagine she'll object."

"There are two other things you might want to mention to her."

"I'm listening."

"Vincent is travelling with a man named Suen, who works for a colleague of mine. You might want to arrange to meet the two of them at Heathrow. Vincent could probably use some public relations advice that Suen isn't qualified to give. Since you're breaking the story in the U.K., I thought you might want to have at least short-term control over the people that Vincent will be talking to there."

"Will you send me their flight number?"

"I will as soon as I hang up, and I'll tell my colleague to text Suen and let him know what's going on."

"What else?"

"The *Wall Street Tribune* is going to publish its story. By this evening in London, you should be able to see it online, and by tomorrow morning it will be in print. I thought you should know. I don't want you to think that we've given preferential treatment to anyone. They aren't going to highlight the Calhoun connection, but instead will focus on the general theme of corruption at the highest levels of government in China. It also appears that some American laws were broken as well as British ones. They've identified and will name at least one U.S. corporation that has bribed its way through the Tsai family into a very profitable business."

"You've been busy."

"I try."

"Okay, I'll call Tamara in a few minutes. I'm quite sure she'll want us to go ahead at full speed. I have the entire story written, except for Calhoun's comments," he said. "And as a caveat, I do have to say that when the story is published might depend on what Dennis Calhoun has to say. We can't assume he doesn't have a reasonable explanation for what has transpired, and that will give us more work to do."

"What kind of explanation could he have?"

"He might say that Vincent Yin concocted the entire scheme with the Tsai family."

"Meaning that Calhoun didn't understand a single word

that was said in the meetings, and Yin interpreted every-thing to suit his own purposes?"

"Something like that."

"You can't believe that."

"Of course I don't, not for a second, and neither does Tamara, but our lawyer raised the possibility — however far-fetched — and we can't ignore it. We do have to expect Calhoun to do some equivocating. That is just one example."

"Who will be the person to contact Calhoun?"

"Me."

"Good, and when will that be?"

"After I talk to Tamara. We have a list of questions we prepared yesterday. I'm ready to go."

"You're not mentioning Yin, are you?"

"Not up front. Our plan is to refer to 'a reliable source.' If Calhoun gets sticky, though, I won't have any choice. Besides, Yin's name is going to come out sooner or later."

"I understand, and so does Vincent. I just think it would be nice to get him landed and in a hotel before that happens."

"Given that you've given us exclusive access to him, I think you can accept that those would be our wishes as well."

"Well, then, Michael, go to it, and good hunting. If I don't hear from you, I'll assume everything is going as planned."

"I will phone to let you know when we intend to publish."

Ava ended the call and sat still for a moment before flop-ping back onto the bed. Her conversation with Dillman had on the surface gone well enough, but all she could think of was his comment about the *Herald*'s lawyer. Calhoun was a prominent Conservative. Maybe the lawyer was a Tory supporter. Maybe he was looking for a way to muddy the waters. Maybe he was trying to find an out for Calhoun.

Stop fixating, she told herself. *Stop being so damn negative.* They had facts and they had corroboration. Nothing was going to go wrong.

48

WHEN AVA EMERGED FROM THE BEDROOM, AUNTIE Grace was in the kitchen stirring something on the stove. There was no sign of Xu.

"Did you nap?" Auntie Grace asked.

"I think I must have. One minute my mind was doing somersaults and the next minute I nodded off. I can hardly believe it was possible after the good night's sleep I had."

"It's good you can sleep. It helps deal with stress. Xu can't do that."

"Where is he?"

"He's gone to talk to Lop, and then he has a meeting with one of the people he was talking to on the phone."

"Did he say when he'd be back?"

"An hour or two, but that was over an hour ago, so he could be home anytime."

Ava went to the kitchen cupboard and took out a cup. A jar of Nescafé instant coffee sat next to the hot water Thermos. She put two large teaspoons of coffee into the cup and filled it with water.

She sat at the kitchen table, holding the cup between her palms and wondering if Dillman had confronted Dennis Calhoun yet. The nap hadn't helped her get rid of the feeling that Calhoun wasn't going to be easy to deal with. She looked at her phone to see if she'd missed any calls while she slept. There were none, and she couldn't decide if that was good or bad.

"You look worried," Auntie Grace said.

"I am. I hate it when I have to depend on other people."

Auntie Grace started to speak, but Ava's phone rang and both women were startled by it.

"Hello," Ava said.

"Are you okay?" May said.

"Why?"

"You sound distant."

"I just woke up from a nap."

"Well, I have some news that might wake you up a bit more," May said. "The Lane Crawford deal closed ten minutes ago. Three looks times four pieces. Hong Kong and the New Territories are the only exclusive markets. We had to give them those markets for a year but it was worth it. The girls and Clark are ecstatic."

"That's fantastic."

"It sets us up for business in Asia, and when we've got that base established, then look out, world. Gillian and Chi-Tze are already talking about doing one of the fashion weeks next year, in New York, London, Milan, or Paris."

"It sure beats doing business on Negros Island in the Philippines, or a hundred other backwaters I've worked."

"Or in Wuhan, but don't ever tell Changxing I said that."

"Congratulate the girls for me."

"Congratulate them yourself, once you dig yourself out of the hole the Tsai family has put you in," May said.

"What hole? Have you heard something new?" Ava said.

"Well, that made you perk up."

"It's weighing on me, and as happy as I am about Lane Crawford, the Tsais are all I'm really thinking about right now."

"No, I haven't heard anything, but I made those phone calls you wanted me to make and I found the reaction fascinating," May said. "No one, and I mean no one, discounted the idea that someone might be that corrupt. Some of them acted like they had nothing to worry about but were intensely curious all the same. Others were more than curious. I was bombarded with questions about which newspapers, what kind of timing, and what names I'd heard mentioned. I didn't imagine that quite so many of them would feel they had something that large to hide."

"So the pot has been well stirred?"

"Absolutely, and the people I called are connected. You can be sure they're phoning their friends and contacts right now. This will spread. My only concern is that the Tsai family will get wind of it."

"Xu expressed the same concern, but we're in this too deep to back off," Ava said.

"What kind of reaction did Xu and Lop get from the people they called?"

"I don't know."

"I can't imagine them getting anything but the same."

"If they did, then hopefully the stage is set to make life uncomfortable for the Tsais."

"I'm sure it is."

"Thanks for making the calls, May, and for lifting my spirits. I'll be in touch when I hear more."

Ava checked the time. She still had hours to wait until the *Tribune* story broke, and maybe even longer before Dillman got back to her about Calhoun. She had time to kill, and her energy level was so high she knew that just sitting around wasn't an option. She headed for the bedroom and took her running gear from the bag. When she walked back into the living room, Auntie Grace looked at her in surprise.

"I don't think you should be straying too far from the house," Auntie said.

"I'll run in the alley. It's long enough that I can work up a sweat."

The men in the courtyard stood up when she emerged from the house. The gate was closed and they made no move to open it when Ava walked towards them.

"Open the gate, please," she said. "I'm going to stay in the alley."

They still seemed doubtful, and Ava began to get impatient.

"Don't go past the fruit wagons," one finally said.

"I promise."

He swung the gate open and she stepped into the alley. It was quiet. The only sign of life was at the fruit carts at either end, each with two other men.

As she started to run towards one end, the men seemed to brace themselves as if they might have to intercept her. She waved at them when she drew near, stopped just short, turned, and sprinted towards the other end, where she did the same thing. By her fourth lap, they had resumed their normal position and were generally ignoring her.

She had no specific idea how long she ran, but she guessed that the alley was 300 metres long and she had done thirty laps, about nine kilometres. The sky was overcast, but it was warm and muggy and she very quickly worked up a sweat. By the time she finished, she was dripping, the sweat washing away some of the tension she'd been carrying.

There was no sign of Auntie Grace when Ava went back into the house. In the cool interior of the kitchen, she drank two large glasses of cold water and then wrapped a towel around her shoulders to absorb the sweat. She knew that it would take at least fifteen minutes for her to cool down sufficiently to be able to shower. She sat at the kitchen table and waited, her mind drawn to London and New York, to Sam Curry and Michael Dillman.

As Ava left the kitchen to go to the bathroom, Auntie Grace was coming out of her own bedroom. "It was my turn to nap," she said.

"Did you hear from Xu?"

"Not yet, but that's not unusual. He's not a man who's married to time when business is concerned."

"I'm going to shower."

"He could be back by the time you're finished," she said.

Ava adjusted the shower head to its most powerful setting, turned the water temperature as high as she could bear, and stepped into the stall. For ten minutes she let the water batter her, and as it did, her thoughts, for the first time that entire day, drifted away from the Tsai family. When she finished, she found that the combination of the run and the shower had actually relaxed her.

She took her time drying her hair and then muddled around with clothes before predictably putting on a T-shirt and her Adidas pants. She checked her phone and computer and saw nothing indicating that anything had changed. With a sigh, she wandered into the kitchen to make another coffee.

Auntie Grace was working at the sink, but stopped when she saw Ava. "He's back," she said. "He's sitting by the fish pond."

Ava walked into the courtyard with a mug of coffee in her hand. Xu was sitting in a wooden chair, his cigarette pack and lighter resting on a small table next to him. It was becoming a familiar scene to her.

"Come and sit," he said, rising to unfold another chair that was leaning against a brick wall near the pond.

"How was your afternoon?" she asked.

"Less strenuous than yours, evidently. The men aren't accustomed to seeing someone running up and down the alley."

"I needed to work off some tension. I'm not good at waiting."

"There are a lot of people in this city, in this province, and in Beijing who are doing some anxious waiting themselves right now."

"Your phone calls went well?"

"It was almost ridiculously easy to get some of them wound up."

"May had the same kind of success."

"Lop too, but in his case the reaction was a bit different."

"How so?"

"The people he spoke to weren't that worried about themselves. They were keen, though, to get a name."

"To go after?"

"You would like to think so, but Lop says that isn't necessarily the case. If the person or persons named are in a position to benefit the military or are currently allies of the military, they might move to defend them rather than prosecute them."

"Does he think that Tsai Lian has that kind of influence?"

"No, but that's only a guess on his part."

"Oh," Ava said.

"There's no reason to be disappointed," Xu said. "We've all done what we can. We've supplied the ammunition — now it's up to the newspapers to load the guns, and the people we've spoken to to fire them."

"There has to be something else we can do," Ava said.

Xu lit a cigarette, inhaled deeply, and blew the smoke in the direction of the gate. As he did, one of the guards took a step forward and pressed a bud into his ear. He listened intently for a few seconds and then trotted towards Ava and Xu.

"There are some unmarked military vehicles circling the neighbourhood," he said.

"Close to us?" Xu said.

"Not yet."

"Does Lop know?"

"He's checking them out."

"Does it appear they're headed in any specific direction?"

"No, sir."

"Keep me posted," Xu said, and then turned to Ava. "This isn't that unusual."

"How do you know they're military if they're unmarked?"

"They drive ordinary Jeeps and Range Rovers and they don't all wear uniforms, but they use a series of licence plates that is reserved for them."

"That's careless."

"Not many people know."

"How do you?"

"We've hired them from time to time."

"Lop was a former colleague of theirs?"

"Once or twice removed, but they're still part of the same band of brothers. That said, they don't take orders from him anymore."

"That isn't comforting."

"I'm not particularly worried."

"Oh god, I just want —" Ava began, but was cut off by her phone.

"This is Michael Dillman," the now familiar voice said.

"I didn't expect to hear from you so soon," she said.

"I thought you'd like to know that I had a talk with Dennis Calhoun, and that Tamara and our lawyer just got off the phone with his lawyer."

"I see," Ava said, not pleased with his neutral tone.

"It has been a most eventful couple of hours."

"What is that supposed to mean?"

"You sound almost alarmed," Dillman said.

"I've been worried about your caveat. I kept thinking that Calhoun would throw smoke and mirrors at you and that your lawyer would buy in to some of it."

"If I had given Calhoun a chance to dance around the subject, he might have. But I didn't."

"So it went well?" Ava said, rising from the chair.

"It went wonderfully well," Dillman said.

Ava smiled, clenched a fist, and punched it in the air. Xu looked up at her, a grin now splitting his face.

"Tell me about it," she said.

"I reached him at his home. He was happy enough to take my call, and when I said I wanted to talk about doing business in China, he was immediately garrulous. I let him run on for a bit and then mentioned that what I really wanted to discuss was Mega Metals' connections to senior levels of the Jiangsu provincial government. He hemmed and hawed and made some general meaningless remark about how it was important for any business to maintain some kind of relationship with government authorities in China," Dillman said. "That's when I said I was referring to a relationship that appeared to be corrupt."

"You were that direct?"

"Yes. Tamara saw no reason for us to be coy."

"How did he react?"

"He said he had no idea what I was talking about, so I told him."

"Specifically?"

"Yes."

"And?"

"Our talk went straight downhill. I listened to several minutes of blustery denials mixed in with libel threats. When I didn't back down, he hung up on me."

"That's it? He hung up on you?"

"Yes."

"So where does that leave things?"

"Normally we would have waited and then gone back to give him another chance to respond, but he — or rather his lawyer — decided to get aggressive. The lawyer put in a call to us half an hour after I'd talked to Calhoun, and our lawyer and Tamara took it. Without even asking what information we had or how we came to have it, he went directly into attack mode. He threatened to sue the paper, the company that owns the paper, and every one of us individually. That was a huge mistake. Tamara responds to facts and reasoned logic. You don't ever threaten or try to bully her. As soon as she hung up the phone, she said, 'That story runs today.'"

"Today?"

"Front page, centre."

"That's just great."

"Tamara is working with some other editors on the headline. They're trying for something dramatic."

"Please thank her for me."

"I will."

"Michael, one last thing. The *Tribune* story is going to break online before it appears in print. Is your paper going to use the same approach?"

"Indeed it is, and with any luck the story should be up in a few hours."

49

AVA PACED BACK AND FORTH ACROSS THE COURT-
yard. Xu watched her from his chair, another cigarette balanced between his fingers and a quizzical look on his face.

"It was good news," she had said as she hung up from
Dillman. "But I'm too hyper to sit. Give me a few minutes."

He didn't speak until she finally sat down again. "Explain
what you mean by good news," he said.

"First, I forgot to ask you to text or leave a voicemail for
Suen. He needs to know that the *Herald* will be sending
someone to Heathrow to meet him and Yin. The paper will
look after their accommodation and help Yin handle the
other media."

"I'll do it after you tell me what you mean by good news."

"Sorry," Ava said, taking a deep breath. "The *Herald* story
will be online in a short while, and in print by tonight. They
spoke to Dennis Calhoun. He went legal on them and it
didn't work in his favour."

"Calhoun will undoubtedly call Tsai Men, and maybe
even the Governor."

"I imagine that's exactly what he will do."

"That's unfortunate."

"There was no other way to handle it."

"I know," Xu said, taking his phone from his jacket pocket.

"Are you calling Tsai Men?" Ava asked.

"I have the ring volume turned down. I was just checking to see if he has tried to call me. He hasn't."

"That's a surprise."

"Maybe Calhoun hasn't contacted him yet. Maybe Calhoun and his lawyer are trying to come up with some kind of story they can spin to cover his butt."

"Do you think so?"

"Not really."

"So why haven't you heard from Men?"

"If they know, they only just know. They could still be digesting the news and planning some kind of strategic response."

"Maybe there isn't that much to digest. I mean, Calhoun hasn't actually seen the story."

"And the Tsais have no idea how deeply they're implicated. They might figure that it's only Calhoun who has the problem. They might want to sit back and do nothing until they know what they're actually dealing with."

"They haven't sat back up till now."

"Yes, but it has only been between me and them, and then them and us. A small circle that they can contain and control. A respectable British newspaper with an international readership is a different animal."

"Do you think they might help Calhoun?"

"Perhaps they'll think about it if there isn't any risk and it doesn't cost them anything."

"If the newspaper story is as hard-hitting and sensational as Dillman hints it is, I think Calhoun is toast. The British tabloids and online media will have a field day with this."

"Then the Tsai family won't want to be anywhere near him. They'll want him to go under by himself, and as quickly and quietly as possible. And Ava, they're smart enough to give him an extra shove out the door to make it look like he is the villain and they were just one of his victims."

Ava shook her head. "All this conjecture is starting to make me a little crazy. We need to see that story."

"Well, there isn't anything we can do from here," Xu said. "Why don't we go inside? I feel like some comfort food and I asked Auntie Grace to make some fresh congee. You can set up your computer in the kitchen and we'll track the newspapers from there."

Auntie Grace was standing at the stove when they entered the kitchen.

"We'll eat now," Xu said.

"I'll get my computer," Ava said, and went to the bedroom. When she returned, the table was set with two large, steaming bowls of congee and side plates with duck eggs, chopped spring onions, and diced Chinese ham. She put her computer on the counter and sat at the table.

Xu filled his bowl with some of everything. Ava just sprinkled onions and white pepper on her congee. She hadn't felt hungry all afternoon, but now the aroma wafting from her bowl released her appetite. She skimmed a layer off the top with her spoon and then kept eating until the bowl was empty and she was ready for another.

"I'd like more, please," she said to Auntie Grace.

"You eat like a man," Xu said.

"What kind of thing is that to say to Ava?" Auntie said.

"I meant it as a compliment. She eats as much as I do and stays so damn thin and fit. I don't know how she does it."

"My mother says it's going to catch up with me one day, that I'll wake up and have gained twenty pounds overnight."

Clucking her tongue at Xu, the old woman refilled both bowls and then stood to one side and watched as they dug in.

When they finished, Ava took her computer from the counter and put it on the table. She found the *Economic Herald* online and opened it.

"There's nothing yet," she said to Xu as she scanned the front page. "The lead story is from yesterday's edition."

"It's early."

"I know, but I was hoping."

"Check the *Tribune*."

"Same thing," Ava said a few minutes later.

"I'm going back outside for a smoke," Xu said.

"Have you sent the text to Suen?"

"I'll do it right away."

She thought about going outside with him but didn't want to leave the computer. She flitted back and forth between the two websites, her impatience growing. *Give it a break*, she thought, and pushed herself away from the table. As she did, her phone rang and she saw the country code for the U.K.

"Yes?" she almost shouted.

"It's Dillman again. Sorry if I'm pestering you," he said.

"Hardly."

"I thought you'd like to know that the story will be up on our site in about half an hour."

Ava drew a deep breath. "Will it be prominent?"

"The headline is front page centre. It reads, 'Chairman Calhoun Bribed Chairman Tsai,' and underneath, 'How Dennis Calhoun Really Made His Money and Reputation in China.'"

"That's quite harsh, and very direct."

"His lawyer shouldn't have threatened Tamara."

"I like the chairman connection."

"Calhoun won't."

"Tsai Lian won't like it any better, particularly since he isn't a chairman and the party has been rather careful about avoiding that title."

"What he may like even less is the sidebar story we're running. It details the Tsai empire using your chart, except that we ran out of space and couldn't get all the companies onto it. We ended up listing them separately. It's still impressive."

"Thank you for that," Ava said.

"You have to expect that the Calhoun story will be the one that's going to get the big play here. The other papers are going to be all over it," Dillman said. "Does anyone else know when Vincent Yin is arriving?"

"No, you're the only one."

"And you'll let them know we'll be meeting them and that we can be trusted?"

"It's being done now."

"Okay, then good luck to you."

Ava ended the call and glanced at her computer. Despite what Dillman had said, she couldn't resist looking at the *Herald*'s website. It was still the same day-old headline. She switched to the *Tribune* and found herself staring at an enlarged photo of Tsai Lian wearing his aviator glasses. She read the headline and then stopped, stood up, and ran towards the door.

"Xu, get in here," she shouted. "Things are starting to move."

50

THEY SAT SIDE BY SIDE AT THE KITCHEN TABLE, AVA'S computer screen filled with the front page of the *Tribune*. The headline on the right side of the page read: "Meet Tsai Lian: The Princeling of Nanjing and His Royal Chinese Family." Underneath it read: "From Son of Communist Peasant Leader to Twenty-Billion-Dollar Man in One Generation."

The story began:

> If you want to conduct business successfully in Jiangsu, one of China's most populous and wealthiest provinces, there is only one path to follow, and that's to the door of any member of the Tsai family.
>
> It is a lesson that Patriot General Insurance of Hartford, Connecticut, learned after ten years of trying and failing to get a foothold in China. One phone call to a senior family member led to a meeting with another. Six months later, Patriot

funnelled $150 million to a company called AKG Consulting, officially owned by a man named Zhu Huan. Zhu is the husband of Ying Jie, who is the daughter of Ying Fa, the Communist Party secretary in Jiangsu and cousin to Tsai Lian, the governor of Jiangsu. AKG promptly transferred the $150 million to another firm, Mother of Pearl Investments, which is controlled by Wu Wai Wai, the sister of Tsai Lian. Mother of Pearl used the $150 million to buy all of Jiangsu Insurance. Patriot was given a 49 percent stake for putting up 100 percent of the money used to buy the local insurance company.

Why was Patriot so generous? Why were they willing to settle for a minority share after putting up all of the money?

Within a year, nearly all of the provincial government's insurance business was flowing through Jiangsu Insurance, and the company's value had increased fourfold. Within three years, other American and European companies that wanted to do business in the province found it wise to have their insurance needs met by Jiangsu. The company's value rose to close to ten times the original purchase price, and Patriot's $150 million investment had turned into nearly half a billion in equity. Moreover, Jiangsu was churning out profits

about 30 percent higher than the industry norm. Why? Because it didn't have to
worry about competition.

The California Technical Trust Bank of
San Francisco had the same good fortune.
It established a subsidiary in Jiangsu called
California Asian Trust. That company put
a lot of cash into AKG and another firm,
New Age Capital. New Age is owned by
Ying Jie and Hu Chi. Ying Jie is the wife
of Zhu Huan of AKG and the daughter
of Ying Fa. Hu Chi is the husband of Tsai
Bik, Tsai Lian's daughter. California Asian
Trust's money — cycled through AKG and
New Age — eventually bought an appliance company called Kitchen Giant. The
purchase was made through a provincial
government auction that some losing parties claim was rigged. For their 100 percent
investment, Trust got a 49 percent stake in
a business that experts tell us should have
been sold for about half a billion — more
than three times the amount that was paid.

Ava scrolled down and saw the chart representing the
Tsai family holdings. She smiled. It looked even more pol-
ished and authoritative than it had in the version Curry
had sent her. Tsai Lian was positioned at the top of the family and too many companies to quickly count, all of them
interconnected like a spider's web. They had even found
photos of some of the major players.

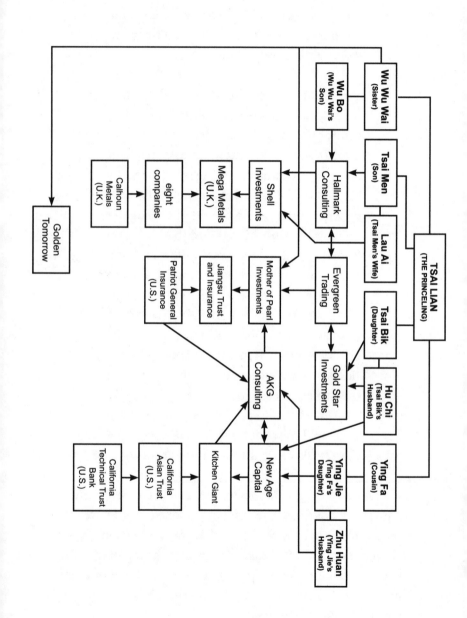

Xu read quietly, his face expressionless, and Ava wondered what was going through his mind. Their war with the Tsai family had now moved from theory to fact. Bridges had been burned, completely and dangerously. It was too late to have second thoughts, but it wasn't too late to have regrets.

"Lian looks quite arrogant in that shot," Xu finally said.

"That's appropriate," Ava said. "What do you think about the story?"

"It's even more powerful than I expected."

"Dillman called and read me the headline from the *Herald*," she said. "That story will be available online any minute now."

"And how strong is it?"

"Equally, and it refers to Tsai Lian as 'Chairman Tsai.'"

Xu shook his head as if that was information he didn't want to hear.

"What do you think?" Ava asked, deciding to push. "What kind of reaction do you think these stories will generate?"

Xu sat back in his chair and turned to Ava. His face was firmly set, and if he had any doubts about the path they'd taken, Ava couldn't detect them.

"Ask me in an hour," he said.

"Why?"

"Because we need to get busy. I have to call Lop, and you should call May. We have to let everyone we contacted know that the stories are public and Tsai Lian has been named as the government official. How they react will tell us what the impact might be."

"The only weakness I can see is that the *Tribune* story doesn't link Lian directly to any of the deals."

"Given everything else in it, I don't think that will matter, but we'll find out," Xu said.

"I'll phone May."

"I'm going to make my calls outside."

Ava punched in May's cell number as Xu left the house. The call went to voicemail, so Ava tried her private office line. It rang once.

"Ava," May said.

"May, the story about the Tsai family just appeared on the *Wall Street Tribune*'s website. The *Economic Herald* story will be available in a few minutes," Ava said in a rush.

"How is the *Tribune* story?"

"Take a look for yourself and tell me what you think."

"Give me a few minutes. Don't hang up."

"I'll wait."

Auntie Grace was still in the kitchen. Ava had been so caught up in what she was doing that she hadn't noticed. "Could I have more coffee, please," she said to her, holding out her mug. While Auntie Grace was making her coffee, Ava checked the *Herald* again. The story was up. The headline was gigantic, even larger than Dillman had indicated, and Ava wondered if this was another bit of the revenge that Tamara Klinger was taking on Calhoun.

"May, are you still on the line?" Ava asked.

"Yes, I'm reading the *Tribune*. Sorry to be so slow but my English is not as good as yours."

"When you're finished, go to the *Herald* website. You can read that story now too."

While May was reading the articles, Auntie Grace quietly placed the cup of coffee in front of Ava. She gave her a pat on the shoulder and went back to the stove.

"It's almost hard to believe." May finally said.

"Which story?"

"Take your pick. Either of them would be a bombshell on its own. Together, God knows what damage they'll cause. I can't remember the last time I was so shocked."

"I've been telling you what I've been finding and what I was doing."

"Yes, but seeing it in large print in two such respected papers makes it appear even worse than I imagined," May said. "And I can tell you that the *Herald* referring to Tsai as 'Chairman Tsai' will make some people very, very angry."

"I thought the *Tribune* calling him the 'Princeling of Nanjing' and 'head of the new Chinese royalty' would be more infuriating."

"Neither description does him any good."

"May, Xu is calling the people he phoned earlier to let them know the stories have broken. He thinks you should be doing the same."

"Of course."

"What will they think?"

"I don't want to guess."

"Can you phone them now and get back to me?"

"Yes. I've been getting calls all day from them, wondering when the stories were going to break. I'm sure they'll be happy to hear from me," May said.

Ava put her phone down and sat back in the chair.

"Can I get you anything else?" Auntie Grace asked.

"No, I'm fine."

"You look more relaxed than you did half an hour ago."

"We've had good news, or at least the beginning of something that could be good news."

"I'm happy for you."

"It isn't over yet," Ava said, sipping her coffee. She then got up to go to the bathroom.

She took her time standing over the sink, looking at herself as she washed her hands. She had no real idea, she realized, what would be the outcome of what she had started. The same was often true of jobs she'd undertaken with Uncle, but the difference this time — and it was a huge difference — was that on past jobs, her failure to collect money was just that, and she knew there would be another day and another job. Now, if the Tsai family survived, or possibly even continued to thrive, there might not be another day. She shuddered and thought of her mother, who, for as long as she could remember, had chided her for her constant risk-taking. It was her nature, and it was only recently that her mother had seemed to accept that. *Maybe she shouldn't have*, Ava thought.

She was now closer to forty than to thirty, but she had the face and the body of a woman in her twenties. She had her mother's and father's genes to thank for that. Her mind was a different age entirely, and that had everything to do with the experiences and memories etched into it. She wondered how old she was inside. Certainly forty, and maybe even fifty. One of her mother's pat descriptions of Ava was that she had an old head on a young body. It was a cliché, but like all clichés it had a kernel of truth. And what that old head was telling her right now was that whatever was going to happen was going to happen fast. She glanced down at her T-shirt and Adidas training pants. *This isn't what I should be wearing*, she thought.

She went into the bedroom, brushed her hair, and fixed

it with the ivory chignon pin. She put on makeup. She took a pink shirt and a black skirt from her bag, slipped them on, and then added the green jade cufflinks and her Cartier watch. She looked at her shoes and opted for the high heels she'd worn to the PÖ launch, which seemed like a lifetime ago. Now fully dressed, she lowered herself onto her knees by the side of the bed and prayed again to Saint Jude. She could not remember ever praying to him so often over the course of a few days, but then she had never needed him more.

When she had finished, she sat on the bed. There was nothing for her to do except wait for Xu, Lop, and May to make their phone calls, and waiting alone was something she was accustomed to. She had her phone next to her, and her ears were attuned to the sound of the door opening and Xu's shoes crossing the living room floor. When she heard the door, she slid from the bed. When she heard the sound of his steps, she left the bedroom.

He was taking a chair at the kitchen table when she entered the room.

"You look like you're going to a meeting," he said, glancing at her.

"I'm not, but that's how I feel. Whenever I was on a job with Uncle, it seems as though I was dressed like this when we closed it successfully," Ava said. "I can't help being superstitious."

"I never discount luck," he said.

"What kind of reaction are you getting on the Tsai Lian stories?" she said as she took a seat.

"The most common one is shock, but not shock that he's been using his position to line the family's pockets — that's to be expected. It's more about the extent of the wealth and the way it's been accumulated. No one cares about the consulting fees and commissions, but the Mega Metals and Jiangsu Insurance deals can't be explained away. They're clearly corrupt deals and couldn't have happened without his active support."

"Do they think they're enough to bring him down?"

Xu shrugged. "Everyone I spoke to is convinced he'll fight to survive."

"What does he have to fight with?"

"They tell me that his father's name and reputation still have currency. There are his years of service to the province. And of course he will call in favours from those who owe him, and he'll threaten those he has something on."

"Could that work?"

"All anyone is sure about is that he will try, but I've been told that one sure sign that he has support will be if the websites carrying the stories are blocked. That can't happen without someone very senior in Beijing giving the order."

"Is that possible?"

"Websites crash all the time. Firewalls mysteriously appear. Newspapers are seized or told to cancel distribution until further notice. If Beijing decides to back Tsai, then it's possible the stories could be restricted to outlets outside China, although many of the people Lop and I spoke to probably have VPNs."

"What is a VPN?"

"The government routinely blocks Facebook and YouTube and other Western sites, but VPNs — virtual private networks — are a way around the blocks. We call it *fan qiang*."

"Climbing over the wall?"

"Yeah, and the term couldn't be more appropriate."

Ava looked at her computer and hit the *Tribune* and the *Herald* tabs. "The sites are still live," she said.

"That's good, but it's very early. We'll have to keep an eye on them."

"And if they don't get blocked?"

"I think it will indicate the stories and their claims are too big for Beijing to ignore, and then officials will have to decide if they're going to stand by Lian or throw him overboard. If they choose to defend him, they'll have to stick out their own necks and reputations. If they don't support him, they will be almost compelled to go after him. Indifference isn't an option."

"What did Lop's people have to say?"

"He says that they're angry beyond belief. Tsai is the son of a general, of a legend of the revolution. He is bringing disgrace to his father and everything he fought for and that they are honour-bound to maintain. Calls are already being made to politicians."

"Do they have that much influence?"

"We'll see," Xu said. "The people I called also have their own circles, and I'm sure that May Ling's contacts have enough power to pull some strings. It adds up."

"So what's the end?"

"Well —" Xu began but was cut off when Ava's cellphone rang.

Ava looked at him. "It's May," she said.

He nodded.

"Hey, I'm with Xu. We're going over this Tsai thing," Ava said.

"You mean Chairman Tsai, the twenty-billion-dollar man?"

"Is that what your contacts are calling him?"

"And worse. I don't know if their rage is coming from jealousy or some genuine anger at the level of his corruption, but it is definitely rage."

"So no one doubts the veracity of the stories?"

"These newspapers have terrific reputations, even here, and there's far too much detail and too much data for the reports to be anything but true."

"Xu is worried about the websites being blocked."

"Changxing made the same comment to me, but then he saw that the *Herald* story is already up on some other sites. It will be tough to shut them all down."

"That's comforting," Ava said. "Now tell me, what do your contacts want to happen to Tsai?"

"Some would like to see him shot, but that's just raw emotion. They know he's too prominent for that. They'd probably be happy with a jail term and the family losing its status and money."

"I'll tell Xu what you're hearing."

"And you'll keep me posted from your side?"

"We will."

May paused and then said, "Ava, please be careful. Wounded animals are the most dangerous."

"I know, and don't worry. I'm in a safe place and staying put until this thing is over."

"What did May have to say?" Xu asked once Ava had put away her phone.

"Other websites are now running the stories."

"That's great."

"And the people she's talking to think the Tsai family has to be held accountable."

"Every hour those websites remain active increases the chance they will stay that way. All we can do is wait and hope."

Ava shook her head. "I thought the hard part was over."

"It is, and we've done everything we can and we've done it as well as we can. Now the big boys will decide if it's enough."

"I'm not good at waiting."

"Lop and I have asked our contacts to call us as soon as they know which way this is going to break. The moment we hear something, you will. That's all we can do for now," Xu said. "Look, I'm going with Lop to a meeting about ten minutes from here by car. Why don't you join us? It will be a distraction."

"Nothing is going to get my mind off those websites," Ava said. "All I keep thinking is that Tsai has to be buried or he's going to bury us."

"Well, we'll know soon enough," Xu said calmly.

51

AVA SEARCHED FOR SOMETHING TO DO THAT WOULD occupy her mind. Finally, almost in desperation, she took out the files on the carbon-fibre containers and made an attempt to analyze the numbers, but every few minutes her fingers would be almost magnetically drawn to the keyboard of her computer and the *Tribune* and *Herald* websites. They remained live, and when she accessed a Chinese search engine and typed in "Tsai family financial scandal," she saw at least ten other media sites that were promoting the story. She was scanning them when she heard a noise at the front door. Then she heard Auntie Grace's footsteps and a few seconds later the sound of the door opening and the voices of the housekeeper and a man.

Ava rose from her chair and walked towards the door. Auntie Grace was in animated conversation with one of the men who was normally stationed at the gate.

"What's going on?" Ava said.

"There are two Range Rovers filled with men at one end of our alley, and a third is parked near the exit at the other end. The fruit vendor called as soon as he saw them, but then his phone went dead," Auntie Grace said. "Wen says they're paramilitary."

"What are they doing?"

"Just a second," Auntie Grace said, and then she stepped outside and spoke so quietly to Wen that Ava couldn't hear her. Whatever she said was enough to send him running back to the gate, where two more of Xu's men stood just inside the courtyard.

Ava watched the three of them take turns looking down the alley. Wen ran back to Ava and Auntie Grace.

"They've split up into two teams, and it looks like they're doing house-to-house searches," he said.

"How many men?" Ava asked.

"Ten in total."

"Are they armed?"

"Yes," Wen said. "They all have batons and pistols, and at least two of them have submachine guns."

"Call Xu," Auntie Grace said.

"My orders were to phone Lop if anything happened," Wen said.

"You do that," Ava said. "I'll call Xu."

Wen took a phone from his pocket and walked towards the gate.

Ava ran into the house to retrieve her phone from the kitchen, Auntie Grace following. She found Xu's number and hit it. The phone rang four times and cut out. She remembered that he'd turned down the volume on his phone. She tried again, with the same result. "Shit, I can't reach him," she said.

"Maybe Wen has had better luck with Lop," Auntie Grace said.

They were almost back at the front door when Ava's phone rang and she saw Xu's number. "The military is in the alley," she said in a rush.

"I know. Lop just told me."

"I think they're looking for me."

"That's most likely the case."

"What do we do?"

"I want you to do nothing except stay inside the house."

"I'm not much good at doing nothing."

"Ava, you have Wen and his men, and there are more men on the way. Give them a chance to get in place."

"Then what?"

"We need time. Lop has already instructed Wen what to do. Let him do it."

"Xu, I'm not going to let them take me without a fight."

"If it comes to that, you'll have plenty of support on your side. But it isn't going to come to that, and no one is going to take you anywhere," he said. "Look, we're no more than fifteen to twenty minutes away from the house. Be patient until we get there."

Ava stepped into the courtyard and saw Wen at the gate, looking down the alley.

"How fast are those men moving?" she shouted.

"They're already at the next set of houses. It won't be more than ten minutes before they get here," he yelled back.

"Did you hear that?" she said to Xu.

"I did, and we're moving as fast as we can," he said. "Lop has already left and I'm only a few minutes behind him."

The word "hurry" crossed her mind. She ended the call and walked towards Wen. He turned as she drew close, and she saw that he was armed with a Cobray M11 semi-automatic. It was Sonny's weapon of choice. She glanced at the other two men and saw they carried the same gun. She started to comment, but two of the men she'd seen earlier at one of the fruit carts appeared in the gateway. Right behind them came two more she didn't know.

"The guns are in the garage, in the trunk of the BMW," Wen said to them.

The four walked to the garage. Before they exited, two more men came into the courtyard. Wen repeated the information about the guns.

"We should go into the house," Auntie Grace said.

"No, I'm going to stay out here," Ava said. "I want to see and hear whatever is going to happen. If I sit inside, everything will be left to my imagination, and it can run wild."

"It's safer in the house."

"If those men get into the courtyard they'll be in the house ten seconds later," Ava said. "It will be the same result, just marginally delayed."

All six of the new arrivals were now armed with a variety of semi-automatic and automatic weapons and were grouped around Wen in the middle of the courtyard. "Close the gate," he told two of his men.

They swung the wooden doors together and secured them with a long, thick crossbeam.

"You should go inside," Wen said to Ava and Auntie Grace.

"I'm staying here," Ava said.

"There's no point arguing with her," Auntie Grace said to him. "And I'm not leaving unless she does."

"You don't have to do this," Ava said to Auntie Grace.

"I'm at an age where I don't have to do anything I don't

want to do, and that includes leaving you out here by your-self. So, I'm staying."

Wen sighed and looked troubled. Ava was sure Lop had instructed him to make sure she and Auntie Grace were indoors.

"We'll sit by the pond," Ava said to him. "That way we're out of the line of sight of the gate."

"If any violence breaks out, if they throw tear gas over the wall . . ."

"We'll go inside."

"Okay, that will have to do," Wen said reluctantly. He turned to the men. "Spread out. Get as much space between each other as you can while maintaining a clear view of the gate."

Ava unfolded chairs for herself and Auntie Grace. As they sat, Ava glanced at the older woman. Her face was impassive, her hands were folded in her lap, and there wasn't a hint of tension in her body.

"You act like you've been through this before," Ava said.

"Hopefully, when this is over, I'll be able to tell you that I've been through much worse."

"Indeed," Ava said.

She noticed that the entire courtyard had become silent; there wasn't so much as a whisper. Wen stood in the middle with one of the men. The others had fanned out on either side of them. Every eye was focused on the gate. Ava's atten-tion was on what was occurring in the alley, and her head was turned in the direction from which the soldiers would come. She strained to hear the sound of vehicles, of boots striking cobblestones, of closing doors and gates. But it was so quiet she could hear her heart beating. She looked at her watch. It had to have been at least five minutes since she'd spoken to Xu. Was it possible Lop could get to the house before the soldiers? But what difference would it make if he did? Had the soldiers left? Why was Xu letting Lop travel back here by himself? Ava drew a deep breath. Her mind was in overdrive. She reached for Auntie Grace's hand. The older woman placed Ava's hand between hers. That was when Ava heard voices.

It was a buzz at first, the words indistinct. Then she heard nervous laughter and someone shouting, "No one's here," and gradually the sound of men walking and more voices added to the mix. They were close now, maybe two or three houses away. Auntie Grace squeezed her hand. She saw the man standing next to Wen whisper something to him. Wen nodded and stepped closer to the gate.

Ava checked her watch. Three minutes had passed, though it seemed like an hour. She heard what she thought was a door closing, and then footsteps and clear voices. She counted four voices and assumed there was a fifth if they were searching houses in two teams. The gate rattled as someone pushed against it.

"This fucking thing is locked," a voice said.

"Here, let me," another said, and pushed, with the same result.

Someone knocked, the noise loud and sharp as if the butt of a gun was being used.

"Who are you?" Wen shouted.

"Officers in the Special Unit, attached to the People's Armed Police."

"What do you want?"

"We want you to open the gate."

Wen paused, and his lips moved as if he was counting. "Why?" he finally said.

"We're conducting a neighbourhood search."

"Why?"

"We believe that some people who've broken the law are hiding in the vicinity."

"There's no one here who broke any law."

"Open the gate," the man insisted.

"This is private property," Wen said.

Ava heard more footsteps and new voices outside the gate. She guessed the remaining five officers had arrived.

"This is Sergeant Tang. I'm in charge here. We need you to open this gate, and open it now," a more authoritative voice said.

"This is private property," Wen repeated.

"We'll break down the gate unless you open it voluntarily."

"You'll have to pay for the damage if you do."

"Don't be so thick," Tang said.

Wen paused again, and then pointed his Cobray at the middle of the gate. "Don't touch the gate," he said.

"Get the ram," Tang said.

Auntie Grace tightened her grip and a nail penetrated Ava's flesh. "When they start to break down the gate, I think we should go inside," Auntie said. "It's better they find us there than out here, where we could get hit by a stray bullet."

"Yes," Ava said.

There was no sound from the other side of the gate. Wen and his men were in position, their guns locked on the gate. None of them moved a muscle. *They're really going to shoot*, Ava thought.

"This is your last chance," Tang suddenly shouted.

Wen shook his head wordlessly.

Seconds later, there was a *boom* as the ram crashed into the wood. Auntie Grace stood and tugged at Ava. "Come," she said.

Ava struggled to her feet, her attention fixed on the gate. The ram hit it again, and she saw the first splinters. Two or three more blows would do the job. She was turning to walk with Auntie Grace into the house when she heard a familiar voice. She stopped. "That's Lop," she said.

Wen nodded but he didn't lower his gun.

Ava stood and waited. All she could hear was voices. Auntie Grace's grip on Ava's hand began to relax, and Ava's breathing slowed.

Minutes passed, and Ava was starting to feel her anxiety build again when Lop shouted, "Wen, open the gate."

He hesitated and then motioned for the men on both sides to move forward. When they'd taken positions on both sides of the gate, he raised the crossbeam and pulled the gate open.

Lop stood in the middle of a group of ten men. Their weapons hung down by their sides. When Lop nodded at him, Wen lowered his gun and the other men followed suit.

"As Captain Bao said, Tang, there was no reason for any of this," Lop said to the man standing next to him.

"No, sir," Tang replied.

"Now, why don't you clear the alley and let the people here go about their normal business."

"Yes, sir," Tang said, but hesitated.

"You don't have to worry about the gate," Lop said. "I'm sure the owner will bear the costs of any repairs."

"Then we'll be off," Tang said.

Lop remained in position as the men moved away. When there was no further sign of them, Ava expected him to come into the courtyard, but he stayed where he was, looking down the alley. She was starting to walk towards him when he took several steps back and Xu's Mercedes slid into view.

Ava froze and then retreated as the car turned into the courtyard. It came to a stop just inside. The back door opened and Xu stepped out. His face was grim.

52

XU AND AVA SAT IN THE WOODEN CHAIRS BY THE pond. Auntie Grace had gone inside. Lop was in the house several doors away. There were only three men in the courtyard and they were unarmed.

"What happened?" she finally asked.

He took out a cigarette and lit it. He inhaled deeply, then raised his head and blew a stream of smoke up into the air, where it hung for a second like a thin grey shroud.

"I'm sorry we weren't here when the military arrived. We had gone into Shanghai to meet with one of the key military commanders of the region. He is one of the men Lop phoned earlier. They were in Special Services together and have a strong bond. We were with him when Wen called Lop and told him about the house search. The commander arranged to have it called off, but it took more time than we'd have liked for them to contact the unit."

"I was lucky you were there."

"Maybe we both were."

"Why were you meeting with him in the first place?"

"We wanted to know what was going to happen to Tsai

Lian. This man is our best source."

"And what did he have to say?"

"I would have phoned you but I thought I should tell you in person."

"Is it that bad?" Ava said, feeling a flutter in her stomach.

"No," Xu said with a firm shake of his head. "Tsai Lian and Ying Fa are under house arrest until they will be told to visit the Nanjing office of the security section of the PLA. 'Visit' is a code word for surrender. If they don't go voluntarily, orders have been issued for them to be taken into custody."

"How does he know that?"

"The man in Beijing who gave the order is a colleague of the man we saw here. He was also part of our phone loop and was waiting to see who was named."

"Beijing moved so quickly."

"The general opinion is that the size of the crimes that were committed justified it."

"You actually believe that's going to be the final outcome?" she said.

"It isn't an outcome, it's the start of a process."

"And you're sure they're going to be taken out of circulation?"

"They took too much. They offended too many. As soon as the numbers became apparent and people spoke to each other, the depth of the reaction was as intense as it was fast."

"Good god."

He took a deep drag from his cigarette, and then shrugged. "Ava, do you remember the night when you, May, and I had dinner, and I offered to put money into the Three Sisters?"

"Of course."

"May commented at the time that there were no longer vendors on the Bund, and I said that one day the government simply decided that it didn't want them there."

"I remember that."

"The next day every vendor was gone and it was as if they'd never been there, as if they'd never existed. The same thing will happen to the Tsais."

"The decision is already made?"

"The order for them not to leave their homes came from Beijing, so yes, some kind of decision has been made."

"Charges will be laid?"

"Our man thinks that's the strongest probability, given the publicity the stories have generated."

"No trial?"

"We're told there will likely be a trial. Appearances have to be maintained. But if they agree to plead guilty, the trial can be held in public within a few weeks and they'll have the chance to look humble and beg for mercy. If they decide to fight, it will be held in secret and be over just as fast. But they, especially Tsai Lian, are too smart to fight."

"Why do you say that?"

"He knows that if he's charged, his allies have deserted him. He knows that if he pleads not guilty, it could be seen as being unrepentant and arrogant and dismissive of the government. Those are attitudes that could turn a jail term into an execution and eradication of the entire family's wealth."

"A guilty plea will protect the family's money?"

"Probably not all of it, but if Lian is particularly humble and co-operative I can envision a more modest jail sentence and some preservation of the family's wealth. They might also let some of them leave the country. Why have them hanging around here as a reminder?"

"What a system."

"Why do you say that?"

"Why bother with a trial at all?"

"The public needs to see that the government is serious about fighting corruption, and that no man is above the law."

"It's still a farce."

"It works in its own way, and maybe more effectively than the American or French or Italian system."

"How so?"

"Public opinion has power everywhere, except that here it may be even more potent."

"That's only because there's virtually no law that can't be bent to suit a particular need or end. In the U.S., Tsai Lian would actually go to court and face a trial that didn't have a predetermined outcome."

"I understand that you're theorizing, so let me do so as well," Xu said. "In the U.S., a man like Lian would hire an army of lawyers and public relations specialists and would buy himself years of time before anything ever went to trial. It isn't that laws aren't bent in the U.S. to suit needs; it's more that the laws don't apply to men who have his kind of wealth. Now you tell me, which system is more fair?"

"I don't know why we're talking about this — neither of us is a political scientist or a social philosopher. I'm a debt collector and you're a gangster," Ava said with a broad smile.

"You were a debt collector, and I am a gangster in transition."

"Agreed."

He picked up his lighter and turned it over in his hand.

"Xu, I thought you would be pleased with this news. When you arrived at the house, you looked upset and I actually thought you had heard the opposite."

"I'm relieved and grateful that we prevailed, but I can't find any joy in it."

"It is what you wanted."

"No, all I wanted was not to be forced back into the drug business, but things have a way of becoming connected, and roads we drive down end up in places we never imagined," he said. "I called Tsai Men from my car after I spoke to Lop. I wanted to let him know that I'd seen the stories and that I had concern for him and his family."

"Did he believe that? About your concern, I mean."

"It was real enough, but I was more concerned about feeling out where his head and emotions were. I didn't want him going rogue on us and seeking some pointless revenge. Besides, he's smart and I'm sure he'll bounce back in some way. We might even be able to do business together again at some point in time."

"No business I'd get involved in."

"I understand, but I live here and you don't. He could become part of my life again."

"But you believe that things are really settled for now?"

"Yes, and unless I'm misreading the situation entirely, you should be able to leave here whenever you wish," he said.

"There's no point in moving to a hotel, so I'll stay here for another night. That is, if you don't mind."

"You know I'm happy to have you. Where will you go from here?"

"May Ling and Suki Chan have a project that I'd like to

look at more closely, and there's still unfinished business in Hong Kong. Then I'll head back to Toronto. My mother's had a gambling windfall, and she wants to take me and my girlfriend to Italy. I think I should take her up on it before she loses everything she won."

"You will stay in touch?"

"Of course."

"I wouldn't blame you if you were hesitant after all the trouble I've been attracting."

Ava reached for the hand that held the lighter. "You know, this may sound a bit strange, but I don't mind a little trouble. It gets my blood flowing and puts my mind into overdrive. As much as I like the idea of business and I love the people I'm working with, there isn't the same kind of buzz."

"Did this give you a buzz?"

"Maybe that's the wrong word, but I'm not sure what word to use," Ava said. "All I know is that when I saw the *Tribune* and *Herald* stories, I thought, *I got them*, and I felt this surge of some weird mixture of relief and exhilaration and satisfaction. It's exactly the same feeling I had on every successful job I did with Uncle."

"You did remarkable work with Uncle, and on this."

"I never found any of it that remarkable. All I've ever done is apply the processes and the lessons I learned working with Uncle."

"Then you've had a wonderful education."

"You know, that's true, and maybe I'm just beginning to appreciate it," Ava said. "I'm also starting to believe that instead of trying to escape my past, I should accept it and maybe even embrace it. It made me who I am. And there is a lot I like about who I am."

53

THE NEXT MORNING, AVA FOUND AUNTIE GRACE alone in the kitchen. Despite Xu's assurances that the Tsais no longer posed any threat, she had slept fitfully and woken several times. The first time, she thought she heard voices near the house. The next time she was convinced that trucks were moving down the alley. Even when she realized there was no one around, she had trouble getting back to sleep. There had been too many twists and turns over the past few days, too many unpleasant surprises for her to take anything for granted.

"How did you sleep?" Auntie Grace asked.

"Not well. My imagination wouldn't leave me in peace."

"Mine neither. I kept hearing strange noises," Auntie said. "I kept thinking those soldiers were going to break down our doors."

"Well, they didn't," Ava said.

"I told Xu how I felt and he said the danger had passed," Auntie Grace said. "Then I asked him why six men were still in the courtyard."

"How did he reply?"

"He just smiled and said the fact that there was no danger was no reason to be careless."

"Where is he?" Ava said.

"He went to meet with Lop about an hour ago. He asked that you call him before you leave," Auntie Grace said. "Assuming you're still leaving."

"I have to get on with my other life."

Auntie Grace started to say something and then stopped. She smiled at Ava. "There's congee on the stove."

"I'll just make myself a coffee."

"No, let me."

Before Ava could respond, Auntie Grace was already reaching for the jar of Nescafé.

Ava sat at the kitchen table and checked her voicemail. There were two messages from Michael Dillman, and one each from May Ling and Brenda Burgess. Dillman first reported that Vincent Yin and Suen had landed and were in a secure place. His second message simply said, "Call me." May Ling and Brenda's messages were similarly succinct.

As she was calling Dillman, Auntie Grace put a steaming cup of coffee in front of her. It was one o'clock in the morning in London and she half expected to hear his voicemail message.

He answered after one ring. "I've been waiting for you to get back to me."

"Thanks for taking care of Vincent and Suen," she said. "What else has been going on? You sound rather excited."

"What hasn't been going on? None of us at the *Herald* can remember the last time this paper broke the news and became part of the news at the same time, and in such a major way."

"We saw online that other papers picked up your story."

"Papers, radio, television, web news organizations — the lot of them. It's been an absolutely crazy day."

"You seem to be holding up rather well."

"Let's see how I feel this time tomorrow. Vincent and I are scheduled to be on a TV breakfast show in the morning, and then we're off to the BBC to do both radio and television interviews."

"You're doing them together?"

"The PR person thinks it buttresses the credbility of both of us, and it's a way for me to provide support for Vincent if he needs it."

"Is the news focus on Calhoun?"

"Of course."

"How is he responding?"

"He isn't directly. His lawyer has said the charges are bogus and that Calhoun will answer them specifically when the time is right. No one believes any of it, particularly the Conservative Party. I'm told that Calhoun will be resigning the chairmanship later today, before he's thrown overboard. And about six hours ago, the Minister of Justice announced that his department would be looking into the accusation that Calhoun violated the U.K. Bribery Act."

"Congratulations to you and Tamara."

"Don't be silly. All we did was fire the gun; you and Vincent loaded it," he said. "Tamara and I want to thank you, and we hope that things are going as well for you in China."

"It's too soon to tell for certain, but all indications are that things are moving in the right direction."

"Wonderful."

"Give my best to Vincent and tell Suen we miss him," Ava said. "Let me know if anything changes on your end. Otherwise, I don't imagine there will be any reason for us to talk again."

"Probably not, so cheers again."

Ava ended the call and sat back in the chair. She had finished her coffee without being aware she was drinking it.

"Everything okay?" Auntie Grace said.

"More than okay, it seems," Ava said.

"Another coffee?"

"Please," Ava said, hitting Brenda Burgess's number.

"I'm sorry, Ms. Burgess is in a meeting and can't be disturbed," the receptionist said.

"Can I leave her a voice message?"

"Of course."

"Brenda, this is Ava Lee and I'm in Shanghai," she said when she was connected. "I'm calling to thank you, Vanessa, Richard, and the rest of your team for the help you've given me over the past week. As I'm sure you know, the stories have made an impact. It looks as though Dennis Calhoun is finished, and Richard deserves a lot of credit for that. We're still waiting to find out the ultimate decision regarding what will happen to the Tsai family. Whatever it is, it's safe for all of us to assume they've lost most of the power they had and, with that, the ability to strike back. I'm going to be in Hong Kong before heading to Canada. I'm not sure when that will be, but I'll call when I know and would love to set up dinner with you, Vanessa, Richard — if he's back — and Amanda."

Auntie Grace waited for Ava to finish her call before putting the second cup of coffee on the table. "What time do you plan to leave?" she asked. "I should tell Wen so he can organize the car for you."

"I have one more phone call to make. It shouldn't take too long, and I'm already packed. So, ten minutes?"

"I'll let him know," Auntie Grace said and then left the kitchen.

Ava phoned Wuhan. "Hey you," she said when May answered.

"Hey you, yourself. How are you feeling?"

"What have you heard?"

"The Tsais are in the kind of trouble you don't get out of."

"We're hearing the same thing," Ava said. "So, in answer to your question, I'm feeling just fine."

"Presuming things stay that way, what are your plans?"

"I've been thinking about our business."

"I am so pleased to hear that."

"I'm sorry for having dumped everything on you over the past few days."

"You don't have to apologize for anything. I understood."

"I know you did, but it didn't make me feel any less guilty."

"Feeling guilty was so unnecessary. The only thing that matters is that you're ready to step back in."

"Absolutely."

"So you could stay in Shanghai for another day or two?"

"Sure. I'm still at Xu's house, but I'm going to move back to the Peninsula this morning. I can stay as long as is necessary."

"Great. I've been thinking about this carbon-fibre container project. Suki has been calling. She's afraid the opportunity to invest is going to be lost unless we move quickly."

"What does she want?"

"For you and her to meet again with Mr. Wang."

"Is she expecting us to make a commitment?"

"Maybe something short-term so we will have the time we need to make a more thorough assessment."

"I actually reviewed the proposal yesterday. It is really interesting. I wish I hadn't been so distracted when I met with him the first time."

"Will you contact her and let her know you're prepared to meet?"

"Gladly."

"I also think that while you're still there, you should sit down with Chi-Tze, Gillian, and Clark to talk about the next six months for PÖ. Getting a foothold in Asia is fantastic, but we need to start thinking about introducing the line in the West. The fashion weeks in February would be an ideal time to launch."

"All of them?"

"There's no way that's possible. They are very difficult to get into, especially for an unknown designer. I'm told that getting into just one would be a big achievement."

"Clark is a graduate of Central Saint Martins, so he must have some London contacts. I'll ask him about who he knows and what influence they might have."

May paused and then said slowly, "Ava, I can't tell you how nice it is to talk about our business rather than those damn Tsais."

"My feelings exactly."

"You'll call me after you meet with Suki and Mr. Wang?"

"Of course. I'll stay in touch," Ava said, ending the conversation. She rose from the chair to leave the kitchen. Auntie Grace stood at the entrance. Ava walked past her on the way to the bedroom to get her bags. When she came back, Auntie Grace had moved to the front door and was talking to Wen. As Ava approached them, Wen nodded and then started to walk towards the car. Auntie Grace held out her arms and the two women hugged.

"Thank you for everything," Ava said.

Auntie Grace shook her head. "Every time you come here, you make me feel more alive. Make sure you keep coming."

"*Xiao lao ban* is ready to leave. Start the car," Ava heard Wen shout.

"What did he say?" Ava asked Auntie Grace.

"He told them to start the car."

"No, what was that name he used?"

"*Xiao lao ban* — Little Boss."

"Who calls me that?"

"I think it was Suen who started it after Hong Kong, but everyone does now."

"Everyone?"

"Even Xu when you're not here."

"That's silly."

"I like it, and don't say anything unpleasant to Wen about it. He means it as a compliment."

Ava walked to the car. Wen opened the back door and stood to one side as she got in. She started to say something but saw Auntie Grace staring at her from the doorway.

"The Peninsula Hotel," she said to the driver.

Xiao lao ban, she thought, and smiled.

COMING SOON
From House of Anansi Press
in Fall 2017

Read on for a preview of the next thrilling
Ava Lee novel, *The Couturier of Milan*

(1)

AVA LEE THOUGHT SHE KNEW LONDON. SHE'D BEEN
there as a tourist and on business countless times. After
nine months of owning part of a designer clothing line,
she also thought she was beginning to understand the
fashion industry. But three days into London Fashion
Week, she felt far removed from any sense of her usual
reality. When she voiced this feeling to May Ling Wong,
her friend and business partner, May's reaction was
surprise.

"What are you talking about?" May said. "You've been
the only calm one this week. Everyone else is running
around like headless chickens, me included."

"What you think is calmness is actually me not knowing
how to react to so much chaos. Between preparations for
the show, all the public relations activity, and the hosting of
lunches and dinners for existing and potential customers,
I've had more contact with people in my three days here
than I've had over the past three months."

"It does seem a bit mad, I admit, but according to our
show director and the public relations people, it's very

typical for fashion week here, or any of the big four fashion weeks, for that matter."

"What a crazy business," Ava said. "New York, London, Milan, and Paris in four consecutive weeks, and twice every year. I don't know how people survive it."

"We're thankful we got into even one of them. It isn't easy for new designers to be accepted into the official part of the week."

"Clark did graduate from Central Saint Martins," Ava said, referring to the famous London design school.

"He does have contacts, thank goodness, but we still had to lobby."

"I've been thinking that I should have arrived only the day before, as I did for the launch in Shanghai. Everything moved so fast there that I didn't have time to feel out of place."

"And what would we have done with Pang Fai? You're the only reason she's here."

Pang Fai was the most talented and famous actress in Chinese cinema and had a massive following in Asia. Her films were now being screened in the West, and her fame there was on a rapid upswing. Her popularity had grown accordingly, and in the past few months she'd made many of the "Most Beautiful Women" and "Sexiest Women" lists in the West. Her decision to promote the PÖ line was a coup.

"She's being paid well enough."

"We both know that she's never promoted any products, let alone a fashion designer, before. She only agreed to do it because of you, and she only came to London because of you. I don't know what happened between you and her in

Shanghai, but you certainly made an impact."

Ava shrugged and then shivered. It was late February, and a cold, damp winter still had its grip on London. She and May Ling were standing outside the Corinthia Hotel waiting for their partner, Ava's sister-in-law Amanda Yee, to join them for the taxi ride to the Shard, the tallest building in the European Union. There, in just over an hour, they were scheduled to introduce their PÖ fashion line to the European market and the Western world.

Despite having already been featured on the cover of Hong Kong *Vogue*, and having had a remarkable initial selling season in Asia, PÖ wasn't a known brand in Europe or North America. Their hope was that the launch at the Shard would correct that, and Pang Fai was an important part of their strategy.

While it wasn't uncommon for actresses to affiliate themselves with specific fashion designers and to attend shows to give support, Pang was going several steps further. Although no one outside the PÖ inner circle knew it, she was going to model in the show. And that was even more remarkable because Pang zealously guarded her privacy and was rarely seen in public outside of film promotion activities.

Ava had originally come up with the idea of having Pang Fai promote the PÖ brand and had secured the actress's agreement. But the decision had been made to withhold any public mention of her involvement until London Fashion Week. Instead, a stealth campaign was set in motion by the PÖ partners and their British and Chinese PR companies. Hints were dropped on social media and in the local press about the possibility of Pang Fai's presence and participation in London. The fashion and style magazines were quietly contacted and told to expect a major surprise at the PÖ launch. When they asked if the rumours about Pang were true, no one from PÖ either confirmed or denied the possibility, fuelling even greater interest and making the brand's debut one of the most anticipated events at London Fashion Week.

Ava believed in luck, but she knew that one of the key elements in good fortune is timing. It seemed to her that things had fallen into place for the PÖ business in an almost preordained way. She had managed to secure Pang Fai's agreement just before the actress's profile began to rise in the West. Asia was now the fastest-growing market for the luxury brand companies, and there was an increasing Asian presence on runways and in magazines. A few Chinese designers had made an impact in the West, but there was still the anticipation that a star was going to emerge. Those factors, the PÖ launch, and the promise of Pang Fai's presence had galvanized public attention, and Ava couldn't help but feel that the stars were aligned to make PÖ an international hit.

"She's going to cause a sensation," May said. "I just hope it doesn't distract from the clothes."

We'll find out soon enough, Ava thought as she checked her watch. Amanda was running a little late and Ava hoped there wasn't a last-minute crisis.

Amanda, May Ling, and Ava owned an investment company called the Three Sisters. Amanda, still in her late twenties, handled the day-to-day operations from their office in Hong Kong. May Ling, who was in her mid-forties but looked at least ten years younger, lived in the city of Wuhan in central China and acted as senior advisor and strategist. She and Ava had put in most of the money and were majority shareholders. Ava's role in the business wasn't as clearly defined but was no less important. Since the company's inception her involvement had cut across finance, marketing, planning, and the building of relationships.

The Three Sisters had put money into a furniture manufacturing company in Borneo, a warehouse and distribution firm that operated out of Shanghai and Beijing, a Hong Kong trading business, and a start-up company that was making revolutionary — or so they hoped — carbon-fibre containers for ocean and air freight shipments. They had decided to gamble on the talents of Clark Po by putting more than $10 million into his Shanghai-based fashion line.

Despite the Asian location of all the businesses, Ava still lived in Toronto. The distance and time difference between the partners didn't present any real difficulties. None of them worked regular eight-hour days, and they were able to communicate well enough by phone, text, email, and Skype. It helped that, in addition to being partners, the women were extremely close and shared an extraordinary level of trust.

"I'm sorry for being late," a voice said.

Ava turned to see Amanda rushing towards them.

"Was there a problem?" she asked.

"No, just the opposite," Amanda said breathlessly. "Chi-Tze called to tell me that the event site is already buzzing. They're expecting a full house, and the PR people are predicting that Pang Fai's appearance is going to generate outstanding press coverage."

"Did Chi-Tze mention how Pang Fai is doing?"

"She's as cool as can be. The other girls, especially the Chinese ones, aren't quite so composed. The fact that they're going to be sharing the runway with her might have something to do with it."

"Do we know what she will be wearing?" Ava asked.

"I don't have a clue, and neither does Chi-Tze or Gillian. Clark and the show director have been huddling together for days, and Pang Fai was with them yesterday. None of them are talking about what she's going to wear or when she'll make her entrance."

"We should be going," May interrupted.

They stepped into a taxi and started the trip that would take them across London Bridge to Southwark, on the south side of the Thames River. Ava gazed out of the window. The last time she'd been to London she had been working for the debt-collection company she ran with her old partner, Uncle. They had worked together for more than ten years, chasing scam artists and thieves around the world. Uncle had died more than a year ago, but he was still a part of her life, often appearing in her dreams and memories. She had started the transition into the Three Sisters partially at his insistence, just before his death.

"I don't know if I'm more nervous or excited," Amanda said as they neared the bridge.

"How is Clark?" Ava asked

"He's a mess."

"Good. He was the same in Shanghai, and look how well that turned out."

"Is Elsa here?" May asked, referring to Elsa Ngan, a friend of Amanda's and an editor at Hong Kong *Vogue*. Elsa had been one of PÖ's first fans.

"Yes, she said there was no way she was going to miss our introduction to the West," Amanda said. "And, by the way, she told me that Carrie Song flew in from Hong Kong yesterday."

"You say that as if it's unusual. I thought Carrie would have attended these fashion weeks every year."

"Apparently not. Normally it's the head buyers from Lane Crawford and Joyce who come to the shows."

"Thank god for her support," May said. "Getting probably the best retailer of women's clothes in Hong Kong and Asia to carry our line was such a coup."

"Carrying them and selling them are two different things," Amanda said. "I have no doubt that Carrie is here only because we've been selling very well."

"That and the fact that she still feels she owes Ava a debt of gratitude," May said.

"Are you still having doubts about the setting for the show?" Ava asked, slightly uncomfortable about discussing her relationship with Song. She preferred to believe that it was the quality of Clark's clothes, not her *guanxi*, that had been the determining factor in Song's decision to take on the line.

"No. I was thinking about it last night and I believe the director we hired to create the show is being honest when he says it's the coolest venue he's ever worked in."

"Clark loves it," Amanda said.

The show was to be staged on a vacant floor more than halfway up the eighty-seven-storey Shard. With its floor-to-ceiling windows as a dramatic backdrop, the venue had been converted into a theatre with a specially constructed stage and a U-shaped runway extending more than thirty metres. Three rows of seats were placed on each side of the runway for the press, photographers, bloggers, retailers, and purchasing groups. The front-row seats were reserved for the major buyers and people of huge influence in the fashion world.

"It is dramatic," Ava said. "And those silk warlord banners we used in Shanghai are going to look fantastic in that light."

"We debated about using them again," Amanda said. "But they worked so well in Shanghai, and we have almost an entirely different audience here, so the director decided to do it."

"And did you finally decide what to do about music?" May asked.

"We're going with Cantopop — loud and upbeat," Amanda said.

They reached the Thames, crossed the bridge, and in a few minutes found themselves on London Bridge Street looking up at the glass-encased Shard.

"This is crazy," Ava said, as they got out of the taxi and stepped into a crowd of people. "They can't all be here for the launch."

"No, this is a busy building most days," Amanda said. "Follow me."

It took them ten minutes to work their way through the lobby and into an elevator. When they exited, they walked straight into a throng of photographers who were taking shots of people posing on the red carpet against a backdrop emblazoned with the PÖ logo. Ava didn't recognize any of them, but Amanda whispered, "The woman with the red hair is a senior editor at *Elle*." Another crowd was gathered near the door to the venue. Ava had never seen a larger collection of well-dressed people. Inside, at least a third of the seats were already taken, mainly those in the second and third rows. Ava, Amanda, and May had been offered front-row seats, but May had been quick to say no.

"We don't need our egos stroked," she said. "I'd rather have someone who can help make our company a success sit there."

"Do you want to go backstage and wish everyone good luck?" Amanda asked as they stepped inside.

"No," Ava said. "We didn't in Shanghai. I don't want us to jinx them."

"Then I guess that's a no from me as well," May said with a laugh.

They took their seats and looked anxiously around. The runway ran from the far end of the room towards the main entrance. The U-shaped design had the added advantage of enabling a maximum number of front-row seats. Five minutes before the show was scheduled to start, and there was hardly an empty seat. Ava looked at the front-row centre seats and saw they were full. She breathed a sigh of relief. The director had made it clear that if some of the major buyers and media people were running late, the show wouldn't start until they got there.

"I saw Carrie and Elsa arrive," May said. "Besides them, I don't know a soul."

"We're not on home turf anymore," Ava said.

The lights dimmed and Jacky Cheung's voice filled the room. Ava felt a slight breeze, and the banners they had brought from Shanghai began to flutter.

Ava was sitting between May and Amanda, and when

the first model appeared, she reached for their hands. For the next twenty minutes, she didn't let go.

After seeing the show in Shanghai, Ava was familiar with the rhythm of the models appearing seconds apart. She knew they were going to show about forty outfits, or "exits," as the director called them, but she quickly lost count. The show was tightly paced, and because of that, Ava noticed that instead of one outfit being singularly prominent, it was the general impression that stayed with her. In this case, she was taken by how beautifully cut everything was, how vibrant the linens — Clark Po's favourite medium — and how well he straddled East and West, with designs that hinted at a Western sensibility but still had distinctivly Eastern touches such as cheongsam and bell collars and voluminous cuffs.

Unlike the Shanghai show, where the workers from the PÖ sample factory were in attendance and cheered loudly, the reaction in London was muted, although Ava thought she could hear muttering that seemed to indicate approval. But success in the fashion world was all so subjective, she knew, skewed to reputation and expectation, and PÖ still lacked the former. One thing that did bode well, she thought, was the number of people taking photos or filming with their smartphones. It seemed as though every other person had a phone aimed at the runway.

Ava lost track of how many models had walked by, but she knew the end of the show was approaching, and there was still no sign of Pang Fai. "I'm beginning to worry about Fai," she whispered to May. "Maybe she's changed her mind about doing this."

The constant flow of models quite suddenly stopped, and Ava watched the last three women walk past them and disappear backstage. There was a buzz in the air. Ava could detect disappointment in it, and felt a rush of anxiety. Was it possible Pang Fai wouldn't appear?

Then all of the models began streaming onto the runway, followed by Clark, who was wearing white linen slacks with a red silk scarf tied around his waist and a loose-fitting white linen shirt with colourful glass buttons. He took five or six steps forward, stopped, turned, and extended his right arm back towards the runway entrance.

Ava felt time stand still. Seconds seemed to stretch into minutes. Then an extraordinarily tall woman stepped onto the runway. She wore a delicately spun black linen coat shot through with thin strands of red and gold. All three colours shimmered under the lights. The coat was tightly fitted and came to just below the knee. The clean, minimalist cut was juxtaposed with a scalloped hem and bell sleeves. The model's face was obscured by a multi-layered hood trimmed in red.

"Is that Pang?" May said.

The model took three steps forward and then stopped. She rolled her shoulders back and then held out a hand towards Clark. He walked to her, took her hand, and led her slowly down the centre of the runway.

Ava could hear herself breathing and realized that the entire room had fallen silent.

Clark faced the woman and whispered something to her. When she nodded, he began to undo the onyx coat buttons. When he finished, he moved back and took two steps to the side.

Her hands reached up and pulled the coat off. It floated to the floor.

May gasped, and Ava felt her own breathing stop for a second.

Pang Fai raised her head. She wore no makeup and her hair was cut in a simple pageboy. She had on a white linen T-shirt that barely reached her thighs, exposing nearly all of the famous Pang legs. The word "PÖ" was written in red, and along the bottom were the date and the word "London."

The models lined the runway, surrounding Clark and Pang. May, Amanda, and Ava hardly noticed the steadily rising applause. Their attention was fixed on Pang Fai.

"Whoever thought of having her so plain under that coat is a genius," Amanda said.

"So plain?" May said. "I've never seen anyone so beautiful."

Clark picked up the coat and placed it over Pang Fai's shoulders. She smiled affectionately and leaned over and kissed him on the lips.

He turned and bowed, waved to the crowd, and took Pang Fai's hand and led her backstage.

Ava felt her body sag and realized she had been caught up in the drama of it all. The applause abated and the crowd began to disperse. Most people were already making their way towards the exit, while a few headed backstage. The director had warned them about the rapid departures. There were shows going on all over London, and schedules were tight. Ava was turning to talk to May when out of the corner of her eye she saw Carrie Song hurrying towards them.

"What did you think?" Ava said.

"I wouldn't have missed this for anything," Carrie said, shaking her head. "The clothes were wonderful, and Pang Fai — my god, only a real superstar could have pulled that off."

"She was amazing."

"There is something else I want to tell you. Do you see that stocky man in the grey suit and light blue tie?" Carrie said, motioning towards the exit.

"The one surrounded by three or four other men in grey and black suits?"

"Yes."

"Who is he?"

"Dominic Ventola, the chairman of VLG, the world's second largest luxury brand company."

"I know the name, and I know of VLG. Why would he come to our show?"

"Like everyone else, he may have wanted to see if Pang Fai would make an appearance. But I can tell you that once the show started he had his assistants — those other men in suits — taking photographs of every outfit."

"Why would they have such an interest?"

"Not to steal Clark's designs, if that's what you're thinking. They don't operate like that," Carrie said. "But, among other things, Dominic likes to invest in talented young designers."

"We don't need any investors."

"I'm not suggesting you do or that that's what he wants," Carrie said. "I probably shouldn't have said anything at all."

"No, I'm glad you did, and I'm sure Clark will be pleased to hear that a man like Ventola saw fit to attend his show and thought enough of his designs to record them."

"He should be."

"And I need to tell you how pleased I am that you came today," Ava said.

"I feel like I have a stake in all of this and all of you."

"A big enough stake that I can entice you to join us for a celebratory lunch?"

"Will Pang Fai be there?"

"Of course, as well as May, Amanda, Clark, and our entire Shanghai team."

"I didn't mean to sound quite so star-struck," Carrie said with a laugh.

"Fai does that to people."

Carrie looked at her watch. "I have two more shows scheduled over the next two hours. One is in Soho and the other is in the Docklands. I can't miss them."

"I understand, but by the time they're done, in all likelihood we'll just be getting started, and it won't be a problem if you're late."

"I'll try to make it."

"Great. We've reserved the private dining area at Hakkasan Restaurant in Hanway Place. It's near Tottenham Court Road, about a twenty-minute cab ride from here."

"It sounds Chinese," Carrie said.

"It is Chinese, actually Cantonese. We are a predictable bunch."

"That's the very last thing anyone would ever call you."

ACKNOWLEDGEMENTS

This is the latest installment in the Ava Lee series and it was one of the most difficult to write because some of the subject matter was far removed from my own personal experiences. There were four people in particular who helped fill in the blanks for me and I'd like to thank them:

Carrie Kirkman and Mary Turner — both fashion mavens and astute businesswomen in the fashion trade — who educated me on the workings of an industry I didn't know very well.

A trio of eagle eyes scanned the page proofs for me and found a number of errors that even a large amount of diligence hadn't previously discovered — so thanks to Catherine Roseburgh, Carol Shetler, and Robin Spano.

Kristine Wookey, who supplied me with a dizzying amount of information on linen.

Lawrence Wong, a Hong Kong resident, who advised on past and current business practices in China, and other things Chinese.

I also want to thank my publisher, Sarah MacLachlan, and her team at House of Anansi Press. They are unfailingly responsive and supportive. I want to especially mention Laura Meyer, my publicist. Laura is totally efficient and professional, but it is her wonderfully positive attitude and perpetual good cheer that make her a joy to work with.

As always, I need to thank my editor at Anansi, the great Janie Yoon. Even after eight books, she doesn't let me glide. She continues to challenge me and, in her own subtle way, she keeps pushing to make every book better than the one before. At times it can be frustrating, but when I'm done, I'm grateful.

In terms of support, my own very large family continues to promote the books any way they can. My thanks to them all.

My agents, Bruce Westwood and Carolyn Forde, are almost like family now. Their support is also without question, but I value them as much for the honest advice and guidance they provide.

Last, I want to thank some booksellers. Each time we launch a new book I experience mixed feelings of anticipation and dread. We were fortunate to be able to launch the last two books at the Indigo store in the Manulife Centre at Bay and Bloor Streets in Toronto and at the Burlington Central Library, with the support of A Different Drummer Books. I want to personally thank Colleen Logan, general manager at the Manulife Indigo, and Ian Elliot, the owner of A Different Drummer, for their tremendous support.

IAN HAMILTON is the author of seven novels. He has won the Arthur Ellis Award for Best First Novel and been a finalist for a number of awards, including the Barry Award for Best Original Trade Paperback, the Barry Award for Best Thriller, a LAMBDA Literary Award for Lesbian Mystery, and the Arthur Ellis Award for Best Novella. The BBC named him one of the Top Ten Crime Writers to Read Now. A former journalist, businessman, and diplomat, Ian lives in Burlington, Ontario, with his wife, Lorraine.

NOW AVAILABLE
From House of Anansi Press

The first book in the Ava Lee series.

Book 1

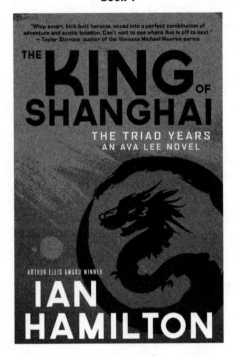

www.houseofanansi.com • www.facebook.com/avaleenovels
www.ianhamiltonbooks.com • www.twitter.com/avaleebooks